The Herald of
the Day of Days

By the same author

'ABDU'L-BAHÁ
The Centre of the Covenant
of Bahá'u'lláh

BAHÁ'U'LLÁH
The King of Glory

BAHÁ'U'LLÁH
A brief life, followed by an essay entitled
THE WORD MADE FLESH

KHADÍJIH BAGUM
The Wife of the Báb

EDWARD GRANVILLE BROWNE AND
THE BAHÁ'Í FAITH

EMINENT BAHÁ'ÍS IN THE TIME OF BAHÁ'U'LLÁH

MUḤAMMAD AND THE COURSE OF ISLÁM

THE BÁB

The Herald of the Day of Days

by

H. M. BALYUZI

GR

GEORGE RONALD

OXFORD

First published 1973 by George Ronald
46 High Street, Kidlington, Oxford, OX5 2DN
Reprinted 1973 and 1974
Paper edition 1975
Reprinted 1994

ISBN 0 85398 054 3

Printed by The Cromwell Press,
Broughton Gifford, Melksham,
Wiltshire SN12 8PH

Contents

Foreword ix

A Note on the Construction of Persian Names xi

Prologue 1

1. All Hail Shíráz 15
2. He Whom They Sought 32
3. Ṭihrán 48
4. The First Martyr 58
5. Pilgrimage to Mecca 69
6. Forces of Opposition Arrayed 76
7. Belief and Denial 85
8. The City of 'Abbás the Great 106
9. The Antichrist of the Bábí Revelation 117
10. Where the Aras Flows 124
11. The Grievous Mountain 134
12. That Midsummer Noon 148
13. The Dawn-Breakers 161

Epilogue 189

APPENDICES

1. The Siege of Karbilá 193
2. The Martyrdom of the Báb 202
3. Prelude to the Episode of Nayríz 204
4. The Seven Martyrs of Ṭihrán 206
5. The Episode of Zanján 209

6. Lord Palmerston's Enquiry 214
7. Myth-Making 217

Bibliography 225
Notes 229
Index 243

TO

THE SHINING MEMORY

OF

A LONE AND NOBLE WOMAN

WHO SUFFERED IN SILENCE

FOR FORTY YEARS

THIS STORY OF HER BELOVED HUSBAND

IS DEDICATED

Foreword

The present book completes the trilogy on the lives of the Founders of the Bahá'í Faith. However, now that additional material is at my disposal, it is my hope to expand at a future date the volume on the life of Bahá'u'lláh, and also to write a supplement to the volume on the life of 'Abdu'l-Bahá.

This book is the first in the range of Bahá'í literature to make extensive use of official documents from governmental archives. I am greatly indebted to Moojan Momen who has generously shared with me the results of his able research in the Public Record Office of London and elsewhere.

The two British Foreign Secretaries who received news and dispatches regarding the Báb and the Bábís were the Earl of Aberdeen, who held office from September 1841 to July 1846, under Sir Robert Peel; and Viscount Palmerston, whose tenure of office extended from July 1846 to January 1852, under Lord John Russell. The British envoy chiefly involved in forwarding such reports to London was Lt.-Col. (later Sir Justin) Sheil, the Minister in Ṭihrán. Lord Palmerston's letters to him (F.O. 248/134) state that his dispatches concerning the Báb and the Bábís were 'laid before the Queen'.

My deep gratitude goes to Abul-Qasim Afnan, who has unstintingly made available to me the chronicle-history and the autobiography of his father, the late Ḥájí Mírzá Ḥabíb-u'lláh, as well as letters written by and to the relatives of the Báb, together with many other documents of inestimable value.

It should be borne in mind that apart from quotations from the Writings of the Báb, speeches attributed to Him or to anyone else in these pages must not be taken as exact reportage of words spoken at the time. They only convey the sense and purport of what was said on those occasions. Obviously no one was taking notes. It is possible, however, that a few short sentences here and there, which immediately engrave themselves on the mind, are exact utterances, the very words spoken.

As the bibliography indicates I have consulted a number of books; but of printed works, the main sources have been *God Passes By* and Nabíl's Narrative, *The Dawn-Breakers*. I am much indebted to the Bahá'í Publishing Trust, Wilmette, Illinois, for permission to quote from these and other sources, as well as to Cambridge University Press, the Public Record Office, George Allen & Unwin Ltd., A. & C. Black Ltd., Faber & Faber Ltd., William Heinemann Ltd., Methuen & Co. Ltd., and *World Order*, A Bahá'í Magazine. Full acknowledgment is made in the bibliography and notes.

I am profoundly grateful to the Hands of the Cause Paul Haney and Abul-Qasim Faizi for reading the manuscript and for their review and advice. As in the past Marion Hofman's generous help has smoothed the path to publication. My indebtedness to her is immense. And without my wife's assistance and support I could not have completed my task.

I should also like to thank Miss Dorothy Wigington, Mr. Farhang Afnan and Mr. Rustom Sabit for their care in reading the proofs, and Mr. Horst W. Kolodziej for his excellent reproduction of a number of old documents and photographs.

Finally, a word as to the Prologue; this in my view provides a necessary background for the story of the Báb. But should the reader find in it too many unfamiliar facts, he may turn immediately to the first chapter.

H. M. BALYUZI

London
October 1972

A Note on the Construction of Persian Names

In times past the people of Persia had no surnames, but in many instances they were known by the name of the district, city, town, or even the village from which they came: for example, Khurásání, Mázindarání, Ṭihrání, Iṣfahání, and Shírází.

There were also various honorific prefixes and suffixes by which a person was distinguished. A descendant of the Prophet Muḥammad had (and has) the prefix of 'Siyyid'. At times, 'Mírzá' took the place of 'Siyyid', and at times the two were used together. 'Mírzá' by itself did not denote any particular ancestry, except when placed after a proper name to mark royal descent.

The suffix 'Khán' served at one time as a title, but with passing years, it became merely honorific, even meaningless, and at no time was it a surname.

The prefix 'Ḥájí' or 'Ḥáj' indicated then, as now, one who had made the pilgrimage to Mecca. Mashhadí and Karbilá'í, as prefixes, marked pilgrimage to Mashhad or Karbilá, but as suffixes pointed out nativity.

There were also innumerable titles conferred by the sovereign in Írán, consisting of diverse combinations, sometimes ludicrous, sometimes grammatically impossible. Occasionally they indicated a definite rank and profession. As time passed, these titles multiplied absurdly, until they were swept away by legislation in the 1920's.

Finally, a person was often distinguished from others by a combination of prefixes and suffixes attached to his name which, if omitted, might cause him to be taken for another person.

Today the situation is much changed, but for the period described in this book, the author can identify people only by the names they then used, however difficult they may be.

Quotations are reproduced in their original form, even though differing from the spelling and transliteration of Persian words adopted in this book. Translations from Persian sources are by the author unless otherwise attributed.

The text of the Authorised Version of the Bible is Crown copyright and the extracts used herein are reproduced by permission.

The Báb, the Exalted One, is the Morn of Truth, Whose Light shineth throughout all regions.

'ABDU'L-BAHÁ

O people of the Báb! sorely persecuted, compelled to silence, but steadfast now as at Sheykh Ṭabarsí and Zanján, what destiny is concealed for you behind the veil of the Future?

EDWARD GRANVILLE BROWNE

PROLOGUE

I

About the time that the thirteen colonies of North America were gaining their independence to form the nucleus of the mighty Republic of the West, France was inching her way towards a revolution such as the world had never seen, and Britain was striding along the road to a revolution of a different kind, industrial, agrarian and economic in nature, a cleric of the Islamic Shí'ah persuasion left his island-home in the Persian Gulf for the great centres of Shí'ah learning and Shí'ah devotion in 'Iráq. His purpose was to find a much larger audience in order to give voice to thoughts and presentiments that had developed with his years.

Shaykh Aḥmad-i-Aḥsá'í (1743–1826), the founder of the Shaykhí school, belonged to the ancient tribe of Banú-Ṣakhr, and his family originated from the region of Aḥsá on the Arabian mainland. His father's name was Shaykh Zayni'd-Dín, and Baḥrayn had been their home. Shaykh Aḥmad first visited Najaf, where the Tomb of 'Alí, the first Imám, cousin and son-in-law of the Prophet Muḥammad, is situated. Then in Karbilá, close by the Shrine of the martyred Ḥusayn, the third Imám, he began to preach and a circle of earnest students gathered round him. He asked the leading Shí'ah divines of the holy cities of 'Iráq to issue him a licence which would give him recognition as a mujtahid in his own right, that is, a divine empowered to interpret and prescribe. They all declared that they considered Shaykh Aḥmad to be a man of knowledge and talent superior to their own, and that their testimonial was written solely at his request.

The fame of Shaykh Aḥmad soon spread throughout Írán. Fatḥ-'Alí Sháh (reigned 1797–1834) and Muḥammad-'Alí Mírzá,* a son of the Sháh who held the life-long tenure of the governorship of Kirmánsháh, were particularly desirous to meet him. But Shaykh Aḥmad preferred to go to Írán by way of Búshihr (Bushire) in the south, rather than by the nearer and more accessible route of Kirmánsháh in the west. From Búshihr he went to Shíráz and thence to Yazd, where he stayed for a number of years. Siyyid Káẓim-i-Rashtí, a young man barely out of his teens, who shared the same views, joined him there (sometime in 1231 A.H.: 1815–16). Shaykh Aḥmad was then making his final arrangements to go on pilgrimage to the holy city of Mashhad,† prior to his visit to Ṭihrán. He received Siyyid Káẓim with great affection and asked him to remain at Yazd to take up his own patient work of many years. In Mashhad and later in Ṭihrán, Shaykh Aḥmad was shown every mark of high respect and reverence.

Eventually Siyyid Káẓim travelled north to be in his company, and together they went to Kirmánsháh, as the Prince-Governor had been urgently begging his father to let Shaykh Aḥmad visit him. They stayed in Kirmánsháh as long as the Governor lived. After his premature death, they departed for Karbilá, where Shaykh Aḥmad, his zeal unabated and his powers untouched by advancing years, preached and taught. He was in his early eighties when he took the road to Mecca and Medina. From that journey he did not return and lies buried in the famed cemetery of Baqi', in the vicinity of the Tomb of the Prophet Muḥammad.

Shaykh Aḥmad's constant theme was the near advent of

* The Rukni'd-Dawlih.

† Mashhad (Meshed) contains the Shrine of Imám Riḍá, the eighth Imám.

the Deliverer of the Latter Days, promised to the world of Islám, the Qá'im of the House of Muḥammad or the Mihdí (Mahdí).[1] In the course of his last pilgrimage to the holy cities of Arabia, he told a merchant from Iṣfahán* who was with him: 'You will attain the presence of the Báb; salute Him on my behalf.'[2] Shaykh Aḥmad did not believe in physical resurrection nor in the physical ascent (Mi'ráj)† of the Prophet Muḥammad to heaven on the night that the Angel Gabriel took Him to view the celestial world. Mi'ráj was an experience of the spirit, Shaykh Aḥmad maintained. Moreover he asserted that the signs and portents of the coming of the Qá'im, given by the Prophet and the Imáms, were allegorical. These and similar doctrines were anathema to the orthodox, but while Shaykh Aḥmad lived, royal patronage muted their hostile criticism.

Siyyid Káẓim (1793–1843), who, in accordance with the will of Shaykh Aḥmad, succeeded him in guiding his disciples, was the son of Siyyid Qásim of Rasht, a town in northern Írán close to the Caspian Sea. He came from a family of well-known merchants and was no more than thirty-three years old when he occupied the seat of authority. The orthodox divines now began their vitriolic assaults in earnest until, at last, Siyyid Káẓim felt that he

* Ḥájí Muḥammad-Ismá'íl-i-Gulpáygání.

† The following verse in the Qur'án (xvii, 4) refers to the Mi'ráj:

> Glory be to Him, who carried His servant by night
> from the Holy Mosque to the Further Mosque
> the precincts of which We have blessed,
> that We might show him some of Our signs.
> He is the All-hearing, the All-seeing.
>
> —Arberry, *The Koran Interpreted*

The Holy Mosque (Masjid-al-Ḥarám) is the Ka'bah in Mecca; the Further Mosque (Masjid-al-Aqṣá) is in Jerusalem.

needed solid support in Írán from the ranks of the orthodox. For that purpose he chose one of his ablest disciples, Mullá Ḥusayn, a native of the small town of Bushrúyih in Khurásán, to go to Iṣfahán and secure the aid of Ḥájí Siyyid Muḥammad-Báqir-i-Rashtí, a noted divine whose influence was felt far and wide. Mullá Ḥusayn succeeded brilliantly in accomplishing the mission entrusted to him, obtained the support of that famous man in writing, and then proceeded to Mashhad to acquire a similar pledge from yet another powerful divine.

In the meantime not only did Siyyid Káẓim suffer from the intrigues and onslaughts of his adversaries headed by Siyyid Ibráhím-i-Qazvíní, but the whole of Karbilá was thrown into turmoil. These disorders were of long standing and gradually the authority of the Ottoman government had ceased to exist. Within the town there were several factions at odds with one another, but all determined to resist the re-establishment of Ottoman power. Two successive Válís (governor-generals) of 'Iráq tried to force the people of Karbilá to submission, but failed conspicuously. However, in the closing months of the year 1842, Najíb Páshá, a man resolute and even obstinate, came to occupy the post of Válí. Affairs in Karbilá had gradually gone from bad to worse. Lawlessness had increased and mob rule prevailed. Najíb Páshá's first thought was to resolve this problem which had baffled his predecessors. He tried to negotiate a settlement, but neither he nor the rebels of Karbilá could really trust one another. Najíb Páshá moved near-by to Musayyib and sent Sar'askar (Colonel) Sa'du'lláh Páshá with a small force to reduce the town. Negotiations proceeded apace. Emissaries came and went. Persian princes, who lived in Karbilá, took part in the negotiations, but nothing was achieved.

During those fatal weeks, at the end of the year 1842 and the beginning of 1843, Siyyid Káẓim, who was greatly respected both for his wisdom and humanity,* took a leading role, urging all parties to act with moderation and in a spirit of conciliation. Twice, in company with a small delegation, he visited the camps of Najíb Páshá and Sa'du'lláh Páshá outside Karbilá. Lieutenant-Colonel Farrant, the British Special Commissioner, reported his efforts to Constantinople:

> The Chief Priest Hajee Seid Kausem did all in his power to prevent hostilities, he preached against their proceedings, he was abused and threatened, they would not listen to him—this I have heard from many people at Kerbella—at this time all were unanimous in defending the place
>
> ... to the very last he entreated them to listen to the

* 'Abdu'l-Bahá has related this story of Siyyid Káẓim's works of charity: ''Alí-Sháh [the Ẓillu's-Sulṭán, see Prologue II, p. 10] claimed the throne of Írán. He showed great benevolence towards the divines of Karbilá and Najaf, sent them money and stood up for them. However, he was unsuccessful and betook himself to Karbilá. There he fell on hard times and suffered poverty. He expected the divines to come to his help and applied to them, one by one. But none heeded him. One night he and his family had to go to bed hungry. At midnight he heard a knock on his door. When he opened it he found someone, who had pulled his 'abá over his head so as to hide his face. This man put a purse with money in it into his hands and went away.

'Time passed. Indigence and want recurred. Again the same person, head covered with 'abá, came at midnight, handed a sum of money and went away without a word. To the repeated question "who are you?" he gave no answer. Then, that man came a third time with a purse containing money. This time 'Alí-Sháh followed him and saw him enter the house of Ḥájí Siyyid Káẓim and shut the door. 'Alí-Sháh related this event in many gatherings. He used to say: "O people! I am not a Shaykhí, but this deed is the work of righteousness. None but a man of truth would act in this way." '[3]

Pacha but without avail, he shewed great courage on the occasion, as he had all the chief Geramees* and Mollahs against him.[4]

Unhappily, his counsel was ignored by both rebels and Turks. In January 1843, after a siege of twenty-four days, the holy city was taken by assault, causing great suffering to the innocent inhabitants. The files of the Public Record Office in London contain several documents that throw light on this episode, as well as on the central part played by Siyyid Káẓim. (See Appendix 1.)

During the siege Ḥájí Siyyid Káẓim had spent himself in an effort to forestall violence and protect all parties to the conflict. Although only fifty years of age, he became aware that his life was nearing its close. He was warned of this, we are told, by the dream of an Arab shepherd who recounted it to him. When his disciples expressed their distress, Siyyid Káẓim replied:

> Is not your love for me for the sake of that true One whose advent we all await? Would you not wish me to die, that the promised One may be revealed?[5]

The year 1844 was about to dawn when Siyyid Káẓim breathed his last and was laid to rest near the tomb of Imám Ḥusayn. His death was reported by Farrant, who wrote on January 24th 1844 to Sir Stratford Canning, sending a copy in February to Lt.-Col. (later Sir) Justin Sheil,[6] the British chargé d'affaires in Ṭihrán:

> Hajee Seid Kausem one of the Chief Priests of Kerbella died lately on his return from a visit to Samerrah—Seid Ibrahim Kasveenee the other Chief Priest who was greatly opposed to him, will now enjoy full power, and all contention between the two religious parties will cease.[7]

* Probably 'yárámáz', meaning 'good-for-nothing'.

When Mullá Ḥusayn-i-Bu<u>sh</u>rú'í returned to Karbilá from his highly successful mission in Írán, his teacher was dead. He had not appointed anyone to succeed him.

II

To follow the events of this narrative, it may be helpful to consider their background in some aspects of Iranian history.*

Muḥammad <u>Sh</u>áh, the third monarch of the Qájár dynasty, ruled the land in 1843, but real power rested in the hands of Ḥájí Mírzá Áqásí, his unprepossessing Grand Vizier. The Qájárs were a tribe of Turkish origin. Áqá Muḥammad <u>Kh</u>án, a eunuch chieftain of this tribe, arose in the year 1779 to carve out a kingdom for himself. Fifteen years later he finally won the crown of Írán when he captured and brutally murdered Luṭf-'Alí <u>Kh</u>án, the last ruler of the Zand dynasty, who was brave and high-minded but piteously young. The eunuch king was utterly and savagely ruthless, and he managed to hold off the Russians in the area of the Caucasus until 1797 when he was struck down by three assassins. He was succeeded by his nephew, Fatḥ-'Alí <u>Sh</u>áh, a man of soft heart and weak will, who was highly uxorious. At his death in 1834, fifty-three sons and forty-six daughters survived him.

During the reign of Fatḥ-'Alí <u>Sh</u>áh, Írán lost heavily to Russia in a series of disastrous wars. Her ministers, comfortably cocooned in their isolation from the currents of world affairs, and totally ignorant of the realities of the European situation, believed that with the aid of the Emperor of France the Russian menace could be thwarted. Hard on the heels of General Gardanne, Bonaparte's envoy, not

* For other aspects the reader is referred to the Introduction of Nabíl's *The Dawn-Breakers*.

one but two envoys from the more familiar 'Ingríz' (English) came in 1808. Sir Harford Jones had been dispatched from the court of King George III and Sir John Malcolm from India. In 1801 the latter, on behalf of the Marquis of Wellesley, Governor-General of India, concluded an abortive treaty with the shrewd and immensely ambitious Grand Vizier* of Fatḥ-'Alí Sháh. But in the intervening years Bonaparte, subsequent to his *débacle* in Egypt and Syria, showered his dubious favours on the Persians, and the British connexion was conveniently ignored by the ministers of Fatḥ-'Alí Sháh, who had entered into the Treaty of Finkenstein (1807) with the French. Moreover, in the same period, the most capable Ḥájí Ibráhím Khán, who had contributed more than anyone to the downfall of the Zand dynasty and the ensuing victories of the eunuch king, fell from power and, as legend has it, met his death in a boiling cauldron.

Indeed, high hopes centred on what the Emperor of France would do for Írán, only to be dashed by Bonaparte's change of policy; when he met Tsar Alexander I at Tilsit (1807) he did not remember any of his promises. And so General Gardanne was ignominiously ousted from Ṭihrán, and Sir Harford Jones and Sir John Malcolm were left at peace, to glower at each other, much to the amusement and also surprise and embarrassment of the Persian ministers. But as Napoleon's star waned, so did the interest of the British in Persian affairs. The wars with Russia went on until the Persians acknowledged defeat in the Treaty of Gulistán of 1813.

Amidst abysmal ignorance, nepotism and malpractice which abounded in the realm, there stood two men in particular, untouched by corruption, who were fully aware of the needs of their country: Prince 'Abbás Mírzá, the heir to the throne, and his vizier, Mírzá Abu'l-Qásim, Qá'im-

* Ḥájí Ibráhím Khán (the I'timádu'd-Dawlih).

Maqám-i-Faráhání. But their attempts at reform could not obtain the success they deserved because of the obscurantism surrounding the person of the sovereign. It was this Crown Prince who sent the first group of Iranian students to Britain to learn the crafts of the West. Their story, which does no credit to the government in London, is preserved in a number of documents lodged in the Public Record Office. Incidentally, one of these men, a student of medicine, was named Mírzá Ḥájí Bábá, the eponym of the chief character of James Morier's well-known satire.

Prince 'Abbás Mírzá, worsted in the field by the Russians, now tried to provide his country with a modern army and engaged British instructors. As in the past, Ṭihrán gave him little help. Yet he was under constant pressure to resume hostilities. The divines, particularly, were urging it.* Yet Russia had no desire to fight; nor had Fatḥ-'Alí Sháh: war was too expensive. Prince Menchikov arrived from St. Petersburg (the present-day Leningrad) not to dictate but to negotiate. But the demands of those who sought war—the clerics and the powerful court faction of Alláh-Yár Khán †—proved irresistible; Menchikov returned to St. Petersburg.

In the war that soon followed the Persians were soundly beaten and Russian forces surged forward to occupy the city of Tabríz. The first to abandon the field was a group of clerics, who, with raised standards, had accompanied the army. By the Treaty of Turkumancháy (1828), onerous and humiliating in the extreme, Írán was excluded from the Caucasus. In addition to the payment of heavy indemnities, she lost her rights in the Caspian Sea and the frontier between Russia and Írán was fixed on the river Aras.

* This incident is referred to by Bahá'u'lláh in His Tablet to Náṣiri'd-Dín Sháh.

† The Áṣafu'd-Dawlih, who later rose in rebellion against the central government during the reign of Náṣiri'd-Dín Sháh.

Prince 'Abbás Mírzá was now a sad and broken man. Rash actions forced upon him had brought total desolation. His modern army was shattered. Because he knew of the intrigues that plagued his father's court, and to make certain that his eldest son would not be left undefended, he asked for guarantees from the Tsar, which were readily given. After this ordeal of defeat and submission Prince 'Abbás Mírzá did not live long. He died at the age of forty-five, and a year later his father followed him to the grave.

The eldest son of 'Abbás Mírzá, named heir-apparent by Fatḥ-'Alí Sháh, came into his heritage by a combination of the assured support of Britain and Russia, and the wise strategy of Qá'im-Maqám. Sir John Campbell, the British Minister in Ṭihrán, and Sir Henry Lindesay Bethune, who took command of the forces loyal to the son of 'Abbás Mírzá, brought him safely from Tabríz to Ṭihrán. Qá'im-Maqám, in the meantime, secured the backing of influential men in the capital, where another son of the late king had styled himself 'Adil Sháh* and was claiming the throne. But his reign was brief, and soon Muḥammad Sháh, the heir-apparent, was well entrenched in Ṭihrán, for Sir Henry Lindesay Bethune (whom a Persian historian calls Mr. Lenzi) easily routed other pretenders.[8]

Muḥammad Sháh did not wish to seem beholden to the British officials who had helped him to his throne, nor did he show much gratitude to Qá'im-Maqám, the architect of his victory. Within a year he contrived the death of that great minister who had served him and his father so well. By the death of Qá'im-Maqám, treacherously designed, Írán sustained a tremendous and irreparable loss. Qá'im-Maqám was not only a brilliant statesman, but also a master

* In reality 'Alí-Sháh, the Ẓillu's-Sulṭán, not to be confused with Prince Sulṭán Mas'úd Mírzá, the Governor-General of Iṣfahán, who had the same title in later years.

of prose whose style rescued the language from encrusted artificialities.*

His successor as the Grand Vizier was Ḥájí Mírzá Áqásí, a man ignorant and devoid of all graces, affecting deep piety. This is how Sir Henry Layard[9] saw him in 1840:

> We waited upon the Prime Minister, the Haji Mirza Agasi, who was then the man of the greatest influence, power and authority in Persia. The Shah had committed to him almost the entire government of his kingdom, occupying himself but little with public affairs, aware of his own incapacity for conducting them. 'The Haji'—the name by which he was familiarly known—was, by all accounts, a statesman of craft and cunning, but of limited abilities. He was cruel and treacherous, proud and overbearing, although he affected the humility of a pious mulla who had performed the pilgrimage to Mecca and the holy shrines of the Imaums. The religious character which he had assumed made him intolerant and bigoted, and he was known to be a fanatical hater of Christians. He had been the Shah's tutor and instructor in the Koran, and had acquired a great influence over his pupil, who had raised him to the lofty position which he then held. He had the reputation of being an accomplished Persian and Arabic scholar, but he was entirely ignorant of all European languages. His misgovernment, and the corruption and general oppression which everywhere existed had brought Persia to the verge of ruin. Distress, misery, and discontent prevailed to an extent previously unknown. He was universally execrated as the cause of the misfortunes and misery from which the people and the State were suffering. We found him seated on his hams, in the Persian fashion, on a fine Kurdish carpet spread in a handsome hall. Before him was a large tray filled with ices

* See Balyuzi, *'Abdu'l-Bahá*, p. 373 and note.

and a variety of fruit . . . He was a man of small stature, with sharp and somewhat mean and forbidding features, and a loud shrill voice. His dress was simple—almost shabby—as became a mulla and a man devoted to religious life . . . It was evident that the Haji suspected that we were spies and agents of the British Government. However, he declared that the Shah was willing that we should visit any part of his territories where we could travel in safety, and that orders had been issued for the preparation of our farman [royal decree]; for his Majesty had said that we belonged to a friendly nation, and his quarrel was not with England but with Lord Palmerston, who had treated Persia ill, and had recalled the Queen's Ambassador[10] without sufficient cause . . .

Nor was Írán on good terms with the Ottomans. Layard's book, *Early Adventures*, indicates the considerable extent of the incursions which the Turks had made into Iranian territory. The meeting between Layard and Ḥájí Mírzá Áqásí in 1840 took place in Hamadán, not far from the frontier, where Muḥammad Sh̲áh was encamped with his army. The relations between the Ottoman and Iranian governments were further strained by the storming and sacking of Karbilá in January 1843, where the chief sufferers were Persian. We have seen how the Persian princes living in Karbilá at the time of its investment by the troops of Najíb Pás̲há took a hand in negotiations. They were exiles and fugitives who had contested with Muḥammad Sh̲áh and offended him, and senior among them was 'Alí-Sh̲áh, the Ẓillu's-Sulṭán.

Yet another issue reared its ugly head to exacerbate relations between Írán and the Ottoman Empire, that of Sh̲í'ah against Sunní. Sheil, the British Minister in Ṭihrán, reported to the Foreign Secretary, the Earl of Aberdeen:

> If the Moollahs, and in particular the chief priest of Ispahan, Hajee Syed Moollah Mahomed Baukir, whose religious influence in Persia is powerful, should use the present opportunity for regaining their former position by exerting their authority among the people, and preaching a crusade against the rival branch of Mahommedanism, it is not easy to foresee the consequences.[11]

Indeed, reported Sheil, the Persian Foreign Minister and Ḥájí Mírzá Áqásí were considering the possibility of war.[12]

This chief priest of Iṣfahán, mentioned by Sheil, was the same divine from whom Mullá Ḥusayn-i-Bus͟hrú'í obtained unqualified support for Siyyid Káẓim-i-Ras͟htí.

It is helpful to compare the authority of the divines of these two great branches of Islám. The S͟hí'ah divine in contradistinction to the Sunní has the power of 'Ijtihád', that is, issuing *ex cathedra* decrees and judgments. His position is, in a sense, analogous to that of the English judge who can, within the boundaries of equity and common law, establish precedents. The Sunní divine belongs to one of the four schools of Islamic jurisprudence: the Ḥanafí, the S͟háfi'í, the Málikí and the Ḥanbalí. The jurisconsults, who founded these four schools or rites, which are named after them, set certain standards from which the Sunní divine cannot deviate. The S͟hí'ah divine, on the other hand, relies exclusively on the text of the Qur'án and the Traditions ascribed to the Prophet and the Imáms, all of which are wide open to interpretation. Moreover, the S͟hí'ah mujtahid—the divine who pronounces *ex cathedra*—does so, it is understood, as the deputy of the Ṣáḥibu'z-Zamán, the Lord of the Age.

CHAPTER I

ALL HAIL SHÍRÁZ

All hail, Shiraz, hail! Oh site without peer!
May God be the Watchman before thy gate,
That the feet of Misfortune enter not here!
Lest my Ruknabad be left desolate . . .
—Ḥáfiẓ

In the afternoon of May 22nd 1844 a traveller stood outside the gates of Shíráz. He had come from Karbilá, on a spiritual quest to his native land of Írán. A boat had taken him to Búshihr on the Persian Gulf. From that insalubrious port his route had lain over forbidding mountains to the renowned city of Shíráz. He was accompanied by his brother and his nephew, both barely twenty years old, and he himself but in his early thirties. They had undertaken this journey for a purpose which to many seemed fantastic. But for themselves and many more like them it was real and urgent.

This traveller was the same Mullá Ḥusayn-i-Bushrú'í, who, after the accomplishment of his highly fruitful mission in Írán on behalf of Siyyid Káẓim-i-Rashtí, had reached Karbilá only to find his teacher dead. He had learned that Siyyid Káẓim's parting counsel to his disciples had been to leave their homes and their cloisters, to abandon their studies and their debates and go out into the world to seek 'the Lord of the Age' (Ṣáḥibu'z-Zamán) whose advent had for centuries been the hope of countless millions. His supernal light would soon break upon the world, Siyyid Káẓim had said. Mullá Ḥusayn together with a number of Siyyid Káẓim's disciples kept vigil for forty days in the old mosque of Kúfih, nearly in ruins, and then set out on different routes to do their master's bidding.

Mullá Ḥusayn was a man of profound scholarship and unbending will. Nothing daunted him. Now, reaching the gates of Shíráz, he sent his companions into the city to obtain lodgings, but he himself tarried for a while in the fields. His mind was occupied with the object of his quest, a quest that had brought him all those wearisome miles to Shíráz, the home and the resting-place of two of the greatest poets of Írán. Here, some five hundred years before, Ḥáfiẓ had composed his superb, ethereal lyrics. Here Sa'dí had lived a good part of his life and had written his lucid prose, his lambent verse. Here had worked and died a host of men celebrated both in their own days and thereafter. The air of Shíráz, the plain of Shíráz, the roses of Shíráz, the cypresses of Shíráz, have all been lavishly praised.

Forty-four years later, the young Edward Granville Browne, the future eminent orientalist of the University of Cambridge, looked at the plain of Shíráz from the heights facing the road to Búshihr, that mountain pass which is named Alláh-u-Akbar (God is the Greatest) because the traveller thus expresses his wonderment at beholding such a beauteous plain. Browne wrote:

> Words cannot describe the rapture which overcame me as, after many a weary march, I gazed at length on the reality of that whereof I had so long dreamed, and found the reality not merely equal to, but far surpassing, the ideal which I had conceived. It is seldom enough in one's life that this occurs. When it does, one's innermost being is stirred with an emotion which baffles description, and which the most eloquent words can but dimly shadow forth.[1]

This was the city that Mullá Ḥusayn was about to enter. It was as if a magnet had drawn him, with his brother and his nephew, to Shíráz. Nor were they alone in being thus drawn.

On this hot afternoon of May 22nd, Mullá Ḥusayn was fatigued after the trying journey from the coast up the precipitous tracks of the rising plateau. But his mind was alert and his soul yearned for that peace which the attainment of his goal would bring him. As he walked and pondered he came face to face with a Youth of striking appearance. That young Man, who was gentle and gracious and whose turban proclaimed His descent from the Prophet Muḥammad, greeted him with great kindness. Mullá Ḥusayn was amazed and overwhelmed by the warmth of this unexpected welcome. It was the courtesy coupled with the dignified mien of this young Siyyid* which particularly impressed him. Then the young Man invited him to be His guest and to partake of the evening meal at His house. Mullá Ḥusayn mentioned that his companions had gone ahead and would be awaiting him, to which the young Siyyid replied: 'Commit them to the care of God; He will surely protect and watch over them'.†

'We soon found ourselves standing at the gate of a house of modest appearance,' Mullá Ḥusayn has recounted. 'He knocked at the door, which was soon opened by an Ethiopian servant. "Enter therein in peace, secure,"‡ were His words as He crossed the threshold and motioned me to follow Him. His invitation, uttered with power and majesty, penetrated my soul. I thought it a good augury to be addressed in such words, standing as I did on the threshold of the first house I was entering in Shíráz, a city the very atmosphere of which had produced already an indescribable impression upon me.'

* A descendant of the Prophet Muḥammad.

† The quotations in this chapter without reference numbers are taken from Nabíl, *The Dawn-Breakers*, ch. III.

‡ Qur'án XV, 46.

Shíráz had cast its spell upon Mullá Ḥusayn. But little did he think that his youthful Host, whose utterance rang with authority, was that 'Lord of the Age', that 'Qá'im of the House of Muḥammad' whom he was seeking. Yet he could not escape the feeling that the unexpected encounter might in some way bring him near the end of his quest. At the same time he was uneasy at having left his brother and nephew with no news of himself. He further recounts: 'Overwhelmed with His acts of extreme kindness, I arose to depart. "The time for evening prayer is approaching," I ventured to observe. "I have promised my friends to join them at that hour in the Masjid-i-Ílkhání".* With extreme courtesy and calm He replied: "You must surely have made the hour of your return conditional upon the will and pleasure of God. It seems that His will has decreed otherwise. You need have no fear of having broken your pledge."' Such undoubted assurance should have made Mullá Ḥusayn aware that he was about to experience the supreme test of his life.

They prayed together. They sat down to converse. And suddenly his Host asked Mullá Ḥusayn: 'Whom, after Siyyid Káẓim, do you regard as his successor and your leader?' Furthermore, He asked: 'Has your teacher given you any detailed indications as to the distinguishing features of the promised One?' Mullá Ḥusayn replied that Siyyid Káẓim had laid the injunction upon his disciples to disperse after his death and seek 'the Lord of the Age', and indeed he had given them indications by which they could come to recognize Him. 'He is of a pure lineage, is of illustrious descent,' said Mullá Ḥusayn, 'and of the seed of Fáṭimih.† As to His age, He is more than twenty and less than thirty. He is endowed with innate knowledge, . . . abstains from smoking, and is free from bodily deficiency.'

* A well-known mosque in Shíráz.

† The daughter of the Prophet Muḥammad, and the wife of 'Alí, the first Imám.

There was silence—the pause that precedes the breaking of the dawn. Mullá Ḥusayn has told us that the silence was broken with 'vibrant voice' by his Host who declared to him:

Behold, all these signs are manifest in Me.

Mullá Ḥusayn was for the moment shocked and bewildered. He tried to resist a claim so breath-taking. But Truth looked him in the face. He marshalled arguments. But Truth is its own argument.

Mullá Ḥusayn said: 'He whose advent we await is a Man of unsurpassed holiness, and the Cause He is to reveal [is] a Cause of tremendous power. Many and diverse are the requirements which He who claims to be its visible embodiment must needs fulfil. How often has Siyyid Káẓim referred to the vastness of the knowledge of the promised One! How often did he say: "My own knowledge is but a drop compared with that with which He has been endowed. All my attainments are but a speck of dust in the face of the immensity of His knowledge. Nay, immeasurable is the difference!" '

In days gone by Mullá Ḥusayn had written a dissertation on some of the abstruse doctrines and teachings which Shaykh Aḥmad and Siyyid Káẓim had enunciated. He carried a copy of this treatise with him. He now presented it to his Host and asked Him to peruse it, and elucidate the mysteries which it contained. Not only did his Host after a rapid look through that treatise shed light upon it, He went far beyond it. Then Mullá Ḥusayn was given the proof of which he had ample knowledge. There is a Súrih (Arabic 'Súrah': chapter) in the Qur'án entitled the Súrih of Joseph.* It tells the story of Joseph, the son of Jacob, he whom his brothers betrayed and sold into slavery, who suffered imprisonment in Egypt, but rose to rule that land. It is highly allegorical. Siyyid

* Súrih xii.

Káẓim had told Mullá Ḥusayn, when requested by him to write a commentary on that chapter of the Qur'án: 'This is, verily, beyond me. He, that great One, who comes after me will, unasked, reveal it for you. That commentary will constitute one of the weightiest testimonies of His truth, and one of the clearest evidences of the loftiness of His position.'

Mullá Ḥusayn's Host told him: 'Now is the time to reveal the commentary on the Súrih of Joseph.'

'He took up His pen,' Mullá Ḥusayn related, 'and with incredible rapidity revealed the entire Súrih of Mulk, the first chapter of His commentary on the Súrih of Joseph. The overpowering effect of the manner in which He wrote was heightened by the gentle intonation of His voice which accompanied His writing. Not for one moment did He interrupt the flow of the verses which streamed from His pen. Not once did He pause till the Súrih of Mulk was finished. I sat enraptured by the magic of His voice and the sweeping force of His revelation.'

But Mullá Ḥusayn was anxious to rejoin his companions. Since that afternoon—and long ago it seemed—when he had sent them into the city and had himself lingered outside the city-gates, he had had no news of them nor they of him. So he rose and asked to be permitted to depart. His Host smilingly told him: 'If you leave in such a state, whoever sees you will assuredly say: "This poor youth has lost his mind."' 'At that moment,' Mullá Ḥusayn has said, 'the clock registered two hours and eleven minutes after sunset.'

In that moment a new Dispensation was born.

'This night,' said He who ushered in the new Dispensation, He who was to herald a new cycle, 'this very hour will, in the days to come, be celebrated as one of the greatest and most significant of all festivals.'*

The evening meal was now served. Mullá Ḥusayn after-

* Today that night and that hour are celebrated with joy and reverence and gratitude all over the world.

wards recalled: 'That holy repast refreshed alike my body and soul. In the presence of my Host, at that hour, I felt as though I were feeding upon the fruits of Paradise . . . Had my youthful Host no other claim to greatness, this were sufficient—that He received me with that quality of hospitality and loving-kindness which I was convinced no other human being could possibly reveal.

'I sat spellbound by His utterance, oblivious of time and of those who awaited me . . . Sleep had departed from me that night. I was enthralled by the music of that voice which rose and fell as He chanted; now swelling forth as He revealed verses of the Qayyúmu'l-Asmá',* again acquiring ethereal, subtle harmonies as He uttered the prayers He was revealing. At the end of each invocation, He would repeat this verse: "Far from the glory of thy Lord, the All-Glorious, be that which His creatures affirm of Him! And peace be upon His Messengers! And praise be to God, the Lord of all beings!"†' Such was Mullá Ḥusayn's recollection of that momentous night.

Then He who stood as the Vicegerent of God on earth thus addressed Mullá Ḥusayn, who only a few hours before had been so anxious, tormented and unsure:

> O thou who art the first to believe in Me! Verily I say, I am the Báb, the Gate of God, and thou art the Bábu'l-Báb, the gate of that Gate. Eighteen souls must, in the beginning, spontaneously and of their own accord, accept Me and recognise the truth of My Revelation. Unwarned and uninvited, each of these must seek independently to find Me. And when their number is complete, one of them must needs be chosen to accompany Me on My pilgrimage to Mecca and Medina. There I shall deliver the Message of God to the Sharíf of Mecca.

* The commentary on the Súrih of Joseph.

† Qur'án xxxvii, 180.

And then He laid this injunction upon 'the first to believe' in Him: 'It is incumbent upon you not to divulge, either to your companions or to any other soul, that which you have seen and heard.'

'This Revelation,' Mullá Ḥusayn has further related, 'so suddenly and impetuously thrust upon me, came as a thunderbolt which, for a time, seemed to have benumbed my faculties. I was blinded by its dazzling splendour and overwhelmed by its crushing force. Excitement, joy, awe, and wonder stirred the depths of my soul. Predominant among these emotions was a sense of gladness and strength which seemed to have transfigured me. How feeble and impotent, how dejected and timid, I had felt previously! Then I could neither write nor walk, so tremulous were my hands and feet. Now, however, the knowledge of His Revelation had galvanised my being. I felt possessed of such courage and power that were the world, all its peoples and its potentates, to rise against me, I would, alone and undaunted, withstand their onslaught. The universe seemed but a handful of dust in my grasp.'

On that early morning of May 23rd 1844 when Mullá Ḥusayn stepped out into the streets of Shíráz, his heart brimming with joy, he abandoned a priestly career which would have brought him high honours. He abandoned it willingly and knowingly for a task which, though great and noble, would bring him jeers and humiliation. He was well-known amongst the circle of the divines who exercised authority. He had the capacity, the intelligence and the learning which would have placed him in years to come in the forefront of the spiritual guides of the nation. Power and riches would have been his. But by giving his allegiance to the young Siyyid of Shíráz whom he had met under such strange circumstances, Mullá Ḥusayn renounced all this, and chose a path in the opposite direction.

Mullá Ḥusayn was not alone in his high resolve. Others

with similar prospects of a clerical vocation journeyed to Shíráz in search of light and truth. They too had set out at the bidding of Siyyid Káẓim. As if by a magnet, they were drawn to Shíráz. How can one explain it otherwise? They had no intimation that in this city lived the One whom they sought. A force far greater than themselves led their steps to Shíráz, to their journey's end. As ordained by the Báb, they found Him, each one, independently. They were true, sincere and eager and they had their reward.

The last to arrive was a youth of twenty-two, whose home was in Bárfurúsh* in the province of Mázindarán which borders the Caspian Sea. When he was a boy in his early teens, his father, Áqá Muḥammad-Ṣáliḥ, had died. Devoting himself to the pursuit of learning he had joined the circle of Siyyid Káẓim in Karbilá. Eventually, he became an outstanding disciple of that remarkable teacher. It is recorded that the night before this youth, whose name was Mullá Muḥammad-'Alí, reached Shíráz, the Báb told Mullá Ḥusayn that on the following day one would arrive whose acceptance of the new theophany would 'complete the number of My chosen disciples'. Next evening as the Báb, accompanied by Mullá Ḥusayn, was going towards His house, they encountered a young man whose dress and appearance showed the effects of a long journey. The newcomer went to Mullá Ḥusayn whom he knew well as a fellow-disciple of Siyyid Káẓim, greeted him and immediately asked whether he had found the object of his quest. Mullá Ḥusayn was not at liberty to divulge the fact that he had, and he tried to pacify his friend and avoid the subject. It was useless, for that youth had seen the Báb. His retort to Mullá Ḥusayn was astounding: 'Why seek you to hide Him from me? I can recognise Him by His gait. I confidently testify that none besides Him, whether in the East or in the West, can claim to be the Truth. None other can manifest the power and majesty

* Now named Bábul.

that radiate from His holy person.' Mullá Ḥusayn was amazed, and leaving the newcomer he walked on and told the Báb what had transpired. Having already anticipated the arrival of that youth, although he had certainly not received any word from him, the Báb observed: 'Marvel not at his strange behaviour. We have in the world of the spirit been communing with that youth. We know him already . . . Go to him and summon him forthwith to Our presence.' Thus did Mullá Muḥammad-'Alíy-i-Bárfurúshí, whom the Báb honoured with the title of Quddús (the Most Holy), attain his heart's desire.

These disciples of the Báb are called the Letters of the Living.* All but one met the Báb face to face, and recognized in Him the Lord of the Age whom they sought. That single exception was a gifted woman, an accomplished writer of verse, courageous, a total stranger to fear, of whom Lord Curzon says:

> Beauty and the female sex also lent their consecration to the new creed, and the heroism of the lovely but ill-fated poetess of Kazvin, Zerin Taj† (Crown of Gold), or Kurrat-el-Ain (Solace of the Eyes), who, throwing off the veil, carried the missionary torch far and wide, is one of the most affecting episodes in modern history.[2]

And here is the tribute of another eminent Englishman, Edward Granville Browne, to this unique woman:

> The appearance of such a woman as Ḳurratu'l-'Ayn is in any country and any age a rare phenomenon, but in such a country as Persia it is a prodigy—nay, almost a miracle. Alike in virtue of her marvellous beauty, her

* Ḥurúf-i-Ḥayy. Ḥayy (the Living) is an Arabic word, numerically equivalent to eighteen.

† Zarrín-Táj.

rare intellectual gifts, her fervid eloquence, her fearless devotion and her glorious martyrdom, she stands forth incomparable and immortal amidst her countrywomen. Had the Bábí religion no other claim to greatness, this were sufficient—that it produced a heroine like Ḳurratu'l-'Ayn.[3]

Qurratu'l-'Ayn belonged to a family famed for its learning. Her father, Ḥájí Mullá Ṣáliḥ, and her uncle, Ḥájí Mullá Muḥammad-Taqí,[4] were both leading figures among the clergy. But they were far too orthodox for this great woman's spiritual susceptibilities, although a younger uncle, Ḥájí Mullá 'Alí, had become a supporter of the Shaykhí school.* Qurratu'l-'Ayn was married to the son of Ḥájí Mullá Muḥammad-Taqí—her cousin, Mullá Muḥammad. They had children, but their marriage was disastrous. Mullá Muḥammad was even more fanatical and narrow-minded than his father and a wide gulf yawned between husband and wife.

Qurratu'l-'Ayn had another cousin, Mullá Javád, who had accepted the rational views of Shaykh Aḥmad and Siyyid Káẓim. Having learned in this cousin's library of the teaching of the illustrious sage of Karbilá who had gone far beyond the limits of orthodoxy, Qurratu'l-'Ayn corresponded with Siyyid Káẓim and gave him her allegiance. From him she received the name Qurratu'l-'Ayn. In vain did her elders attempt to dampen her enthusiasm. No persuasion or threat could stop the tide of her newly-found devotion. And when she decided to leave her home and her family and join the circle of Siyyid Káẓim, nothing could thwart her purpose. To appreciate the boldness and gravity of her action, one must realize how sheltered were the Eastern women of those days; her behaviour could be seen only as scandalous and almost unprecedented. However, she reached Karbilá too

* The school of Shaykh Aḥmad.

late. Ten days prior to her arrival Siyyid Káẓim had passed away. Qurratu'l-'Ayn remained in Karbilá. She was convinced that before long the One promised to them would appear. Now, many of the disciples of Siyyid Káẓim were setting out on their search. One of them was Qurratu'l-'Ayn's brother-in-law, the husband of her younger sister Marḍíyyih. She gave this relative, Mírzá Muḥammad-'Alí, a sealed letter and told him to deliver it to the One whom they expected and sought. A verbal message in verse was added to the letter: 'Say to Him, from me,' she said,

> 'The effulgence of thy face flashed forth and
> the rays of thy visage arose on high;
> Then speak the word, "Am I not your
> Lord?" and "Thou art, Thou art!"
> we will all reply.'[5]

When Mírzá Muḥammad-'Alí reached the presence of the Báb, he gave Him the letter and the message; and the Báb numbered her among the Letters of the Living. Thus it was that this fearless, eloquent pioneer of woman's emancipation joined the ranks of the first disciples of the Báb. Qurratu'l-'Ayn is better known as Ṭáhirih—the Pure One—a designation by which she will ever be remembered.*

The Letters of the Living, the eighteen disciples who found the Báb 'independently and of their own accord', were:

Mullá Muḥammad-'Alíy-i-Bárfurú<u>sh</u>í, entitled Quddús.
Mullá Ḥusayn-i-Bu<u>sh</u>rú'í, entitled Bábu'l-Báb.
Mírzá Muḥammad-Ḥasan-i-Bu<u>sh</u>rú'í, brother of Mullá Ḥusayn.
Mírzá Muḥammad-Báqir, nephew of Mullá Ḥusayn.
Mírzá Muḥammad-'Alíy-i-Qazvíní, brother-in-law of Ṭáhirih.
Mullá Aḥmad-i-Ibdál-i-Mará<u>gh</u>í'í.

* We shall see on p. 163 how she acquired this name.

Mullá Yúsuf-i-Ardibílí.
Mullá Jalíl-i-Urúmí.
Mullá Maḥmúd-i-Khu'í.

These nine were martyrs who fell during 'the Mázindarán upheaval' (see p. 175).

Mullá 'Alíy-i-Basṭámí, the first martyr of the Bábí Dispensation. He was put to death somewhere in 'Iráq.

Qurratu'l-'Ayn, Ṭáhirih, whose original name was Umm-Salamih.

Siyyid Ḥusayn-i-Yazdí, known as Kátib (the Amanuensis), and also 'Azíz.

Ṭáhirih and Siyyid Ḥusayn-i-Yazdí suffered martyrdom in the holocaust of August 1852, subsequent to the attempt made by two Bábís on the life of Náṣiri'd-Dín Sháh.

Shaykh Sa'íd-i-Hindí (the Indian). He met his death somewhere in India, though no one knows how and where.

Mullá Báqir-i-Tabrízí. He lived on to the advent of Bahá'u'lláh and believed in Him.

Mírzá Hádíy-i-Qazvíní, son of Ḥájí Mírzá 'Abdu'l-Vahháb, and brother of Mírzá Muḥammad-'Alí (the fifth name above). Mírzá Hádí remained apart from other Bábís and taught the Faith with caution.

Mírzá Muḥammad Rawḍih-Khán-i-Yazdí. He too remained apart from other Bábís and was generally known as a Shaykhí. But he never renounced his faith and taught it whenever he could.

Mullá Khudá-Bakhsh-i-Qúchání, later known as Mullá 'Alíy-i-Rází. He died a natural death, but his son Mashíyyatu'lláh later met with martyrdom in his youth.

Mullá Ḥasan-i-Bajistání. Doubts assailed him after the martyrdom of the Báb, because he did not consider himself worthy of the station given to him. Forced to leave his home, he went to 'Iráq and attained the presence of Bahá'u'lláh.

Mullá 'Alíy-i-Basṭámí was given the mission to return to 'Iráq and inform the people in that heartland of the Shí'ah persuasion that the Báb had appeared, but not to divulge, as yet, any particulars that might reveal His identity. To him the Báb said:

> Your faith must be immovable as the rock, must weather every storm and survive every calamity. Suffer not the denunciations of the foolish and the calumnies of the clergy to afflict you, or to turn you from your purpose. For you are called to partake of the celestial banquet prepared for you in the immortal Realm. You are the first to leave the House of God, and to suffer for His sake. If you be slain in His path, remember that great will be your reward, and goodly the gift which will be bestowed upon you.

Mullá 'Alí was soon on his way to 'Iráq. Then the Báb called together the other sixteen disciples and spoke to them, adjuring them to go out into the world and serve their God in the light of the faith given to them:

> O My beloved friends! You are the bearers of the name of God in this Day. You have been chosen as the repositories of His mystery. It behoves each one of you to manifest the attributes of God, and to exemplify by your deeds and words the signs of His righteousness, His power and glory. The very members of your body must bear witness to the loftiness of your purpose, the integrity of your life, the reality of your faith, and the exalted character of your devotion. For verily I say, this is the Day spoken of by God in His Book: 'On that day will We set a seal upon their mouths; yet shall their hands speak unto Us, and their feet shall bear witness to that which they shall have done.'* Ponder the words of Jesus addressed to His disciples, as He sent them forth to

* Qur'án xxxvi, 65.

propagate the Cause of God. In words such as these, He bade them arise and fulfil their mission: 'Ye are even as the fire which in the darkness of the night has been kindled upon the mountain-top. Let your light shine before the eyes of men. Such must be the purity of your character and the degree of your renunciation, that the people of the earth may through you recognise and be drawn closer to the heavenly Father who is the Source of purity and grace. For none has seen the Father who is in heaven. You who are His spiritual children must by your deeds exemplify His virtues, and witness to His glory. You are the salt of the earth, but if the salt have lost its savour, wherewith shall it be salted? Such must be the degree of your detachment, that into whatever city you enter to proclaim and teach the Cause of God, you should in no wise expect either meat or reward from its people. Nay, when you depart out of that city, you should shake the dust from off your feet. As you have entered it pure and undefiled, so must you depart from that city. For verily I say, the heavenly Father is ever with you and keeps watch over you. If you be faithful to Him, He will assuredly deliver into your hands all the treasures of the earth, and will exalt you above all the rulers and kings of the world.' O My Letters! Verily I say, immensely exalted is this Day above the days of the Apostles of old. Nay, immeasurable is the difference! You are the witnesses of the Dawn of the promised Day of God. You are the partakers of the mystic chalice of His Revelation. Gird up the loins of endeavour, and be mindful of the words of God as revealed in His Book: 'Lo, the Lord thy God is come, and with Him is the company of His angels arrayed before Him!'* Purge your hearts of worldly desires, and let angelic virtues be your adorning. Strive that by your deeds you may bear witness to the truth of these words of God, and beware lest, by 'turning back',† He may 'change you for another people',† who

* Qur'án lxxxix, 23.

† *ibid.*, xlvii.

'shall not be your like',* and who shall take from you the Kingdom of God. The days when idle worship was deemed sufficient are ended. The time is come when naught but the purest motive, supported by deeds of stainless purity, can ascend to the throne of the Most High and be acceptable unto Him. 'The good word riseth up unto Him, and the righteous deed will cause it to be exalted before Him.'* You are the lowly, of whom God has thus spoken in His Book: 'And We desire to show favour to those who were brought low in the land, and to make them spiritual leaders among men, and to make them Our heirs.'† You have been called to this station; you will attain to it, only if you arise to trample beneath your feet every earthly desire, and endeavour to become those honoured servants of His who speak not till He hath spoken, and who do His bidding'. You are the first Letters that have been generated from the Primal Point [the Báb], the first Springs that have welled out from the Source of this Revelation. Beseech the Lord your God to grant that no earthly entanglements, no worldly affections, no ephemeral pursuits, may tarnish the purity, or embitter the sweetness, of that grace which flows through you. I am preparing you for the advent of a mighty Day. Exert your utmost endeavour that, in the world to come, I, who am now instructing you, may, before the mercy-seat of God, rejoice in your deeds and glory in your achievements. The secret of the Day that is to come is now concealed. It can neither be divulged nor estimated. The newly born babe of that Day excels the wisest and most venerable men of this time, and the lowliest and most unlearned of that period shall surpass in understanding the most erudite and accomplished divines of this age. Scatter throughout the length and breadth of this land, and, with steadfast feet and sanctified hearts, prepare the way for His coming. Heed not your weaknesses and frailty; fix

* Qur'án.

† *ibid.*, xxviii, 4.

your gaze upon the invincible power of the Lord, your God, the Almighty. Has He not, in past days, caused Abraham, in spite of His seeming helplessness, to triumph over the forces of Nimrod? Has He not enabled Moses, whose staff was His only companion, to vanquish Pharaoh and his hosts? Has He not established the ascendancy of Jesus, poor and lowly as He was in the eyes of men, over the combined forces of the Jewish people? Has He not subjected the barbarous and militant tribes of Arabia to the holy and transforming discipline of Muḥammad, His Prophet? Arise in His name, put your trust wholly in Him, and be assured of ultimate victory.

CHAPTER 2

HE WHOM THEY SOUGHT

The gentle spirit of the Bāb is surely high up in the cycles of eternity. Who can fail, as Prof. Browne says, to be attracted by him?

—T. K. Cheyne, D.Litt., D.D.

Siyyid (or Mírzá) 'Alí-Muḥammad, known to history as the Báb, was the son of Siyyid (or Mír) Muḥammad-Riḍá, a mercer of Shíráz.[1] He was born on October 20th 1819 (Muḥarram 1st, 1235 A.H.). Through both His father and His mother He was descended from Imám Ḥusayn,* the third Imám. Thus He stood in direct line of descent from the Prophet Muḥammad. According to Mírzá Abu'l-Faḍl-i-Gulpáygání, Siyyid Muḥammad-Riḍá, the Báb's father, died when his only child was an infant, unweaned. Then the care of the child devolved upon a maternal uncle, Ḥájí Mírzá Siyyid 'Alí. He was the only relative of the Báb to espouse His Cause openly during His lifetime and, as will be seen, to accept martyrdom for His sake. But according to a manuscript history of the Bábí-Bahá'í Faith in Shíráz by Ḥájí Mírzá Ḥabíbu'lláh-i-Afnán,† Siyyid Muḥammad-Riḍá passed away when his son was nine years old, and 'Abdu'l-Bahá appears to confirm this account.‡

Two of Siyyid Muḥammad-Riḍa's paternal cousins rose

* He was the son of Fáṭimih and 'Alí.

† Ḥájí Mírzá Ḥabíbu'lláh's father, Áqá Mírzá-Áqá, was a nephew of the wife of the Báb, and his paternal grandfather, Áqá Mírzá Zaynu'l-'Ábidín, was a paternal cousin of the father of the Báb. (See Foreword for other details of the manuscript.)

‡ Browne (ed.), *A Traveller's Narrative*, Vol. II, p. 2.

to eminence in the ranks of the Shí'ah divines, and both bore allegiance, in strict secrecy, to their kinsman when His claim to be 'the Qá'im of the House of Muḥammad' became publicly known. Of the two, the more famed and distinguished was Ḥájí Mírzá Muḥammad-Ḥasan (1815–95), known as Mírzáy-i-Shírází, who, like all the leading Shí'ah divines, resided in 'Iráq. He was the most influential ecclesiastic of his time, powerful enough to wreck the Tobacco Régie, the monopoly concession which Náṣiri'd-Dín Sháh (reigned 1848–96) gave to Major Gerald F. Talbot, a British citizen, in the summer of 1889.[2] Mírzáy-i-Shírází put the use of tobacco under an interdict and the people of Írán, even the women in the Sháh's harem, ceased to use it. Náṣiri'd-Dín Sháh was forced early in 1892 to cancel the concession and pay the Tobacco Corporation an indemnity of £500,000. The father of Mírzáy-i-Shírází, named Mírzá Maḥmúd, was a noted calligraphist, and was uncle to the father of the Báb.

The other celebrated ecclesiastic, cousin to Siyyid Muḥammad-Riḍá, was Ḥájí Siyyid Javád, the Imám-Jum'ih* of Kirmán. It was Quddús who gave this dignitary the news of the advent of the Báb. Ḥájí Siyyid Javád extended his protection to Quddús, despite the clamour of his adversaries.

The mother of the Báb was Fáṭimih-Bagum. She was the daughter of Mírzá Muḥammad-Ḥusayn, a merchant of Shíráz, and had three brothers. Of these, Ḥájí Mírzá Siyyid 'Alí became the guardian of the Báb, while Ḥájí Mírzá Siyyid Muḥammad and Ḥájí Mírzá Ḥasan-'Alí, although not enlisted in the ranks of the followers of their illustrious Nephew, feature in His story.

Every account that we have of Siyyid 'Alí-Muḥammad's childhood indicates that He was not an ordinary child.

* Literally, 'The Leader of Friday'—the leading imám (he who leads the congregation in prayer) in a town or city.

When He was sent to school, He so surprised the schoolmaster, Shaykh 'Ábid, with His wisdom and intelligence that the bewildered man took the child back to His uncle, and said that he had nothing to teach this gifted pupil: 'He, verily, stands in no need of teachers such as I.' The uncle had already noticed the remarkable qualities of his ward, and it is recorded that on this occasion he was very stern with Him: 'Have You forgotten my instructions? Have I not already admonished You to follow the example of Your fellow-pupils, to observe silence, and to listen attentively to every word spoken by Your teacher?' It was totally alien to the nature of that gentle child to disregard the wishes of His guardian. He returned to school and conducted Himself on the pattern of other children. Nothing, however, could restrain the superior mind and intelligence possessed by that exceptional boy. As time went on, the schoolmaster became convinced that he could not help his student; in the role of instructor he felt as the instructed.

It should also be said that schools such as that attended by Siyyid 'Alí-Muḥammad, which were common in those days, were one-man affairs and matters taught were elementary, although pupils were trained to read the Qur'án, even if they could not possibly understand the meaning of the sacred text which is of course in Arabic. The Báb did not go beyond this school nor the tuition of Shaykh 'Ábid. Thus His schooling was meagre.

The Báb was only five years old when He was sent to receive tuition from Shaykh 'Ábid. Ḥájí Mírzá Ḥabíbu'lláh's narrative contains an account of His first day at school, related by Áqá Muḥammad-Ibráhím-i-Ismá'íl Bag, a well-known merchant of Shíráz, who was a fellow-scholar at the age of twelve. The Báb had taken a seat, with great courtesy, in between this boy and another pupil who was also much older than Himself. His head was bowed over the primer put in front of Him, the first lines of which He had been taught to repeat. But He would not utter a word. When asked why He did not read aloud as other boys were doing He made no reply. Just then two boys, sitting near them, were heard to recite a couplet from Ḥáfiẓ, which runs thus:

From the pinnacles of Heaven they call out unto thee;
I know not what hath thee here entrapped.[3]

'That is your answer,' said the Báb, turning to Áqá Muḥammad-Ibráhím.

Ḥájí Mírzá Ḥabíbu'lláh also tells us that, apart from teaching boys, Shaykh 'Ábid had a regular class for theological students. On one occasion some of these students posed a question which after a long period of discussion remained unresolved. Shaykh 'Ábid told them that he would consult some authoritative works that same night and on the morrow present them with the solution. Just then the Báb, who had been listening, spoke and with sound reasoning propounded the answer which they sought. They were wonder-struck, for they had no recollection of discussing that particular subject within earshot of the Báb, who might then have looked up references in books and memorized them to repeat parrot-wise. Shaykh 'Ábid asked Him where He had gained that knowledge. The boy replied smilingly with a couplet from Ḥáfiẓ:

Should the grace of the Holy Spirit once again deign to assist,
Others will also do what Christ could perform.[3]

Not only did the mental faculties of the Báb astound the schoolmaster; the nobility of His character impressed him even more. Indeed all those who were close or near to His person could not but yield to the charm of His being. Years later, when the Báb had raised the call of a new theophany, the schoolmaster casting his mind over the past told Ḥájí Siyyid Javád-i-Karbilá'í, a learned scion of a celebrated priestly family (the Baḥru'l-'Ulúm*), that Siyyid 'Alí-Muḥammad was always dignified and serene, that He was very handsome and cared little for the pastimes of other boys. Some mornings, the schoolmaster recalled, He was late coming to school and when asked the reason He remained silent. On occasions Shaykh 'Ábid sent other pupils to call at His home and ask Him to come to school. They would return to say that they had found Him at His devotions. One day, when He had come late to school and was questioned by Shaykh 'Ábid, the Báb said quietly that He had been in the house of His 'Grandfather'. Thus do the Siyyids refer to their ancestor the Prophet Muḥammad. To the schoolmaster's remonstrances that He was only a child of ten from whom such rigorous attention to devotions was not demanded, He replied quietly again, 'I wish to be like My Grandfather'. At that time, Shaykh 'Ábid said, he had taken the words of Siyyid 'Alí-Muḥammad as childish *naïveté*.[4]

A certain book-binder of Shíráz named Siyyid Muḥammad, whose house neighboured that of the Báb's, but who in later years removed to Saráy-i-Amír † in Ṭihrán to ply his trade, had heard Shaykh 'Ábid relate that it was customary, when the season was clement, for the boys to invite their teacher and their fellow-pupils on Fridays (the day of rest) to an outing in one of the numerous gardens which bordered the city of Shíráz. At times they would find that the Báb had betaken Himself to a shaded, secluded spot in a corner of the orchard to pray and meditate.

Ḥájí Siyyid Javád-i-Karbilá'í had himself encountered the Báb in the years of His childhood. He was normally a resident of Karbilá and had attended regularly the discourses of Siyyid Káẓim-i-Rashtí, eventually becoming one of his ardent disciples. But he was also a man of travel who em-

* Literally, the 'Sea of All Knowledge'.
† A well-known inn (caravanserai).

barked now and then on long journeys. Twice he went on pilgrimage to Mecca and spent some time there teaching and discoursing. He visited India and stayed in Bombay for a while. One of his journeys took him to Shíráz, at a time when the Báb was about nine years old. Being well acquainted with Ḥájí Siyyid Muḥammad (one of the Báb's maternal uncles), Ḥájí Siyyid Javád visited him occasionally. Decades later he recalled that on one of these visits he could hear the intonations of a melodious, enraptured voice, coming from the direction of the alcove reserved for devotions. Before long a boy stepped out of the recess and Ḥájí Mírzá Siyyid Muḥammad introduced Him as his nephew who was orphaned. Another visit coincided with the Báb's return from school. Ḥájí Siyyid Javád noticed that He held a batch of papers and asked what they were. Very courteously the boy replied that they were His calligraphic exercises. When Ḥájí Siyyid Javád inspected them he marvelled at their excellence.

On yet another and later occasion, when the Báb was for a time engaged in trading in the port of Búshihr, Ḥájí Siyyid Javád spent six months in that town, living in the same inn as the Báb. Thus they often met. Still later, in Karbilá, Ḥájí Siyyid Javád again met the Báb, who by then was in His early twenties.

When Mullá 'Alíy-i-Basṭámí reached 'Iráq with the tidings of the advent of the Báb, the news spread rapidly among the divines and the students of theology. Ḥájí Siyyid Javád was one of those particularly attracted, and he often urged Mullá 'Alí to divulge the name of Him who had put forth such a tremendous claim. But the Báb had emphatically forbidden Mullá 'Alí to mention His name or give any clue to His identity. To all insistent requests Mullá 'Alí merely said that before long His identity would be revealed to them. No one, according to the testimony of Ḥájí Siyyid Javád, suspected that the Báb could be the young merchant of Shíráz who had only recently lived among them. Most of the Shaykhís believed that the Báb must be one of the close disciples of Siyyid Káẓim.

Then it occurred to Ḥájí Siyyid Javád to invite Mullá 'Alí to his own home and question him more closely. Seated on the roof of the house, in the neighbourhood of the Shrine of Imám Ḥusayn, the two of them conversed at length about the 'Great Event', but no matter how hard he tried, Ḥájí Siyyid Javád could not induce his guest to disclose the secret which he had been bidden to withhold. So frustrated did he feel that, on his own admission, Ḥájí Siyyid Javád gripped the arms of Mullá 'Alí, pushed him hard against the wall and exclaimed: 'What am I to do with you, Mullá 'Alí! Kill you? Won't you say who that wondrous Being is? Won't you relieve us of this misery?' Gasping for breath, Mullá 'Alí replied: 'Siyyid Javád! It is forbidden. You yourself are a man of learning. You should know better. It is forbidden.' And then quite unexpectedly and without knowing why, Mullá 'Alí added that the Báb had specially mentioned that all His letters extant in 'Iráq, whoever the recipient might have been, ought to be sent to Shíráz. No sooner had Mullá 'Alí spoken than Ḥájí Siyyid Javád had, in a flash, a mental picture of Siyyid 'Alí-Muḥammad, whom he had known and admired since His childhood. He ran down the stairs to the room where he kept his papers, gathered up the letters he had received from Siyyid 'Alí-Muḥammad and hurried back to the roof. The moment Mullá 'Alí caught sight of the seal on those letters he burst into tears, and so did Ḥájí Siyyid Javád. They wept for joy, and between his sobs Mullá 'Alí kept repeating: 'Áqá Siyyid Javád! Áqá Siyyid Javád! I did not mention any name to you. It is forbidden to mention His blessed name. Don't mention His name to anyone.'[5]

Thus did Ḥájí Siyyid Javád-i-Karbilá'í find his new Faith, to which he remained steadfastly loyal throughout his long life. We shall hear later a good deal more of this remarkable man.

Siyyid 'Alí-Muḥammad had some six to seven years of schooling with Shaykh 'Ábid. In all probability He left the school at the Qahviy-i-Awlíyá' before He was thirteen. According to Ḥájí Mírzá Ḥabíbu'lláh's narrative, He joined Ḥájí Mírzá Siyyid 'Alí, His uncle-guardian, in business when He was fifteen years old,* and shortly afterwards moved to Búshihr. Pages of commercial accounts which He kept put it beyond doubt that the Báb left Shíráz for Búshihr when He was nearly sixteen. There can be little doubt that at an early age the Báb took over the complete management of the trading-house in Búshihr. His scrupulous attention to detail and His undeviating fairness in transactions became widely known in the region. A man who had consigned to Him some goods to sell was astonished to find, when he received his money, that it was more than could be obtained at current prices. He wanted to return some of it. The Báb told him that it was only fair and just that he should be given that particular sum, because his goods would have fetched exactly that amount had they been offered for sale when the market was at its best.

A.-L.-M. Nicolas maintains that the Báb was also engaged in writing and composing, during this period of His sojourn in Búshihr. He mentions a treatise, the *Risáliy-i-Fiqhíyyih*, as having come from the pen of the Báb during those years.[6] His statement is corroborated by Ḥájí Mírzá Ḥabíbu'lláh's narrative:

> One day in Egypt during the time when Mírzá Abu'l-Faḍl was occupied with writing his book, the *Fará'id*,

* Islamic law specifies fifteen as the age of maturity.

we came to talk about the early years of the Báb, prior to His declaration, and the period when He was engaged in trading. Mírzá Abu'l-Faḍl related the following to me: 'I myself heard the late Ḥájí Siyyid Javád-i-Karbilá'í say that when the Báb was pursuing the career of a merchant in Búshihr, he . . . because of his friendship with the uncles of the Báb used to stay with them whenever he visited either Shíráz or Búshihr. One day Ḥájí Mírzá Siyyid Muḥammad came to him with a request. "Give some good counsel to my nephew . . . tell Him not to write certain things which can only arouse the jealousy of some people: these people cannot bear to see a young merchant of little schooling show such erudition, they feel envious." Ḥájí Mírzá Siyyid Muḥammad had been very insistent that Ḥájí Siyyid Javád should counsel the Báb to desist from writing. Ḥájí Siyyid Javád had however replied with these lines of verse: "The fair of face cannot put up with the veil; Shut him in, and out of the window will he show his visage," and had added: "We are earth-bound and He is celestial. Our counsel is of no use to Him." '

Mullá Muḥammad-i-Zarandí, Nabíl-i-A'ẓam, lays particular stress on the Báb's strict regard for His devotions on Fridays. Even the torrid conditions of Búshihr, he states, did not deter the Báb. Writers of such histories as the *Násikhu't-Taváríkh*,[7] hostile to the Báb, have alleged that long exposure to the severe heat of the sun in that seaport, while engaged in prayers, affected His mind. They have gone on to assert that it was this derangement of mind which led Him to make extravagant claims. But Ḥájí Mírzá Jání of Káshán refutes any suggestion that the Báb deliberately practised austerities, or that He found Himself a 'murshid' (spiritual guide) to direct Him along such lines.

Unfortunately records of the years that the Báb spent in Búshihr are scant. We cannot be certain as to the exact dates when He took over the complete management of the trading-house and when He retired. Ḥájí Mu'ínu's-Salṭanih of Tabríz states in his chronicle that the Báb assumed direct responsibility at the age of twenty. If that statement be correct, the period during which He acted on His own was quite brief. According to Mírzá Abu'l-Faḍl of Gulpáygán, He journeyed to the holy cities of 'Iráq in the spring of 1841, stayed in 'Iráq for nearly seven months and returned to His 'native province of Fárs' in the autumn of that year. Ḥájí Mírzá Ḥabíbu'lláh states that the Báb's sojourn in Búshihr lasted six years. According to him, when the Báb decided to go on pilgrimage to the holy cities of 'Iráq, He wrote to His uncles in Shíráz asking them to come and take over the business from Him. His uncles, however, procrastinated, whereupon the Báb settled all the outstanding matters in Búshihr Himself, brought His books up to date, locked and sealed the door of the office and left the keys with the gate-keeper of the caravanserai, to be handed over to any one of His uncles. He informed His uncles of what He had done and explained that since they had not heeded His repeated pleas He had no other alternative, determined as He was to go on pilgrimage to the holy cities.* Ḥájí Mírzá Siyyid Muḥammad was greatly perturbed lest their credit be damaged and their clients suffer serious loss. But Ḥájí Mírzá Siyyid 'Alí assured him that their nephew would never do anything to compromise them and that all accounts would be found in perfect order. Ḥájí Mírzá Siyyid Muḥammad hurried to Búshihr where a close inspection of the books satisfied him that nothing had been left to chance.

* The holy cities of 'Iráq are: (1) Najaf and (2) Karbilá (both already mentioned), which have within them the shrines of the first and the third Imáms, respectively; (3) Káẓimayn, in the close vicinity of Baghdád, which harbours the shrines of Imám Músá al-Káẓim, the seventh Imám, and Imám Muḥammad al-Taqí, the ninth Imám; (4) Sámarrá, where the shrines of the tenth and the eleventh Imáms, 'Alí an-Naqí and Ḥasan al-'Askarí, are situated.

While in Karbilá the Báb visited Siyyid Káẓim-i-Rashtí and attended his discourses. But these occasional visits did not and could not make Him a pupil or disciple of Siyyid Káẓim. His adversaries have alleged that He sat at the feet of Siyyid Káẓim for months on end to learn from him. But accounts that we have from close associates of Siyyid Káẓim all indicate that the Shaykhí leader welcomed and received Siyyid 'Alí-Muḥammad, on every occasion, with great reverence. Here is a long account by Shaykh Ḥasan-i-Zunúzí:

> My days were spent in the service of Siyyid Káẓim, to whom I was greatly attached. One day, at the hour of dawn, I was suddenly awakened by Mullá Naw-rúz, one of his intimate attendants, who, in great excitement, bade me arise and follow him. We went to the house of Siyyid Káẓim, where we found him fully dressed, wearing his 'abá, and ready to leave his home. He asked me to accompany him. 'A highly esteemed and distinguished Person,' he said, 'has arrived. I feel it incumbent upon us both to visit Him.' The morning light had just broken when I found myself walking with him through the streets of Karbilá. We soon reached a house, at the door of which stood a Youth, as if expectant to receive us. He wore a green turban, and His countenance revealed an expression of humility and kindliness which I can never describe. He quietly approached us, extended His arms towards Siyyid Káẓim, and lovingly embraced him. His affability and loving-kindness singularly contrasted with the sense of profound reverence that characterised the attitude of Siyyid Káẓim towards Him. Speechless and with bowed head, he received the many expressions of affection and esteem with which that Youth greeted him. We were soon led by Him to the upper floor of that house, and entered a chamber bedecked with flowers and redolent of the loveliest perfume. He bade us be seated. We knew not, however, what seats we actually occupied, so over-

powering was the sense of delight which seized us. We observed a silver cup which had been placed in the centre of the room, which our youthful Host, soon after we were seated, filled to overflowing, and handed to Siyyid Káẓim, saying: 'A drink of a pure beverage shall their Lord give them.'* Siyyid Káẓim held the cup with both hands and quaffed it. A feeling of reverent joy filled his being, a feeling which he could not suppress. I too was presented with a cupful of that beverage, though no words were addressed to me. All that was spoken at that memorable gathering was the above-mentioned verse of the Qur'án. Soon after, the Host arose from His seat and, accompanying us to the threshold of the house, bade us farewell. I was mute with wonder, and knew not how to express the cordiality of His welcome, the dignity of His bearing, the charm of that face, and the delicious fragrance of that beverage. How great was my amazement when I saw my teacher quaff without the least hesitation that holy draught from a silver cup, the use of which, according to the precepts of Islám, is forbidden to the faithful. I could not explain the motive which could have induced the Siyyid to manifest such profound reverence in the presence of that Youth—a reverence which even the sight of the shrine of the Siyyidu'sh-Shuhadá'† had failed to excite. Three days later, I saw that same Youth arrive and take His seat in the midst of the company of the assembled disciples of Siyyid Káẓim. He sat close to the threshold, and with the same modesty and dignity of bearing listened to the discourse of the Siyyid. As soon as his eyes fell upon that Youth, the Siyyid discontinued his address and held his peace. Whereupon one of his disciples begged him to resume the argument which he had left unfinished. 'What more shall I say?' replied Siyyid Káẓim, as he

* Qur'án lxxvi, 21.

† 'Siyyidu'sh-Shuhadá'' can be variously translated as the 'Head', the 'Chief', the 'Master' or 'Prince of the Martyrs'. It is applied to Imám Ḥusayn (the grandson of the Prophet Muḥammad) who was the third Imám.

turned his face toward the Báb. 'Lo, the Truth is more manifest than the ray of light that has fallen upon that lap!' I immediately observed that the ray to which the Siyyid referred had fallen upon the lap of that same Youth whom we had recently visited. 'Why is it,' that questioner enquired, 'that you neither reveal His name nor identify His person?' To this the Siyyid replied by pointing with his finger to his own throat, implying that were he to divulge His name, they both would be put to death instantly. This added still further to my perplexity. I had already heard my teacher observe that so great is the perversity of this generation, that were he to point with his finger to the promised One and say: 'He indeed is the Beloved, the Desire of your hearts and mine,' they would still fail to recognise and acknowledge Him. I saw the Siyyid actually point out with his finger the ray of light that had fallen on that lap, and yet none among those who were present seemed to apprehend its meaning. I, for my part, was convinced that the Siyyid himself could never be the promised One, but that a mystery inscrutable to us all, lay concealed in that strange and attractive Youth. Several times I ventured to approach Siyyid Káẓim and seek from him an elucidation of this mystery. Every time I approached him, I was overcome by a sense of awe which his personality so powerfully inspired.[8]

Shaykh Ḥasan-i-Zunúzí has gone on to relate:

I often felt the urge to seek alone the presence of that Háshimite* Youth and to endeavour to fathom His mystery. I watched Him several times as He stood in an attitude of prayer at the doorway of the shrine of the Imám Ḥusayn. So wrapt was He in His devotions that He seemed utterly oblivious of those around Him. Tears rained from His eyes, and from His lips fell words of

* Háshim was the great-grandfather of the Prophet Muḥammad.

glorification and praise of such power and beauty as even the noblest passages of our sacred Scriptures could not hope to surpass. The words 'O God, my God, my Beloved, my heart's Desire,' were uttered with a frequency and ardour that those of the visiting pilgrims who were near enough to hear Him instinctively interrupted the course of their devotions, and marvelled at the evidences of piety and veneration which that youthful countenance evinced. Like Him they were moved to tears, and from Him they learned the lesson of true adoration. Having completed His prayers, that Youth, without crossing the threshold of the shrine and without attempting to address any words to those around Him, would quietly return to His home. I felt the impulse to address Him, but every time I ventured an approach, a force that I could neither explain nor resist, detained me. My inquiries about Him elicited the information that He was a resident of Shíráz, that He was a merchant by profession, and did not belong to any of the ecclesiastical orders. I was, moreover, informed that He, and also His uncles and relatives, were among the lovers and admirers of Shaykh Aḥmad and Siyyid Káẓim. I learned that He had departed for Najaf on His way to Shíráz. That Youth had set my heart aflame. The memory of that vision haunted me. My soul was wedded to His till the day when the call of a Youth from Shíráz, proclaiming Himself to be the Báb, reached my ears. The thought instantly flashed through my mind that such a person could be none other than that selfsame Youth whom I had seen in Karbilá, the Youth of my heart's desire.[9]

According to Ḥájí Mírzá Ḥabíbu'lláh's narrative, as the sojourn of the Báb in the holy cities lengthened into months, His mother, anxious to have her only son back in Shíráz, asked her brother, Ḥájí Mírzá Siyyid 'Alí, to go to 'Iráq and persuade Him to return. He could not deny his sister's request, but when he reached 'Iráq he found that his nephew, who had once been his ward, was unwilling to leave the holy cities. Thereupon he appealed to Ḥájí Siyyid Javád-i-Karbilá'í for help, who was at first reluctant to lend his support, not wishing to lose the company of the young Shírází Siyyid whom he had over the course of years so tremendously admired. However, when he learned that His mother was greatly concerned, he consented to intervene. At last the Báb complied with their request and agreed to return. After a few months in Shíráz He declared His intention of going once again to 'Iráq. His mother, alarmed and agitated by this decision, once more sought the aid of her brother. Their efforts resulted in the marriage of the Báb to Khadíjih-Bagum, daughter of Ḥájí Mírzá 'Alí,[10] the paternal uncle of His mother. The marriage took place in August 1842. Khadíjih-Bagum had two brothers: Ḥájí Mírzá Abu'l-Qásim and Ḥájí Mírzá Siyyid Ḥasan, and both of them, though not counted among His followers in His lifetime, have a place in the story of the Báb. The descendants of these two brothers-in-law of the Báb, and the descendants of His maternal uncles, are known as the Afnán (the Twigs).

A son was born to Siyyid 'Alí-Muḥammad and Khadíjih-Bagum in the year 1843, whom they named Aḥmad, but he did not live long. Ḥájí Mírzá Ḥabíbu'lláh states that the child was still-born. The Báb notes the birth of Aḥmad in the *Qayyúmu'l-Asmá'*, His commentary on the Súrih of Yúsuf (Joseph). Speaking of His wedding with His well-beloved, who was herself descended from the Well-Beloved (Muḥammad is known as Ḥabíbu'lláh—the Well-Beloved of God), and relating how He had called upon the angels of Heaven and the cohorts of Paradise to witness that wedding, the Báb then addresses His wife:

> O well-beloved! Value highly the grace of Dhikr [the Báb],[11] the Greatest, for it comes from God, the Loved

One. Thou shalt not be a woman, like other women, if thou obeyest God in the Cause of Truth . . . and take pride in being the consort of the Well-Beloved, who is loved by God the Greatest. Sufficient unto thee is this glory which cometh unto thee from God, the All-Wise, the All-Praised. Be patient in all that God hath ordained concerning the Báb and His Family. Verily, thy son, Aḥmad, is with Fáṭimih,* the Sublime, in the sanctified Paradise.[12]

And there is this further reference to Ahmad in the *Qayyúmu'l-Asmá'*:

> All praise be to God Who bestowed upon the Solace of the Eyes,† in His youth, Aḥmad. We did verily raise him up unto God . . . O Solace of the Eyes! Be patient in what thy God hath ordained for thee. Verily He doeth whatsoever He willeth. He is the All-Wise in the exercise of His justice. He is thy Lord, the Ancient of Days, and praised be He in whatever He ordereth.[12]

* The daughter of the Prophet Muḥammad.

† The Báb refers to Himself time and again in this Book as 'Qurratu'l-'Ayn'—the Solace of the Eyes.

CHAPTER 3

ṬIHRÁN

Rejoice with great joy, for God hath made thee 'the Day-Spring of His light', inasmuch as within thee was born the Manifestation of His Glory. Be thou glad for this name that hath been conferred upon thee—a name through which the Day-Star of grace hath shed its splendour, through which both earth and heaven have been illumined.

—Bahá'u'lláh, addressing the city of Ṭihrán

. . . We stand, life in hand, wholly resigned to His will; that perchance, through God's loving kindness and His grace, this revealed and manifest Letter may lay down His life as a sacrifice in the path of the Primal Point,* the most exalted Word.

—Bahá'u'lláh, from the *Kitáb-i-Íqán*

Mullá Ḥusayn was sorely disappointed when he realized that he was not to be the companion of the Báb, on His pilgrimage to Mecca. But for the man who was the first to find Him and believe in Him the Báb had marked out a task infinitely glorious. Mullá Ḥusayn was to go from Shíráz to Ṭihrán, where the fulfilment of that task awaited him. He had travelled to Shíráz on a quest. There he had reached its end, had found the Qá'im of the House of Muḥammad. Now he was to undertake another quest, and he was not entirely aware of the consequences that would attend its success. To him the Báb said:

In this pilgrimage upon which We are soon to embark, We have chosen Quddús as Our companion. We have

* 'Nuqṭiy-i-Úlá'—the Báb.

left you behind to face the onslaught of a fierce and relentless enemy. Rest assured, however, that a bounty unspeakably glorious shall be conferred upon you. Follow the course of your journey towards the north, and visit on your way Iṣfahán, Ká<u>sh</u>án, Qum, and Ṭihrán. Beseech almighty Providence that He may graciously enable you to attain, in that capital, the seat of true sovereignty, and to enter the mansion of the Beloved. A secret lies hidden in that city. When made manifest, it shall turn the earth into paradise. My hope is that you may partake of its grace and recognise its splendour. From Ṭihrán proceed to <u>Kh</u>urásán, and there proclaim anew the Call. From thence return to Najaf and Karbilá and there await the summons of your Lord. Be assured that the high mission for which you have been created will, in its entirety, be accomplished by you. Until you have consummated your work, if all the darts of an unbelieving world be directed against you, they will be powerless to hurt a single hair of your head.[1]

When the time came for Mullá Ḥusayn to leave <u>Sh</u>íráz, the Báb told him:

Grieve not that you have not been chosen to accompany Me on My pilgrimage to Ḥijáz. I shall, instead, direct your steps to that city which enshrines a Mystery of such transcendent holiness as neither Ḥijáz nor <u>Sh</u>íráz can hope to rival. My hope is that you may, by the aid of God, be enabled to remove the veils from the eyes of the wayward and to cleanse the minds of the malevolent. Visit, on your way, Iṣfahán, Ká<u>sh</u>án, Ṭihrán, and <u>Kh</u>urásán. Proceed thence to 'Iráq, and there await the summons of your Lord, who will keep watch over you and will direct you to whatsoever is His will and desire. As to Myself, I shall, accompanied by Quddús and My Ethiopian servant,* proceed on My pilgrimage to Ḥijáz. I shall join the company of the pilgrims of Fárs, who will shortly be sailing for that land. I shall visit Mecca and Medina, and

* His name was Mubárak.

there fulfil the mission* with which God has entrusted Me. God willing, I shall return hither by the way of Kúfih, in which place I hope to meet you. If it be decreed otherwise, I shall ask you to join Me in Shíráz. The hosts of the invisible Kingdom, be assured, will sustain and reinforce your efforts. The essence of power is now dwelling in you, and the company of His chosen angels revolves around you. His almighty arms will surround you, and His unfailing Spirit will ever continue to guide your steps. He that loves you, loves God; and whoever opposes you, has opposed God. Whoso befriends you, him will God befriend; and whoso rejects you, him will God reject.[2]

Mullá Ḥusayn was known in Iṣfahán, for there he had obtained testimonials from the great mujtahid, Ḥájí Siyyid Muḥammad-Báqir, in support of Siyyid Káẓim-i-Rashtí. That eminent divine was now dead, but his son, Ḥájí Siyyid Asadu'lláh, walking in the footsteps of his illustrious father, refused to associate himself with the adversaries of Mullá Ḥusayn. Another noted divine, Ḥájí Muḥammad-Ibráhím-i-Kalbásí, did likewise, and sternly admonished those who opposed Mullá Ḥusayn to cease their clamouring and investigate dispassionately whatever he was advocating. The Governor, Manúchihr Khán, the Mu'tamidu'd-Dawlih, similarly declined to heed their strictures.

The first person in Iṣfahán to embrace the new Faith was a youth, a sifter of wheat. The Báb immortalizes his memory in the Persian *Bayán*:[3]

Iṣfahán, that outstanding city, is distinguished by the religious fervour of its shí'ah inhabitants, by the learning of its divines, and by the keen expectation, shared by high and low alike, of the imminent coming of the Ṣáḥibu'z-Zamán.† In every quarter of that city, religious institu-

* To raise the Call of the Qá'im.

† The Lord of the Age.

tions have been established. And yet, when the Messenger of God had been made manifest, they who claimed to be the repositories of learning and the expounders of the mysteries of the Faith of God rejected His Message. Of all the inhabitants of that seat of learning, only one person, a sifter of wheat, was found to recognise the Truth, and was invested with the robe of Divine virtue![4]

Others eventually followed the example of that youth,* among them Mírzá Muḥammad ʻAlíy-i-Nahrí and his brother, Mírzá Hádí, who were Siyyids and highly respected. Mullá Ṣádiq-i-Muqaddas-i-Khurásání was another convert. Siyyid Káẓim had told Mullá Ṣádiq to establish his residence in Iṣfahán and pave the way for the coming of the Qá'im. That man of iron courage (whom we shall encounter again in the course of this story) met Mullá Ḥusayn in the home of Mírzá Muḥammad-ʻAlíy-i-Nahrí. Mullá Ṣádiq himself relates:

> I asked Mullá Ḥusayn to divulge the name of Him who claimed to be the promised Manifestation. He replied: 'To enquire about that name and to divulge it are alike forbidden.' 'Would it, then, be possible,' I asked, 'for me, even as the Letters of the Living, to seek independently the grace of the All-Merciful and, through prayer, to discover His identity?' 'The door of His grace,' he replied, 'is never closed before the face of him who seeks to find Him.' I immediately retired from his presence, and requested his host to allow me the privacy of a room in his house where, alone and undisturbed, I could commune with God. In the midst of my contemplation, I suddenly remembered the face of a Youth whom I had often observed while in Karbilá, standing in an attitude of prayer, with His face bathed in tears, at the entrance

* He is usually known as Gandum-Pák-Kun (the Sifter of Wheat); his name was Mullá Ja'far. He was one of the martyrs of Shaykh Ṭabarsí.

of the shrine of the Imám Ḥusayn. That same countenance now reappeared before my eyes. In my vision I seemed to behold that same face, those same features, expressive of such joy as I could never describe. He smiled as He gazed at me. I went towards Him, ready to throw myself at His feet. I was bending towards the ground, when, lo! that radiant figure vanished from before me. Overpowered with joy and gladness, I ran out to meet Mullá Ḥusayn, who with transport received me and assured me that I had, at last, attained the object of my desire. He bade me, however, repress my feelings. 'Declare not your vision to anyone,' he urged me; 'the time for it has not yet arrived. You have reaped the fruit of your patient waiting in Iṣfahán. You should now proceed to Kirmán, and there acquaint Ḥájí Mírzá Karím Khán with this Message.* From that place you should travel to Shíráz and endeavour to rouse the people of that city from their heedlessness. I hope to join you in Shíráz and share with you the blessings of a joyous reunion with our Beloved.'[5]

In Káshán, Mullá Ḥusayn found a responsive and eager heart in a well-known merchant of that town, named Ḥájí Mírzá Jání.† He too features prominently in the story of the Báb. The next stage in Mullá Ḥusayn's journey was the city of Qum, where the shrine of Ma'ṣúmih, the sister of Imám Riḍá, the eighth Imám, is situated. He found no attentive ears in Qum. Then came the crucial stage of his journey, when he entered the capital city of Írán, for there lay the 'Mystery' which the Báb had mentioned.

In Ṭihrán Mullá Ḥusayn took a room in a theological institution called the madrisih (school) of Mírzá Ṣáliḥ,

* Ḥájí Mírzá Muḥammad-Karím Khán-i-Kirmání considered himself to be the successor to Siyyid Káẓim. He fostered bitter opposition to the Báb within the Shaykhí school.

† He was the first to attempt to write a history of the new theophany.

alternatively the madrisih of Páminár.* The director of the institution, Ḥájí Mírzá Muḥammad-i-Khurásání, was the leading Shaykhí in the capital. He not only refused to heed what Mullá Ḥusayn imparted, but severely remonstrated with him and accused him of having betrayed the trust of Siyyid Káẓim. Ḥájí Mírzá Muḥammad made it clear that in his view Mullá Ḥusayn's presence in Ṭihrán posed a threat to the Shaykhí community. Mullá Ḥusayn replied that he did not intend to stay long in Ṭihrán, nor had he done or said anything which detracted from the position of the founders of the Shaykhí school.

As far as he could, Mullá Ḥusayn kept away from the madrisih of Mírzá Ṣáliḥ. He went out early in the mornings and returned after sunset. Mullá Muḥammad-i-Mu'allim,† a native of the district of Núr in Mázindarán, has described how Mullá Ḥusayn accomplished his mission:

> I was in those days recognised as one of the favoured disciples of Ḥájí Mírzá Muḥammad, and lived in the same school in which he taught. My room adjoined his room, and we were closely associated together. On the day that he was engaged in discussion with Mullá Ḥusayn, I overheard their conversation from beginning to end, and was deeply affected by the ardour, the fluency, and learning of that youthful stranger. I was surprised at the evasive answers, the arrogance, and contemptuous behaviour of Ḥájí Mírzá Muḥammad. That day I felt strongly attracted by the charm of that youth, and deeply resented the unseemly conduct of my teacher towards him. I concealed my feelings, however, and pretended to ignore his discussions with Mullá Ḥusayn. I was seized with a passionate desire to meet the latter, and ventured, at the hour of midnight, to visit him. He did not expect me, but I knocked at his door, and found him awake seated

* Páy-i-Minár, named after the quarter of the city where it was located.

† Teacher or tutor.

beside his lamp. He received me affectionately, and spoke to me with extreme courtesy and tenderness. I unburdened my heart to him, and as I was addressing him, tears, which I could not repress, flowed from my eyes. 'I can now see,' he said, 'the reason why I have chosen to dwell in this place. Your teacher has contemptuously rejected this Message and despised its Author. My hope is that his pupil may, unlike his master, recognise its truth. What is your name, and which city is your home?' 'My name,' I replied, 'is Mullá Muḥammad, and my surname Mu'allim. My home is Núr, in the province of Mázindarán.' 'Tell me,' further inquired Mullá Ḥusayn, 'is there to-day among the family of the late Mírzá Buzurg-i-Núrí, who was so renowned for his character, his charm, and artistic and intellectual attainments, anyone who has proved himself capable of maintaining the high traditions of that illustrious house?' 'Yea,' I replied, 'among his sons now living, one has distinguished Himself by the very traits which characterised His father. By His virtuous life, His high attainments, His loving-kindness and liberality, He has proved Himself a noble descendant of a noble father.' 'What is His occupation?' he asked me. 'He cheers the disconsolate and feeds the hungry,' I replied. 'What of His rank and position?' 'He has none,' I said, 'apart from befriending the poor and the stranger.' 'What is His name?' 'Ḥusayn-'Alí.' 'In which of the scripts of His father does He excel?'* 'His favourite script is shikastih-nasta'líq.' 'How does He spend His time?' 'He roams the woods and delights in the beauties of the countryside.' 'What is His age?' 'Eight and twenty.' The eagerness with which Mullá Ḥusayn questioned me, and the sense of delight with which he welcomed every particular I gave him, greatly surprised me. Turning to me, with his face beaming with satisfaction and joy, he once more enquired: 'I presume you often meet Him?' 'I frequently visit His home,' I replied. 'Will you,' he said, 'deliver into His hands a trust from me?' 'Most

* Bahá'u'lláh's father was famed for his calligraphy.

assuredly,' was my reply. He then gave me a scroll wrapped in a piece of cloth, and requested me to hand it to Him the next day at the hour of dawn. 'Should He deign to answer me,' he added, 'will you be kind enough to acquaint me with His reply?' I received the scroll from him and, at break of day, arose to carry out his desire.

As I approached the house of Bahá'u'lláh, I recognised His brother Mírzá Músá, who was standing at the gate, and to whom I communicated the object of my visit. He went into the house and soon reappeared bearing a message of welcome. I was ushered into His presence, and presented the scroll to Mírzá Músá, who laid it before Bahá'u'lláh. He bade us both be seated. Unfolding the scroll, He glanced at its contents and began to read aloud to us certain of its passages. I sat enraptured as I listened to the sound of His voice and the sweetness of its melody. He had read a page of the scroll when, turning to His brother, He said: 'Músá, what have you to say? Verily I say, whoso believes in the Qur'án and recognises its Divine origin, and yet hesitates, though it be for a moment, to admit that these soul-stirring words are endowed with the same regenerating power, has most assuredly erred in his judgment and has strayed far from the path of justice.' He spoke no more. Dismissing me from His presence, He charged me to take to Mullá Ḥusayn, as a gift from Him, a loaf of Russian sugar and a package of tea, and to convey to him the expression of His appreciation and love.

I arose and, filled with joy, hastened back to Mullá Ḥusayn, and delivered to him the gift and message of Bahá'u'lláh. With what joy and exultation he received them from me! Words fail me to describe the intensity of his emotion. He started to his feet, received with bowed head the gift from my hand, and fervently kissed it. He then took me in his arms, kissed my eyes, and said: 'My dearly beloved friend! I pray that even as you have rejoiced my heart, God may grant you eternal felicity and fill your heart with imperishable gladness.' I was amazed at the behaviour of Mullá Ḥusayn. What could be,

I thought to myself, the nature of the bond that unites these two souls? What could have kindled so fervid a fellowship in their hearts? Why should Mullá Ḥusayn, in whose sight the pomp and circumstance of royalty were the merest trifle, have evinced such gladness at the sight of so inconsiderable a gift from the hands of Bahá'u'lláh? I was puzzled by this thought and could not unravel its mystery.

A few days later, Mullá Ḥusayn left for Khurásán. As he bade me farewell, he said: 'Breathe not to anyone what you have heard and witnessed. Let this be a secret hidden within your breast. Divulge not His name, for they who envy His position will arise to harm Him. In your moments of meditation, pray that the Almighty may protect Him, that, through Him, He may exalt the downtrodden, enrich the poor, and redeem the fallen. The secret of things is concealed from our eyes. Ours is the duty to raise the call of the New Day and to proclaim this Divine Message unto all people. Many a soul will, in this city, shed his blood in this path. That blood will water the Tree of God, will cause it to flourish, and to overshadow all mankind.'[6]

From Mashhad, the holy city that has within it the Shrine of the eighth Imám, Mullá Ḥusayn addressed his first letter to the Báb. He gave, as instructed by Him, the full details of his journey from Shíráz to Khurásán. He presented the list of names of those who had responded to the call of the new theophany: a list which had become further enriched in Khurásán by the enrolment of Mírzá Aḥmad-i-Azghandí, the most learned of the divines of that renowned province; Mullá Mírzá Muḥammad-i-Furúghí, another divine of immense learning; Mírzá Muḥammad-Báqir-i-Qá'iní, whose house in Mashhad was to gain the distinction of being known as the Bábíyyih, since its doors would be always open to those who sought Mullá Ḥusayn and to all the Bábís; Mullá Aḥmad-i-Mu'allim, who had been a tutor to the sons of

Siyyid Káẓim; and Mullá Shaykh 'Alí, to whom the Báb gave the title of 'Aẓím (Great). But above all, Mullá Ḥusayn recounted what had transpired in Ṭihrán, culminating in the gracious response of the nobleman of Núr. He sent his letter, again as instructed by the Báb, to Ṭabas (a town in the province of Khurásán) where agents of Ḥájí Mírzá Siyyid 'Alí received it and dispatched it to Yazd, whence it reached Shíráz. The arrival of Mullá Ḥusayn's letter and the tidings which it conveyed brought unbounded joy to the Báb. Soon after, in the month of September, He left Shíráz, accompanied by Quddús, and the faithful Ethiopian servant, Mubárak.

From Búshihr, while waiting to take the boat to Jiddah (Jaddah), the Báb wrote His first letter to His wife. It opens with these moving words:

'In the Name of God, exalted is He. My sweet love, may God preserve thee.' 'God is my witness,' He continues, 'that since the time of separation sorrow has been so intense that it cannot be described,' and adds His hope that God, 'the Lord of the world,' may 'facilitate the return journey in the best manner.' Two days previously He had reached Búshihr, and informs His wife that 'the weather is exceedingly hot, but God, the Lord of the world, is the Protector.' The boat, it seemed, would be sailing the same month; 'God, the Lord of the world, will provide protection by His grace.' He had not been able to see His mother at the time of His departure, and asks His wife to give her His salutation (salám) and request her prayers. He would write to Bombay for the goods required. And the letter ends thus: 'God willing, that which is decreed will come to pass. Peace be upon thee and the mercy of God and His blessings.'[7]

The ship, bearing pilgrims to Jiddah, set sail on the nineteenth day of Ramaḍán 1260—October 2nd 1844.[8]

CHAPTER 4

THE FIRST MARTYR

The world turns and the world changes,
But one thing does not change.
In all of my years, one thing does not change.
However you disguise it, this thing does not change:
The perpetual struggle of Good and Evil.
—T. S. Eliot

Lady Sheil, whose husband was the British envoy in Ṭihrán,* states in her book, *Glimpses of Life and Manners in Persia*, that the Báb declared His mission in Káẓimayn, near Baghdád, and that 'Incensed at this blasphemy, the Turkish authorities issued orders for his execution, but he was claimed by the Persian consul as a subject of the Shah, and sent to his native place'.[1] Obviously Lady Sheil was confused. She had heard of the arrest of Mullá 'Alíy-i-Basṭámí in 'Iráq and of his imprisonment. She mistook him for the Báb.

Mullá 'Alí, as we have seen, was directed to 'Iráq by the Báb, and took with him a copy of the *Qayyúmu'l-Asmá'*, the commentary on the Súrih of Yúsuf (Joseph). The news and the message that he gave aroused eager interest and ready response from his hearers. But hostile reaction was also swift. It was Mullá 'Alí who, in Karbilá, informed Qurratu'l-'Ayn of the advent of the Báb. He was not at liberty to mention His Name. We do not know whether, in view of the fact that Qurratu'l-'Ayn had been elevated to the high and honoured position of a Letter of the Living, Mullá 'Alí gave

* See note 6, Prologue.

her any information other than the tidings of the appearance of the Báb. The disciples of Siyyid Káẓim were in a much stronger position there than in Najaf, in spite of the fact that in Karbilá they had a redoubtable opponent in the person of Siyyid Ibráhím-i-Qazvíní. There in Karbilá, Mullá 'Alí remained safe. But the story was different in Najaf. Nabíl-i-A'ẓam writes:

> In the presence of Shaykh Muḥammad-Ḥasan, one of the most celebrated ecclesiastics of shí'ah Islám, and in the face of a distinguished company of his disciples, Mullá 'Alí announced fearlessly the manifestation of the Báb, the Gate whose advent they were eagerly awaiting. 'His proof,' he declared, 'is His Word; His testimony, none other than the testimony with which Islám seeks to vindicate its truth. From the pen of this unschooled Háshimite Youth of Persia there have streamed, within the space of forty-eight hours, as great a number of verses, of prayers, of homilies, and scientific treatises, as would equal in volume the whole of the Qur'án, which it took Muḥammad, the Prophet of God, twenty-three years to reveal!' That proud and fanatic leader, instead of welcoming, in an age of darkness and prejudice, these life-giving evidences of a new-born Revelation, forthwith pronounced Mullá 'Alí a heretic and expelled him from the assembly. His disciples and followers, even the Shaykhís, who already testified to Mullá 'Alí's piety, sincerity, and learning, endorsed, unhesitatingly, the judgment against him. The disciples of Shaykh Muḥammad-Ḥasan, joining hands with their adversaries, heaped upon him untold indignities. They eventually delivered him, his hands bound in chains, to an official of the Ottoman government, arraigning him as a wrecker of Islám, a calumniator of the Prophet, an instigator of mischief, a disgrace to the Faith, and worthy of the penalty of death. He was taken to Baghdád under the escort of government officials, and was cast into prison by the governor of that city.[2]

Áqá Muḥammad-Muṣṭafáy-i-Baghdádí,[3] in a short autobiography which he wrote at the instance of Mírzá Abu'l-Faḍl, describes Mullá 'Alí's arrival in 'Iráq and the events which followed:

> The messenger, Mullá 'Alí al-Basṭámí,* reached Kúfih in the year A.H. 1260 [A.D. 1844] and distributed books, treatises and tablets amongst the divines. Due to this a body of the divines in Najaf and Karbilá were seized with consternation. They arose in opposition and stirred themselves to vociferous denunciation. The Government hearing of what had transpired, became concerned lest disorders might ensue, and deemed it politic to imprison the messenger, confiscate the books and tablets in his possession and send him to the seat of the province, that is Baghdád. The Válí, at that time, was Najíb Páshá, the same man who captured Karbilá . . .†
>
> When the messenger reached Baghdád the Válí kept him in prison and placed the books and the treatises in the council-chamber. My father, Shaykh Muḥammad, visited the messenger every day in the prison, and heard the Word of God from him for three months. Whatever he heard he imparted to those who were seekers, so that, during this short time, a large number of people came to believe. Shaykh Bashír an-Najafí was one of them, a mujtahid seventy-five years old. Then there were Shaykh Sulṭán al-Karbilá'í and a group with him in Karbilá; Siyyid Muḥammad-Ja'far, Siyyid Ḥasan Ja'far, and Siyyid 'Alí Bishr and a group with him in the town of Káẓimíyyah; Shaykh Muḥammad Shibl [the author's father], Siyyid Muḥsin al-Káẓimí, Shaykh Ṣáliḥ al-Karímí and a group with them of villagers like Shaykh 'Abbás, Mullá Maḥmúd, 'Abdu'l-Hádí and Mihdí . . .
>
> When the Government noticed that the Cause was gaining ground day by day, the afore-mentioned Válí, Najíb Páshá, ordered the divines of all the regions to come to

* Áqá Muḥammad-Muṣṭafá wrote in Arabic.

† See Prologue I.

Baghdád . . .[4] They summoned my father, Shaykh Muḥammad, to present himself. But my father left Baghdád in disguise, because he had learned that the Válí intended to make him give witness against the Cause of the Day of Judgment. They brought the messenger to this terrible assembly and asked him who the Lord of the Cause was. He answered: 'The awaited Spirit of Truth hath come. He is the One promised in the Books of God.' Then he read them some verses and prayers and called upon them to believe. It went hard with them to accept the Cause. They arose to deny and to reject it, full of haughtiness. They agreed to denounce the messenger as a heretic and passed the sentence of death upon him, and thus ended that assemblage of ill omen. The Válí sent the account of the proceedings to the Sublime Porte, whence came the orders that the messenger should be sent in fetters, together with his books, to the capital. The messenger languished for six months in the gaol of Baghdád and was then dispatched to the Sublime Porte, under escort, by way of Mosul. The fame of the Cause was noised abroad in Mosul, and when he passed Mosul nothing more was heard of him.[5]

The circumstances of Mullá 'Alí's arrest were also noted by Major Henry Rawlinson,[6] then British Political Agent in Baghdád, who, on January 8th 1845, reported to Sir Stratford Canning, the Ambassador in Istanbul:

I have the honor to report for Your Excellency's information the following circumstances which are at present causing much excitement at this place, and which threaten in their consequences to give rise to renewed misunderstanding between the Persian & Turkish Govts.

About three months ago, an inferior priest of Shiraz appeared in Kerbela, bearing a copy of the Koran, which he stated to have been delivered to him, by the forerunner of the Imam Mehdi, to be exhibited in token of his approaching advent. The book proved on examination to have been altered and interpolated in many essential passages, the object being, to prepare the Mohammedan world for the immediate manifestation of the Imam, and to identify the individual to whom the emendations of the text were declared to have been revealed, as his inspired & true precursor. It was in consequence pronounced by a part of the Sheeah divines at Nejef and Kerbela, to be a blasphemous production, and the priest of Shiraz was warned by them of the danger; which he incurred in giving currency to its contents—but a considerable section nevertheless of the Sheeahs of Nejef, who under the name of *Usúlí*, or 'Transcendentalists', have lately risen into notice as the disciples of the High Priest Sheikh Kazem, and who are in avowed expectation of the speedy advent of the Imam, adopted the proposed readings, and declared themselves ready to join the Precursor; as soon as he should appear amongst them—These parties owing to local dissensions, were shortly afterwards denounced to the Govt. by the orthodox Sheeas as heretics, and attention being thus drawn to the perverted copy of the Koran, upon which they rested their belief, the volume was seized & its bearer being brought to Bagdad, was cast into prison, as a blasphemer against Islam and a disturber of the public peace.*[7]

* Major Rawlinson nowhere mentions the name of the priest who is alleged to have been the possessor of a 'spurious' version of the Qur'án. It is obvious that the priest, about whom he was writing, could have been none other than Mullá 'Alíy-i-Basṭámí, whom he wrongly designated as 'Shirazee' for the simple reason that he had come from Shíráz. His frequent references to the disciples of Siyyid Káẓim as '*Usúlí*' indicate that his knowledge of the issue was meagre, for these disciples were known as Shaykhís. The term could have been more appropriately applied to the opponents of Siyyid Káẓim. They and their counterpart, the 'Akhbárís', followed different methods of interpretation within the Shí'ah fold. For a description of these schools of thought, see Browne, *A Literary History of Persia*, Vol. IV, pp. 374–6.

Mullá 'Alí was the first martyr of the Bábí Faith. Though his arrest and sufferings lasted only a few months, he was the centre of conjecture, the subject of official report, and the cause of increased rancour between the Sunní and Shí'ah sects, and the Ottoman and Iranian governments. European officials who were drawn into this obscure drama included Major Rawlinson, who submitted frequent and lengthy reports to Sir Stratford Canning in Istanbul and Lt.-Col. Sheil in Ṭihrán, and received their advice and instructions; M. de Titow, Russian envoy in Istanbul who joined Canning in urging the Sublime Porte to restrain Najíb Páshá from putting 'the Persian Priest' to death, and instead to inflict on him only 'the mildest punishment consistent with the public tranquillity'; and Lord Aberdeen, the British Foreign Secretary in London, who was apprised of the final outcome.

Although the dispatches of Major Rawlinson are in certain aspects subject to grave reservations, for his knowledge was sometimes meagre and at second hand, even inaccurate, they do portray the agitation, confusion and opposition created by the claim of the Báb and the teaching of Mullá 'Alí. Thus he wrote to Canning:

> The Soonnee Priesthood have taken up the case in a rancorous spirit of bigotry, and their inveteracy has enlisted the sympathies of the entire Sheeah sect, in favor of the imprisoned Persian . . . the question has now become one of virulent contest, between the Soonee & Sheeah sects, or which is the same thing in this part of the Ottoman Empire, between the Turkish & Persian population . . .[8]

It was the Governor (Válí) of Baghdád, Najíb Páshá, who bore the responsibility of controlling these passions; but being himself a fanatical Sunní, he was resolved that the Shí'ahs should submit to the Sunní authority, and determined to bar any intrusions of the Persians into the affairs of his Páshálik.* Nevertheless, as reported by Rawlinson:

> Nejib Pasha at the same time, to give all due formality to his proceedings, and to divest the affair of the appearance of mere sectarian persecution, has brought in the chief Priests from Nejef & Kerbela, to hold a solemn Court of Inquisition in conjunction with the heads of the Soonnee religion in Bagdad, but I do not anticipate much benefit from this compulsory & most unwilling attendance of the former parties—They will probably make an effort to save the life of their unfortunate countryman, proposing the banishment of the messenger and of the heads of the *Usúlí* sect, as the simplest method of suppressing the heresy, but they will be intimidated & overruled . . .[9]

Indeed, such an unwieldy court of Sunní and Shí'ah divines could come to no agreement about Mullá 'Alí's punishment. On January 16th 1845, Rawlinson wrote to Sheil, in Ṭihrán:

> The Court of Inquisition convened for the trial of the Persian priest, was held on Monday last [January 13th], H.E. Nejib Pasha presiding, and Moola Abdool Azeez being also present, to afford his countenance to the accused—The perverted copy of the Koran being produced in Court, was unanimously condemned as a blasphemous production, and parties avowing a belief in the readings which it continued [sic], were declared to be liable to the punishment of death—It was then argued whether or not the Shirazee had thus avowed his belief in a blasphemous production—he himself distinctly repudiated the charge, and although witnesses were brought forward, who stated that he had in their presence

* His province.

declared his adoption of the spurious text, of which he was the bearer, yet as there was reason to suspect the fidelity of their evidence, the Sheeah divines were disposed to give him the benefit of his present disavowal—After much discussion the Soonee law-officers adjudged the culprit to be convicted of blasphemy & passed sentence of death on him accordingly, while the Sheeahs returned a verdict, that he was only guilty of the dissemination of blasphemy, & liable in consequence to no heavier punishment than imprisonment or banishment . . .

To this Rawlinson added:

I understand that considerable uneasiness is beginning to display itself at Kerbela & Nejef, in regard to the expected manifestation of the Imam, and I am apprehensive that the measures now in progress will rather increase than allay the excitement.*[10]

* Rawlinson's letter to Sheil carries the statement that Mullá 'Alí abjured his faith. Apart from the evidence of the devotion and heroism of the disciples of the Báb, which history amply provides, several factors must be considered. Major Rawlinson was not present at that meeting of the divines, which he termed 'the Court of Inquisition'. Therefore his information was second-hand. The emergence of Sunní-Shí'ah antagonism was another factor which would certainly have clouded the issue. The 'advent of the Imam' need not, necessarily, have troubled the Sunní conscience, because Sunnís have never believed in the Imámate and the occultation of the Twelfth Imám. Furthermore, that which Mullá 'Alí is supposed to have rejected, according to Rawlinson, was a 'perverted copy of the Koran'. Would Mullá 'Alí ever have an interpolated copy of the Qur'án to announce the message he had to give, or to prove it? And then the question must also be asked: if Mullá 'Alí, the man who brought the news of the advent of the Báb, had recanted, how was it that 'considerable uneasiness' was becoming perceptible in Karbilá and Najaf, 'in regard to the expected manifestation of the Imam'?

The personal intervention of Najíb Pá<u>sh</u>á had served also to influence the course of events in another way. By referring the matter to the Sublime Porte, he prevented the extradition of the Persian prisoner to his native land, as requested by the Iranian Prime Minister, Ḥájí Mírzá Áqásí.

A similar request for the transfer of Mullá 'Alí to Persian jurisdiction was made to Major Rawlinson by the Governor of Kirmán<u>sh</u>áh, Muḥibb-'Alí <u>Kh</u>án, for, as he wrote:

> In the first place it is improper to arrest and imprison anyone on a mere accusation, which may be true or false, —and in the second place, supposing that he (the Shirázee) were guilty; as a subject of the exalted Govt. of Persia, he ought not to be subject to arrest—if his crime were proved, his punishment should be that of banishment from the Turkish territory—I have therefore considered it necessary to represent this matter to you my friend, and to request that, as a well wisher to the preservation of friendship between the two Governments, You will communicate with H. Excy. Nejib Pasha on the subject, and will suggest to him, that if the guilt of the Persian be fully substantiated, he may be sent to Kermanshah, in order that I may transfer him to Tehran for punishment—and if on the other hand, the accusations against him prove to be malicious and without foundation, he may be at once released and set at liberty.
>
> Under any circumstances his continued imprisonment is unbecoming and contrary (to custom).[11]

This request was duly submitted by Rawlinson to Najíb Pá<u>sh</u>á but, as the Governor had already referred the matter to the Sublime Porte after the religious court's examination, the prisoner remained in Turkish custody.

It was on April 15th that Rawlinson reported to Canning that 'Nejib Pasha received orders by yesterday's post to transmit to Constantinople the Persian priest who has been in confinement for the last 3 months at Bagdad . . . His

Excy. is preparing to obey these instructions with all available despatch.' He also says in the same letter:

> . . . [the] more in fact these Mujtiheds* are degraded by the Turkish Govt., the more complete, I think, will be their ascendancy over the minds of their disciples and the only results, therefore, which are likely to attend the proscription of their public duties, are the more complete isolation of the Persian community of this province, and an increase of the rancorous feeling with which the dominant Soonee party is regarded—[12]

On the last day of April, Rawlinson wrote once more to Canning:

> I take this opportunity of reporting that the Persian priest of Shiraz so long detained in confinement at this place, was sent a prisoner to Constantinople in company with the Tartar † who conveyed the last Bagdad post.[13]

Meanwhile, as early as February, Major Rawlinson came to an erroneous conclusion about the Báb, which subsequent events belied. He wrote to Canning on the 18th:

> . . . the excitement which has been for some time prevalent in this vicinity among the Sheeah sect in connection with the expected manifestation of the Imam Mehdi, is beginning gradually to subside, the impostor who personated the character of the forerunner of the Imam . . . having been deterred by a sense of personal danger from a further prosecution of the agitation, which he set on foot at Kerbela in the Autumn on his passage from Persia to Mecca.[14]

He was also in error in stating to Sheil, ten days later, that 'the impostor . . . joined as a private individual the Caravan

* Shí'ah divines.
† Official courier.

of pilgrims which is travelling to Persia by the route of Damascus and Aleppo'.[15]

In considering this episode of the arrest, imprisonment and banishment of the first Bábí martyr, there are four aspects which deserve special note. First is the fact that while the Bábís in Shíráz were being punished by Ḥusayn Khán, Governor of the province of Fárs,* the Persian Government was trying to rescue Mullá 'Alí in Baghdád. Secondly, whereas the Shí'ah divines were demanding a light punishment, the Sunnís were clamouring for the death penalty. A third point, important to students of the Bábí Faith, is that from the earliest stage of its history rumours and misinformation about the Báb abounded. It is also of considerable interest that this episode was reported to Lord Aberdeen, the British Foreign Secretary in London.

As to Mullá 'Alí, what precisely happened to him, how and where he died and where he was interred, have all remained mysteries. It has been said that he died in the prison of Karkúk, but no definite proof exists. He was the first of the concourse of martyrs whose numbers were soon to swell into hundreds and thousands.

* Mullá 'Alí was before long caught up in a furore of agitation and oppression, was apprehended, put on trial and condemned to death. It has always been assumed that he was put to death somewhere in 'Iráq (either in Mosul or beyond), while being taken to Istanbul, because nothing more was ever heard of him after he reached Mosul. But recent research in official archives has established the fact that he arrived in the Ottoman capital, was once again put on trial and was condemned to hard labour in the dockyards, where he died towards the end of 1846. (For most of this information the author is much indebted to Mr Sami Doktoroglu.)

CHAPTER 5

PILGRIMAGE TO MECCA: THE HOUSE OF KA'BAH

Vaunt not thyself, O thou who leadeth the pilgrims on their way,
That which thou seest is the House, and that which I see is the Lord of that House.

—Ḥáfiẓ

The Báb embarked for Jiddah, probably on an Arab sailing-boat named *Futúḥ-ar-Rasúl*—Victories of the Messenger. If so, He had as fellow-passenger a maternal uncle of Muḥammad Sháh, Muḥammad-Báqir Khán, the Biglarbagí* of Ṭihrán, who was attended by Shukru'lláh Khán-i-Núrí, a prominent official of the province of Fárs. We know for certain that two of His fellow-townsmen on the boat were Ḥájí Abu'l-Ḥasan, who pursued the same trade as the Báb's father, and Shaykh Abú-Háshim, brother of Shaykh Abú-Turáb, the Imám-Jum'ih of Shíráz. The former was captivated by the charm and the sublime bearing of his compatriot, the young Siyyid of whose claim he was unaware, and gave Him his allegiance without the slightest hesitation when he learned of His claim. Shaykh Abú-Háshim, however, was already jealous of the respect commanded by the Báb and became His implacable enemy, even though his brother, the Imám-Jum'ih, served the interests of the Báb to the best of his ability.[1]

Ḥájí Abu'l-Ḥasan has related[2] that during the voyage Shaykh Abú-Háshim became daily more arrogant and

* The principal official responsible for public order in a town or city.

quarrelsome, molesting the passengers and making the young Siyyid a particular target for his invective. When the Arab captain could no longer tolerate his insolent behaviour, he ordered him to be seized and thrown into the sea. According to Ḥájí Abu'l-Ḥasan, it was the Báb who stepped forward to intercede for him. However, the captain was determined to be rid of the troublesome Shaykh. And when the Báb noticed that the sailors were about to throw Shaykh Abú-Háshim overboard, He hurled Himself upon him, caught hold of him and earnestly requested the captain to pardon the wrong-doer. The Arab captain was astonished, because it had been the young Siyyid who had suffered most from the Shaykh's malice. But the Báb replied that, since people who behaved in that manner harmed only themselves, one should be tolerant and forgiving.

The rites of the Ḥajj (pilgrimage to Mecca) are to be performed on the ninth and tenth days of the month of Dhi'l-Ḥijjah, the last month of the Muslim lunar year. On the tenth day the 'Íd-al-Aḍḥá (the Festival of Sacrifices) is celebrated throughout the Muslim world.* It commemorates the sacrifice offered by Abraham of His son. Whenever the 'Íd-al-Aḍḥá falls on a Friday, the Ḥajj of that year is termed the Ḥajj-i-Akbar (the Greatest Ḥajj). In the year 1260, the tenth of Dhi'l-Ḥijjah was a Friday (December 20th 1844), and therefore the number of pilgrims was commensurately greater. An Islamic tradition points to the appearance of the Qá'im in a year of the Ḥajj-i-Akbar.

Another particularly notable pilgrim in that year 1260 was a divine of high repute, Siyyid Ja'far-i-Kashfí, whose son Siyyid Yaḥyá (later known as Vaḥíd) was to become one of the most distinguished followers of the Báb.

The journey to Jiddah was long, tedious and exhausting. Seas were rough and storms frequent. An Arab sailing-boat did not afford much comfort. 'For days we suffered

* In Persia this Feast is usually called 'Íd-i-Qurbán.

from the scarcity of water. I had to content myself with the juice of sweet lemon,' the Báb writes in the Persian *Bayán*.[3] Ḥájí Abu'l-Ḥasan recounts:

> During the entire period of approximately two months, from the day we embarked at Búshihr to the day when we landed at Jaddih, the port of Ḥijáz, whenever by day or night I chanced to meet either the Báb or Quddús, I invariably found them together, both absorbed in their work. The Báb seemed to be dictating, and Quddús was busily engaged in taking down whatever fell from His lips. Even at a time when panic seemed to have seized the passengers of that storm-tossed vessel, they would be seen pursuing their labours with unperturbed confidence and calm. Neither the violence of the elements nor the tumult of the people around them could either ruffle the serenity of their countenance or turn them from their purpose.[4]

At Jiddah the Báb and His companions put on the iḥrám,* the garb of the pilgrim. He travelled to Mecca on a camel, but Quddús would not mount and walked all the way, keeping pace with it. On the tenth day of Dhi'l-Ḥijjah the Báb offered the prescribed sacrifice. The meat of the nineteen lambs which He bought was all given to the poor and the needy; nine of the animals were sacrificed on His own behalf, seven on behalf of Quddús and three for Mubárak.[5]

Ḥájí Mírzá Ḥabíbu'lláh-i-Afnán, quoting Ḥájí Abu'l-Ḥasan, relates in his chronicle that after the completion of the rites of the Ḥajj, at a time when the court of the House of Ka'bah and the roofs of adjoining houses teemed with pilgrims, the Báb stood against the structure of the Ka'bah, laid hold of the ring on its door and thrice repeated, in a clear voice:

> I am that Qá'im whose advent you have been awaiting.

* A sheet of cloth, unstitched.

Ḥájí Abu'l-Ḥasan recalled, many years later, that a sudden hush fell upon the audience. The full implication of those momentous words must, at the time, have eluded that vast concourse of people. But the news of the claim of the young Siyyid soon spread in an ever-widening circle.

One day in Mecca, the Báb came face to face with Mírzá Muḥammad-Ḥusayn-i-Kirmání, known as Muḥíṭ.* They happened to meet close by the sacred Black Stone (Ḥajar al-Aswad). The Báb took Muḥíṭ's hand, saying:

> O Muḥíṭ! You regard yourself as one of the most outstanding figures of the shaykhí community and a distinguished exponent of its teachings. In your heart you even claim to be one of the direct successors and rightful inheritors of those twin great Lights, those Stars that have heralded the morn of Divine guidance. Behold, we are both now standing within this most sacred shrine. Within its hallowed precincts, He whose Spirit dwells in this place can cause Truth immediately to be known and distinguished from falsehood, and righteousness from error. Verily I declare, none besides Me in this day, whether in the East or in the West, can claim to be the Gate that leads men to the knowledge of God. My proof is none other than that proof whereby the truth of the Prophet Muḥammad was established. Ask Me whatsoever you please; now, at this very moment, I pledge Myself to reveal such verses as can demonstrate the truth of My mission. You must choose either to submit yourself unreservedly to My Cause or to repudiate it entirely. You have no other alternative. If you choose to reject My message, I will not let go your hand until you pledge your word to declare publicly your repudiation of the Truth which I have proclaimed. Thus shall He who speaks the Truth be made known, and he that speaks falsely shall be condemned to eternal misery and shame. Then shall the way of Truth be revealed and made manifest to all men.

* He had pretensions to leadership of the Shaykhí sect after the death of Siyyid Káẓim.

Muḥíṭ was taken by surprise and was overwhelmed. He replied to the Báb:

> My Lord, my Master! Ever since the day on which my eyes beheld You in Karbilá, I seemed at last to have found and recognised Him who had been the object of my quest. I renounce whosoever has failed to recognise You, and despise him in whose heart may yet linger the faintest misgivings as to Your purity and holiness. I pray You to overlook my weakness, and entreat You to answer me in my perplexity. Please God I may, at this very place, within the precincts of this hallowed shrine, swear my fealty to You, and arise for the triumph of Your Cause. If I be insincere in what I declare, if in my heart I should disbelieve what my lips proclaim, I would deem myself utterly unworthy of the grace of the Prophet of God, and regard my action as an act of manifest disloyalty to 'Alí, His chosen successor.

The Báb knew how vacillating Muḥíṭ was, and answered:

> Verily I say, the Truth is even now known and distinguished from falsehood. O shrine of the Prophet of God, and you, O Quddús, who have believed in Me! I take you both, in this hour, as My witnesses. You have seen and heard that which has come to pass between Me and him. I call upon you to testify thereunto, and God, verily, is, beyond and above you, My sure and ultimate Witness. He is the All-Seeing, the All-Knowing, the All-Wise. O Muḥíṭ! Set forth whatsoever perplexes your mind, and I will, by the aid of God, unloose My tongue and undertake to resolve your problems, so that you may testify to the excellence of My utterance and realise that no one besides Me is able to manifest My wisdom.[6]

Muḥíṭ presented his questions and then departed hurriedly for Medina. The Báb, in answer to them, revealed the *Ṣaḥífiy-i-Baynu'l-Ḥaramayn*, which, as its name 'The Epistle Between the Two Shrines' indicates, was composed on the road to the city of the Prophet (Medina). Muḥíṭ, contrary to his promise, did not remain long in Medina, but received the Báb's treatise in Karbilá. To the end of his days, Muḥíṭ was shifty and irresolute, and the headship of the Shaykhí community did not go to him, but to Ḥájí Muḥammad-Karím Khán-i-Kirmání.

The last act of the Báb in Mecca was to address a Tablet to the Sharíf (Sherif) of Mecca, in which He proclaimed His advent and His Divine mandate. Quddús delivered it together with a volume of the Writings of the Báb. But the Sharíf was preoccupied and ignored the communication put in his hands. Ḥájí Níyáz-i-Baghdádí recounts:

> In the year 1267 A.H. [A.D. 1850–51], I undertook a pilgrimage to that holy city, where I was privileged to meet the Sherif. In the course of his conversation with me, he said: 'I recollect that in the year '60, during the season of pilgrimage, a youth came to visit me. He presented to me a sealed book which I readily accepted but was too much occupied at that time to read. A few days later I met again that same youth, who asked me whether I had any reply to make to his offer. Pressure of work had again detained me from considering the contents of that book. I was therefore unable to give him a satisfactory reply. When the season of pilgrimage was over, one day, as I was sorting out my letters, my eyes fell accidentally upon that book. I opened it and found, in its introductory pages, a moving and exquisitely written homily which was followed by verses the tone and language of which bore a striking resemblance to the Qur'án. All that I gathered from the perusal of the book was that among the people of Persia a man of the seed of Fáṭimih and descendant of the family of Háshim, had raised a new call, and was announcing to all people the appearance of the promised Qá'im. I remained, however, ignorant of the name of the author of that book, nor was I informed of the

circumstances attending that call.' 'A great commotion,' I remarked, 'has indeed seized that land during the last few years. A Youth, a descendant of the Prophet and a merchant by profession, has claimed that His utterance was the Voice of Divine inspiration. He has publicly asserted that, within the space of a few days, there could stream from His tongue verses of such number and excellence as would surpass in volume and beauty the Qur'án itself—a work which it took Muḥammad no less than twenty-three years to reveal. A multitude of people, both high and low, civil and ecclesiastical, among the inhabitants of Persia, have rallied round His standard and have willingly sacrificed themselves in His path. That Youth has, during the past year, in the last days of the month of Sha'bán [July 1850], suffered martyrdom in Tabríz, in the province of Ádhirbáyján. They who persecuted Him sought by this means to extinguish the light which He kindled in that land. Since His martyrdom, however, His influence has pervaded all classes of people.' The Sherif, who was listening attentively, expressed his indignation at the behaviour of those who had persecuted the Báb. 'The malediction of God be upon these evil people,' he exclaimed, 'a people who, in days past, treated in the same manner our holy and illustrious ancestors!' With these words the Sherif concluded his conversation with me.[7]

The Báb reached Medina on the first day of the year A.H. 1261: Friday, January 10th 1845.[8] It was the first of Muḥarram and the day of His birth. From Medina He proceeded to Jiddah, where He took a boat bound for the port of Búshihr.

CHAPTER 6

FORCES OF OPPOSITION ARRAYED

But man, proud man,
Drest in a little brief authority,
Most ignorant of what he's most assured,
His glassy essence, like an angry ape,
Plays such fantastic tricks before high heaven
As makes the angels weep . . .
—Shakespeare

The London *Times* of Wednesday, November 19th 1845, carried this item of news on its third page, taken from the *Literary Gazette* of the preceding Saturday:

MAHOMETAN SCHISM.—A new sect has lately set itself up in Persia, at the head of which is a merchant who had returned from a pilgrimage to Mecca, and proclaimed himself a successor of the Prophet. The way they treat such matters at Shiraz appears in the following account (June 23):—Four persons being heard repeating their profession of faith according to the form prescribed by the impostor, were apprehended, tried, and found guilty of unpardonable blasphemy. They were sentenced to lose their beards by fire being set to them. The sentence was put into execution with all the zeal and fanaticism becoming a true believer in Mahomet. Not deeming the loss of beards a sufficient punishment, they were further sentenced the next day, to have their faces blacked and exposed through the city. Each of them was led by a mirgazah* (executioner), who had made a hole in his nose and passed through it a string, which he sometimes

* Mír-Ghaḍab.

pulled with such violence that the unfortunate fellows cried out alternately for mercy from the executioner and for vengeance from Heaven. It is the custom in Persia on such occasions for the executioners to collect money from the spectators, and particularly from the shop-keepers in the bazaar. In the evening when the pockets of the executioners were well filled with money, they led the unfortunate fellows to the city gate, and there turned them adrift. After which the mollahs at Shiraz sent men to Bushire, with power to seize the impostor, and take him to Shiraz, where, on being tried, he very wisely denied the charge of apostacy laid against him, and thus escaped from punishment.

An American quarterly, the *Eclectic Magazine of Foreign Literature, Science, and Art*,[1] in its issue of January–April 1846, reproduced the same item of news which was again taken in full from the *Literary Gazette* of London. As far as is known, these were the earliest references to the Faith of the Báb in any Western publication. British merchants, who then happened to be in S͟híráz, were responsible for that report, which, as we shall see, although correct in its essentials, was not devoid of error.

The Báb, returning from His pilgrimage to Mecca, arrived at Bús͟hihr sometime in the month of Ṣafar 1261 A.H. (February–March 1845). There He parted from Quddús, saying:

> The days of your companionship with Me are drawing to a close. The hour of separation has struck, a separation which no reunion will follow except in the Kingdom of God, in the presence of the King of Glory.[2]

Quddús left for S͟híráz and took with him a letter from the Báb addressed to His uncle, Ḥájí Mírzá Siyyid 'Alí. Meeting Quddús and hearing all he had to impart convinced Ḥájí

Mírzá Siyyid 'Alí of the truth of the Cause of his Nephew, and he immediately pledged Him his unqualified allegiance.

Mullá Ṣádiq-i-Muqaddas now reached S͟híráz, accompanied by Mullá 'Alí-Akbar-i-Ardistání, who had once been his pupil in Iṣfahán. Mullá Ṣádiq established himself in a mosque known as Báqir-Ábád, where he led the congregation in prayer. But as soon as he received a Tablet from the Báb, sent from Bús͟hihr, he moved to the mosque adjoining His house. There he carried out the specific instruction of the Báb to include in the traditional Islamic Call to Prayer— the Ad͟hán—these additional words: 'I bear witness that He whose name is 'Alí Qabl-i-Muḥammad ['Alí preceding Muḥammad, the Báb] is the servant of Baqíyyatu'lláh [the Remnant of God, Bahá'u'lláh].'[3]

Then the storm broke. S͟hayk͟h Abú-Hás͟him, notorious for his behaviour on the pilgrim boat, had already written to his compatriots in S͟híráz to arouse their fury. Now the divines of that city, led by S͟hayk͟h Ḥusayn-i-'Arab,* Ḥájí S͟hayk͟h Mihdíy-i-Kujúrí and Mullá Muḥammad-'Alíy-i-Maḥallátí, were demanding blood. Quddús, Muqaddas and Mullá 'Alí-Akbar were arrested, hauled before the Governor-General, and mercilessly beaten, after which they suffered the punishments and indignities described in the London report already quoted (see p. 76). But there were three of them, not four.†

The Governor-General of the province of Fárs was

* The Názimu's͟h-S͟harí'ih, who universally earned the epithet of 'Ẓálim', the Tyrant.

† *Táríḵ͟h-i-Jadíd* (p. 202) names a fourth person, a certain Mullá Abú-Ṭálib, a friend of Mullá Ṣádiq-i-Muqaddas. His identity is unknown. A letter exists, written by Mullá 'Alí-Akbar-i-Ardistání to the Báb, when he was seeking permission to visit Him. Since their chastisement, he says, he had been living in ruins outside S͟híráz. The letter makes it absolutely certain that he was the only one who had remained and that both Quddús and Muqaddas had gone.

Ḥusayn Khán, who was called Ájúdán-Báshí (the adjutant-major), and had also the titles of Ṣáḥib-Ikhtíyár and Niẓámu'd-Dawlih. Ḥusayn Khán was a native of Marághih in Ádharbáyján, and had served as Persian envoy both to London and Paris. In London, in June 1839, Lord Palmerston was at first inclined not to meet him, but then decided to receive him unofficially. At that time relations between Britain and Írán had reached a low point. Captain Hennell, the British Political Agent, had been forced to withdraw from Búshihr, and at the same time a British naval force had occupied the island of Khárg (Karrack). Palmerston thundered at Ḥusayn Khán: 'Had the Admiral on arriving on board turned his guns upon the town [Búshihr] and knocked it about their ears, in my opinion he would have been justified in so doing'.[4] When the envoy returned home, Muḥammad Sháh was so displeased that he had him severely bastinadoed. Nor had Ḥusayn Khán's mission to France, it would seem, been any more successful, although some obscurity surrounds his dealings with the French. In Paris he engaged a number of officers to train the Persian army, and there were irregularities in the matter of their travelling expenses. But more serious issues were involved, which are described by Sir Henry Layard* in the following passage:

> M. Boré,† with all his learning and enlightenment, was a religious fanatic and profoundly intolerant of heretics. After residing with him for a fortnight, and having been treated by him with great kindness and hospitality, I found myself compelled, to my great sorrow, to

* See note 9, Prologue.

† M. Boré resided in Julfa, Iṣfahán. He was a layman sent by the French Government to obtain a foothold for the French in Írán. Later he became a Jesuit priest, and was the head of a Jesuit establishment in Galata when Layard met him in Constantinople. It is likely he sent copious notes to his superiors about the Báb and the Bábís.

> leave his house [in 1840] under the following circumstances. The Embassy which the King of the French* had sent to the Shah had not succeeded in obtaining the object of its mission, and had left Persia much irritated at its failure, which was mainly attributed by it and the French Government to English intrigues. The truth was, I believe, that they had been duped by Hussein Khan, who had been sent as ambassador to Paris. The subject was an unpleasant one for me to discuss, and I avoided it in conversation with my host. One day, however, at dinner, it was raised by M. Flandin,[5] the French artist, who denounced my country and countrymen in very offensive terms, M. Boré himself joining in the abuse. They accused the English Government and English agents of having had recourse to poison to prevent Frenchmen from establishing themselves and gaining influence in Persia, and of having actually engaged assassins to murder M. Outray, when on his way on a diplomatic mission to Tehran. I denied, with indignation, these ridiculous and calumnious charges, and high words having ensued, I moved from M. Boré's house to a ruined building occupied by Mr. Burgess.†[6]

Failure in London and tortuosity in Paris did not commend themselves to Muḥammad Sháh; and so, for the next few years, Ḥusayn Khán lived under a cloud. But in 1845 we find him riding high in the province of Fárs. He had been given that governorship because he was reputed to be a man stern in his judgments, and Fárs needed an iron hand.

Indeed Fárs had been in a terrifying plight. The people of Shíráz, high and low alike, had effectively played cat and mouse with the governors sent from Ṭihrán to rule over them. Firaydún Mírzá, the Farmán-Farmá, Muḥammad Sháh's own brother, much favoured by Ḥájí Mírzá Áqásí

* Louis-Philippe.

† An English merchant in Tabríz.

and much detested by the Shírázís, was ousted by a combination of the grandees and the mob.

Mírzá Nabí Khán-i-Qazvíní, the Amír-i-Díván,[7] was also forced out, not once, but twice. On the second occasion many leading citizens—headed by Ḥájí Qavámu'l-Mulk[8] and Muḥammad-Qulí Khán-i-Ílbagí, a powerful chieftain of the Qashqá'í tribe—went to Ṭihrán, to demand the reinstatement of Firaydún Mírzá, whom they had previously challenged and maligned. Muḥammad Sháh kept them waiting in the capital. Mírzá Riḍá (Meerza Reza), the acting British Agent in Shíráz, reported on August 7th 1844 to Captain Hennell in Búshihr:

> On the Evening of the 11th Rajab [July 28th] one of the King's Chapurs [couriers] arrived at Shiraz, bringing two Royal Firmans [edicts] which had been issued at the instance of His Excellency Colonel Sheil, to be published at Shiraz and Bushire . . .
>
> One day the people, consisting of the principal and respectable Inhabitants and Merchants, were assembled in the Mosque, in order to hear the Firman from the Pulpit, when the turbulent and evil [sic] disposed tumultuously rushed in to prevent its being read, because addressed to the Ameer [Amír, the Governor]; These were of the followers of the Hajee Kuwaum [Ḥájí Qavám]. The Ameer then gave the Shiraz Firman into the hands of Resheed Khan, Surteep [Rashíd Khán-i-Sartíp], who took it to the New Mosque in the Naamutee [Ni'matí-Khánih] Quarter,[9] where it was published from the Reading Desks to the assembled Moollahs, respectable Inhabitants, and Merchants.
>
> On the following day when the Ameer directed that the Firman should be read in the Dewan Khaneh [Díván-Khánih—the Court], the rioters fully armed again rushed in impetuously. Syed Hussein Khan and Resheed Khan then assembled their followers and topchees [túpchí: gunner], and complaining bitterly, requested permission

to meet them . . . nor was it without difficulty and much persuasion that the Ameer could induce them to desist pending instructions from the Capital.

The several Quarters of Shiraz are for the most part at feud—Thieving and disturbance are on the increase—The Ameer has not been dismissed nor has a new Governor been appointed.[10]

And matters went from bad to worse. Mírzá Riḍá's report to his chief, the following November 24th, was one long catalogue of woes, not totally devoid of amusing points:

Last Friday, from the ten Quarters of Hyedree [Ḥaydarí] and Naamutte [Ni'matí] a Mob and Crowd was again collected in the open plain, which has ever been the scene of their conflicts, for the purpose of fighting. From Midday to Sunset they fought with slings and stones, sticks and arms . . . As Meerza Mahomed Ali, the secretary of Hajee Kuwam [Ḥájí Qavám], a fine intelligent youth, was leaving his dwelling about midday upon some business, a drunken lootee,* without reason or previous quarrel, plunged a dagger into his right side . . . two cousins, both young, in a state of Drunkenness, were disputing regarding a woman, no person not even the woman being present, when one struck a dagger into the thigh of the other, who expired two days after . . . some men of the Fehlee† Tribe were sitting together one night, talking over occurrences of former years, when . . . an excellent horseman, was shot in the side with a pistol, and immediately yielded his life.[11]

Qubád Khán, a nephew of the Ílkhání (the supreme head of the Qashqá'í tribe), who governed Fírúzábád in the heart of the Qashqá'í terrain, had, for a financial consideration,

* 'Lúṭí': mobster, bravo.
† Faylí: a clan of the Qashqá'ís.

put armed men at the disposal of some headmen of the village of Maymand to settle a vendetta—and so the story trails on.

Towards the end of the year 1844 Ḥusayn Khán was given the governorship of Fárs, but as late as December 21st and December 24th Mírzá Riḍá was still pouring out tales of woe to Captain Hennell in Búshihr. Matters had reached such a pitch, he said, that people were stripped naked in plain daylight in public thoroughfares, and if anyone offered resistance he was repeatedly stabbed; at night so many matchlocks were fired at random that no sleep was possible, and in any case people had to keep awake to guard their homes. The unpleasant yet humorous experience of a physician clearly shows the breakdown of law in Shíráz at that time:

> . . . some of the Alwat* brought a horse to the door of a Physician's Dispensary, whose equipment and clothes were of the best, saying, 'We have an invalid who is very ill, take the trouble to come to him and we will attend you.' The Poor Physician starts for the sickman's [sic] dwelling, and they take him through two or three streets when they desire him to be so good as to dismount from the horse; he does so, and they strip him from head to foot and go their way.[12]

During that period of anarchy the Báb was on pilgrimage and absent from Shíráz. Ḥusayn Khán arrived at his post in the early part of 1845, when the Báb was about halfway back to His native land. The new Governor set about with all dispatch to give the Shírázís a lesson which he was certain they would take to heart. There were mutilations and executions until order was finally restored. But in little more than three years when Muḥammad Sháh died, Shírázís, headed

* 'Alváṭ': plural of 'Lúṭí'.

once again by the astute Ḥájí Qavámu'l-Mulk and the headstrong Muḥammad-Qulí Khán (the Ílbagí* of the Qashqá'ís), rebelled and forced the dismissal of Ḥusayn Khán.

Ḥusayn Khán was the first official in Persia to raise his hand against the Báb and His people. Having meted out cruel punishments to Quddús and the other two Bábís, and having acquainted himself with the identity of the Báb and ascertained that He had arrived at Búshihr, Ḥusayn Khán commissioned a body of horsemen to go to that port, arrest the Báb and bring Him to Shíráz. In the meantime the Báb had completed His arrangements to return to the city of His birth.

At Dálakí, some forty miles to the north-east of Búshihr, where the coastal plain ends and the plateau begins to rise, Ḥusayn Khán's horsemen encountered the Báb. He was the first to notice them and sent His Ethiopian servant to call them to Him. They were reluctant to approach Him, but Aṣlán Khán, a man senior in their ranks, accepted the invitation. However, to the Báb's query regarding the purpose of their mission they evasively replied that the Governor had sent them to make some investigation in that neighbourhood. But the Báb said to them:

> The governor has sent you to arrest Me. Here am I; do with Me as you please. By coming out to meet you, I have curtailed the length of your march, and have made it easier for you to find Me.[13]

* The chieftain next in rank to the Ílkhání. The central government made these appointments.

CHAPTER 7

BELIEF AND DENIAL

Know then thyself, presume not God to scan;
The proper study of Mankind is Man.
Plac'd on this isthmus of a middle state,
A being darkly wise, and rudely great:

. . .

Created half to rise, and half to fall;
Great lord of all things, yet a prey to all;
Sole judge of Truth, in endless Error hurl'd:
The glory, jest and riddle of the world!

—Alexander Pope

The Báb was now a captive, and a captive, apart from a few short months, He remained to the very end. The escort, which should have arrested Him and taken Him in chains to the city of His birth, was subdued and reverent. He rode to Shíráz almost in triumph. It would have been feasible to avoid Ḥusayn Khán's horsemen and seek a safe retreat; but He Himself chose to reveal Himself to His would-be captors. Even more, He said to their spokesman who was enthralled by His unrivalled act, and was entreating Him to take the road to safety, to go to Mashhad and find refuge in the shrine of the eighth Imám:

> May the Lord your God requite you for your magnanimity and noble intention. No one knows the mystery of My Cause; no one can fathom its secrets. Never will I turn My face away from the decree of God. He alone is My sure Stronghold, My Stay and My Refuge. Until My last hour is at hand, none dare assail Me, none can

frustrate the plan of the Almighty. And when My hour is come, how great will be My joy to quaff the cup of martyrdom in His name! Here am I; deliver Me into the hands of your master. Be not afraid, for no one will blame you.[1]

When the identity of the Báb became known some members of His family felt concern, even alarm, lest great harm might come to Him, and they themselves suffer in the process. Only one uncle, Ḥájí Mírzá Siyyid 'Alí, His former guardian, who had reared Him and established Him in the world of commerce, believed in His Divine Mission. So did His wife. But the rest, even His mother, were sceptical and one or two were definitely antagonistic.

When Muḥammad, the Arabian Prophet, refused to bend to the dictates of His tribe, the elders of Quraysh went to His aged uncle, Abú-Ṭálib, in whose home He had grown to manhood, and demanded that Muḥammad be put under restraint. Abú-Ṭálib urged his Nephew to be moderate, but finding Muḥammad determined to pursue His course, assured Him that his protection would never waver. The elders of Quraysh then decided on a stratagem to erode the support that Muḥammad received from His clan—the Banú-Háshim. A boycott was ordered, but the descendants of Háshim, with the solitary exception of Abú-Lahab,* one of the several uncles of the Prophet, moved to a section at the edge of the town and lived for three years in a state of siege, in defence of Muḥammad, although most of them still worshipped their old idols.

The relatives of the Báb did as Muḥammad's relatives

* Such was the verdict of the Qur'án (cxi) on Abú-Lahab:

Perish the hands of Abu Lahab, and perish he!
His wealth avails him not, neither what he has earned;
he shall roast at a flaming fire
and his wife, the carrier of the firewood,
upon her neck a rope of palm-fibre.[2]

before them. Whatever doubts they may have had, they stood by Him.

Ḥájí Mírzá Siyyid Muḥammad, another maternal uncle of the Báb, did not come to believe in his Nephew as the Qá'im of the House of Muḥammad until more than a decade later, when he presented his questions and his doubts to Bahá'u'lláh and received in answer the *Kitáb-i-Íqán—The Book of Certitude*. Yet, such were the magnetic powers of the Báb that when He reached Búshihr and was welcomed by this uncle, the latter wrote in these terms to his family in Shíráz:

> It has gladdened our hearts that His Honour the Ḥájí [the Báb] has arrived safely and is in good health. I am at His service and honoured to be in His company. It is deemed advisable that He should stay here for a while. God willing, He will, before long, honour those parts with His presence, be assured . . . His blessed Person is our glory. Be certain of His Cause and do not let people's idle talk cause doubts to creep into your hearts. And have no fear whatsoever. The Lord of the world is His Protector and gives Him victory . . .

At the end of his letter Ḥájí Mírzá Siyyid Muḥammad sent a message, on behalf of his wife, to the mother of the wife of the Báb: 'You have a son-in-law who is peerless in the world. All the peoples of the world ought to obey Him.'[3]

And in a letter written shortly after, to Ḥájí Mírzá Muḥammad-'Alí, one of his sons, the same Ḥájí Mírzá Siyyid Muḥammad quoted the Báb as saying: My proof is My Book—let him who can, produce the like of these verses.

Similarly, Muḥammad had said in the Qur'án:[4]

> Say: 'Bring a Book from God that gives
> better guidance than these, and follow it,
> if you speak truly.'

> Then if they do not answer thee, know that
> they are only following their caprices;
> and who is further astray than he who
> follows his caprice without guidance from
> God? Surely God guides not the people
> of the evildoers.
>
> —xxviii, 49–50.

> Those are the signs of God that We recite to thee in truth;
> in what manner of discourse then, after God and His signs,
> will they believe?
>
> —xlv, 5.

The Báb's entry into Shíráz was truly majestic. It bore no resemblance to the condition envisaged by the Governor. He had ordered the Báb to be brought to Shíráz in chains. Instead, there was the Báb riding, calm and serene, at the head of the horsemen. They went straight to the citadel where the Governor resided. Ḥusayn Khán received the Báb with overbearing insolence: 'Do you realise what a great mischief you have kindled? Are you aware what a disgrace you have become to the holy Faith of Islám and to the august person of our sovereign? Are you not the man who claims to be the author of a new revelation which annuls the sacred precepts of the Qur'án?'[5] The Báb spoke in reply these words from the Qur'án:[6]

> O believers, if an ungodly man
> comes to you with a tiding, make
> clear,* lest you afflict a people
> unwittingly, and then repent of
> what you have done.
>
> —xlix, 6.

* Rodwell translates this as 'clear it up at once . . . '

Ḥusayn Khán was beside himself with rage, and ordered an attendant to strike the Báb's face. His turban fell off but was replaced gently by Shaykh Abú-Turáb, the Imám-Jum'ih, who treated the Báb with respect and consideration. On the other hand, Shaykh Ḥusayn-i-'Arab, the Tyrant, who was also present, following the example set by the arrogant Governor of Fárs, assailed the Báb vehemently both with hand and tongue. In the meantime news had reached the mother of the Báb of this shameless behaviour towards her Son. Moved by her pleadings, Ḥájí Mírzá Siyyid 'Alí hurried to the citadel to demand the release of his Nephew. Ḥusayn Khán agreed to let the Báb go to His home, if His uncle would promise that apart from the members of His family no one else would be allowed to meet Him. Ḥájí Mírzá Siyyid 'Alí protested that he himself was a well-known merchant of the city, with many connections and a host of friends and acquaintances, all of whom would wish to visit his Nephew, who had just returned from pilgrimage to the holy cities of Mecca and Medina. Ḥusayn Khán, realizing that an immediate ban was not possible, set a time limit of three days, after which the Báb should be kept incommunicado.

The months during which the Báb lived under surveillance in His native town saw the birth of the Bábí community. Hitherto His identity had remained unrevealed, and only individuals, here and there and unrelated to one another, were Bábís. Apart from the first few months of His Ministry, when the body of the Letters of the Living was gradually forming, the Báb had not had a group of disciples around Him. Even then, because of the condition which the Báb had laid down for the attainment of those who were to be the first believers,* cohesion as one firmly-knit body was not feasible. And as soon as the requisite number was enrolled,

* They were to find Him 'independently and of their own accord'.

the Báb sent them out into the world to spread the glad tidings of the New Day. But, once again in Shíráz, despite the oppressive measures of Ḥusayn Khán, an appreciable number of Bábís came into the presence of the Báb, consorted with Him and received instruction and Tablets from Him. Viewed in this light, this Shíráz episode would seem the most fecund period in the short Ministry of the Báb.

Ḥájí Siyyid Javád-i-Karbilá'í, who, as we have seen, had known the Báb from His childhood, now hurried to Shíráz; and soon after came a man destined to achieve high fame in the ranks of the 'Dawn-Breakers'. He was Siyyid Yaḥyá of Dáráb, the son of the same greatly-revered Siyyid Ja'far-i-Kashfí, whom we noted before as a fellow-pilgrim of the Báb. Siyyid Yaḥyá was a divine of great erudition, and he thought that he could easily overcome the Báb in argument. As he lived in Ṭihrán, close to royal circles, Muḥammad Sháh asked Siyyid Yaḥyá to go to Shíráz and investigate the claim of the Báb. In Shíráz he was the guest of the Governor. Ḥájí Siyyid Javád-i-Karbilá'í arranged a meeting between the Báb and Siyyid Yaḥyá in the house of Ḥájí Mírzá Siyyid 'Alí. At that first encounter Siyyid Yaḥyá, proud of his vast knowledge, brought out one abstruse point after another from the Qur'án, from Traditions, from learned works. To all of them the Báb listened calmly, and gave answers concise and convincing. Siyyid Yaḥyá was subdued, but still he searched for a test which would relieve him from the necessity of giving his allegiance to the Báb. He told Ḥájí Siyyid Javád-i-Karbilá'í that if only the Báb would show forth a miracle, his lingering doubts would vanish, to which Ḥájí Siyyid Javád replied that to demand the performance of a miracle, when faced with the brilliance of the Sun of Truth, was tantamount to seeking light from a flickering candle. Siyyid Yaḥyá has himself related:

> I resolved that in my third interview with the Báb I would in my inmost heart request Him to reveal for me a

commentary on the Súrih of Kaw<u>th</u>ar.* I determined not to breathe that request in His presence. Should He, unasked by me, reveal this commentary in a manner that would immediately distinguish it in my eyes from the prevailing standards current among the commentators on the Qur'án, I then would be convinced of the Divine character of His Mission, and would readily embrace His Cause. If not, I would refuse to acknowledge Him. As soon as I was ushered into His presence, a sense of fear, for which I could not account, suddenly seized me. My limbs quivered as I beheld His face. I, who on repeated occasions had been introduced into the presence of the <u>Sh</u>áh and had never discovered the slightest trace of timidity in myself, was now so awed and shaken that I could not remain standing on my feet. The Báb, beholding my plight, arose from His seat, advanced towards me, and, taking hold of my hand, seated me beside Him. 'Seek from Me,' He said, 'whatever is your heart's desire. I will readily reveal it to you.' I was speechless with wonder. Like a babe that can neither understand nor speak, I felt powerless to respond. He smiled as He gazed at me and said: 'Were I to reveal for you the commentary on the Súrih of Kaw<u>th</u>ar, would you acknowledge that My words are born of the Spirit of God? Would you recognise that My utterance can in no wise be associated with sorcery or magic?' Tears flowed from my eyes as I heard Him speak these words. All I was able to utter was this verse of the Qur'án: 'O our Lord, with ourselves have we dealt unjustly: if Thou forgive us not and have not pity on us, we shall surely be of those who perish.'

It was still early in the afternoon when the Báb requested Ḥájí Mírzá Siyyid 'Alí to bring His pen-case and some paper. He then started to reveal His commentary on the Súrih of Kaw<u>th</u>ar. How am I to describe this scene of inexpressible majesty? Verses streamed from His pen with a rapidity that was truly astounding. The incredible swiftness of His writing, the soft and gentle murmur of

* Qur'án, cviii. Kaw<u>th</u>ar is said to be a river in Paradise.

His voice, and the stupendous force of His style, amazed and bewildered me. He continued in this manner until the approach of sunset. He did not pause until the entire commentary of the Súrih was completed. He then laid down His pen and asked for tea. Soon after, He began to read it aloud in my presence. My heart leaped madly as I heard Him pour out, in accents of unutterable sweetness, those treasures enshrined in that sublime commentary. I was so entranced by its beauty that three times over I was on the verge of fainting. He sought to revive my failing strength with a few drops of rose-water which He caused to be sprinkled on my face. This restored my vigour and enabled me to follow His reading to the end.[7]

The Báb's conquest of Siyyid Yaḥyá was total. That night and the two following nights, as instructed by the Báb, Siyyid Yaḥyá remained a guest in the house of Ḥájí Mírzá Siyyid 'Alí, until he himself and Mullá 'Abdu'l-Karím-i-Qazvíní, the scribe, (later known as Mírzá Aḥmad-i-Kátib), completed the transcription of the Báb's commentary. Siyyid Yaḥyá has stated:

> We verified all the traditions in the text and found them to be entirely accurate. Such was the state of certitude to which I had attained that if all the powers of the earth were to be leagued against me they would be powerless to shake my confidence in the greatness of His Cause.[8]

Siyyid Yaḥyá had stayed away for such a long time from the Governor's residence that Ḥusayn Khán's suspicions were aroused. To his impatient queries, Siyyid Yaḥyá replied:

> No one but God, who alone can change the hearts of men, is able to captivate the heart of Siyyid Yaḥyá. Whoso can ensnare his heart is of God, and His word unquestionably the voice of Truth.[9]

Ḥusayn Khán was nonplussed and, for the moment, could only hold his peace; but he wrote bitterly to Muḥammad Sháh to denounce Siyyid Yaḥyá. Nabíl-i-A'ẓam states that Muḥammad Sháh reprimanded his Governor, replying:

> It is strictly forbidden to any one of our subjects to utter such words as would tend to detract from the exalted rank of Siyyid Yaḥyáy-i-Dárábí. He is of noble lineage, a man of great learning, of perfect and consummate virtue. He will under no circumstances incline his ear to any cause unless he believes it to be conducive to the advancement of the best interests of our realm and to the well-being of the Faith of Islám.[10]

Nabíl has also recorded that

> Muḥammad Sháh . . . was reported to have addressed these words to Ḥájí Mírzá Áqásí: 'We have been lately informed that Siyyid Yaḥyáy-i-Dárábí has become a Bábí. If this be true, it behoves us to cease belittling the cause of that siyyid.'[10]

'Abdu'l-Bahá has stated that Siyyid Yaḥyá

> wrote without fear or care a detailed account of his observations to Mírzá Luṭf-'Alí, the chamberlain in order that the latter might submit it to the notice of the late king, while he himself journeyed to all parts of Persia, and in every town and station summoned the people from the pulpit-tops in such wise that other learned doctors decided that he must be mad, accounting it a sure case of bewitchment.[11]

At the bidding of the Báb, Siyyid Yaḥyá went first to Burújird in the province of Luristán, where his father lived, to give that much-revered divine the tidings of the New Day. The Báb expressly told him to treat his father with great gentleness. Siyyid Ja'far-i-Kashfí* did not wholly turn away from the Faith which his illustrious son was fervently professing and advocating, but showed no desire to identify himself with it. Siyyid Yaḥyá, as commanded by the Báb, did not burden his father more and went his own way which he had gladly chosen—the way that was to lead him to martyrdom. Siyyid Yaḥyá is known as Vaḥíd—the Unique One—a designation given to him by the Báb.†

The divines of Shíráz were insistent that the Báb should attend a Friday gathering in one of the mosques and clarify his position. What they really demanded was the complete renunciation of any claim. This attendance in a mosque on a Friday did take place, but the date of it is not known.

Nabíl-i-A'ẓam thus describes the summoning of the Báb to the Mosque of Vakíl:[12]

> The Báb, accompanied by Ḥájí Mírzá Siyyid 'Alí, arrived at the Masjid at a time when the Imám-Jum'ih had just ascended the pulpit and was preparing to deliver his sermon. As soon as his eyes fell upon the Báb, he publicly welcomed Him, requested Him to ascend the pulpit, and called upon Him to address the congregation. The Báb, responding to his invitation, advanced towards him and, standing on the first step of the staircase, prepared to address the people. 'Come up higher,' interjected the Imám-Jum'ih. Complying with his wish, the Báb ascended two more steps. As He was standing, His head hid the breast of Shaykh Abú-Turáb, who was occupying the pulpit-top. He began by prefacing His public

* 'The Discloser': he was called 'Kashfí' because of the powers of divination attributed to him.

† A letter has survived in the handwriting of Vaḥíd, addressed to Ḥájí Mírzá Siyyid Muḥammad, the uncle of the Báb. Therein Vaḥíd presents proof to convince him of the truth of the claim of his Nephew. See Plate facing p. 81 for an example of Vaḥíd's handwriting.

declaration with an introductory discourse. No sooner had He uttered the opening words of 'Praise be to God, who hath in truth created the heavens and the earth,' than a certain siyyid known as Siyyid-i-Shish-Parí, whose function was to carry the mace before the Imám-Jum'ih, insolently shouted: 'Enough of this idle chatter! Declare, now and immediately, the thing you intend to say.' The Imám-Jum'ih greatly resented the rudeness of the siyyid's remark. 'Hold your peace,' he rebuked him, 'and be ashamed of your impertinence.' He then, turning to the Báb, asked Him to be brief, as this, he said, would allay the excitement of the people. The Báb, as He faced the congregation, declared: 'The condemnation of God be upon him who regards me either as a representative of the Imám or the gate thereof. The condemnation of God be also upon whosoever imputes to me the charge of having denied the unity of God, of having repudiated the prophethood of Muḥammad, the Seal of the Prophets, of having rejected the truth of any of the messengers of old, or of having refused to recognise the guardianship of 'Alí, the Commander of the Faithful, or of any of the imáms who have succeeded him.' He then ascended to the top of the staircase, embraced the Imám-Jum'ih, and, descending to the floor of the Masjid, joined the congregation for the observance of the Friday prayer. The Imám-Jum'ih intervened and requested Him to retire. 'Your family,' he said, 'is anxiously awaiting your return. All are apprehensive lest any harm befall you. Repair to your house and there offer your prayer; of greater merit shall this deed be in the sight of God.' Ḥájí Mírzá Siyyid 'Alí also was, at the request of the Imám-Jum'ih, asked to accompany his nephew to his home. This precautionary measure which Shaykh Abú-Turáb thought it wise to observe was actuated by the fear lest, after the dispersion of the congregation, a few of the evil-minded among the crowd might still attempt to injure the person of the Báb or endanger His life. But for the sagacity, the sympathy, and the careful attention which the Imám-

Jum'ih so strikingly displayed on a number of such occasions, the infuriated mob would doubtless have been led to gratify its savage desire, and would have committed the most abominable of excesses. He seemed to have been the instrument of the invisible Hand appointed to protect both the person and the Mission of that Youth.[13]

Regarding that gathering in the Mosque of Vakíl, 'Abdu'l-Bahá has written:

> One day they summoned him to the mosque urging and constraining him to recant, but he discoursed from the pulpit in such wise as to silence and subdue those present and to stablish and strengthen his followers. It was then supposed that he claimed to be the medium of grace from His Highness the Lord of the Age* (upon him be peace); but afterwards it became known and evident that his meaning was the Gate-hood [*Bábiyyat*] of another city and the mediumship of the graces of another person whose qualities and attributes were contained in his books and treatises.[14]

Ḥájí Mírzá Ḥabíbu'lláh-i-Afnán has this record in his chronicle:

'The late Ḥájí Mírzá Muḥammad-Sádiq-i-Mu'allim [Teacher], who was a man of good repute, was relating the story of that day for the late 'Andalíb.[15] My brother, Ḥájí Mírzá Buzurg, and I were present. This is the summary of what he said: "I was about twenty-five years old and able to judge an issue. It was noised abroad that the Governor, by the request of the divines, had ordered that the people of Shíráz, of all classes, should gather in the Masjid-i-Vakíl, as the Siyyid-i-Báb was going to renounce His claim. I too went to the mosque to find a place near [the pulpit] so that

* Ṣaḥibu'z-Zamán, i.e., the Qá'im, the Mihdí (Mahdí).

I might hear well all that He had to say. From the morning onwards, people, group by group, thronged the mosque. Three hours before sunset there was such a press of people in the mosque that the cloisters and the courtyard and the roofs, even the minarets, were fully crowded. The Governor, the divines, the merchants and the notables were sitting in the cloisters, near the stone pulpit. (This is a pulpit carved out of one piece of marble. It has fourteen steps.) I was also sitting near it. Voices were heard in the courtyard, saying: 'He is coming.' He came through the gate, accompanied by ten footmen and 'Abdu'l-Ḥamíd Khán-i-Dárúghih [chief of police], and approached the pulpit. He had His turban on and an 'abá on His shoulders. He displayed such power and dignity and His bearing was so sublime that I cannot describe it adequately. That vast gathering seemed as naught to Him. He paid no heed to that assemblage of the people. He addressed Ḥusayn Khán and the divines: 'What is your intention in asking Me to come here?' They answered: 'The intention is that you should ascend this pulpit and repudiate your false claim so that this commotion and unrest will subside.' He said nothing and went up to the third step of the pulpit. Shaykh Ḥusayn, the Tyrant, said with utmost vehemence: 'Go to the top of the pulpit so that all may see and hear you.' The Báb ascended the pulpit and sat down at the top. All of a sudden, silence fell upon that assemblage. It seemed as if there was not a soul in the mosque. The whole concourse of people strained their ears. He began to recite at the start a homily in Arabic on Divine Unity. It was delivered with utmost eloquence, with majesty and power. It lasted about half an hour, and the concourse of people, high and low, learned and illiterate alike, listened attentively and were fascinated. The people's silence infuriated Shaykh Ḥusayn, who turned to the Governor and said: 'Did you bring this Siyyid here, into the presence of all these people, to prove His Cause, or did you bring Him to recant and renounce His false claim? He will soon with these words win over all these people to His side. Tell Him to say what He has to say. What are all these idle tales?' Ḥusayn Khán, the Ṣáḥib-Ikhtíyár, told the Báb: 'O Siyyid! say what you have been told to say. What is this idle chatter?' The Báb was silent for a moment and then He addressed the crowd: 'O people! Know this well that I speak what My Grandfather, the Messenger of God, spoke twelve hundred and sixty years ago, and I do not speak what My Grandfather did not. "What Muḥammad made lawful remains lawful unto the Day of Resurrection and what He forbade remains forbidden unto the Day of Resurrection",* and according to the Tradition that has come down from the Imáms, "Whenever the Qá'im arises that will be the Day of Resurrection".' The Báb, having spoken those words, descended from the pulpit. Some of the people, who had been inimical and hostile, that day foreswore their antagonism. But when the Báb came face to face with Shaykh Ḥusayn, that enemy raised his walking-stick to strike Him. The late Mírzá Abu'l-Ḥasan Khán, the Mushíru'l-Mulk,† who was then a young man, brought forward his shoulder to ward off the attack, and it was his shoulder that was hit."

'That Ḥájí [Ḥájí Mírzá Muḥammad-Ṣádiq], who was not a believer but a well-wisher, related this story to the late 'Andalíb. His meaning was that the Báb, on that occasion, affirmed His Cause and completed His proof before the concourse of people.'

Ḥájí Mírzá Ḥabíbu'lláh goes on to say: 'Then the divines came together and passed a sentence of death on the Báb. They wrote out their verdict and affixed their seals to it. The

* The Báb was quoting a Muslim Tradition.

† He and his father, Mírzá Muḥammad-'Alí, the first Mushíru'l-Mulk, were the Viziers of Fárs, in succession, over a period of forty years.

instigator of this move and the source of all mischief was Shaykh Ḥusayn, the Tyrant, who held the title of Náẓim'ush-Sharíy'ih. Their numbers included Shaykh Abú-Háshim, Shaykh Asadu'lláh, Shaykh Mihdíy-i-Kujúrí and Mullá Muḥammad-'Alíy-i-Maḥallátí. Next they took what they had written and sealed to the late Shaykh Abú-Turáb, the Imám-Jum'ih, because he had refused to heed their pleas and had declined to attend their meeting. Now they presented their paper to the Imám-Jum'ih and asked him to put his seal on it that "we may finish off this Siyyid". Shaykh Abú-Turáb, on perusing the verdict, became very angry, threw that piece of paper on the ground and said, "Have you gone out of your minds? I will never put my seal on this paper, because I have no doubts about the lineage, integrity, piety, nobility and honesty of this Siyyid. I see that this young Man is possessed of all the virtues of Islám and humanity and of all the faculties of intellect. There can be only two sides to this question: He either speaks the truth, or He is, as you allege, a liar. If He be truthful I cannot endorse such a verdict on a man of truth, and if He be a liar, as you aver, tell me which one of us present here is so strictly truthful as to sit in judgment upon this Siyyid. Away with you and your false imaginings, away, away!" No matter how hard they tried and how much they insisted, the late Shaykh Abú-Turáb did not grant them their wish; and because he declined to put his seal on their paper, their plan was brought to naught and they did not succeed in achieving their objective.'

According to Nicolas, Muḥammad Sháh asked Siyyid Yaḥyáy-i-Dárábí to go to Shíráz and investigate the Cause of the Báb, when the account of the gathering in the Mosque of Vakíl was presented to him.[16]

'Abdu'l-Bahá tells us that when the news of the journeys of Siyyid Yaḥyáy-i-Dárábí and the anger provoked by them reached Zanján, Mullá Muḥammad 'Alí the divine, who was a man of mark possessed of penetrating speech, sent one of those on whom he could rely to Shíráz to investigate this matter. This person, having acquainted himself with the details of these occurrences in such wise as was necessary and proper, returned with some [of the Báb's] writings. When the divine heard how matters were and had made himself acquainted with the writings, notwithstanding that he was a man expert in knowledge and noted for profound research, he went mad and became crazed as was predestined: he gathered up his books in the lecture-room saying, 'The season of spring and wine has arrived,' and uttered this sentence:–'*Search for knowledge after reaching the known is culpable.*' Then from the summit of the pulpit he summoned and directed all his disciples [to embrace the doctrine], and wrote to the Báb his own declaration and confession . . .

Although the doctors of Zanján arose with heart and soul to exhort and admonish the people they could effect nothing. Finally they were compelled to go to Teherán and made their complaint before the late king Muḥammad Sháh, requesting that Mullá Muḥammad 'Alí be summoned to Teherán.

Now when he came to Teherán they brought him before a conclave of the doctors . . . after many controversies and disputations nought was effected with him in that assembly. The late king therefore bestowed on him a staff and fifty *túmáns* for his expenses, and gave him permission to return.[17]

The confidant whom Mullá Muḥammad-'Alí of Zanján, better known as Ḥujjat (the Proof),* sent to Shíráz to investigate the Cause of the Báb was named Mullá Iskandar. Nabíl-i-A'ẓam describes his return:

* He was called Ḥujjatu'l-Islám (The Proof of Islám), an appellation given to highly-placed and well-recognized divines. The Báb gave him the designation: Ḥujjat-i-Zanjání.

He arrived at a time when all the leading 'ulamás of the city had assembled in the presence of Ḥujjat. As soon as he appeared, Ḥujjat enquired whether he believed in, or rejected, the new Revelation. Mullá Iskandar submitted the writings of the Báb . . . and asserted that whatever should be the verdict of his master, the same would he deem it his obligation to follow. 'What!' angrily exclaimed Ḥujjat. 'But for the presence of this distinguished company, I would have chastised you severely. How dare you consider matters of belief to be dependent upon the approbation or rejection of others?' Receiving from the hand of his messenger the copy of the Qayyúmu'l-Asmá', he, as soon as he had perused a page of that book, fell prostrate upon the ground and exclaimed: 'I bear witness that these words which I have read proceed from the same Source as that of the Qur'án. Whoso has recognised the truth of that sacred Book must needs testify to the Divine origin of these words, and must needs submit to the precepts inculcated by their Author. I take you, members of this assembly, as my witnesses: I pledge such allegiance to the Author of this Revelation that should He ever pronounce the night to be the day, and declare the sun to be a shadow, I would unreservedly submit to His judgment, and would regard His verdict as the voice of Truth.'[18]

Mullá Muḥammad-'Alí of Zanján, who, like Siyyid Yaḥyá of Dáráb, was destined to become a brilliant star in the Bábí firmament, was a practitioner of the Akhbárí school,[19] and that had placed him oftentimes at odds with other divines of his rank and station. Beyond that variance Mullá Muḥammad-'Alí was always very forceful and emphatic in the expression of his views. That forthrightness, sustained by his vast knowledge and lucid speech, had led to serious disputations with his peers. Time and again the mediation of no less a person than the monarch himself had saved the situation from deterioration into violence. He had once before been summoned to Ṭihrán, where, in the presence of Muḥammad Sháh, he had worsted his opponents. As the common parlance has it, he was not a man to mince his words.

There were a number of Bábís in Karbilá eagerly awaiting the arrival of the Báb. The news that the Báb had changed His route shook the faith of a few of them. As instructed by the Báb Himself, these Bábís left Karbilá for Iṣfahán. At Kangávar, situated between Kirmánsháh and Hamadán, they encountered Mullá Ḥusayn, the Bábu'l-Báb, and his brother and nephew, whose destination was Karbilá. But, hearing what had happened, Mullá Ḥusayn decided to accompany them to Iṣfahán. There he received the news from Shíráz that the Báb was under constraint. He determined to continue on to Shíráz, accompanied, as before, by his brother and nephew. He took off his turban and clerical robes and put on the accoutrements of a horseman of the Hizárih tribe in Khurásán. Thus he entered the gate of Shíráz and reached the house of Ḥájí Mírzá Siyyid 'Alí. Some days later Mírzá Muḥammad-'Alíy-i-Nahrí with his brother Mírzá Hádí, and Mullá 'Abdu'l-Karím-i-Qazvíní arrived at Shíráz, and with them were Mullá 'Abdu'l-'Alíy-i-Hirátí and Mullá Javád-i-Baraghání, who were fickle and deeply jealous of Mullá Ḥusayn. In spite of Mullá Ḥusayn's disguise, the enemies of the Báb soon recognized him, and the cry went up denouncing his presence in Shíráz. Then the Báb directed Mullá Ḥusayn to Yazd, whence he was to proceed to Khurásán. Others He also told to leave; only Mullá 'Abdu'l-Karím remained to be His scribe. Those who had professed the Faith of the Báb to gain their own ends, such as Mullá 'Abdu'l-'Alíy-i-Hirátí, went to Kirmán and attached themselves to Ḥájí Muḥammad-Karím Khán-i-Kirmání, who, by this date, had assumed the leadership of the Shaykhí community.

A number of other Bábís, as previously mentioned, also
repaired to S̲h̲íráz and attained the presence of the Báb.
One of them was Mullá S̲h̲ayk̲h̲ ʻAlí of K̲h̲urásán, whom the
Báb designated as ʻAẓím* (Great). He was still in S̲h̲íráz
when Siyyid Yaḥyáy-i-Dárábí came to make his investigation. S̲h̲ayk̲h̲ Ḥasan-i-Zunúzí was another. Moreover, S̲h̲íráz
itself had by this time a group of native Bábís. Ḥájí Abu'l-
Ḥasan, the Báb's fellow-pilgrim, was one; another was a
nephew of S̲h̲ayk̲h̲ Abú-Turáb, the Imám-Jumʻih, a youth
named S̲h̲ayk̲h̲-ʻAlí Mírzá; yet another, Ḥájí Muḥammad-
Bisát, a close friend of the same Imám-Jumʻih; and to name
a few more: Mírzá-Áqáy-i-Rikáb-Sáz (Stirrup-maker),
destined to fall a martyr, one of the very few who quaffed
the cup of martyrdom in S̲h̲íráz itself; Luṭf-ʻAlí Mírzá, a
descendant of the Afs̲h̲ár kings (1736–95), whom we shall
meet in a subsequent chapter; Áqá Muḥammad-Karím, a
merchant, who was eventually compelled by continued persecution to abandon his native city; Mírzá Raḥím, a baker,
who became an ardent teacher of the Faith; Mírzá ʻAbdu'l-
Karím, who had the office of key-holder to the shrine known
as S̲h̲áh-C̲h̲irág̲h̲† (King of the Lamp) where Mír Aḥmad, a
brother of the eighth Imám, is buried; Mas̲h̲hadí Abu'l-
Qásim-i-Labbáf (Quilt-maker), whose son Ḥis̲h̲mat achieved
fame as a poet; Mírzá Mihdí, a poet of note, whose soubriquet was Ṣábir (Patient), and his son, Mírzá ʻAlí-Akbar.
Most of these native Bábís of S̲h̲íráz embraced the Faith
after hearing the Báb from the pulpit of the Mosque of Vakíl.

By the summer of 1846, the Báb had cleared the way for
another chapter in the progress of His Ministry. He be-
queathed all His property jointly to His mother and to His
wife, who was to inherit subsequently the whole estate.‡

---

* ʻAẓím is numerically equivalent to S̲h̲ayk̲h̲ ʻAlí.

† Many of the relatives of the Báb, including His uncle, Ḥájí
Mírzá Siyyid Muḥammad, were buried inside this shrine.

‡ See Plate facing p. 193.

Then He took up His residence in the house of His uncle, Ḥájí Mírzá Siyyid ʿAlí. That was the house where He was born and where He had spent much of His childhood. At the time of this move, He told those of His followers who had come to make their home in S͟híráz to go to Iṣfahán. Included in that group were Siyyid Ḥusayn-i-Yazdí, one of the Letters of the Living, who later became the amanuensis of the Báb, S͟hayk͟h Ḥasan-i-Zunúzí and Mullá ʿAbduʾl-Karím-i-Qazvíní, the scribe.

One evening it was reported to the Governor that a large number of Bábís had gathered in the house of Ḥájí Mírzá Siyyid ʿAlí. Ḥusayn K͟hán ordered ʿAbduʾl-Ḥamíd K͟hán, the Dárúg͟hih (chief constable) of S͟híráz, to rush the house of the uncle of the Báb, surprise its occupants and arrest everyone he found there. According to Nicolas, Ḥájí Mírzá Áqásí had instructed the Governor to put the Báb to death in secret. It was apparently Ḥusayn K͟hán's intention to carry out the orders of the Grand Vizier that night. However, that very night a severe cholera epidemic swept the city,* and Ḥusayn K͟hán fled precipitately. The chief constable and his men entered Ḥájí Mírzá Siyyid ʿAlí's house by way of the roof-top, but found no one with the Báb, except His uncle and one disciple, Siyyid Káẓim-i-Zanjání. With the Governor gone, the chief constable decided to take the Báb to his own house. Reaching his home, ʿAbduʾl-Ḥamíd K͟hán

---

* On October 15th 1846, Major Hennell reported from Bús͟hihr to Sheil in Ṭihrán that cholera reached S͟híráz about September 22nd, and that 'immediately the fact was ascertained' Ḥusayn K͟hán left S͟híráz and went well away. At the time of his writing, Hennell states, the Governor had come back, to Bág͟h-i-Tak͟ht, a garden and palace on the northern heights overlooking S͟híráz. On November 16th, Hennell reported that 'the cholera has ceased its ravages at Shiraz', that it had spread as far away as Fasá and Jahrum, that there had been no fatal cases in Bús͟hihr, and that Baṣrah and Bag͟hdád in Turkish domains had suffered most, deaths numbering up to 200 a day in Baṣrah. (F.O. 268/113.)

found, to his horror and distress, that within the few hours of his absence his sons had been struck by cholera. He pleaded with the Báb for their recovery. It was now the hour of dawn and the Báb was preparing to say His morning prayer. He gave 'Abdu'l-Ḥamíd Khán some of the water with which He was making His ablutions and told him to take it to his sons to drink; they would recover, the Báb assured the chief constable. They recovered indeed, and 'Abdu'l-Ḥamíd Khán was so overwhelmed with joy and gratitude that he sought out the Governor and begged Ḥusayn Khán to permit him to release the Báb. 'Abdu'l-Bahá states in *A Traveller's Narrative* that Ḥusayn Khán consented on condition that the Báb agreed to depart from Shíráz.[20]

NOTE

When this book had reached the stage of paginated proofs, the writer received a number of very important documents, one of which is a historical find of prime importance. It is a letter from the Báb to His uncle, Ḥájí Mírzá Siyyid 'Alí, written at Kunár-Takhtih, a stage further from Dálakí, on the Búshihr-Shíráz road. It was at Dálakí that He encountered the horsemen sent to arrest Him. He mentions the esteem shown to Him by those horsemen. But the importance of this letter lies in the fact that it is precisely dated: 24th of the 2nd Jamádí 1261, which corresponds to June 30th 1845. The date of the Báb's departure from Búshihr had nowhere been recorded and had remained unknown. It must have taken Him another week, at least, to reach Shíráz. Departing for Iṣfahán in the last days of September 1846, His sojurn in His native city was, thus, less than fifteen months.

CHAPTER 8

THE CITY OF 'ABBÁS THE GREAT

The garlands wither on your brow,
  Then boast no more your mighty deeds;
Upon Death's purple altar now
  See where the victor-victim bleeds:
    Your heads must come
    To the cold tomb;
Only the actions of the just
Smell sweet and blossom in the dust.
—James Shirley

Autumn was setting in when the Báb left the house of 'Abdu'l-Ḥamíd Khán, turned His back on Shíráz and took the road to Iṣfahán. He was attended by Siyyid Káẓim-i-Zanjání.[1] No opportunity had there been for Him to see His mother and His wife, and they never met again. But He said farewell to His uncle, Ḥájí Mírzá Siyyid 'Alí.

His family was in great distress, and the confounded and frustrated Governor turned upon them to give vent to his fury. First he seized and chastised the venerable Ḥájí Mírzá Siyyid 'Alí, then had his men break into the house of Ḥájí Mírzá Abu'l-Qásim, the brother-in-law of the Báb, who was dangerously ill in bed. He was dragged out, carried to the Governor's residence, threatened, reviled and fined. Porters took him back to his house, slinging him over their shoulders since he was unable to walk. The people of Shíráz were warned that if a single sheet of the writings of the Báb was found in their possession, they would be severely punished. In their panic, scores dashed to the house of Ḥájí Mírzá Abu'l-Qásim with bundles of the writings of the Báb, all written in His own hand, threw them into the open portico of the house and dashed away, lest they might be seen with the incriminating material. Ḥájí Mírzá Siyyid 'Alí advised the members of that household to wash away the ink and bury the sodden paper.*

A day or two before the house of Ḥájí Mírzá Siyyid 'Alí was raided, Ḥájí Mírzá Abu'l-Qásim wrote to Ḥájí Mírzá Siyyid Muḥammad, who was still in Búshihr, in tones of great dismay: opposition was mounting, even a relative by marriage was vociferously denouncing the Báb (whom he names as Ḥájí Mírzá 'Alí-Muḥammad throughout his letter) and Ḥájí Mírzá Siyyid 'Alí. As there were certain matters which Ḥájí Mírzá Siyyid 'Alí could not manage by himself, he desired Ḥájí Mírzá Siyyid Muḥammad to come as soon as possible from Búshihr, to do all that was needed to settle their affairs. 'Some people may feel ashamed and keep within bounds when they see you,' he wrote. He wanted to be freed of their trading engagements so that he could take his family and leave Shíráz, to avoid any further injustices.

Iṣfahán, towards which the Báb set His face, was and is, *par excellence*, the city of 'Abbás the Great, the most illustrious of the Ṣafavid monarchs (1501–1732), who is best known in the West because of his association with the Sherley brothers and the East India Company, with whose aid he drove the Portuguese out of the Persian Gulf. He is 'The Great Sophy' of Shakespeare. Iṣfahán had been the capital of the Saljúqs (Seljucids), centuries before, but it had suffered neglect in the intervening years. Sháh 'Abbás

* The present writer remembers hearing from his mother her recollections of her paternal grandmother, the wife of Ḥájí Mírzá Abu'l-Qásim, which included an account of the washing away of the writings of the Báb. Huge copper collanders were used for the purpose. The paper was either buried or thrown into wells.

moved his capital from Qazvín to Iṣfahán, and began restoring the city which was to be styled, erelong, Niṣf-i-Jahán—Half-the-World. Magnificent mosques and colleges and pavilions, and the largest public square in the world, are prominent among that great ruler's works, and are there today to inspire wonder and admiration. But with the decline and eventual fall of the Ṣafavids, Iṣfahán, too, declined and met with repeated misfortunes in the days of the Qájárs, who pulled down or painted over Ṣafavid buildings.

In that autumn of 1846, the Governor-General of Iṣfahán was a Georgian eunuch: Manúchihr Khán, the Mu'tamidu'd-Dawlih. He had been, writes Layard,

> purchased in his childhood as a slave, had been brought up a Musulman, and reduced to his unhappy condition. Like many of his kind, he was employed when young in the public service, and had by his remarkable abilities risen to the highest posts. He had for many years enjoyed the confidence and the favour of the Shah. Considered the best administrator in the kingdom, he had been sent to govern the great province of Isfahan, which included within its limits the wild and lawless tribes of the Lurs and Bakhtiyari, generally in rebellion, and the semi-independent Arab population of the plains between the Luristan Mountains and the Euphrates. He was hated and feared for his cruelty, but it was generally admitted that he ruled justly, that he protected the weak from oppression by the strong, and that where he was able to enforce his authority life and property were secure.[2]

Layard established a close friendship with Muḥammad-Taqí Khán, the chieftain of the Chahár-Lang section of the Bakhtíyárís. Manúchihr Khán captured this chieftain, after lengthy manoeuvres, and sent him with his family to Ṭihrán, where he died. Chiefly for that reason Layard is not at all complimentary in his copious writings about

Manúchihr Khán. There is no doubt that the Bakhtíyárí chieftain was in rebellion against the central government and even intended to take himself and his territory out of its jurisdiction. The proof is afforded by the fact that he sent Henry Layard to the island of Khárg, then occupied by British forces, to sound the British authorities for support. Hennell told Layard that although Britain was in a state bordering on war with Írán, she would not countenance or encourage insurrection or secession.

Disregarding Layard's prejudices, the fact remains that historical evidence exists in plenty to prove that Manúchihr Khán had, in the company of his peers, his ample share of avarice and cruelty. He had been a faithful servant of Muḥammad Sháh, had fought battles for him to make his throne secure, and had, in successive appointments, pacified a vast area of the country, stretching from Kirmánsháh in the west to Iṣfahán in the central regions, and to the waters of the Persian Gulf in the south. When he served as the Vizier of the province of Fárs, he put down an uprising, brought some seventy to eighty prisoners with him to Shíráz, and outside the gate of Bágh-i-Sháh had a tower erected with their living bodies, which was held firm by mortar.

The Báb, as He approached Iṣfahán, wrote a letter to Manúchihr Khán in which he asked for shelter. Siyyid Káẓim-i-Zanjání took the letter to the Governor, who, greatly impressed by it, sent it on to Siyyid Muḥammad, the Sulṭánu'l-'Ulamá, the Imám-Jum'ih of Iṣfahán, and requested that high dignitary to open his home to the Báb. The Imám-Jum'ih dispatched a number of people close to himself, amongst them his brother,* some distance out of the city to escort the Báb to Iṣfahán, and at the city-limits he

* This man in future years proved so hostile, bloodthirsty and rapacious that Bahá'u'lláh designated him as 'Raqshá', the She-Serpent.

himself welcomed the Visitor with respect and reverence. He went far beyond the usual marks of cordial hospitality, even to the extent of pouring water from a ewer over the hands of the Báb, a task normally performed by attendants.

There were, by this time, an appreciable number of Bábís in Iṣfahán, many of them natives of the city and some directed there by the Báb Himself. Amongst the wider public the fame of the Báb spread rapidly. There was one occasion when people came to take away the water He had used for His ablutions, so greatly did they value it. His host was enthralled by the Báb. One night, after the evening meal, he asked his Guest to write for him a commentary on the Súrih of V'al-'Aṣr (Afternoon—Qur'án ciii), one of the shortest Súrihs:

By the afternoon!
Surely Man is in the way of loss,
save those who believe, and do righteous deeds,
and counsel each other unto the truth,
and counsel each other to be steadfast.[3]

The Báb took up His pen and wrote His commentary, there and then, to the astonishment and delight of all who were present. It was past midnight when the assemblage broke up. Mullá Muḥammad-Taqíy-i-Hirátí, one of the divines of Iṣfahán, was so overcome by the power of the Báb's pen and voice that he said with great feeling:

> Peerless and unique as are the words which have streamed from this pen, to be able to reveal, within so short a time and in so legible a writing, so great a number of verses as to equal a fourth, nay a third, of the Qur'án, is in itself an achievement such as no mortal, without the intervention of God, could hope to perform.[4]

People of all ranks flocked to the house of the Imám-Jum'ih. Manúchihr Khán himself called there to meet the Báb. He was a proud man and a powerful Governor, ruling over an important section of the realm. His visit to a young Siyyid, hitherto unknown, indicates the measure of change wrought in him by that one letter which he had received from the Báb. Indeed, Manú͟chihr K͟hán was to become a changed man under the influence of the Báb, who had been a fugitive and an exile at his door. He now asked the Báb for a treatise on 'Nubuvvat-i-K͟háṣṣih'—the specific station and mission of the Prophet Muḥammad. Again surrounded by a number of the leading divines of Iṣfahán, the Báb wrote instantaneously the treatise which the Governor desired. Within two hours He produced a disquisition of fifty pages, superbly reasoned, proving unassailably the claim and the achievement of Islám, and ending His theme on the subject of the advent of the Qá'im and the Return of Imám Ḥusayn (Rijʻat-i-Ḥusayní). Manú͟chihr K͟hán's immediate response was:

> Hear me! Members of this revered assembly, I take you as my witnesses. Never until this day have I in my heart been firmly convinced of the truth of Islám. I can henceforth, thanks to this exposition penned by this Youth, declare myself a firm believer in the Faith proclaimed by the Apostle of God. I solemnly testify to my belief in the reality of the superhuman power with which this Youth is endowed, a power which no amount of learning can ever impart.[5]

It was inevitable that soon the jealousy of the clergy would be aroused. Áqá Muḥammad-Mihdí,* the son of the renowned Ḥájí Muḥammad-Ibráhím-i-Kalbásí, began to use the pulpit to insult and disparage the Báb. When Ḥájí Mírzá Áqásí heard of the situation in Iṣfahán, he wrote to upbraid the Imám-Jumʻih for having harboured the Báb.

* Because of his stupidity Áqá Muḥammad-Mihdí was mockingly called Safíhu'l-ʻUlamá—the Foolish One of the Learned.

The Grand Vizier was afraid that Manúchihr Khán, because of the confidence that Muḥammad Sháh reposed in him, might succeed in arranging a meeting between the Báb and the monarch. The hold which Ḥájí Mírzá Áqásí had on Muḥammad Sháh was chiefly due to the quasi-religious nature of their relationship. He was the murshid (spiritual guide) and his king was the muríd (disciple). The Imám-Jum'ih, still loyal, took no step in opposition, but endeavoured to reduce the number of visitors.

As the clamour of the opponents increased, Manúchihr Khán thought of a scheme to silence them. He invited the leading divines to meet the Báb at his home and argue their case. Ḥájí Siyyid Asadu'lláh, the son of the celebrated Ḥájí Siyyid Muḥammad-Báqir-i-Rashtí, declined the invitation and advised the rest to do the same:

> I have sought to excuse myself and I would most certainly urge you to do the same. I regard it as most unwise of you to meet the Siyyid-i-Báb face to face. He will, no doubt, reassert his claim and will, in support of his argument, adduce whatever proof you may desire him to give, and, without the least hesitation, will reveal as a testimony to the truth he bears, verses of such a number as would equal half the Qur'án. In the end he will challenge you in these words: 'Produce likewise, if ye are men of truth.' We can in no wise successfully resist him. If we disdain to answer him, our impotence will have been exposed. If we, on the other hand, submit to his claim, we shall not only be forfeiting our own reputation, our own prerogatives and rights, but will have committed ourselves to acknowledge any further claims that he may feel inclined to make in the future.[6]

Only Ḥájí Muḥammad-Ja'far-i-Ábádi'í took Ḥájí Siyyid Asadu'lláh's advice and kept away. In the presence of Manúchihr Khán, Mírzá Ḥasan-i-Núrí was the first to pose a question. Mírzá Ḥasan was a follower of the Ishráqí school (Platonism), and his question concerned certain elements of the philosophy of Mullá Ṣadrá contained in his celebrated work: the *Ḥikmatu'l-'Arshíyyah* (Celestial or Divine Philosophy).[7] The Báb's answers, even though couched in simple terms, were beyond the grasp of Mírzá Ḥasan's mind. 'The Foolish One of the Learned' was the next to face the Báb, and he began to probe into points of Islamic jurisprudence. Unable to withstand the force of the Báb's exposition he started a verbal assault which the Governor quickly brought to an end. Sensing the mood of the audience, Manúchihr Khán deemed it prudent that the Báb should stay under the protection of his roof and not return to the house of the Imám-Jum'ih, where he had been a guest for forty days.

The next move came from the divines. Like their compatriots in Shíráz, they gathered together and passed a verdict on the Báb which carried with it the sentence of death. Both Ḥájí Siyyid Asadu'lláh-i-Rashtí and Ḥájí Muḥammad-Ja'far-i-Ábádi'í refused to be identified with it, but the Imám-Jum'ih, with an eye to his position, wrote:

> I testify that in the course of my association with this youth I have been unable to discover any act that would in any way betray his repudiation of the doctrines of Islám. On the contrary, I have known him as a pious and loyal observer of its precepts. The extravagance of his claims, however, and his disdainful contempt for the things of the world, incline me to believe that he is devoid of reason and judgment.[8]

Muḥammad Sháh had already instructed Manúchihr Khán to send the Báb to Ṭihrán. The transforming power of the Báb can now be discerned. Manúchihr Khán had served the Qájár monarch faithfully at all times. His generalship had helped to secure Muḥammad Sháh's position. But, once conquered by the Báb and won over to

His Cause, Manúchihr Khán unhesitatingly availed himself of the Sháh's command, not to send the Báb immediately to the capital which would have put Him at the mercy of Ḥájí Mírzá Áqásí, but to shield Him from His enemies. Under public gaze the Báb was escorted out of Iṣfahán, guarded by five hundred horsemen. Nabíl-i-A'ẓam writes:

> Imperative orders had been given that at the completion of each farsang* one hundred of this mounted escort should return directly to Iṣfahán. To the chief of the last remaining contingent, a man in whom he placed implicit confidence, the Mu'tamid confidentially intimated his desire that at every maydán† twenty of the remaining hundred should likewise be ordered by him to return to the city. Of the twenty remaining horsemen, the Mu'tamid directed that ten should be despatched to Ardistán for the purpose of collecting the taxes levied by the government, and that the rest, all of whom should be of his tried and most reliable men, should, by an unfrequented route, bring the Báb back in disguise to Iṣfahán. They were, moreover, instructed so to regulate their march that before dawn of the ensuing day the Báb should have arrived at Iṣfahán and should have been delivered into his custody . . . At an unsuspected hour, the Báb re-entered the city, was directly conducted to the private residence of the Mu'tamid, known by the name of 'Imárat-i-Khurshíd [the Sun-House], and was introduced, through a side entrance reserved for the Mu'tamid himself, into his private apartments. The governor waited in person on the Báb, served His meals, and provided whatever was required for His comfort and safety.[9]

'Abdu'l-Bahá states in *A Traveller's Narrative* that Manúchihr Khán gave secret orders for the return of the Báb when He

* Three miles roughly to a farsang or farsakh.

† Maydán is a public square or an arena; as a measure of distance it was an indeterminate sub-division of a farsang.

and His escort had reached Múrchih-Khár, some thirty-five miles to the north of Iṣfahán.[10]

Wild rumours began to circulate regarding the fate of the Báb. It was believed that He had been executed in Ṭihrán. To allay the fears of the Bábís of Iṣfahán the Báb allowed Mullá ‘Abdu'l-Karím-i-Qazvíní, Siyyid Ḥusayn-i-Yazdí and Shaykh Ḥasan-i-Zunúzí to be brought to meet Him. He entrusted them with the task of transcribing His Writings. Not long afterwards, He instructed them to tell the other Bábís who had moved to Iṣfahán to leave the city and go northwards, to Káshán, or Qum or Ṭihrán.

Not long before his death, Manúchihr Khán offered the Báb all his immense fortune,* and the resources of his army which were considerable, that they might march to Ṭihrán and approach the person of Muḥammad Sháh. Manúchihr Khán was certain that the monarch, who trusted him completely, would listen to his plea, recognize the truth of the Revelation of the Báb, and whole-heartedly lend his support to the promotion of the new Faith. And Manúchihr Khán looked even beyond the frontiers of Írán, for he told the Báb: ‘. . . I hope to be enabled to incline the hearts of the rulers and kings of the earth to this most wondrous Cause . . .’ To this the Báb replied:

> May God requite you for your noble intentions. So lofty a purpose is to Me even more precious than the act itself. Your days and Mine are numbered, however; they are too short to enable Me to witness, and allow you to achieve, the realisation of your hopes. Not by the means which you fondly imagine will an almighty Providence accomplish the triumph of His Faith. Through the poor

* According to Nicolas, the French envoy in Ṭihrán (M. de Bonnière) wrote to the Ministry of Foreign Affairs in Paris, on March 4th 1847, that Mu‘tamidu'd-Dawlih, the Governor of Iṣfahán, had died, leaving a fortune estimated at 40 million francs.[11]

and lowly of this land, by the blood which these shall have shed in His path, will the omnipotent Sovereign ensure the preservation and consolidate the foundation of His Cause. That same God will, in the world to come, place upon your head the crown of immortal glory, and will shower upon you His inestimable blessings. Of the span of your earthly life there remain only three months and nine days, after which you shall, with faith and certitude, hasten to your eternal abode.[12]

The Báb, in His Tablet addressed to Muḥammad Sháh, states that He foretold, in a letter to two divines in Yazd, the date of the death of Manúchihr Khán, eighty-seven days before it occurred. And He mentions that Manúchihr Khán had offered Him all that he possessed, even taking off his rings and placing them before Him.

Manúchihr Khán had come to realize that his wealth was the product of oppression. The Báb accepted both his repentance and his wealth, then returned to him his riches for his use until his death, which occurred in the month of Rabí'u'l-Avval 1263 A.H. (February–March 1847 A.D.)

Even though in his will Manúchihr Khán left all his property to the Báb, his nephew and successor, Gurgín Khán, appropriated everything after his death, and informed Muḥammad Sháh that the Báb was in Iṣfahán, having been kept, well-protected, by the late Governor in the seclusion of 'Imárat-i-Khurshíd. Muḥammad Sháh's trust in Manúchihr Khán was not shaken. He felt certain that that wise man and faithful servant had guarded the Báb against all possible harm until an opportune time when a meeting between himself and the Báb could be arranged. He issued orders for the removal of the Báb to the capital in such wise that He should not be recognized *en route*.

Those four months in the private residence of the Governor of Iṣfahán were the calmest that the Báb was to experience throughout His Ministry.[13]

CHAPTER 9

THE ANTICHRIST OF THE BÁBÍ REVELATION

No! by heav'n, which He
Holds, and the abyss and the immensity
Of worlds and life, which I hold with Him—No!
I have a victor, true, but no superior.
Homage he has from all, but none from me.
I battle it against Him, as I battled
In highest heav'n. Through all eternity
And the unfathomable gulfs of Hades
And the interminable realms of space
And the infinity of endless ages,
All, all, will I dispute. And world by world
And star by star and universe by universe
Shall tremble in the balance, till the great
Conflict shall cease, if ever it shall cease . . .
—Lucifer in *Cain* by Lord Byron

Ḥájí Mírzá Áqásí, the Grand Vizier and the spiritual guide of Muḥammad Sháh, has been called the Antichrist of the Bábí Revelation.[1] He was a man bankrupt of ideas and bereft of graces. A native of Íraván* in the Caucasus, his real name was Mírzá 'Abbás. From the day he learned of the advent of the Báb, he bore Him intense enmity which never abated. It was he who prevented a meeting between the Báb and Muḥammad Sháh, when, by the direct order of the Sháh himself, the Báb was moved from Iṣfahán and it seemed that the cherished hope of Manúchihr Khán for their meeting would at last be realized.

* Yerevan or Erivan, today the capital of the Armenian Socialist Soviet Republic.

Following the instructions of Muḥammad Sháh, Gurgín Khán gave the custody of the Báb to Muḥammad Big-i-Chápárchí (the chief courier). Muḥammad Big belonged to the sect of Ahl-i-Ḥaqq (the People of Truth), commonly known as the 'Alíyu'lláhí, who have had a long tradition of tolerance, liberalism and rectitude.[2] 'Abdu'l-Bahá states in *A Traveller's Narrative* that the guards who escorted the Báb, on this journey to the north, were Nuṣayrí horsemen. Nuṣayrís and 'Alíyu'lláhís are almost identical.

The first town on their road to the capital was Káshán. Ḥájí Mírzá Jání, the Bábí merchant of that town, had dreamt that he beheld the Báb approaching Káshán by the 'Aṭṭár (Druggist) Gate. Keeping watch by that gate, on the eve of Naw-Rúz, he saw his dream fulfilled, for there was the Báb on horseback coming towards Káshán. As he went forward to kiss His stirrup, the Báb told him: 'We are to be your Guest for three nights.'[3] This was exactly what he had heard the Báb say to him in his dream. Muḥammad Big, noticing the warmth of their greeting, thought that the young Siyyid in his charge and the citizen of Káshán were friends of long standing, and he readily agreed to let the Báb stay in the house of Ḥájí Mírzá Jání. A colleague, however, refused to give his consent; he had been told, he said, not to allow the Báb to enter any city *en route*. After a lengthy argument Muḥammad Big succeeded in persuading this colleague to withdraw his objection. Ḥájí Mírzá Jání was prepared to invite the whole escort to be his guests, but the Báb did not permit it. Siyyid Ḥusayn-i-Yazdí, who had already proceeded to Káshán as bidden by the Báb, that night attained His presence. While the Báb was dictating a Tablet to Siyyid Ḥusayn, in honour of Ḥájí Mírzá Jání, a friend of the Káshání merchant was announced. His name was Siyyid 'Abdu'l-Báqí, and he was reputed for his erudition; he sat and listened to the Báb, but failed to be moved by what he heard and noticed. Some days after the Báb left Káshán he learned who that young Siyyid was. He was sorrow-stricken that he had not recognized the powers of the Báb and withdrew from society for the rest of his life.

On the second day after Naw-Rúz the Báb rejoined His escort to journey towards Qum,* the next city on the road to Ṭihrán. They did not enter Qum but went on to the village of Qumrúd, where the entire population was 'Alíyu'lláhí. Nabíl-i-A'ẓam writes:

> At the invitation of the headman of the village, the Báb tarried one night in that place and was touched by the warmth and spontaneity of the reception which those simple folk had accorded Him. Ere He resumed His journey, He invoked the blessings of the Almighty in their behalf and cheered their hearts with assurances of His appreciation and love.[4]

Two days later, in the afternoon of March 28th, they reached the fortress of Kinár-Gird, only twenty-eight miles from Ṭihrán. The long journey from Iṣfahán was almost over. But here Ḥájí Mírzá Áqásí intervened and sent instructions to Muḥammad Big to take the Báb to the village of Kulayn, where the great Shí'ah jurisconsult, Muḥammad ibn-i-Ya'qúb was born and is buried.† Ḥájí Mírzá Áqásí himself was the owner of Kulayn, and a tent which belonged to him was pitched outside the village to accommodate the Báb. It was a delectable spot with lush vegetation, orchards and running brooks. The Báb was delighted, but uncertainties of the future overshadowed Him. Days passed without

* Qum is the second holy city of Írán. Mashhad which holds the Shrine of Imám Riḍá has pride of place.

† Commonly known as al-Kulayní, he died in A.D. 941. He was the author of *Uṣúl al-Káfí* (*Uṣúl-i-Káfí* in Persian usage), one of the four books that form the compendium of the belief and practice of Ithná-'Asharís ('Twelvers'). These are the Shí'ahs who believe in the major occultation of the Twelfth Imám, Muḥammad ibn-i-Ḥasan al-'Askarí.

further instruction from Ṭihrán. Siyyid Ḥusayn-i-Yazdí and his brother Siyyid Ḥasan, as well as Mullá 'Abdu'l-Karím-i-Qazvíní and Shaykh Ḥasan-i-Zunúzí, came to Kulayn to attend the Báb. And from Ṭihrán came Mullá Mihdíy-i-Khu'í accompanied by Mullá Muḥammad-Mihdíy-i-Kindí, the latter bearing a letter and presents from Bahá'u'lláh. Receiving them brought the Báb untold joy.[5]

According to *A Traveller's Narrative* the Báb's sojourn in Kulayn was lengthened into twenty days.[6] During this time a remarkable incident occurred which Mullá 'Abdu'l-Karím has thus related:

> My companions and I were fast asleep in the vicinity of the tent of the Báb when the trampling of horsemen suddenly awakened us. We were soon informed that the tent of the Báb was vacant and that those who had gone out in search of Him had failed to find Him. We heard Muḥammad Big remonstrate with the guards. 'Why feel disturbed?' he pleaded. 'Are not His magnanimity and nobleness of soul sufficiently established in your eyes to convince you that He will never, for the sake of His own safety, consent to involve others in embarrassment? He, no doubt, must have retired, in the silence of this moonlit night, to a place where He can seek undisturbed communion with God. He will unquestionably return to His tent. He will never desert us.' In his eagerness to reassure his colleagues, Muḥammad Big set out on foot along the road leading to Ṭihrán. I, too, with my companions, followed him. Shortly after, the rest of the guards were seen, each on horseback, marching behind us. We had covered about a maydán when, by the dim light of the early dawn, we discerned in the distance the lonely figure of the Báb. He was coming towards us from the direction of Ṭihrán. 'Did you believe Me to have escaped?' were His words to Muḥammad Big as He approached him. 'Far be it from me,' was the instant reply as he flung himself at the feet of the Báb, 'to entertain

such thoughts.' Muḥammad Big was too much awed by the serene majesty which that radiant face revealed that morning to venture any further remark. A look of confidence had settled upon His countenance; His words were invested with such transcendent power, that a feeling of profound reverence wrapped our very souls. No one dared to question Him as to the course of so remarkable a change in His speech and demeanour. Nor did He Himself choose to allay our curiosity and wonder.[7]

Nearly three weeks had passed since His arrival at Kulayn when the Báb wrote to Muḥammad Sháh to ask for a meeting. And now Ḥájí Mírzá Áqásí made the move which consigned the Báb to prison for the rest of his days. According to *A Traveller's Narrative*, he persuasively told Muḥammad Sháh:

> The royal cavalcade is on the point of starting, and to engage in such matters as the present will conduce to the disruption of the kingdom. Neither is there any doubt that the most notable doctors of the capital also will behave after the fashion of the doctors of Isfahán, which thing will be the cause of a popular outbreak, or that, according to the religion of the immaculate Imám, they will regard the blood of this Seyyid as of no account, yea, as more lawful than mother's milk. The imperial train is prepared for travel, neither is there hindrance or impediment in view. There is no doubt that the presence of the Báb will be the cause of the gravest trouble and the greatest mischief. Therefore, on the spur of the moment, the wisest plan is this:–to place this person in the Castle of Mákú during the period of absence of the royal train from the seat of the imperial throne, and to defer the obtaining of an audience to the time of return.[8]

Mírzá Abu'l-Faḍl states that Ḥájí Mírzá Áqásí played on the fears of Muḥammad Sháh by instancing in particular the rebellion in Khurásán of Muḥammad-Ḥasan Khán, the Sálár, and the earlier defiance of the central government by Ḥasan-'Alí Khán, Aga Khan I.* Whatever arguments the Grand Vizier used, he succeeded in preventing a meeting between the Báb and Muḥammad Sháh in that spring of 1847. And it was never to take place.

In April, the Sháh sent a reply to the letter of the Báb which, according to *A Traveller's Narrative*, was couched in these terms:

> Since the royal train is on the verge of departure from Teherán, to meet in a befitting manner is impossible. Do you go to Mákú and there abide and rest for a while, engaged in praying for our victorious state; and we have arranged that under all circumstances they shall shew you attention and respect. When we return from travel we will summon you specially.[9]

Nabíl-i-A'ẓam, in his narrative, gives this version of the contents of Muḥammad Sháh's letter:

> Much as we desire to meet you, we find ourself unable, in view of our immediate departure from our capital, to receive you befittingly in Ṭihrán. We have signified our desire that you be conducted to Máh-Kú, and have issued the necessary instructions to 'Alí Khán, the warden of the castle, to treat you with respect and consideration. It is our hope and intention to summon you to this place upon our return to the seat of our government, at which time we shall definitely pronounce our judgment. We trust that we have caused you no disappointment, and that you will at no time hesitate to inform us in case any grievances befall you. We fain would hope that you will continue

* In the opinion of the present writer, the second revolt of the Aga Khan, in 1840, was entirely due to the tortuous policies and the maladroitness of Ḥájí Mírzá Áqásí himself.

to pray for our well-being and for the prosperity of our realm.[10]

Ḥusayn Khán, the Governor of Fárs, was attending the Sháh in the capital at the very time that Ḥájí Mírzá Áqásí blocked the path of the Báb and prevented His entry into Ṭihrán.

CHAPTER 10

WHERE THE ARAS FLOWS

Over the banks of Aras shouldst thou, O Zephyr, pass,
Kiss the earth of that vale and refreshen thy breath thereby.
—Ḥáfiẓ

Máh-Kú,* a town of the province of Á<u>dh</u>arbáyján, is in the extreme north-west of Írán, close to the point where the Russo-Turkish frontiers meet. Within a short distance of the town of Máh-Kú and its bleak fortress perched on a mountain peak above, the Aras flows, the Araxes of the Greeks. Ḥájí Mírzá Áqásí contrived to have the Báb banished to this remote corner of the land, well away from the capital, and well away from the areas where His Faith was born and nurtured. But the road to Máh-Kú was through Tabríz, the second city of the realm and the seat of the Crown Prince.

The same horsemen, still under the command of Muḥammad Big, were given the task of escorting the Báb to Tabríz. They had, by then, become greatly devoted to Him. His utter kindness coupled with His majesty of bearing had totally captivated them. Two of the followers of the Báb were allowed to remain with Him: Siyyid Ḥusayn-i-Yazdí and his brother, Siyyid Ḥasan.

On the road north, one of the halting-places was the village of Síyáh-Dihán, close by Qazvín. There the Báb addressed a letter to the Grand Vizier, and also wrote to some of the leading divines of Qazvín, including the father and the uncle of Qurratu'l-'Ayn. A number of the Bábís attained His presence in the village of Síyáh-Dihán during

* Also Mákú or Má-Kúh.

His one night there, and among these was Mullá Iskandar of Zanján, the same man who had visited Shíráz as Ḥujjat's emissary to learn what he could about the Báb. Now the Báb entrusted to him a letter for Ḥájí Sulaymán Khán-i-Afshár, who happened to be in Zanján; he had been a fervent supporter of Siyyid Káẓim-i-Rashtí. To him the Báb wrote:

> He whose virtues the late siyyid unceasingly extolled, and to the approach of whose Revelation he continually alluded, is now revealed. I am that promised One. Arise and deliver Me from the hand of the oppressor.[1]

Ḥájí Sulaymán Khán received the letter within three days, but did not heed it and left for the capital.

At that time Ḥujjat* was in Ṭihrán, kept there under surveillance. But the moment he heard of the Báb's letter to Sulaymán Khán, he sent a message to the Bábís of Zanján to march out and rescue the Báb. A sizable number of Bábís from Ḥujjat's native town and from Qazvín and Ṭihrán came together and made a concerted effort to carry out their daring scheme. At midnight they reached the spot where the Báb and His escort were bivouacked. The guards were asleep and there was every opportunity to escape. But the Báb told His would-be rescuers that He would not run away. 'The mountains of Ádhirbáyján too have their claims.'[2]

Before His mission reached its end Muḥammad Big came to believe in the Báb.† Grief-stricken he went to the Báb and asked to be forgiven: 'The journey from Iṣfahán has been long and arduous. I have failed to do my duty and to serve

* See pp. 100–102.

† Muḥammad Big's son, named 'Alí-Akbar Big, became, in future years, a follower of Bahá'u'lláh. Mírzá Abu'l-Faḍl met him in Ṭihrán and heard from him how it happened that his father came to accept the Báb.

You as I ought. I crave Your forgiveness, and pray You to vouchsafe me Your blessings.' To this the Báb replied: 'Be assured. I account you a member of My fold. They who embrace My Cause will eternally bless and glorify you, will extol your conduct and exalt your name.'[3] Later, Muḥammad Big met Ḥájí Mírzá Jání once again, and recounted for him the story of that journey to Tabríz. The Ká<u>sh</u>ání merchant included Muḥammad Big's story in his chronicle, and Mírzá Ḥusayn-i-Hamadání, the author of the *Táríkh-i-Jadíd* (*The New History*) in turn made use of it in his own work:

> ... we proceeded to Mílán,* where many of the inhabitants came to see His Holiness, and were filled with wonder at the majesty and dignity of that Lord of mankind. In the morning, as we were setting out from Mílán, an old woman brought a scald-headed child, whose head was so covered with scabs that it was white down to the neck, and entreated His Holiness to heal him. The guards would have forbidden her, but His Holiness prevented them, and called the child to him. Then he drew a handkerchief over its head and repeated certain words; which he had no sooner done than the child was healed. And in that place about two hundred persons believed and underwent a true and sincere conversion ... on leaving Mílán, while we were on the road His Holiness suddenly urged his horse into so swift a gallop that all the horsemen composing the escort were filled with amazement, seeing that his steed was the leanest of all. We galloped after him as hard as we could, but were unable to come up with him, though the horsemen were filled with apprehension lest he should effect his escape. Presently he reined in his horse of his own accord, and, so soon as we came up to him, said with a smile, 'Were I desirous of escaping, you could not prevent me.' And indeed it was even as he said; had he desired in the least degree to escape, none could

* A village in the vicinity of Tabríz.

have prevented him, and under all circumstances he shewed himself endowed with more than human strength. For example, we were all practised horsemen inured to travel, yet, by reason of the cold and our weariness, we were at times hardly able to keep our saddles, while he, on the other hand, during all this period shewed no sign of faintness or weariness, but, from the time when he mounted till he alighted at the end of the stage, would not so much as change his posture or shift his seat.[4]

The stage beyond the village of Mílán was the city of Tabríz itself. As the news spread that the Báb was approaching the city, the Bábís there tried to go out to meet him, but they were stopped and sent back. Only a youth managed to break through the cordon of guards and soldiers. Barefooted, he ran more than a mile till he reached the Báb and His escort. Such was the state of his ecstasy that he flung himself forward in the path of one of the horsemen, caught the hem of his cloak and eagerly and fervently kissed his stirrup. Addressing them all, he cried out: 'Ye are the companions of my Well-Beloved. I cherish you as the apple of my eye.'[5] And when he came into the presence of the Báb, he fell prostrate on the ground and unrestrainedly wept. The Báb dismounted, raised him up, embraced him and wiped his tears.

The Báb's entry into Tabríz, the scene three years later of His martyrdom in its public square, bears close resemblance to the entry of Jesus into Jerusalem on Palm Sunday, less than a week before He was led to Golgotha to be crucified.

> And they that went before, and they that followed, cried, saying, Hosanna! Blessed *is* he that cometh in the name of the Lord!
>
> Blessed *be* the kingdom of our father David, that cometh in the name of the Lord! Hosanna in the highest!*

* Mark xi, 9–10.

That is how St. Mark recounts the joy of the people who gave Jesus a regal welcome into Jerusalem.

When the Báb was brought into Tabríz the streets were crowded, and amongst the surging mass were Bábís who had been deprived of coming close to their Master; but vast numbers were there who were not His followers. Those narrow thoroughfares echoed with the cry of 'Alláh-u-Akbar'—God is the Greatest—the opening line of the A<u>dh</u>án, the call to prayer which every devout Muslim repeats time and again in the course of his devotions. Officials were alarmed by this wonderful and unprecedented reception, and sent town criers to warn the people against attempting to gain access to the Siyyid-i-Báb.

'Abdu'l-Bahá states that the Báb was kept for forty days in Tabríz.[6] During that time He was strictly secluded, and His only visitors were Ḥájí Muḥammad-Taqíy-i-Mílání, a well-known merchant, and Ḥájí 'Alí-'Askar.* When they first approached the house where the Báb was lodged, guards stopped them, but Siyyid Ḥasan asserted the authority of the Báb and gained them admittance. After that no one ever tried to bar their way, and they attained the presence of the Báb several times.

At last came the orders for the removal of the Báb to Máh-Kú. That town was the birthplace of Ḥájí Mírzá Áqásí, although he is generally known as Íravání‡ because his family originated there. The vast majority of the inhabitants of Máh-Kú and its environs were Kurds who were Sunní by persuasion. 'Alí <u>Kh</u>án, the warden of the castle, was a Kurd, simple, rough and uncouth. He was arrogantly un-

* Persecution forced him to abandon Tabríz. With his family he went to Adrianople and was exiled in the company of Bahá'u'lláh to 'Akká. He features in the *Memorials of the Faithful* by 'Abdu'l-Bahá (pp. 161–4).

‡ From Íraván. See p. 117 and note.

bending at the start of the Báb's incarceration, and would not allow any follower of the Báb to stay in the town, even for one night. When Shaykh Ḥasan-i-Zunúzí reached Máh-Kú he found that the only shelter available to him was a mosque outside the town. But he was able to meet and exchange letters and messages with Siyyid Ḥasan, who came into the town each day with a guard to buy provisions, and thus for a while he maintained a link between the Báb and His people.

But one day the Báb advised Siyyid Ḥasan that these secret contacts with Shaykh Ḥasan were to end; He Himself would tell 'Alí Khán to permit visitors to come and go in peace. Both men were greatly astonished, since they knew well the character and attitude of the warden, who had even tried to prevent the people of Máh-Kú from coming to the foot of the mountain to obtain a glimpse of the Báb. By now the Báb had won the love and esteem of these hardened frontiersmen, who had shown such marked hostility when He was first brought to their fortress, nor could 'Alí Khán prevent their gathering daily at the mountain's base to gaze upwards in the hope of receiving His blessing.

At an early hour on the morning following the Báb's advice to Siyyid Ḥasan, the inmates of the castle were startled by an incessant and agitated knocking. It was 'Alí Khán, peremptorily pounding the gate and shouting at the guardsmen for admittance. A guard rushed in to say that the warden wished to come immediately into the presence of the Báb. Siyyid Ḥusayn presented the request, and the Báb replied that He would receive 'Alí Khán at once. The warden was visibly shaking, obviously caught up by some tremendous emotion. He threw himself at the feet of the Báb and begged to be relieved of his misery:

> 'Deliver me from my perplexity. I adjure You, by the Prophet of God, Your illustrious Ancestor, to dissipate

> my doubts, for their weight has well-nigh crushed my heart. I was riding through the wilderness and was approaching the gate of the town, when, it being the hour of dawn, my eyes suddenly beheld You standing by the side of the river engaged in offering Your prayer. With outstretched arms and upraised eyes, You were invoking the name of God. I stood still and watched You. I was waiting for You to terminate Your devotions that I might approach and rebuke You for having ventured to leave the castle without my leave. In Your communion with God, You seemed so wrapt in worship that You were utterly forgetful of Yourself. I quietly approached You; in Your state of rapture, You remained wholly unaware of my presence. I was suddenly seized with great fear and recoiled at the thought of awakening You from Your ecstasy. I decided to leave You, to proceed to the guards and to reprove them for their negligent conduct. I soon found out, to my amazement, that both the outer and inner gates were closed. They were opened at my request, I was ushered into Your presence, and now find You, to my wonder, seated before me. I am utterly confounded. I know not whether my reason has deserted me.' The Báb answered and said: 'What you have witnessed is true and undeniable. You belittled this Revelation and have contemptuously disdained its Author. God, the All-Merciful, desiring not to afflict you with His punishment, has willed to reveal to your eyes the Truth. By His Divine interposition, He has instilled into your heart the love of His chosen One, and caused you to recognise the unconquerable power of His Faith.'[7]

All the arrogance of the warden left him. He was totally conquered. He became humble. The first words that he uttered were:

> A poor man, a shaykh, is yearning to attain Your presence. He lives in a masjid [mosque] outside the gate of Máh-Kú. I pray You that I myself be allowed to bring him to

> this place that he may meet You. By this act I hope that my evil deeds may be forgiven, that I may be enabled to wash away the stains of my cruel behaviour toward Your friends.[8]

He went away and returned with Shaykh Ḥasan-i-Zunúzí.

'Alí Khán's change of heart and attitude radically altered the situation. The prison gates no longer barred the Báb from His followers. Bábís came from everywhere to attain the presence of their Lord, among them Mullá Ḥusayn, the Bábu'l-Báb. The Báb received him at the gate of the castle and celebrated the Feast of Naw-Rúz with him. Ere his departure, the Báb directed him to visit Tabríz and other towns of the province of Ádharbáyján, and then proceed to Zanján, Qazvín, Ṭihrán, and finally to the province of Mázindarán.

'Alí Khán's devotion to the person of the Báb increased day by day. He did everything possible to mitigate the rigours of prison life. Every Friday he came up the mountain to offer his homage. Ḥájí Mírzá Áqásí was alarmed by the news reaching him from Máh-Kú, and so was the Russian Minister in Ṭihrán, Prince Dimitri Ivanovich Dolgorukov. In dispatches to Count Nesselrode, the Minister of Foreign Affairs, dated February 4th and December 24th 1848, he mentions that, in the previous year, the Báb had been removed from the vicinity of the Russian border by his demand.[9] This assertion is borne out by a letter of Mullá Aḥmad-i-Ibdál, one of the Letters of the Living, written when he was in Káẓimayn, close to Baghdád. It is not clear to whom the letter is addressed, most probably to one of the uncles of the Báb.[10] Mullá Aḥmad writes:

> These days, God willing, I intend to go and attain the presence of my Lord . . . These days pilgrims arrived here from Urúmíyyih. I sought the news of my Lord from them. They said that He was in a district of

Urúmíyyih, called <u>Ch</u>ihrúm [<u>Ch</u>ihríq?]. The Governor of Urúmíyyih wished, at first, to keep Him in the town itself, but the clerics had taken fright lest disturbances might arise, and had refused their consent; curses of God rest upon them. It is said that the Governor is acting with kindness, and from the towns of Á<u>dh</u>arbáyján people come in large groups, attain His presence and return believers. According to what has been related there is a tremendous upsurge, that is to say, many, many people have become devoted to Him . . . And as to the reason for the departure of <u>Dh</u>ikr, on Him be peace from Máh-Kú, it is this, that the Russian Envoy had heard that He was in Máh-Kú, and, being afraid of disturbance, told the Vizier, Ḥájí Mírzá Áqásí: 'Send the <u>Dh</u>ikr, on whom be peace, to some other area of your realms, because Máh-Kú is on the frontier and close to our territory, and we are afraid of disturbances; a few years ago, a certain Mullá Ṣádiq claimed to be the deputy [of the Imám] and within a month gathered 30,000 followers round him.' Russians had witnessed that and had taken fright.

'Abdu'l-Bahá states that the Báb's incarceration in the castle of Máh-Kú lasted nine months. According to Nabíl-i-A'ẓam, on the twentieth day after Naw-Rúz (April 9th 1848), He left that mountain fastness on the Russian and Turkish frontiers.[11]

At Máh-Kú the Báb revealed the *Dalá'il-i-Sab'ih* (The Seven Proofs) and began the composition of the Persian *Bayán** (Exposition or Utterance). Nabíl-i-A'ẓam writes:

I have heard <u>Sh</u>ay<u>kh</u> Ḥasan-i-Zunúzí bear witness to the following: 'The voice of the Báb, as He dictated the teachings and principles of His Faith, could be clearly heard by those who were dwelling at the foot of the

* A copy of the Persian *Bayán*, in the handwriting of Siyyid Ḥusayn-i-Yazdí, to whom He dictated it, exists in the International Archives of the Bahá'í Faith.

mountain. The melody of His chanting, the rhythmic flow of the verses which streamed from His lips caught our ears and penetrated into our very souls. Mountain and valley re-echoed the majesty of His voice. Our hearts vibrated in their depths to the appeal of His utterance.'[12]

CHAPTER 11

THE GRIEVOUS MOUNTAIN

Our little systems have their day;
They have their day and cease to be:
They are but broken lights of thee,
And thou, O Lord, art more than they.
—Alfred, Lord Tennyson

The man chosen by Ḥájí Mírzá Áqásí to take the Báb away from the castle of Máh-Kú was Riḍá-Qulí K͟hán-i-Afs͟hár, an officer with the rank of Sartíp (brigadier, in today's usage). He was the son of Ḥájí Sulaymán K͟hán, the official who, in Zanján, failed to heed the Báb's message to him. Ḥájí Sulaymán K͟hán was intensely devoted to Siyyid Káẓim-i-Ras͟htí, who had told him that he would live to see the advent of the Qá'im; he often expressed surprise that the Qá'im had not appeared for him to recognize, despite this unequivocal promise. Although he met the Báb in Mecca, he attached himself to Ḥájí Muḥammad-Karím K͟hán-i-Kirmání and refused to listen to the Bábís. His devotion to Siyyid Káẓim was of such a character that, having obtained the hand of a daughter of Siyyid Káẓim for his son, he began his day by paying his respects in person to his daughter-in-law. It was this son who was entrusted with the task of moving the Báb from Máh-Kú to Urúmíyyih and C͟hihríq.* And soon he too became captivated by the Prisoner in his charge. Eventually, Riḍá-Qulí K͟hán became an avowed,

* The Báb named C͟hihríq 'Jabal-i-S͟hadíd'—the Grievous Mountain. 'S͟hadíd' is numerically equal to C͟hihríq. He called Máh-Kú 'Jabal-i-Básiṭ'—the Open Mountain. 'Básiṭ' is numerically equal to Máh-Kú.

zealous Bábí, and broke away from his father, who persisted in his hostility to the Báb.

The castle of Chihríq is in the neighbourhood of Urúmíyyih, known today as Riḍá'íyyih. Its warden, Yaḥyá Khán, was a Kurdish chieftain, whose sister was married to Muḥammad Sháh. The son of this union was called 'Abbás Mírzá, after the Sháh's own father, and bore also his title, Náyibu's-Salṭanih (Viceroy or Regent). Because this child was such a favourite of Muḥammad Sháh, the mother of the heir to the throne, Náṣiri'd-Dín Mírzá, was exceedingly jealous of him. Her jealousy put his life in jeopardy after the death of his father, but Colonel Farrant's intervention saved him.† He was exiled to Qum, but even then he was not secure, for he was accused of being in league with the Bábís. Mírzá Ḥusayn-i-Mutavallí (Custodian) of Qum was forced, under torture, to sign a confession implicating 'Abbás Mírzá in faked Bábí plots.‡ This unfortunate prince spent many years of his life in exile, mostly in 'Iráq. He was eventually allowed to return to Írán and was given the title of Mulk-Árá; but he was always close to misfortune and danger.

Yaḥyá Khán, the warden of Chihríq, was harsh and unpredictable, but before long he too felt unable to keep the gates of his castle closed against the Bábís. The same power, which had held 'Alí Khán of Máh-Kú spellbound, captured the heart of Yaḥyá Khán. So many Bábís came to Chihríq that it was impossible to house them and rooms had to be found for them in Iskí-Shahr, which was not far away. Food and all other necessities were purchased in Iskí-Shahr. Once

† 'Abbás Mírzá was then nine years old. Farrant was the British chargé d'affaires in the absence of Sheil.

‡ This man was in the fortress of Shaykh Ṭabarsí and betrayed his fellow-believers. Some years later in Baghdád he fell on evil days and Bahá'u'lláh gave him a monthly allowance.

some honey was bought there for the Báb, but He found the quality to be inferior and the price exorbitant and had it returned.

> Honey of a superior quality [He said] could no doubt have been purchased at a lower price. I who am your example have been a merchant by profession. It behoves you in all your transactions to follow in My way. You must neither defraud your neighbour nor allow him to defraud you. Such was the way of your Master. The shrewdest and ablest of men were unable to deceive Him, nor did He on His part choose to act ungenerously towards the meanest and most helpless of creatures.[1]

Khuy was another town of Ádharbáyján which was not far from Chihríq. Not long had passed since the Báb's arrival at Chihríq when Khuy became aware that a number of its prominent citizens among the siyyids, divines and officials had become Bábís. Mírzá Asadu'lláh, on whom the Báb conferred the designation of Dayyán,[2] was one of them. Dayyán means the conqueror or the judge. Mírzá Asadu'lláh, a proud man, high in the service of the government, and a man of vast learning who wielded a fluent pen,* had for long withstood the attempts of the Bábís to convert him. Not only did he refuse to yield any ground to them, he also proved a vociferous antagonist. Then he had a dream which induced him to write to the Báb. And when he received the answer to his letter he gave the Báb his allegiance with a zeal and fervour that thoroughly alarmed his father, who was a personal friend of the Grand Vizier. He wrote to Ḥájí Mírzá Áqásí, expatiating on his son's bewitchment and deploring his grave aberrations.†

* He was a master of Persian, Arabic, Turkish, Hebrew and Syriac.

† The Báb revealed the *Lawḥ-i-Ḥurúfát* (Tablet of the Letters) in honour of Mírzá Asadu'lláh. 'Had the Point of the Bayán

Once again Ḥájí Mírzá Áqásí found himself thwarted. The Faith of the Báb was spreading and he could not contain it. And now the Grand Vizier had the additional anxiety of watching the rapid deterioration of Muḥammad Sháh's health. The monarch was only forty years old, but as a sufferer from gout his malady was wearing him down.

At Chihríq itself a dervish arrived from India. Who he truly was, no one knew and no one knows even now. The Báb gave him the name Qahru'lláh (the Wrath of God). All that this dervish would say about himself was:

> In the days when I occupied the exalted position of a navváb in India, the Báb appeared to me in a vision. He gazed at me and won my heart completely. I arose, and had started to follow Him, when He looked at me intently and said: 'Divest yourself of your gorgeous attire, depart from your native land, and hasten on foot to meet Me in Ádhirbáyján. In Chihríq you will attain your heart's desire.' I followed His directions and have now reached my goal.[4]

The Báb instructed him to go back to his native land, the same way he had come, as a dervish and on foot. Qahru'lláh would have no companion on that long journey back. His fate remains a mystery, just as does the fate of Shaykh Sa'íd, the Indian Letter of the Living.

The Báb had been in Chihríq for three months when Ḥájí Mírzá Áqásí decided He should be taken, once more, to Tabríz. Before the summons came, the Báb sent away those Bábís who had congregated in and around Chihríq; among them was the redoubtable 'Aẓím.* At the same time, He commissioned Shaykh Ḥasan-i-Zunúzí to collect the

---

[Nuqṭiy-i-Bayán] no other testimony with which to establish His truth,' He states, 'this were sufficient—that He revealed a Tablet such as this, a Tablet such as no amount of learning could produce.'[3]

* See p. 103.

Writings He had revealed in the two castles, and hand them for safe-keeping to Siyyid Ibráhím-i-Khalíl, who resided in Tabríz.

When the Báb reached Urúmíyyih, on his way to Tabríz, the Governor, Malik Qásim Mírzá, a descendant of Fatḥ-'Alí Sháh, received Him reverently. Nevertheless, he decided to pose a test for his Guest. On a Friday, when the Báb planned to go to the public bath, he directed that a particularly unruly horse be brought to convey Him. Those who knew of his plan awaited the outcome with bated breath. Miraculously, the horse stood quietly for the Báb, who mounted and rode it to the bath with perfect control. The Prince-Governor, ashamed and abashed, walked on foot beside the Báb's steed nearly to His destination, until the Báb asked him to return to his house. The news spread and stunned the town. When the Báb came out of the bath and mounted the same horse again, men, women and children rushed in to take away every drop of the water He had used.

From now on the Governor's residence was thronged daily by people who wished to meet the Báb or just to catch a glimpse of Him. During this time, Áqá-Bálá Big, the Naqqásh-Báshí (Chief Painter) made a portrait of the Báb, the only one ever drawn of Him; its story is of tremendous interest.

Áqá-Bálá Big was a native of Shíshván, a village on the banks of Lake Urúmíyyih. Like scores of others, he was attracted to Government House to see the Báb. Years later he related his experience to Varqá, the Bahá'í martyr-poet. He had noticed that as soon as the Báb's eyes alighted on him He arranged His 'abá neatly and looked at him intently. This happened again the next day, and Áqá-Bálá Big realized that the Báb was giving him a sign that he might draw His portrait. The painter made a rough sketch there and then. Later, he composed the portrait in black and white. When Varqá informed Bahá'u'lláh of this, he was instructed to ask the painter to make two copies of the portrait in water colour, one to be sent to the Holy Land and one to be kept by Varqá himself. The copy taken to the Holy Land is in the International Archives of the Bahá'í Faith. The copy which the martyr-poet held was among his possessions, looted at the time of his arrest. The original black and white portrait was discovered years later by Siyyid Asadu'lláh-i-Qumí, who conveyed it to the Holy Land and presented it to 'Abdu'l-Bahá.*

The Báb must have reached Tabríz in the last week of July 1848. Muḥammad Sháh's illness was, by then, giving concern to Ḥájí Mírzá Áqásí, and the wily old Grand Vizier, conscious of his approaching downfall, was already seeking ways and means of softening the blow. Over the course of years he had grown to be a very rich man, owning villages and farmlands and urban property. He knew that with the death of Muḥammad Sháh he would lose not only his position and power, but also his enormous wealth. When Muḥammad Sháh was dying, Ḥájí Mírzá Áqásí was no longer to be seen within the precincts of the palace, for his powerful enemies in the Court, whom he had not been able to destroy,† were ready to pounce on him. He retired to his village of 'Abbásábád. There his body-guard, recruited from his home town of Máh-Kú, disintegrated. The people of Ṭihrán who had suffered so much at their hands now found opportunities to avenge themselves, and Ḥájí Mírzá Áqásí found himself in such straits that he felt constrained to write to the boy-prince, 'Abbás Mírzá, and a number of prominent courtiers, to plead for harmony and friendship. As

* The present writer heard this account from Valíyu'lláh Varqá, the son of the martyr-poet, who had the rank of a Hand of the Cause by appointment of the Guardian of the Bahá'í Faith.

† They included men such as Mírzá Yúsuf, the Mustawfíu'l-Mamálik and 'Abbás-Qulí Khán-i-Javánshír.

no response was forthcoming from these quarters, he put on a bold face and tried to regain his residence in Ṭihrán. But the artillery General, who commanded the royal guard at the citadel, let him know that his stay in Ṭihrán was undesirable. So he tried to reach Ádharbáyján, the province to which he had exiled the Báb, to take refuge with the inhabitants of his native town. He had not gone far from the capital when he was turned back. Deserted and mocked, he had no course open but to seek sanctuary in the shrine of Sháh 'Abdu'l-'Aẓím. Such was the end of all power for Ḥájí Mírzá Áqásí, the Antichrist of the Bábí Revelation.

In Tabríz the Báb was brought before the Crown Prince, Náṣiri'd-Dín Mírzá, who was only seventeen years old and had recently been given the governorship of Ádharbáyján. A panel of the prominent divines of Tabríz gathered to examine the Báb. The leading men of that panel were: Ḥájí Mírzá Maḥmúd, the Niẓámu'l-'Ulamá, who was the chief tutor of the Crown Prince; Mullá Muḥammad-i-Mámaqání, a disciple of Siyyid Káẓim and an outstanding figure among the Shaykhís; Ḥájí Murtiḍá-Qulíy-i-Marandí, the 'Alamu'l-Hudá; Ḥájí Mírzá 'Alí-Aṣghar, the Shaykhu'l-Islám;* and Mírzá Aḥmad, the Imám-Jum'ih. The procedures of that high tribunal were frivolous from beginning to end. Here were the shining lights of the religious hierarchy of Tabríz, assembled to learn from a young Siyyid, who claimed to be the bearer of a Message from God, what the nature of His claim was and what proofs He could adduce to substantiate it. That they failed miserably to be just and to apply themselves to the problem before them need not be sought in the evidence of the followers of the Báb. Two of the best known Persian histories of the time plentifully provide that evi-

* Like the Imám-Jum'ih, the Shaykhu'l-Islám was a leading divine of a city, who enjoyed certain privileges. Although the sovereign appointed the Shaykhu'l-Islám, there were many instances when the position passed from father to son.

dence. These are the *Násikhu't-Tavárikh* by Muḥammad-Taqí Khán of Káshán[5] and the Supplement to the *Rawḍatu's-Ṣafá* of Mírkhund* by Riḍá-Qulí Khán-i-Hidáyat; both works were written during the reign of Náṣiri'd-Dín Sháh. From these two histories, Edward Granville Browne prepared a version of the procès-verbal of that infamous tribunal for the Appendices to his translation of *A Traveller's Narrative*. He also used another book, the *Qiṣaṣu'l-'Ulamá* (Chronicles of the Divines) written in 1873. Typical are these two questions, said to have been put to the Báb by Niẓámu'l-'Ulamá:

'As the Prophet or some other wise man hath said "Knowledge is twofold—knowledge of bodies, and knowledge of religions"; I ask, then, in Medicine, what occurs in the stomach when a person suffers from indigestion? Why are some cases amenable to treatment? And why do some go on to permanent dyspepsia or syncope [swooning], or terminate in hypochondriasis?'

'The science of "Applications" is elucidated from the Book and the Code, and the understanding of the Book and the Code [the Qur'án and the Traditions] depends on many sciences, such as Grammar, Rhetoric, and Logic. Do you who are the Báb conjugate *Ḳála*?' †

The Báb is alleged to have replied that He had learned to conjugate Arabic words in His childhood, but had forgotten the rules. This is supposed to have been the answer of a Person who had revealed the *Qayyúmu'l-Asmá'*, the *Commentary on the Súrih of Kawthar*, the *Commentary on the Súrih of V'al-'Aṣr*—all in Arabic.

When the Báb stated clearly: 'I am that person for whose

* Also, Mírkhwand. He died A.H. 903, A.D. 1497–8.

† Qála, the third person singular of 'to say'.

appearance ye have waited a thousand years,' Nizámu'l-'Ulamá retorted:

'That is to say you are the Mahdí, the Lord of Religion?'

'Yes,' answered the Báb.

'The same in person, or generically?'

'In person.'

'What is your name, and what are the names of your father and mother? Where is your birthplace? And how old are you?'

'My name is 'Alí Muḥammad,' answered the Báb. 'My mother was named Khadíja and my father Mírzá Riẓá the cloth-seller; my birth-place is Shíráz; and of my life, behold, thirty-five years have elapsed.'*

'The name of the Lord of Religion is Muḥammad; his father was named Ḥasan and his mother Narjis; his birth-place was Surra-man-Ra'a; and his age is more than a thousand years. There is the most complete variance. And besides I did not send you.'

'Do you claim to be God?' asked the Báb.

'Such an Imám is worthy of such a God,' replied Niẓámu'l-'Ulamá.

'I can in one day write two thousand verses. Who else can do this?'

'When I resided at the Supreme Shrines I had a secretary who used to write two thousand verses a day. Eventually he became blind. You must certainly give up this occupation, or else you too will go blind.'[6]

Even from these few quotations the absurdity of the trial may be seen.

The authors of *Násikhu't-Taváríkh*, the Supplement to *Rawḍatu'ṣ-Ṣafá* and *Qiṣaṣu'l-'Ulamá* took their material from

* Critics such as Mírzá Káẓim Big (Kazem-Beg) have observed that giving the age of the Báb as thirty-five indicates that the whole account is spurious. Furthermore, it was not the mother of the Báb who was named Khadíjih, but His wife.

a tract written by the same Niẓámu'l-'Ulamá who presided over the tribunal in Tabríz. But Shaykh Muḥammad-Taqí, the son of Mullá Muḥammad-i-Mámaqání, and no less an opponent of the Faith of the Báb than his father, in a book written specifically to refute that Faith, took Niẓámu'l-'Ulamá to task for having perverted the truth. Shaykh Muḥammad-Taqí was himself present at the tribunal; in his book he underlined, one by one, Niẓámu'l-'Ulamá's misrepresentations. His testimony to the powers of the Báb, which he recorded despite his avowed, unrelenting antagonism, has recently been reprinted. Eventually, Niẓámu'l-'Ulamá collected as many copies as he could of his own tract and destroyed them.

Nabíl-i-A'ẓam states, on the authority of Shaykh Ḥasan-i-Zunúzí, that the person most insolent in the course of that mock trial was Mullá Muḥammad-i-Mámaqání.* The Báb was sitting between him and the Crown Prince, and when He affirmed that He was the Qá'im, whose advent they expected, Mullá Muḥammad called out in anger:

'You wretched and immature lad of Shíráz! You have already convulsed and subverted 'Iráq; do you now wish to arouse a like turmoil in Ádhirbáyján?'

The Báb's answer to his outburst was only this: 'Your Honour, I have not come hither of My own accord. I have been summoned to this place.'

Mullá Muḥammad, yet more haughty and disdainful, shouted back: 'Hold your peace, you perverse and contemptible follower of Satan!'

And the Báb replied serenely: 'Your Honour, I maintain what I have already declared.'

Then, according to Nabíl-i-A'ẓam, Niẓámu'l-'Ulamá posed this challenge:

'The claim which you have advanced is a stupendous one;

* It is of interest that another son of Mullá Muḥammad, named Mírzá Ismá'íl, embraced the new Revelation.

it must needs be supported by the most incontrovertible evidence.'

'His own word,' said the Báb, 'is the most convincing evidence of the truth of the Mission of the Prophet of God.' And He quoted from the Qur'án a verse in support of His argument: ' "Is it not enough for them that We have sent down to Thee the Book?" '*

Niẓámu'l-'Ulamá rejoined: 'Describe orally, if you speak the truth, the proceedings of this gathering in language that will resemble the phraseology of the verses of the Qur'án so that the Valí-'Ahd [Crown Prince] and the assembled divines may bear witness to the truth of your claim.'

The Báb had spoken no more than a few words in response to this request when Mullá Muḥammad rudely intervened:

'This self-appointed Qá'im of ours has at the very start of his address betrayed his ignorance of the most rudimentary rules of grammar!'

'The Qur'án itself does in no wise accord with the rules and conventions current amongst men,' said the Báb. 'The Word of God can never be subject to the limitations of His creatures. Nay, the rules and canons which men have adopted have been deduced from the text of the Word of God and are based upon it. These men have, in the very texts of that holy Book, discovered no less than three hundred instances of grammatical error, such as the one you now criticise. Inasmuch as it was the Word of God, they had no other alternative except to resign themselves to His will.'

But Mullá Muḥammad turned a deaf ear to the Báb, and another divine interrupted with an absurd question about the tense of a verb. Then the Báb spoke this verse of the Qur'án: 'Far be the glory of thy Lord, the Lord of all greatness, from what they impute to Him, and peace be upon

* Qur'án xxix, 51.

His Apostles!' And He rose up from His seat and walked out.*[7]

Shortly after these proceedings, it was decided to inflict corporal punishment upon the Báb, and He was taken to the house of Muḥammad-Káẓim Khán, the farrásh-báshí.† As the guards refused to carry out the sentence, Mírzá 'Alí-Aṣghar, the Shaykhu'l-Islám, personally administered the bastinado. When the news reached Urúmíyyih that the Báb had been subjected to such indignity, many of those who had been attracted to His Faith abandoned it. In Tabríz, the Báb was seen by Dr. Cormick, an English physician, the only Westerner ever to have met Him. The Reverend Benjamin Labaree, D.D., of the American Presbyterian Mission

* An undated letter has come to light in the handwriting of Náṣiri'd-Dín Sháh, written during the Ministry of Bahá'u'lláh, and addressed to 'Aláu'd-Dawlih, a governor of Ṭihrán. The Sháh instructed the Governor to put certain questions to the 'Bábís' arrested by Amínu's-Sulṭán, including Áqá Jamál-i-Burújirdí, the only one he mentions by name. Only Amínu's-Sulṭán and Ḥájí Áqá Muḥammad, a divine, should be present for the questioning, he instructed, and the replies of the Bábís were to be recorded and presented to him. He himself, he said, might then have to meet these 'Bábís', to determine exactly what their aims and purposes were.

Náṣiri'd-Dín Sháh's language was abusive, but two points are particularly worth noting in this long tirade: first, his admission that, before the tribunal in Tabríz, the Báb stood firmly by His claim that He was the Qá'im; second, his insistence that he wanted to know what were the beliefs and intentions of the 'Bábís'.

During the governorship of 'Aláu'd-Dawlih, Áqá Najaf-'Alí, a Bahá'í of Tabríz, was arrested, resulting in the apprehension of a number of Bahá'ís in Ṭihrán. Áqá Najaf-'Alí had recently returned from 'Akká and was the bearer of a number of Tablets. He lost his life but the other Bahá'ís were eventually freed.

† Literally, 'chief-lictor', a Roman officer who executed sentences on offenders.

at Urúmíyyih, asked Dr. Cormick for the particulars of his visit. The English physician wrote in answer:

> You ask me for some particulars of my interview with the founder of the sect known as Bábís. Nothing of any importance transpired in this interview, as the Báb was aware of my having been sent with two other Persian doctors to see whether he was of sane mind or merely a madman, to decide the question whether to put him to death or not. With this knowledge he was loth to answer any questions put to him. To all enquiries he merely regarded us with a mild look, chanting in a low melodious voice some hymns, I suppose. Two other *Sayyids*, his intimate friends, were also present, who subsequently were put to death with him,* besides a couple of government officials. He only once deigned to answer me, on my saying that I was not a Musulmán and was willing to know something about his religion, as I might perhaps be inclined to adopt it. He regarded me very intently on my saying this, and replied that he had no doubt of all Europeans coming over to his religion. Our report to the Sháh at that time was of a nature to spare his life. He was put to death some time after by the order of the *Amír-i-Nizám* Mírzá Taqí Khán. On our report he merely got the bastinado, in which operation a *farrásh*, whether intentionally or not, struck him across the face with the stick destined for his feet, which produced a great wound and swelling of the face. On being asked whether a Persian surgeon should be brought to treat him, he expressed a desire that I should be sent for, and I accordingly treated him for a few days, but in the interviews consequent on this I could never get him to have a confidential chat with me, as some Government people were always present, he being a prisoner.
>
> He was very thankful for my attentions to him. He was

* This is a mistake. The two brothers, Siyyid Ḥasan and Siyyid Ḥusayn, were not put to death with the Báb, contrary to Browne's note accompanying this account.

a very mild and delicate-looking man, rather small in stature and very fair for a Persian, with a melodious soft voice, which struck me much. Being a Sayyid, he was dressed in the habits of that sect, as were also his two companions. In fact his whole look and deportment went far to dispose one in his favour. Of his doctrine I heard nothing from his own lips, although the idea was that there existed in his religion a certain approach to Christianity. He was seen by some Armenian carpenters, who were sent to make some repairs in his prison, reading the Bible, and he took no pains to conceal it, but on the contrary told them of it. Most assuredly the Musulmán fanaticism does not exist in his religion, as applied to Christians, nor is there that restraint of females that now exists.[8]

It must have been sometime in the first days of August 1848 that the Báb was restored to Chihríq. From there, He addressed a letter to Ḥájí Mírzá Áqásí:

O thou who hast disbelieved in God, and hast turned thy face away from His signs![9]

That letter, stern and unsparing, is known as the *Khuṭbiy-i-Qahríyyih* (Sermon of Wrath). The Báb sent it to Ḥujjat, who was still in Ṭihrán unable to return to his native town, to give it in person to the Grand Vizier. Ḥujjat carried out the task entrusted to him. By then Ḥájí Mírzá Áqásí had fallen from power, to end his days in obscurity in 'Iráq.

Muḥammad Sháh died on September 4th 1848.* Less than a year later, Ḥájí Mírzá Áqásí followed him to the grave.

* There was a certain Ḥájí Riḍáy-i-Qásí[10] in Shíráz, always ready to start a riot or head a revolt. The present writer recalls being told by his paternal grandmother that one day, at dawn, Ḥájí Qásí came galloping past their door, rattling a long stick (or a lance) in a hole in the wall, shouting: 'O house of the Siyyids, may you rest in safety, Muḥammad Sháh has gone to hell.' She remembered that incident very well, although at the time she was no more than seven or eight years old.

CHAPTER 12

THAT MIDSUMMER NOON

Transcendent Star, past mortal ken
The glory of your Life through all the spheres
Bathes the unending vista of the years.
The radiance of the Light you brought to men
Has purified the planet's heart anew!
Your blood was poured upon its dearth like dew,
Ichor of God's decree, let each drop shed
Raise up the nations, and the living dead,
Revive the vision of the spirit's youth:
Auroral is the fountain of your Truth.

—Beatrice Irwin

The death of Muḥammad S͟háh and the downfall of Ḥájí Mírzá Áqásí were events of far-reaching consequence. The new monarch was very young and inexperienced, while the man who now occupied the seat left vacant by the disappearance of Ḥájí Mírzá Áqásí was capable and uncorrupted, but self-willed and headstrong. Mírzá Taqí K͟hán, the Amír-Niẓám (better known by his later title Amír-i-Kabír) had by sheer force of his abilities raised himself from humble origins to a position of power. His father had been a cook in the employment of the illustrious Qá'im-Maqám. And it had been that great minister who had first noticed high promise in the young Taqí. Although Náṣiri'd-Dín S͟háh now reigned over Írán, it was Mírzá Taqí K͟hán who ruled it.

Once again, within the confines of C͟hihríq, the Báb had uninterrupted communication with His followers. Mullá

Ádí Guzal, a native of Marághih (Ádh-rbáyján), acted as a courier, often traversing vast distances on foot. Decades later 'Abdu'l-Bahá recalled a day when this indefatigable man arrived at Ṭihrán, dressed as a dervish and much travel-stained. Vaḥíd, on learning who he was and from whence he had come, bent low and kissed the mud-encrusted feet of the courier, for he had been in the presence of the Beloved.

One of this courier's journeys took him to Quddús, with the gift of a valuable pen-case and a silk turban sent by the Báb. And when Quddús and Mullá Ḥusayn and their companions died as martyrs in Mázindarán, the Báb chose this same faithful courier to go on pilgrimage in His stead to the land drenched with their blood. Thus Mullá Ádí Guzal was the first Bábí to set eyes on the scenes of that carnage. He was also, for two months, the Báb's personal attendant in the castle of Chihríq.[1]

Sulaymán Khán, the son of Yaḥyá Khán of Tabríz, was one of the prominent followers of the Báb who attained His presence in this castle, after making the journey in disguise.* He had no liking for service at court, and had gone to 'Iráq, to live under the shadow of the Shrine of Imám Ḥusayn. There he found himself attracted to the teachings of Siyyid Káẓim and, hearing later of the advent of the Báb, gave Him his allegiance. The news of the plight of his fellow-believers, who were hounded and besieged in Mázindarán, drew him back to his native land. He reached Ṭihrán dressed as a cleric. Mírzá Taqí Khán, however, made him discard his turban and long cloak, and forced him to wear a military uniform. But he could not prevail upon him to enter the service of the Government. Sulaymán Khán's primary purpose remained unfulfilled: to give aid to Quddús and the Bábu'l-Báb proved impossible, but his sudden

* The father of Sulaymán Khán was an attendant of 'Abbás Mírzá, and then of his son, Muḥammad Sháh.

departure from Karbilá was not to be in vain, or barren of significant result.

Another visitor to Chihríq during the closing months of the life of the Báb was His uncle, Ḥájí Mírzá Siyyid 'Alí. His life too was nearing its end, to be laid down in the path of his Nephew. Two years had passed since the day his Nephew bade him farewell in Shíráz, and Ḥájí Mírzá Siyyid 'Alí could no longer bear the pangs of separation. He settled his accounts, closed his books and took the road to Ádharbáyján. Having attained his heart's desire, he wrote to his brother, Ḥájí Mírzá Siyyid Muḥammad, to help him see the truth of their Nephew's mission. His letter was written on the fifth day of Jamádíu'l-Úlá—the anniversary of the Declaration of the Báb. 'On such a day,' he told his brother, 'the resplendent Light of God shone forth . . . This is the day of Resurrection . . . the day to behold the Visage of God.'[2] The One promised, expected and awaited had indeed come, he asserted, and come with verses constituting the primal proof of all the Manifestations of God. He desired all the members of his family to see his letter. One cannot but marvel at the quality of devotion and certainty that this letter reveals.

To meet, after such a long interval, the uncle who had stood *in loco parentis* to Him when He was orphaned, must have given the Báb intense joy. But within a few months* of His uncle's visit, news came that brought Him unbearable sorrow. At Shaykh Ṭabarsí in Mázindarán a large number of His followers had been massacred, including nine of His first disciples, the Letters of the Living; amongst them were the Bábu'l-Báb who had first believed in Him, and Quddús, His companion on the journey to Ḥijáz, the beloved disciple whose primacy was unquestioned.

According to His amanuensis:

* Towards the end of June 1849.

The Báb was heart-broken at the receipt of this unexpected intelligence. He was crushed with grief, a grief that stilled His voice and silenced His pen. For nine days He refused to meet any of His friends. I myself, though His close and constant attendant, was refused admittance. Whatever meat or drink we offered Him, He was disinclined to touch. Tears rained continually from His eyes, and expressions of anguish dropped unceasingly from His lips. I could hear Him, from behind the curtain, give vent to His feelings of sadness as He communed, in the privacy of His cell, with His Beloved. I attempted to jot down the effusions of His sorrow as they poured forth from His wounded heart. Suspecting that I was attempting to preserve the lamentations He uttered, He bade me destroy whatever I had recorded. Nothing remains of the moans and cries with which that heavy-laden heart sought to relieve itself of the pangs that had seized it. For a period of five months He languished, immersed in an ocean of despondency and sorrow.[3]

Conscious that His own life was fast approaching its end, the Báb put all His Writings, His pen-case, His seals and rings in a box which He entrusted to Mullá Báqir-i-Tabrízí, one of the Letters of the Living, with instructions to deliver it, together with a letter, to Mírzá Aḥmad-i-Kátib (Mullá 'Abdu'l-Karím-i-Qazvíní). Nabíl-i-A'ẓam writes:

Mullá Báqir departed forthwith for Qazvín. Within eighteen days he reached that town and was informed that Mírzá Aḥmad had departed for Qum. He left immediately for that destination and arrived towards the middle of the month of Sha'bán.* I was then in Qum . . . I was living in the same house with Mírzá Aḥmad . . . In those days Shaykh 'Aẓím, Siyyid Ismá'íl, and a number of other companions likewise were dwelling with us. Mullá Báqir delivered the trust into the hands of Mírzá Aḥmad, who, at the insistence of Shaykh 'Aẓím, opened it

* Towards the end of June 1850.

before us. We marvelled when we beheld, among the things which that coffer contained, a scroll of blue paper, of the most delicate texture, on which the Báb, in His own exquisite handwriting, which was a fine shikastih script, had penned, in the form of a pentacle, what numbered about five hundred verses, all consisting of derivatives from the word 'Bahá'.* That scroll was in a state of perfect preservation, was spotlessly clean . . . So fine and intricate was the penmanship that, viewed at a distance, the writing appeared as a single wash of ink on the paper. We were overcome with admiration as we gazed upon a masterpiece which no calligraphist, we believed, could rival. That scroll was replaced in the coffer and handed back to Mírzá Aḥmad, who, on the very day he received it, proceeded to Ṭihrán. Ere he departed, he informed us that all he could divulge of that letter was the injunction that the trust was to be delivered into the hands of Jináb-i-Bahá † in Ṭihrán.[4]

It was also during the last few months of His life that the Báb composed the Arabic *Bayán*, which, in the estimation of Nicolas, is the epitome of the teachings of the Báb.

The man who took the decision to have the Báb executed was Mírzá Taqí Khán, the Grand Vizier of Náṣiri'd-Dín Sháh. His obdurate nature brooked no opposition. Mírzá Áqá Khán-i-Núrí, who had a ministerial post, made a faint protest, but his voice went unheeded. Orders were sent to Ḥamzih Mírzá, the Ḥishmatu'd-Dawlih, Governor-General of Ádharbáyján, to bring the Báb to Tabríz. When these were carried out further orders came from the Grand Vizier, brought by no less a person than his brother, Mírzá Ḥasan Khán, the Vazír Nizám. They were to the effect that the Báb should be executed by a firing squad, in full public view.

* There were 360 derivatives. (Browne, ed., *A Traveller's Narrative*, Vol. II, p. 42.)

† Bahá'u'lláh.

Ḥishmatu'd-Dawlih refused absolutely to be associated in any way with such a dastardly action. His response was: 'I am neither Ibn-i-Zíyád nor Ibn-i-Sa'd* that he should call upon me to slay an innocent descendant of the Prophet of God.'[5]

The Grand Vizier, on being informed by Mírzá Ḥasan Khán of this refusal, instructed his brother to carry out the orders under his own authority. Divested of His turban and sash which indicated His lineage, the Báb and His attendants were taken on foot to the barracks, from the house which the Governor had put at their disposal. On the way to the citadel, a youth, barefoot and dishevelled, threw himself at the feet of the Báb, beseeching Him: 'Send me not from Thee, O Master. Wherever Thou goest, suffer me to follow Thee.' To this the Báb replied: 'Muḥammad-'Alí, arise, and rest assured that you will be with Me. Tomorrow you shall witness what God has decreed.'[6]

This youth, Mírzá Muḥammad-'Alíy-i-Zunúzí, had long been devoted to the Báb, but his stepfather † had used every subterfuge to prevent him from meeting the Báb and voicing his allegiance, even going to the length of locking him up in his own house. Shaykh Ḥasan-i-Zunúzí was related to the family, and thus had access to Mírzá Muḥammad-'Alí. Visiting him one day, Shaykh Ḥasan found the youth transformed, no longer wretched and bemoaning his fate, but happy and at peace. 'The eyes of my Beloved,' he told Shaykh Ḥasan, 'have beheld this face, and these eyes have gazed upon His countenance.' He then recounted an experience he had had:

> Let me tell you the secret of my happiness. After the Báb had been taken back to Chihríq,‡ one day, as I lay confined

* Men responsible for the tragedy of Karbilá, and the martyrdom of Imám Ḥusayn.

† Siyyid 'Alíy-i-Zunúzí.

‡ Following his examination in the summer of 1848.

in my cell, I turned my heart to Him and besought Him in these words: 'Thou beholdest, O my Best-Beloved, my captivity and helplessness, and knowest how eagerly I yearn to look upon Thy face. Dispel the gloom that oppresses my heart, with the light of Thy countenance.' What tears of agonising pain I shed that hour! I was so overcome with emotion that I seemed to have lost consciousness. Suddenly I heard the voice of the Báb, and, lo! He was calling me. He bade me arise. I beheld the majesty of His countenance as He appeared before me. He smiled as He looked into my eyes. I rushed forward and flung myself at His feet. 'Rejoice,' He said; 'the hour is approaching when, in this very city, I shall be suspended before the eyes of the multitude and shall fall a victim to the fire of the enemy. I shall choose no one except you to share with Me the cup of martyrdom. Rest assured that this promise which I give you shall be fulfilled.'[7]

Now, two years later, in a thoroughfare of Tabríz, Mírzá Muḥammad-'Alíy-i-Zunúzí received the same promise and assurance from the Báb.

That night the Báb was joyous. He knew that on the following day He would quaff the cup of martyrdom. He also knew that His Mission on this earth was totally accomplished, despite fierce opposition mounted by the divines and rulers of the land, and despite the tyrannies and indignities to which He had been mercilessly subjected. No power had succeeded in quenching the flame of faith which His Word had set ablaze. He had knowingly sacrificed His life for the sake of the Redeemer promised unto all Faiths. The near advent of 'Him Whom God shall make manifest' (Man-Yuẓhiruhu'lláh) had been His constant theme. He had made the acceptance of His own Book—the mighty *Bayán*—dependent upon the good pleasure of 'Him Whom God shall make manifest', Whom He had addressed in the early days of His Ministry:

> O Thou Remnant of God! I have sacrificed myself wholly for Thee; I have accepted curses for Thy sake, and have yearned for naught but martyrdom in the path of Thy love.[8]

And now on this night—His last on earth—He was happy and contented. He told the faithful disciples who were with Him that He preferred to meet His death at the hand of a friend rather than at the hands of enemies, and invited them to fulfil His wish. Among those men who so dearly loved Him, only Mírzá Muḥammad-'Alí dared to undertake that fearsome task, but his companions restrained him. 'This same youth who has risen to comply with My wish,' the Báb said, 'will, together with Me, suffer martyrdom. Him will I choose to share with Me its crown.' And He added: 'Verily Muḥammad-'Alí will be with Us in Paradise.'[9]

Jesus was crucified with two criminals, and St. Luke tells us:

> And one of the malefactors which were hanged railed on him, saying, If thou be Christ, save thyself and us.
>
> But the other answering rebuked him, saying, Dost not thou fear God, seeing thou art in the same condemnation?
>
> And we indeed justly; for we receive the due reward of our deeds: but this man hath done nothing amiss.
>
> And he said unto Jesus, Lord, remember me when thou comest into thy kingdom.
>
> And Jesus said unto him, Verily I say unto thee, To day shalt thou be with me in paradise.*

In the morning they took the Báb to the homes of the leading divines: Mullá Muḥammad-i-Mámaqání, Mullá Murtiḍá-Qulíy-i-Marandí and Mírzá Báqir, to obtain the death-warrants. These men needed no inducement: they had the warrants written, signed and sealed, ready to

* xxiii, 39–43.

deliver to the farrásh-báshí, and did not even deign to show their faces to the Prisoner.

Again we are reminded of St. Luke:

> And the men that held Jesus mocked him, and smote *him*.
>
> And when they had blindfolded him, they struck him on the face, and asked him, saying, Prophesy, who is it that smote thee?
>
> And many other things blasphemously spake they against him.
>
> And as soon as it was day, the elders of the people and the chief priests and the scribes came together, and led him into their council, saying,
>
> Art thou the Christ? tell us. And he said unto them, If I tell you, ye will not believe:
>
> And if I also ask *you*, ye will not answer me, nor let *me* go.
>
> Hereafter shall the Son of man sit on the right hand of the power of God.
>
> Then said they all, Art thou then the Son of God? And he said unto them, Ye say that I am.
>
> And they said, What need we any further witness? for we ourselves have heard of his own mouth.*

The stepfather of Mírzá Muḥammad-'Alí now made an attempt to save him. Siyyid Ḥusayn-i-Yazdí and his brother, at the instructions of the Báb Himself, had recanted so that they could take to the followers of the Báb His last words and wishes. Mírzá Muḥammad-'Alí refused all blandishments, declared his desire to die with his Master, and told Mullá Muḥammad-i-Mámaqání to his face: 'I am not mad. Such a charge should rather be brought against you who have sentenced to death a man no less holy than the promised Qá'im. He is not a fool who has embraced His Faith and is longing to shed his blood in His path.'[10] His young

* xxii, 63–71.

child was brought to him. They thought that, perchance, the sight of the boy might soften his heart. But Mírzá Muḥammad-'Alí's resolve remained unshaken. God would provide for his child and protect him.

So at noon they led the Báb and His disciple to the square in front of the citadel of Tabríz. Sám Khán, the commander of the Armenian regiment detailed to execute them, was ill at ease. The Prisoner looked kind and compassionate. For what crime was He to be put to death? Unable to still the voice of his conscience, Sám Khán approached the Báb: 'I profess the Christian Faith and entertain no ill will against you. If your Cause be the Cause of Truth, enable me to free myself from the obligation to shed your blood.' To this the Báb replied: 'Follow your instructions, and if your intention be sincere, the Almighty is surely able to relieve you from your perplexity.'[11]

The Báb and His disciple were suspended by ropes from a nail in the wall, the head of Mírzá Muḥammad-'Alí resting on the breast of the Báb. Seven hundred and fifty soldiers were positioned in three files. Roofs of the buildings around teemed with spectators.

Each row of soldiers fired in turn. The smoke from so many rifles clouded the scene. When it lifted the Báb was not there. Only His disciple could be seen, standing under the nail in the wall, smiling and unconcerned. Bullets had only severed the ropes with which they were suspended. Cries rang out from the onlookers: 'The Siyyid-i-Báb has gone from our sight!'

A frantic search followed. The Báb was found, sitting in the same room where He had been lodged the night before, in conversation with His amanuensis. That conversation had been interrupted earlier in the day. Now it was finished and He told the farrásh-báshí to carry out his duty. But the farrásh-báshí was terror-stricken and ran away, nor did he ever return to his post. Sám Khán, for his part, told his superiors that he had carried out the task given to him; he would not attempt it a second time. So Áqá Ján Khán-i-Khamsih and his Náṣirí regiment replaced the Armenians, and the Báb and His disciple were suspended once again at the same spot.

Now the Báb addressed the multitude gathered to see Him die:

> Had you believed in Me, O wayward generation, every one of you would have followed the example of this youth, who stood in rank above most of you, and willingly would have sacrificed himself in My path. The day will come when you will have recognised Me; that day I shall have ceased to be with you.[12]

And St. Luke relates:

> And there followed him a great company of people, and of women, which also bewailed and lamented him.
>
> But Jesus turning unto them said, Daughters of Jerusalem, weep not for me, but weep for yourselves, and for your children.
>
> For, behold, the days are coming, in the which they shall say, Blessed *are* the barren, and the wombs that never bare, and the paps which never gave suck.
>
> Then shall they begin to say to the mountains, Fall on us; and to the hills, Cover us.*

The Náṣirí regiment fired. The bodies of the Báb and His disciple were shattered, and their flesh was united. But the face of the Báb was untouched. Then a storm descended upon Tabríz. Tempestuous winds blew and dust darkened the skies, and the skies remained dark, until the darkness of the day merged into the darkness of the night.

> And it was about the sixth hour, and there was a darkness over all the earth until the ninth hour.

* xxiii, 27–30.

And the sun was darkened, and the veil of the temple was rent in the midst.

And when Jesus had cried with a loud voice, he said, Father, into thy hands I commend my spirit: and having said thus, he gave up the ghost.*

Thus at noon, one midsummer day—Sunday July 9th 1850†—they put to death a Manifestation of God, just as at noon, centuries before, another Manifestation of God was slain.

When night fell, they dragged the bodies through the streets of Tabríz, and threw them on the edge of the moat surrounding the city. Soldiers were stationed there to guard over them, lest the Bábís attempt to retrieve the precious remains. Not far away, two Bábís, feigning madness, kept vigil throughout the night.

Next morning the Russian Consul took an artist with him to make a drawing of the remains of the Báb.

Sulaymán Khán, that loyal disciple who attained the presence of the Báb in Chihríq, reached Tabríz the day after His martyrdom. He had intended to rescue his Master. But that was not to be. Now, he went straightway to Ḥájí Mírzá Mihdí Khán, the Kalántar (Mayor) of Tabríz, who was a friend of long standing, and told him that he had decided to dare everything that very night and carry the bodies away by a surprise attack on the soldiers guarding them on the edge of the moat. The Kalántar told Sulaymán Khán to withdraw for the moment and assured him that there was a much safer and more reliable way to achieve his purpose.

There was in Tabríz a certain Ḥájí Alláh-Yár, a confidant of the Kalántar, well-known for his exploits. Instructed by

* Luke xxiii, 44–6.

† Sha'bán 28th, 1266 A.H.

the Kalántar, Ḥájí Alláh-Yár used such means as he knew best to take the bodies away from under the eyes of the soldiers. He delivered the remains to Sulaymán Khán, who had them moved to the silk factory of Ḥájí Aḥmad, a Bábí of Mílán. There they were enshrouded and hidden under the bales of silk. Next day a casket was made to contain them, and they were sent away to safety. Ḥájí Alláh-Yár refused to accept any reward for his service.[13]

Soldiers reported the disappearance of the bodies. Wild beasts had devoured the remains, they alleged, while they slept. And the divines gave credence to that story and shouted for joy. What better proof could there be to show how false the Siyyid-i-Báb was? Beasts do not, cannot consume the remains of the Imám.*

* See Appendix 2 for extracts from British official documents which report the execution and the disposition of the bodies.

CHAPTER 13

THE DAWN-BREAKERS

Knowest thou what the seekers of life should seek?
Death—and submitting cast their lives at the
Beloved's feet.
He who towards Ka'bah his steps directs
Should not heed the wounding thorn in deserts forlorn.
—'Azízu'lláh Miṣbáḥ

The Báb appeared in a country renowned for a glorious and envied past; but since the beginning of the nineteenth century Írán had declined rapidly. The structure of the State had begun to falter under the Ṣafavid dynasty (1501–1732), enjoying only a brief revival in the next two reigns.* But by the middle of the nineteenth century, Persia was materially impoverished, intellectually stagnant, spiritually moribund. The condition of the peasantry was appalling. Corruption had eaten deep into the vitals of the nation and oppression and tyranny were widespread. It is said that every man has his price; the adage was particularly true of the Persians of the mid-nineteenth century. Offices of State and governorships were shamelessly bought and sold. Taxes and customs revenues were farmed. Bribery, peculation and extortion were legitimized under the respectable name of Madákhil (Perquisites). Historic cities and buildings were falling into ruin. Many a traveller has remarked on the magnificent aspect of famous cities, towns and villages when seen from afar, with their domes and minarets, citadels and gateways,

* Afshárid Nádir Sháh (1736–47) and the Zand ruler, Karím Khán (1750–79).

groves and orchards; but how miserable and dilapidated they were found to be when one entered them. The toll of disease and neglect and insecurity had reduced the population of a country with an area the size of Western Europe to well below ten million.

The burden of a semi-feudal state was indeed onerous, and no less so was the burden of the dominance established by the divines. Certainly, they had in their ranks men of the calibre and quality of Shaykh Aḥmad-i-Aḥsá'í, Siyyid Káẓim-i-Rashtí, Ḥájí Siyyid Muḥammad-Báqir-i-Rashtí* and Shaykh Murtiḍáy-i-Anṣárí, men who had high regard for truth and righteousness; just as there were in the service of the State men of enlightened vision and shining integrity. But collectively the divines abused the power they had obtained with the advent of the Ṣafavid dynasty.

The fall of a nation from the pinnacle of achievement is more marked than the decline from lesser heights.

The Call to a New Day

The Call of the Báb was a call to awakening, a claim that a New Day had dawned. But the magnitude of this claim was not easily realized; one of the first to do so was Qurratu'l-'Ayn. When Mullá 'Alíy-i-Basṭámí was condemned and imprisoned in Baghdád, she was still at Karbilá. Because of complaints by the Shí'ah divines, the Government sent her back to Baghdád, where she lodged in the house of Shaykh Muḥammad Shibl, the father of Áqá Muḥammad Muṣṭafáy-i-Baghdádí, until the Government moved her to the house of the Muftí of Baghdád.† So outspoken was she in her public statements that some of her fellow-believers from Káẓimayn were alarmed and, according to Áqá Muḥammad-Muṣṭafá, agitated against her. Siyyid 'Alí Bishr, the

* Known both as Rashtí and Shaftí.

† In a book which the Muftí, Maḥmúd al-Álúsí, wrote, he spoke of Qurratu'l-'Ayn with great admiration.

most learned of them, wrote a letter on their behalf to the Báb, which Nawrúz-'Alí, once an attendant of Siyyid Káẓim, took to Him in Máh-Kú, returning with His answer which rang with high praise of Qurratu'l-'Ayn. It caused Siyyid 'Alí Bishr and his party from Káẓimayn* to withdraw from the Faith they had previously espoused with enthusiasm. The Báb described Qurratu'l-'Ayn, in that Epistle, as Ṭáhirih, the Pure, and Ṣiddíqih, the Truthful, and laid an injunction on His followers in 'Iráq to accept without question whatever she might pronounce, for they were not in a position to understand and appreciate her station. By this time a large number of Bábís had assembled in Baghdád, and Qurratu'l-'Ayn was constantly and openly teaching the Faith. She had received a copy of the *Commentary on the Súrih of Kawthar*, which the Báb had revealed for Vaḥíd, and she made full use of it, driving the opposing divines to desperation. When she threw down a challenge to them to debate the issue with her, their only reply was vehement denunciation.

Najíb Páshá was still at his post as Válí of Baghdád, but he was now a chastened man. Moreover, the opponents of Qurratu'l-'Ayn were the Shí'ah divines and Najíb Páshá, being a Sunní, would take no action to please them, but he reported to the Sublime Porte that Qurratu'l-'Ayn had challenged them. The authorities in Constantinople were also not prepared to give comfort to Shí'ahs by making a martyr of Qurratu'l-'Ayn. At the same time they had no wish to champion her cause. They told Najíb Páshá that, as Qurratu'l-'Ayn was Persian, she should confine her challenge to the divines of her native land; she should be sent to Persia.† So Qurratu'l-'Ayn (or Ṭáhirih as we shall

* These included Siyyid Ṭáhá and Siyyid Muḥammad-Ja'far.

† Yet only two years before they had refused to hand over Mullá 'Alí to the Persian Government, that he might reach safety.

call her), accompanied by a number of ardent and prominent Bábís,[1] quitted Baghdád and was escorted to the frontier by Muḥammad Áqá Yávar, an officer in the service of Najíb Páshá, who became attracted to the Cause she was advocating.

Various eventful stops were made by Ṭáhirih and her companions in their journey across Persia to Qazvín. In the small town of Kirand, her eloquence and the clarity of her disquisition so impressed the chiefs of that area that they offered to place twelve thousand men under her command, to follow her wherever she went. The great majority (if not all) of the inhabitants of Kirand and its neighbourhood were 'Alíyu'lláhís. Ṭáhirih gave them her blessing, told them to keep to their homes, and moved on to Kirmánsháh. The challenge she presented to Áqá 'Abdu'lláh-i-Bihbihání, the leading divine of that town, thoroughly discomfited him. With the populace clamouring for a positive answer, and the Governor treating Ṭáhirih with great respect, the cornered divine sought to free himself from his dilemma by writing to her father in Qazvín, asking him to send some of his close relatives to remove her from Kirmánsháh. Áqá Muḥammad-Muṣṭafá, himself an eye-witness, vividly describes how four men came from Qazvín, joined forces with a Qazvíní officer stationed in Kirmánsháh, invaded the house where Ṭáhirih's companions resided, and beat and robbed them of all they possessed. When the Governor learned what had happened, he ordered the arrest of the culprits and restored to the Bábís their property. It was soon known that Áqá 'Abdu'lláh had conspired to bring about this situation.

From Kirmánsháh, Ṭáhirih and her companions moved on to fresh scenes of triumph in the small town of Ṣaḥnih, before reaching Hamadán. Here her brothers arrived from Qazvín to beg her to return with them to their native place. She agreed on condition that she should stay in Hamadán long enough to make the public cognizant of the Faith of the Báb. During her days in Hamadán, she issued a challenge to Ra'ísu'l-'Ulamá, the leading divine of the city, whose response was to have the bearer of her treatise, Mullá Ibráhím-i-Maḥallátí, himself a distinguished divine, beaten and thrown out of his house. Mullá Ibráhím lingered between life and death for some days, and although he recovered, his martyrdom was not far off. This reverse was outweighed by Ṭáhirih's success in converting two ladies of the Royal Family, married to scions of the aristocracy of Hamadán, and even more significant were her talks with two of the most learned Jewish rabbis,* which led to attracting members of the Jewish Faith to the Bábí fold.† Hamadán, flourishing on the site of ancient Ecbatana, is the city where the tombs of Esther and Mordecai are situated.

As promised, Ṭáhirih then left for Qazvín in the company of her brothers. Before departing, she asked most of the Arab Bábís, who were with her, to return to 'Iráq. Only a few stayed behind, to join her later in Qazvín, but within a month she requested all of her fellow-believers, Arab and Persian alike, who had travelled with her, to leave her native town. Of the large company who had come from 'Iráq, attending and supporting her, only Mullá Ibráhím-i-Maḥallátí and Shaykh Ṣáliḥ-al-Karímí remained with her in Qazvín.

* Mullá Ilyáhú and Mullá Lálizár.

† The first Jewish Bahá'í was Ḥakím Masíḥ, a doctor (later to become court physician to Muḥammad Sháh) who met Ṭáhirih in Baghdád, and was deeply impressed by her eloquence and masterly exposition. Years later, while attending his son, he met Mullá Ṣádiq-i-Muqaddas, a survivor of Shaykh Ṭabarsí, to whom Bahá'u'lláh had given the designation of Ismu'lláhu'l-Aṣdaq (the Name of God, the Most Truthful). This encounter led Ḥakím Masíḥ to embrace the Bahá'í Faith. He was the grandfather of Dr. Luṭfu'lláh Ḥakím. (See Balyuzi, *'Abdu'l-Bahá*, p. 78n.)

Three of the others* went on to Ṭihrán, where they met the Bábu'l-Báb. In April 1890, Edward Granville Browne, returning from 'Akká, met one of them, Áqá Muḥammad-Muṣṭafá, in Beirut and inquired about that meeting and the appearance of Mullá Ḥusayn. He learned that the Bábu'l-Báb was

> Lean and fragile to look at, but keen and bright as the sword which never left his side.† For the rest, he was not more than thirty or thirty-five years old, and his raiment was white.[2]

At Qazvín, Ṭáhirih refused to be reunited with her husband and went to her father's house. Her impetuous uncle, Ḥájí Mullá Taqí, felt greatly insulted and his wrath knew no bounds. His denunciation of those whom he considered to be responsible for his daughter-in-law's waywardness became fiercer than ever before. Shaykh Aḥmad and Siyyid Káẓim were the particular targets of his vilification. Then, one morning at dawn, he was found in the mosque, fatally stabbed. Immediately the Bábís were accused of his murder, and even Ṭáhirih was considered guilty, was kept under close watch, and her life was in danger. Although a Shírází[3] confessed that he had slain Ḥájí Mullá Taqí because of his rabid animosity towards Shaykh Aḥmad and Siyyid Káẓim, three Bábís, totally innocent of the crime, were put to death —Shaykh Ṣáliḥ-al-Karímí in Ṭihrán, and Mullá Ibráhím-i-Maḥallatí and Mullá Ṭáhir in Qazvín. These three were the first martyrs of the Bábí Faith in Persia itself, and their deaths constituted the first public execution of Bábís.‡

* They were Shaykh Muḥammad Shibl and his son, Áqá Muḥammad-Muṣṭafá, and Shaykh Sulṭán-i-Karbilá'í.

† Mullá Ḥusayn's sword is in the International Archives of the Bahá'í Faith.

‡ It is of interest that Shaykh Ṣáliḥ, martyred in Persia, was a native of 'Iráq, while the first martyr of the Bábí Faith, Mullá 'Alíy-i-Basṭámí, was a Persian who met his death in 'Iráq.

Ḥájí Asadu'lláh, a well-known merchant of the Farhádí family, was also martyred, while in prison, by partisans of Ṭáhirih's husband, the Imám-Jum'ih of Qazvín, and a report was circulated that he had died from natural causes.

Ṭáhirih was now totally isolated. Bahá'u'lláh gave the task of rescuing her to Mírzá Hádí, the nephew of the martyred Ḥájí Asadu'lláh. This young man, who had left Qazvín at the outset of agitation against the Bábís, returned at the risk of his life and successfully carried out his mission. Ṭáhirih reached Ṭihrán in safety. Thus it was that she could be at the conference of Badas͟ht, where she rendered her most signal service to the Faith of the Báb.

The Conference of Badas͟ht

The gathering of the Bábís at Badas͟ht coincided with the removal of the Báb, from the castle of C͟hihríq to Tabríz, for His public examination. Contrary to certain allegations, the Bábís did not congregate in Badas͟ht to concert plans to rescue Him. They came there, guided by Bahá'u'lláh, to settle a vital and cardinal issue: was this persuasion of theirs just an offshoot of Islám, or was it an independent Faith? Until then no public claim had been made that the Báb, as the Qá'im of the House of Muḥammad, was an Inaugurator of a new theophany. Strange it seems, in perspective, that about the time when a decision was being reached in a tiny hamlet on the edge of K͟hurásán, hundreds of miles away in the city of Tabríz, the Báb was announcing His station before a tribunal summoned to question Him.*

'Abdu'l-Bahá states that Bahá'u'lláh and Quddús had agreed that the time had come to declare the advent of a new Dispensation.[4] However, there were faint hearts in the Bábí

* The station of the Báb is discussed and defined by Shoghi Effendi, the Guardian of the Bahá'í Faith, in *The Dispensation of Bahá'u'lláh*, reprinted in the collection of his writings entitled *The World Order of Bahá'u'lláh*, to which the reader is referred.

ranks, as events were to prove. Ṭáhirih had met opposition from fellow-Bábís because she had always been bold enough to assert that this was indeed a new day. Any announcement at Badasht would have to be emphatic and unhedged, to make a persuasive impact. And this it was, in a most dramatic way.

Bahá'u'lláh had rented three gardens in Badasht: Quddús lived in one, Ṭáhirih in the second, and Bahá'u'lláh had a tent pitched in the third. Other Bábís, among whom were a number of the Letters of the Living such as Mírzá Muḥammad-'Alí, the brother-in-law of Ṭáhirih, and Mullá Báqir-i-Tabrízí, lived under tents in the grounds facing the three gardens.*

During the three weeks of the conference, argument and counter-argument were put forward, and differences of view and approach arose between Quddús and Ṭáhirih. At last it was Ṭáhirih's unheard-of gesture, courageous beyond belief and description, followed by Bahá'u'lláh's decisive intervention, which made clear to all that a new Dispensation had begun. Ṭáhirih's brave act was to cast aside her veil. Men were shaken to the depths of their being to see her thus. Some fled with horror from the scene. One, in desperation, tried to cut his throat. When the uproar subsided, Bahá'u'lláh called for a copy of the Qur'án and directed a reciter to read the fifty-sixth súrih, 'al-Wáqi'a': †

> When the inevitable day of judgment shall suddenly come, no soul shall charge the prediction of its coming with falsehood: it will abase some, and exalt others. When

* Mullá Ḥusayn was prevented from reaching Badasht.

† Literally, 'The Event'; Professor Arberry has translated it as 'Terror' and George Sale as 'The Inevitable'. The present writer prefers in this instance Sale's rendering of the whole súrih to Arberry's; verses 1–12 are quoted. The incident is taken from 'Abdu'l-Bahá, *The Memorials of The Faithful*, p. 201, and Cheyne, *The Reconciliation of Races and Religions*, pp. 101–3.

> the earth shall be shaken with a violent shock; and the mountains shall be dashed in pieces, and shall become as dust scattered abroad; and ye shall be separated into three distinct classes: the companions of the right hand (how happy shall the companions of the right hand be!), and the companions of the left hand (how miserable shall the companions of the left hand be!), and those who have preceded others in the faith shall precede them to paradise. These are they who shall approach near unto God: they shall dwell in gardens of delight.

At Badas͟ht the faint-hearted fell away. And when those who had remained steadfast left the hamlet it was to go out into a world, for them, greatly changed. That change was in a sense a reflection of the transformation they had experienced. They were determined to assert their freedom from the fetters of the past. In a country tightly wedded to blind, rigid orthodoxy, the deportment of the Bábís would arouse bitter hostility. There were Bábís, undoubtedly, who in their newly-found consciousness of emancipation, committed repellent excesses, and they deserved rejection by their fellow-countrymen. But for the majority, the animosity now directed against them created a situation which was new, and in turn required counter-measures to ensure their very existence. The opposition they had met in the past was sporadic, and not nation-wide, depending on the character, influence and power of the leaders, directors and instigators of such opposition, in any particular locality. The open welcome which the Báb had received when He reached Iṣfahán, following the barbaric treatment He had suffered at the hands of the Governor-General and the divines of Fárs; the enthusiasm and eagerness with which the people had, at first, greeted Him both in Tabríz and Urúmíyyih; the friendly reception which Quddús had found in Kirmán, after being humiliated in S͟hí͟ráz; the reverence shown conspicuously to Ṭáhirih in Kirand and Kirmáns͟háh; the respect and kindly attention accorded to the Bábu'l-Báb by Ḥamzih Mírzá, the Governor-General of K͟hurásán*—all were to become only memories, sadly lacking counterparts in the era whose opening was marked by the Báb's public declaration of His station as the promised Qá'im during His examination at Tabríz, the echoing affirmation of the dawning of a new and independent religious Dispensation at the conference of Bada͟sht, and by the death of Muḥammad S͟háh.

Hardly had the conference of Bada͟sht ended when the people of the village of Níyálá attacked the Bábís. Nabíl-i-A'ẓam heard the story from Bahá'u'lláh Himself:

> We were all gathered in the village of Níyálá and were resting at the foot of a mountain, when, at the hour of dawn, we were suddenly awakened by the stones which the people of the neighbourhood were hurling upon us from the top of the mountain. The fierceness of their attack induced our companions to flee in terror and consternation. I clothed Quddús in my own garments and despatched him to a place of safety, where I intended to join him. When I arrived, I found that he had gone. None of our companions had remained in Níyálá except Ṭáhirih and a young man from S͟híráz, Mírzá 'Abdu'lláh. The violence with which we were assailed had brought desolation into our camp. I found no one into whose custody I could deliver Ṭáhirih except that young man, who displayed on that occasion a courage and determination that were truly surprising. Sword in hand, undaunted by the savage assault of the inhabitants of the village, who had rushed to plunder our property, he sprang forward to stay the hand of the assailants. Though himself wounded in several parts of his body, he risked his life to protect our property. I bade him desist from his act.

* Also known as Ḥis͟hmatu'd-Dawlih, the brother of Muḥam-mad S͟háh, who, at a later date, was the Governor-General of Ád͟harbáyján, and refused to superintend the execution of the Báb.

When the tumult had subsided, I approached a number of the inhabitants of the village and was able to convince them of the cruelty and shamefulness of their behaviour. I subsequently succeeded in restoring a part of our plundered property.[5]

The Episode of Shaykh Ṭabarsí

It was mid-July 1848 when the Bábís were scattered by the assault of the villagers of Níyálá. They took different routes, but many of them came together again. Bahá'u'lláh travelled to Núr, His home in Mázindarán. Quddús was arrested and taken to the town of Sárí, also in Mázindarán, where he was lodged, under restraint, in the home of Mírzá Muḥammad-Taqí, the leading divine. Ṭáhirih also went to the same province, and she too was arrested. Later, she was sent to the capital and was given into the charge of Maḥmúd Khán, the Kalántar (Mayor) of Ṭihrán, who detained her until the hour of her martyrdom in August 1852.

Mullá Ḥusayn, whose visit to the camp of Ḥamzih Mírzá had prevented him from attending the conference of Badasht, had in the meantime returned to Mashhad, and intended to go to Karbilá. But an emissary of the Báb overtook him with an urgent message. The Báb had conferred on him the name of Siyyid 'Alí, had sent him a green turban of His own to wear, and had instructed him to go to the aid of Quddús with the Black Standard unfurled before him—the Standard of which the Prophet Muḥammad had said:

> Should your eyes behold the Black Standards proceeding from Khurásán, hasten ye towards them, even though ye should have to crawl over the snow, inasmuch as they proclaim the advent of the promised Mihdí, the Vicegerent of God.[6]

Mullá Ḥusayn began his long march to Mázindarán to rescue Quddús, accompanied by many of the Bábís who had scattered after the incident in Níyálá, and some of the newly-converted who ranged themselves behind the Black Standard. Their numbers, on that journey, swelled into hundreds. On their way they raised the call of the New Day, finding eager supporters, but also such venomous hostility that they could not take residence in any town or village. Yet they did not intend to engage in combat with anyone, let alone the forces of the State. They were only demonstrating their belief and their vision.

As they approached Bárfurúsh, its leading divine, Sa'ídu'l-'Ulamá, was so vituperative in denouncing Mullá Ḥusayn that the whole town rose up to oppose the Bábís. Clashes and casualties were inevitable. Mullá Ḥusayn himself, in the fray, cut through the trunk of a tree and the barrel of a gun, in one stroke of his sword, to fell an adversary.* The people of Bárfurúsh were worsted and asked for a truce, and because of their unrest, their leaders begged Mullá Ḥusayn to leave on the morrow for Ámul. 'Abbás-Qulí Khán-i-Láríjání, whom Nicolas names as 'the chief military personage of the province,'[7] gave Mullá Ḥusayn a solemn promise, fortified by an oath on the Qur'án, that Khusraw-i-Qádí-Kalá'í and his horsemen would escort the Bábís to safety through the forests. This military chief impressed on Khusraw the need to do his duty by Mullá Ḥusayn, and to show him respect and consideration. But Sa'ídu'l-'Ulamá corrupted Khusraw by telling him that he personally would accept responsibility before God and man for any injury, or even death, that might be inflicted on the Bábís. Once in

* The fame of this feat spread far and wide. Later, when the Grand Vizier reprimanded Prince Mihdí-Qulí Mírzá, commander of an army sent against the defenders of Shaykh Ṭabarsí, because he had fled before them, the Prince sent him pieces of the musket-barrel smashed by the sword of Mullá Ḥusayn, with this message: 'Such is the contemptible strength of an adversary who, with a single stroke of his sword, has shattered into six pieces the tree, the musket, and its holder.'[8]

the depths of the forest, Khusraw and his hundred men treacherously attacked the Bábís. He received his desert at the hands of a man* of learning, not a hardened trooper, who at the first opportunity stabbed and killed Khusraw with a dagger.

The Grand Vizier was particularly irked and infuriated that the Bábís could defeat and put to flight his force, although, for the most part, they were untrained in the arts of war. True, one could find in their ranks men such as Riḍá Khán-i-Turkamán,† an accomplished young courtier, whose father was the Master of the Horse in the royal establishment. But these were exceptions. The vast majority were artisans, small traders, merchants, students of theology, divines.

Khusraw's treachery and death, and raids by hostile villagers on the exposed flanks of the Bábí camp, forced Mullá Ḥusayn to seek a place where the Bábís could be safely lodged. Arriving on October 12th 1848 at the shrine of Shaykh Aḥmad ibn-i-Abí-Ṭálib-i-Ṭabarsí, about fourteen miles south-east of Bárfurúsh, he gave orders for the construction of a fortress round the shrine, under the supervision of the builder of the Bábíyyih in Mashhad (see p. 56). They were harassed at every stage by neighbouring villagers and had often to defend themselves. No sooner was their work finished than they received a visit from Bahá'u'lláh, who advised Mullá Ḥusayn to seek the release of Quddús, that he might be with them. This mission was soon accomplished and, towards the end of that year, Quddús joined them in the newly-built fortress, to be acknowledged by Mullá Ḥusayn as above him in rank.

On January 30th 1849, Lt.-Col. Farrant, then chargé d'affaires in Ṭihrán, reported to Lord Palmerston that some five hundred persons, 'disciples of a Fanatic, who calls

* Mírzá Muḥammad-Taqíy-i-Juvayní.

† A martyr of Shaykh Ṭabarsí.

himself the door, or gate of the true Mahomedan Religion', had assembled in Mázindarán, that fighting had broken out, and that 'Abbás-Qulí K̲h̲án-i-Láríjání had been ordered to proceed to that province and arrest the leaders.[9]

The Bábís would gladly have lived peacefully within the four walls they had erected around the shrine of S̲h̲ayk̲h̲ Ṭabarsí. But the continuous clamouring of the divines, led by Sa'ídu'l-'Ulamá of Bárfurús̲h̲, and the despotic, obstinate and haughty nature of the Grand Vizier, combined to deny them peace and security. One army after another was sent to reduce them. In sorties from their fortress they inflicted heavy losses on the besieging forces, causing commanders to flee for their lives. Some of the commanders* died on the battlefield, while Quddús, during one of the sorties, received a bullet wound in his mouth.

Bahá'u'lláh, accompanied by His brother Mírzá Yaḥyá, with Ḥájí Mírzá Jání of Kás̲h̲án, and Mullá Báqir of Tabríz (one of the Letters of the Living), set out from Ṭihrán to join the defenders of S̲h̲ayk̲h̲ Ṭabarsí, but they were intercepted and taken to Ámul. Bahá'u'lláh offered to bear the punishment intended for the others, and was bastinadoed.

At dawn of February 2nd 1849, Mullá Ḥusayn led his last sortie. 'Abbás-Qulí K̲h̲án, in joint command of the Government forces, had climbed a tree and, picking out the figure of Mullá Ḥusayn on horseback, shot him in the chest. He did not know whom he had mortally wounded, until a timorous siyyid from Qum † turned traitor and informed him. Mullá Ḥusayn was carried by his companions to the fort, where he died and was buried inside the shrine. He was thirty-five years old. Bahá'u'lláh wrote of him in the *Kitáb-i-Íqán—The Book of Certitude*:—'But for him, God

---

* Such as 'Abdu'lláh K̲h̲án-i-Turkamán and Ḥabíbu'lláh K̲h̲án-i-Afg̲h̲án.

† Mírzá Ḥusayn-i-Mutavallí.

would not have been established upon the seat of His mercy, nor ascended the throne of eternal glory.'[10]

Now Mírzá Muḥammad-Báqir-i-Qá'iní replaced Mullá Ḥusayn in leading the companions. But the end could not be far off. Of the three hundred and thirteen defenders of the fortress, a number had died, many were wounded, and a few wavered in their resolve. The pressure of the forces arrayed against them increased. Cannon were levelled at them. Food became scarce and they ate grass, leaves of trees, the skin and ground bone of their slaughtered horses, the boiled leather of their saddles. 'Abdu'l-Bahá speaks of their sufferings in the *Memorials of the Faithful*:

> For eighteen days they remained without food. They lived on the leather of their shoes. This too was soon consumed, and they had nothing left but water. They drank a mouthful every morning, and lay famished and exhausted in their fort. When attacked, however, they would instantly spring to their feet, and manifest in the face of the enemy a magnificent courage and astonishing resistance . . . Under such circumstances to maintain an unwavering faith and patience is extremely difficult, and to endure such dire afflictions a rare phenomenon.[11]

The end came not through abject surrender, but through the perfidy of the foe. Prince Mihdí-Qulí Mírzá, brother of Muḥammad Sháh, took a solemn oath on the Qur'án that their lives and property would be inviolate should they come out of the fortress and disperse in peace. A horse was sent for Quddús to take him to the camp of the Prince. But once the companions had been lured out of the fortress, the oath was conveniently forgotten. The Bábís were massacred, the fortress was pillaged and razed to the ground. Hideous outrages were committed upon the corpses of the slain, and a vast area of the forest was strewn with their remains: disembowelled, hacked to pieces, burned. Survivors were few. No more than three or four were kept to be heavily ransomed. A few who were left for dead recovered. Still a few others were sold into slavery and eventually found their way back to the company of their fellow-believers. All the dead were Persians except two Arabs of Baghdád who had come out with Ṭáhirih from 'Iráq.[12]

Quddús was taken to Bárfurúsh, his native town, where Sa'ídu'l-'Ulamá, his pitiless foe, awaited him. Prince Mihdí-Qulí Mírzá, oblivious to his pledge, forsook Quddús and gave him into the hands of that bloodthirsty priest. Imprecations were heaped upon the head of the captive. He was made to suffer refined tortures and searing agonies which an insanely jealous adversary had devised for him. At the height of his torments he was heard to say:

> Forgive, O my God, the trespasses of this people. Deal with them in Thy mercy, for they know not what we already have discovered and cherish.[13]

In the public square of Bárfurúsh (the Sabzih-Maydán), Sa'ídu'l-'Ulamá struck Quddús down with an axe, and any instrument which a frenzied mob could lay its hands on was used to tear his flesh and dismember him. Then they threw his shattered, mutilated body onto a blazing fire lit in the square. That night, when all were gone, Ḥájí Muḥammad-'Alíy-i-Ḥamzih, a divine, humane and compassionate, universally acclaimed for his integrity, collected from the dying embers what remained of the body of the martyr, and reverently buried it.

The martyrdom of Quddús took place in the month of May 1849, seven months after his fellow-Bábís had first taken refuge in the fort of Shaykh Ṭabarsí.[14] It marked the end of an episode which had begun, eleven months before, with the raising of the Black Standard on the plain of Khurásán; during which deeds of incredible heroism by some three hundred Bábís had stunned and humiliated opposition forces vastly outnumbering them; which had witnessed the deaths of half the Letters of the Living, including the first, the Bábu'l-Báb, and Quddús, the last and greatest; and which closed with acts of treachery and atrocious cruelty. Words which Quddús spoke during their occupation of the fort are a fitting commentary upon the spirit of those who defended it:

> Never . . . have we under any circumstances attempted to direct any offensive against our opponents. Not until they unchained their attack upon us did we arise to defend our lives. Had we cherished the ambition of waging holy war against them, had we harboured the least intention of achieving ascendancy through the power of our arms over the unbelievers, we should not, until this day, have remained besieged within these walls. The force of our arms would have by now, as was the case with the companions of Muḥammad in days past, convulsed the nations of the earth and prepared them for the acceptance of our Message. Such is not our way, however, which we have chosen to tread. Ever since we repaired to this fort, our sole, our unalterable purpose has been the vindication, by our deeds and by our readiness to shed our blood in the path of our Faith, of the exalted character of our mission. The hour is fast approaching when we shall be able to consummate this task.[15]

The Year 1850

While Quddús and his companions were defending themselves at Shaykh Ṭabarsí, Bábís in other parts of Persia were increasingly the victims of an intense and systematic persecution on the part of both civil and ecclesiastical authorities. The reason was not far to seek and was stated by Sheil, once more at his post in Ṭihrán after a long period of absence, when he addressed Lord Palmerston on February 12th 1850:

> . . . unluckily the proselytes are all of the Mahommedan faith, which is inflexible in the punishment of a relapsed Mussulman. Thus both the temporal and religious authorities have an interest in the extermination of this sect.
>
> It is conjectured that in Teheran this religion has acquired votaries in every class, not even excluding the artillery and regular Infantry—Their numbers in this city, it is supposed, may amount to about two thousand.[16]

Sheil's dispatches took note of four occurrences in particular, in the year 1850: the execution of the Báb,* the episodes of Nayríz and Zanján, and the public martyrdom of seven Bábís in Ṭihrán.

The Episode of Nayríz

The incomparable Vaḥíd—Siyyid Yaḥyáy-i-Dárábí—the trusted emissary whom Muḥammad Sháh had sent to investigate the claims of the Báb and who had returned His devoted supporter—was in Yazd in the early weeks of 1850, fearlessly proclaiming the advent of the Qá'im in the person of the Báb. Unwise acts by a purported fellow-believer put his life in danger in that city, and he was forced to leave secretly for Nayríz in the province of Fárs.† On hearing of his approach, the people of his native quarter of Chinár Súkhtih who loved and honoured Vaḥíd, together with a number of the notables of Nayríz, went out to meet him, thus bringing on their families threats of dire punishment by the Governor of Nayríz, Zaynu'l-'Ábidín Khán, who was fearful and desired to prevent Vaḥíd's entry to the

* See ch. 12.

† See Appendix 3. Vaḥíd, as a man of influence, possessed houses in Yazd, Nayríz, and his native town of Dáráb.

town.[17] But these warnings went unheeded; Vaḥíd continued his journey and on arrival at his native quarter, went straight to the Masjid-i-Jum'ih where, ascending the pulpit, he addressed a congregation estimated to have numbered fifteen hundred. He said:

> My sole purpose in coming to Nayríz is to proclaim the Cause of God. I thank and glorify Him for having enabled me to touch your hearts with His Message. No need for me to tarry any longer in your midst, for if I prolong my stay, I fear that the governor will ill-treat you because of me. He may seek reinforcement from Shíráz and destroy your homes and subject you to untold indignities.[18]

But the people refused to let him go, for they were willing and prepared, they assured him, to meet any misfortune and hardship that might overtake them.

Zaynu'l-'Ábidín Khán, thwarted in his efforts to prevent Vaḥíd's entrance into Nayríz, and aroused to fury by the influence he was exerting on the populace, schemed to entrap and arrest him. For this purpose he recruited a thousand trained soldiers. Some of those who had joined Vaḥíd now broke away and forsook him, thus adding to the strength of his opponents. The menace posed by the Governor became so severe that Vaḥíd could find no way to secure the safety of his people and himself, other than by taking refuge with seventy-two of his companions in the fort of Khájih outside Nayríz. The Governor sent his brother, 'Alí-Aṣghar Khán, to attack this small band with the force he had gathered. They did not succeed, but his brother was killed in the engagement. The Bábís now lived under conditions of siege, and their water supply was cut off. They built a water-cistern, strengthened their fort, and were reinforced by additional residents of Nayríz. Meanwhile, appeals were being made by Zaynu'l-'Ábidín Khán for assistance from Shíráz, until the Governor-General of

Fárs, Prince Fírúz Mírzá (the Nuṣratu'd-Dawlih), who had ordered the extermination of the besieged Bábís, sent an army to conclude the affair.[19] Even this large force could not overcome the resistance of the defenders of the fortress. Not only did victory elude it, but heavy losses were suffered.*

What had happened at Shaykh Ṭabarsí was now re-enacted in Nayríz. Zaynu'l-'Ábidín Khán and his associates resorted to fraud to overcome the Bábís. They suspended their attack and sent a written message to Vaḥíd, which said, in effect:

> Hitherto, as we were ignorant of the true character of your Faith, we have allowed the mischief-makers to induce us to believe that every one of you has violated the sacred precepts of Islám. Therefore did we arise against you, and have endeavoured to extirpate your Faith. During the last few days, we have been made aware of the fact that your activities are untinged by any political motive, that none of you cherish any inclination to subvert the foundations of the State. We also have been convinced of the fact that your teachings do not involve any grave departure from the fundamental teachings of Islám. All that you seem to uphold is the claim that a man has appeared whose words are inspired and whose testimony is certain, and whom all the followers of Islám must recognise and support. We can in no wise be convinced of the validity of this claim unless you consent to repose the utmost confidence in our sincerity, and accept our request to allow certain of your representatives to emerge from the fort and meet us in this camp, where we can, within the space of a few days, ascertain the character of your belief. If you prove yourselves able to demonstrate the true claims of your Faith, we too will readily

* Sheil, reporting to Lord Palmerston on July 22nd 1850, stated that the defenders 'twice repulsed the Shah's troops.' (F.O. 60/152.)

embrace it, for we are not the enemies of Truth, and none of us wish to deny it. Your leader we have always recognised as one of the ablest champions of Islám, and we regard him as our example and guide. This Qur'án, to which we affix our seals, is the witness to the integrity of our purpose. Let that holy Book decide whether the claim you advance is true or false. The malediction of God and His Prophet rest upon us if we should attempt to deceive you. Your acceptance of our invitation will save a whole army from destruction, whilst your refusal will leave them in suspense and doubt. We pledge our word that as soon as we are convinced of the truth of your Message, we shall strive to display the same zeal and devotion you already have so strikingly manifested. Your friends will be our friends, and your enemies our enemies. Whatever your leader may choose to command, the same we pledge ourselves to obey. On the other hand, if we fail to be convinced of the truth of your claim, we solemnly promise that we shall in no wise interfere with your safe return to the fort, and shall be willing to resume our contest against you. We entreat you to refuse to shed more blood before attempting to establish the truth of your Cause.[20]

Vaḥíd was well aware of the dishonesty of this message; nevertheless, he walked out in person, with five attendants, into the camp of his enemies, where he was received for three days with great ceremony. But all the while they were planning a stratagem to overcome the occupants of the fort. Under duress, they compelled Vaḥíd to write a letter to his people, assuring them that a settlement had been reached, and that they should abandon the fortress and return to their homes. Vaḥíd attempted to caution his companions against this treachery in a second letter which was never delivered to them. Thus, within a month, did the defenders of the fort of Kh̲ájih meet the same fate as the defenders of Sh̲ayk̲h̲ Ṭabarsí.

Four years later, a divine of Nayríz,* a man who was just and truthful and courageous, wrote the whole story of that episode high on an inner wall of the Masjid-i-Jum'ih in the Bázár quarter. Although he had to write with circumspection to avoid being denounced, he composed his narrative in such a way that one can, without difficulty, read more of it between the lines. His account bears out the fact that Vaḥíd was given solemn assurances, that he was received with great esteem and reverence, that those who had pledged their word broke their pledges, that the quarter of Chinár-Súkhtih, which was then a stronghold of the Bábís of Nayríz,† and the quarter of the Bázár were sacked, that houses were demolished, huge sums of money extorted, and Nayríz was reduced to a state of desolation.

The circumstances of Vaḥíd's martyrdom recall the tragedy of Karbilá. All alone, he was assailed in the streets of Nayríz, as Imám Ḥusayn, whose descendant he was, had been assailed on the Euphrates plain. There the body of the Imám had been trampled into the dust by the hooves of horses, and in Nayríz the corpse of Vaḥíd suffered similar indignities. When the victorious army marched back to Shíráz, it took as prisoners women and children, with the heads of the martyrs of Nayríz raised aloft on lances. Damascus had witnessed a similar scene centuries before, when the family of the martyred Ḥusayn, which included his only surviving son, was paraded in its streets, to be led into the court of the tyrant Yazíd, preceded by the head of the Imám and those of his sons and brothers and nephews—the flower of the House of Muḥammad.

The Seven Martyrs of Ṭihrán

At the beginning of 1850, seven Bábís were arrested in Ṭihrán, charged with plotting to assassinate the Grand

* Siyyid Ibráhím, the son of Siyyid Ḥusayn.

† It is populated today by Bahá'ís.

Vizier. They are known as the Seven Martyrs of Ṭihrán. The accusation was palpably false. There were many Bábís in Ṭihrán better equipped to engage in such an exercise. But more significant, all seven were men of outstanding character and repute, and respected by their countrymen. The real reason for their arrest was their espousal of the Faith of the Báb. Although efforts were made by men high in the professions they represented, to persuade them to give lip-denial to their most sacred beliefs, they steadfastly refused and were beheaded.

The Guardian of the Bahá'í Faith has vividly described this terrible scene, which was enacted in a public square of Ṭihrán (the Sabzih-Maydán):

> The defiant answers which they flung at their persecutors; the ecstatic joy which seized them as they drew near the scene of their death; the jubilant shouts they raised as they faced their executioner; the poignancy of the verses which, in their last moments, some of them recited; the appeals and challenges they addressed to the multitude of onlookers who gazed with stupefaction upon them; the eagerness with which the last three victims strove to precede one another in sealing their faith with their blood; and lastly, the atrocities which a bloodthirsty foe degraded itself by inflicting upon their dead bodies which lay unburied for three days and three nights in the Sabzih-Maydán, during which time thousands of so-called devout Shí'ahs kicked their corpses, spat upon their faces, pelted, cursed, derided, and heaped refuse upon them—these were the chief features of the tragedy of the Seven Martyrs of Ṭihrán, a tragedy which stands out as one of the grimmest scenes witnessed in the course of the early unfoldment of the Faith of Bahá'u'lláh.[21]

Ḥájí Mírzá Siyyid 'Alí, the uncle of the Báb, was one of these martyrs. He had recently returned from his visit to the Báb in Chihríq (see p. 150) and could easily have left the capital, when rumours were rife following the events of Mázindarán and Yazd. But he fearlessly stayed on, spurned all efforts made to induce him to recant, and met death gladly in the path of his Nephew.

The other six were: Mírzá Qurbán-'Alí of Bárfurúsh, Ḥájí Mullá Ismá'íl-i-Qumí, Siyyid Ḥusayn-i-Turshízí, Ḥájí Muḥammad-Taqíy-i-Kirmání, Siyyid Murtaḍáy-i-Zanjání and Áqá Muḥammad-Ḥusayn-i-Marághi'í.

Mírzá Qurbán-'Alí had been a Ni'matu'lláhí dervish, and a leading figure of that mystic order. He was well-known in the ruling circles of the capital and greatly respected. Mírzá Taqí Khán (the Grand Vizier) particularly wished to save him, but the faith of the dervish remained unshakable. At his execution, the first blow of the executioner's sword only knocked his turban off his head, whereupon he recited aloud:

Happy he whom love's intoxication
So hath overcome that scarce he knows
Whether at the feet of the Beloved
It be head or turban which he throws![22]

Ḥájí Mullá Ismá'íl had been a disciple of Siyyid Káẓim. Even at the moment of his execution, someone came up to him with a message from a friend, pleading with him to recant, but his answer was:

Zephyr, prythee bear for me a message
To that Ishmael* who was not slain,
'Living from the street of the Beloved
Love permits not to return again.'[23]

Ḥájí Muḥammad-Taqí and Siyyid Murtaḍá were merchants of note, and Siyyid Ḥusayn had been a divine famed

* Ishmael (Ismá'íl), the son of Abraham, by Hagar.

for his piety. Siyyid Murtaḍá was a brother of that Siyyid Káẓim-i-Zanjání who attended the Báb during His journey to Iṣfahán and later fell a martyr at Shaykh Ṭabarsí. Áqá Muḥammad-Ḥusayn had been tortured to betray his companions, but he would not implicate innocent men in fictitious plots.

The Báb, from his remote prison in Chihríq and already overwhelmed by calamity, eulogized these heroic men as the 'Seven Goats' of Islamic tradition, who would precede the promised Qá'im, their true Shepherd, to His own martyrdom.*

The Episode of Zanján

The fiercest and most devastating of the three military actions against the Bábís began in Zanján, in May 1850, after the return of Ḥujjat from his detention in Ṭihrán. (See p. 125.) Although he had enjoyed the protection of Muḥammad Sháh in his defence of the Faith of the Báb, he was feared and hated as an infidel by the divines of Zanján. With the death of the Sháh and the accession to power of Mírzá Taqí Khán under the succeeding reign, he was the object of a concealed hostility on the part of the authorities, while enjoying the devoted loyalty and affection of countless men and women of his native town.

A small quarrel between children, in which Ḥujjat intervened to save the Bábí child, sparked into flame the smouldering animosity against Ḥujjat and a plan was made to seize and bring him before the Governor. Failing in this, his opponents subjected one of his companions to painful injury and death. Then, by the Governor's decree, Zanján was split into two opposing camps, a large number of men were recruited from surrounding villages, and Ḥujjat and his companions were forced to seek safety in the nearby fort of 'Alí-Mardán Khán. Counting women and children, about

* See Appendix 4.

three thousand of Ḥujjat's supporters entered the fort, which they held against repeated attack and siege for almost nine months.

Edward Granville Browne, who visited Zanján nearly forty years later, could find no natural advantages in the fort to account for the 'desperate resistance offered by the Bábís', and concluded that their success in holding off the vastly superior regiments of the Sháh should 'be attributed less to the strength of the position which they occupied than to the extraordinary valour with which they defended themselves'.[24] They were sustained in their cruel ordeal by the indomitable Ḥujjat, whom no calamity could overcome, and by the tenacity of their own devotion to the Báb, their promised Qá'im. A British observer in the 'Persian camp before Zenjan' reported to Sheil in Ṭihrán:

> They [the Bábís] fight in the most obstinate and spirited manner, the women even, of whom several have been killed, engaging in the strife—and they are such excellent marksmen that up to this time a good many have fallen of the Government troops.[25]

The most celebrated of the women was a village girl, Zaynab, who dressed as a man and, for five months until her death in the struggle, guarded the ramparts with the men. Ḥujjat gave her the name of Rustam-'Alí.

Finding that all efforts to defeat the Bábís were fruitless, the commander determined to adopt the same treacherous tactics as had succeeded at Ṭabarsí and Nayríz. He drew up a proposal for peace, assuring the defenders of the forgiveness of the Sháh and pledging with a sealed copy of the Qur'án the safety of all who would leave the fort. Ḥujjat, fully conscious of their intentions but honouring the Qur'án, sent a delegation of nine young children and men over eighty to the camp of the commander. They were insolently received and most were thrown into a dungeon. It was the signal for a final month-long siege, in which some eighteen regiments were brought into action, subjecting the now famished and depleted Bábís to a constant bombardment of cannon. With the wounding of Ḥujjat, the fort was captured, but its occupants continued their struggle from nearby houses, throwing the opposing army into despair. Then Ḥujjat's wife and baby son were killed, and a few days later he himself died of his wounds. There were left of the Bábís only two hundred able-bodied men who were struck down in a fierce attack. When the survivors had been inhumanly tortured, killed and their bodies mutilated, the body of Ḥujjat was discovered and exposed for three days to dishonour in the public square. Hands unknown rescued and carried it away. Already Ḥujjat's eight-year-old son had been 'literally cut into small pieces', and the wives and daughters of the Bábís were handed over to the soldiers.[26] *

Yet never had the martyrs of Zanján sought a holy war, nor contemplated disloyalty to their country and sovereign. Assailed by enemies who purposed only their destruction, they had courageously defended themselves. The spirit of their defence shines in these words of Ḥujjat in his last days:

> The day whereon I found Thy beloved One, O my God, and recognised in Him the Manifestation of Thy eternal Spirit, I foresaw the woes that I should suffer for Thee . . . Would that a myriad lives were mine, would that I possessed the riches of the whole earth and its glory, that I might resign them all freely and joyously in Thy path.[27]

On January 6th 1851 Sheil closed his reports on Zanján:

> For the present, the doctrines of Bâb have received a check—In every part of Persia his disciples have been

* See Appendix 5.

crushed or scattered—But though there is a cessation of the open promulgation of his tenets, it is believed that in secret they are not the less cherished . . .[28]

The Dawn-Breakers had paid dearly with their lives that the Faith of the Báb might live on. And it did live on, to attain its efflorescence in the Revelation of Bahá'u'lláh.

EPILOGUE

I am the Primal Point from which have been generated all created things . . . I am the Countenance of God Whose splendour can never be obscured, the Light of God Whose radiance can never fade . . . I am one of the sustaining pillars of the Primal Word of God. Whosoever hath recognized Me, hath known all that is true and right, and hath attained all that is good and seemly.

—The Báb

On the third day after the martyrdom of the Báb, His remains, inextricably united with those of His heroic, faithful disciple, were placed in a casket and taken to a locality which was safe and secure.

What happened, during the next fifty years, to the remains of the Báb cannot be better summarized than in the words of Shoghi Effendi, the Guardian of the Bahá'í Faith:

> Subsequently, according to Bahá'u'lláh's instructions, they were transported to Ṭihrán and placed in the shrine of Imám-Zádih Ḥasan. They were later removed to the residence of Ḥájí Sulaymán Khán* himself in the Sar-Chashmih quarter of the city, and from his house were taken to the shrine of Imám-Zádih Ma'ṣúm, where they remained concealed until the year 1284 A.H. (1867–1868), when a Tablet, revealed by Bahá'u'lláh in Adrianople, directed Mullá 'Alí-Akbar-i-Shahmírzádí † and Jamál-i-Burújirdí to transfer them without delay to some other

* He was, as we have seen, instrumental in rescuing the remains of the Báb.

† Also known generally as Ḥájí Ákhund. He was a Hand of the Cause, appointed by Bahá'u'lláh.

spot, an instruction which, in view of the subsequent reconstruction of that shrine, proved to have been providential.

Unable to find a suitable place in the suburb of Sháh 'Abdu'l-'Aẓím, Mullá 'Alí-Akbar and his companion continued their search until, on the road leading to Chashmih-'Alí [the 'Alí Springs], they came upon the abandoned and dilapidated Masjid-i-Mashá'u'lláh, where they deposited, within one of its walls, after dark, their precious burden, having first re-wrapt the remains in a silken shroud brought by them for that purpose. Finding the next day to their consternation that the hiding-place had been discovered,* they clandestinely carried the casket through the gate of the capital direct to the house of Mírzá Ḥasan-i-Vazír, a believer and son-in-law of Ḥájí Mírzá Siyyid 'Alíy-i-Tafrishí, the Majdu'l-Ashráf, where it remained for no less than fourteen months.† The long-guarded secret of its whereabouts becoming known to the believers, they began to visit the house in such numbers that a communication had to be addressed by Mullá 'Alí-Akbar to Bahá'u'lláh, begging for guidance in the matter. Ḥájí Sháh Muḥammad-i-Manshádí, surnamed Amínu'l-Bayán, was accordingly commissioned to receive the Trust from him, and bidden to exercise the utmost secrecy as to its disposal.

* Thieves must have seen Ḥájí Ákhund and Jamál-i-Burújirdí place the casket in a niche and brick it up. Whoever they were, they moved some of the bricks and broke open the casket, but finding that it did not contain any valuables they left it alone.

† In the house of Mírzá Ḥasan-i-Vazír, the remains were either deposited in a new casket, or the original broken casket was put inside a larger one. Some pieces of blood-stained and torn linen must have fallen out, when the remains were being secured. Many years later, Dr. Yúnis Khán-i-Afrúkhtih, in the course of professional attendance upon the family of Majdu'l-Ashráf, learned that they had in their possession pieces of linen soaked with the blood of the Báb. Dr. Afrúkhtih persuaded them to part with those precious relics. They are now in the International Archives of the Bahá'í Faith.

Assisted by another believer, Ḥájí Sh͟áh Muḥammad buried the casket beneath the floor of the inner sanctuary of the shrine of Imám-Zádih Zayd, where it lay undetected until Mírzá Asadu'lláh-i-Iṣfahání was informed of its exact location through a chart forwarded to him by Bahá'u'lláh. Instructed by Bahá'u'lláh to conceal it elsewhere, he first removed the remains to his own house in Ṭihrán, after which they were deposited in several other localities such as the house of Ḥusayn-'Alíy-i-Iṣfahání and that of Muḥammad-Karím-i-'Aṭṭár, where they remained hidden until the year 1316 (1899) A.H., when, in pursuance of directions issued by 'Abdu'l-Bahá, this same Mírzá Asadu'lláh, together with a number of other believers, transported them by way of Iṣfahán, Kirmáns͟háh, Bag͟hdád and Damascus, to Beirut and thence by sea to 'Akká, arriving at their destination on the 19th of the month of Ramaḍán 1316 A.H. (January 31, 1899), fifty lunar years after the Báb's execution in Tabríz.[1]

Forty years after the martyrdom of the Báb, on a day in spring, Bahá'u'lláh was standing under the shade of a cluster of cypress trees on the slopes of Mount Carmel. In front of Him stretched the curve of the Bay of Haifa, beyond which loomed a sinister sight, the grim citadel of 'Akká—His first abode when He was brought, a Prisoner and an Exile, to the Holy Land. In darkest days He had told His people not to grieve, the prison gates would open and He would raise His tent on the fair mountain across the bay.

He it was Whose advent the Báb had come to herald. For Him—He Whom God shall make manifest—the young Martyr-Prophet had suffered tribulations, had sacrificed His life. In His Dispensation, the Dispensation of His Forerunner had found its fulfilment, regained its splendour. And now as Bahá'u'lláh—the Lord of Hosts—looked at the expanse of rock below those cypress trees (which today still stand, firm and proud), He told His Son, 'Abdu'l-Bahá, who would shortly wield authority in His Name, that a mausoleum should be raised on that mountain-mass to receive the remains of the Báb.

A decade went by before 'Abdu'l-Bahá could carry out that command. The sons of Bahá'u'lláh, who had strayed away from His Covenant, strove hard to block the enterprise. But at last the land was secured, the access route was obtained, the foundation-stone was laid, and construction work had begun. Then the mischief wrought by those violators of the Covenant of Bahá'u'lláh led to the incarceration of 'Abdu'l-Bahá within the walls of 'Akká. His life was in peril, but though, for a while, all His activities were either curtailed or stopped, the work of constructing that mausoleum on Mount Carmel was never allowed to lapse.

In the year 1908, the despotism of the Ottoman rulers came to an end, and 'Abdu'l-Bahá found His freedom. The next year on Naw-Rúz Day—March 21st—in a vault beneath the building which He had raised with undaunted resolution and with heart-ache, He deposited the casket containing the remains of the Báb within a marble sarcophagus, the gift of the Bahá'ís of Rangoon. Nearly forty years later, Shoghi Effendi, the Guardian of the Bahá'í Faith, undertook to adorn the Shrine of the Báb with a superstructure, both strong and beautiful, crowned with a golden dome. Today it shines dazzlingly in the heart of Mount Carmel—the Mountain of God—a spiritual home for a flourishing world community and a beacon of hope for the whole of mankind.

APPENDIX I

THE SIEGE OF KARBILÁ

The best and fullest account of the upheavals in Karbilá is contained in a sixty-six-page dispatch from Lt.-Col. Farrant, the British Special Commissioner, to Sir Stratford Canning (later Viscount Stratford de Redcliffe), the British Ambassador in Istanbul.[1] His description of the position and the condition of Karbilá is particularly worthy of note:

'The town of Kerbella is situated about four hours distance from the right bank of the Euphrates on the confines of the Syrian desert, south south west of Bagdad about 55 miles distant, and is about $1\frac{3}{4}$ miles in circumference, surrounded by a brick wall about 24 feet high with twenty nine bastions each of which is capable of containing one gun—it contains 3400 houses of a very inferior description; the houses closely crowded together approach within three yards of the wall—the streets are very narrow, the tops of the houses are surrounded by a brick parapet and can be fired from without exposure, it has six gates three of which are very small—The tomb of Imaum Hossein is a fine building and stands nearly in the centre of the town, that of his brother Abbas in the South East quarter about two hundred and fifty yards from the Najif gate. The town is surrounded by gardens which approach close to the walls, leaving only a small footpath. The gardens are filled with huge date trees, intersected with numerous ditches, and extend to some distance from the town which is not perceptible until you are close under the walls. Its strength consists in its situation, but it appeared to me that a few good troops ought to be able to take it in a short time. The houses mostly belonged to Persians who have left their country and settled there for generations. Many of the rich men in Persia have houses and land there, that in time of need they may have a safe place of refuge, or wishing in their old age to retire to a place held in such veneration by them—

'The population varies from ten thousand to twenty thousand and eighty thousand, it is always fluctuating, and I was informed that during the time the pilgrims arrive, the streets are almost impassable—The houses are mostly divided into several small courts, occasionally one hundred persons are crowded into one of these houses, which to outward appearance could with difficulty contain half that number—The poorer pilgrims take up their abodes in the Courts of the Mosques—

'The working classes at Kerbella viz Bakers small shopkeepers day labourers &c were all Persians.'

Najíb Pá<u>sh</u>á had warned the Persian, the British and the French Agents that he intended to attack Karbilá. In a long letter addressed to the Persian Agent in Bag<u>h</u>dád dated <u>Sh</u>avvál 16th 1258 (November 18th 1842), he had, after detailing the history of the rebellion in Karbilá and its consequences, uttered this clear warning:

'Being, however, near the shrines of Ali & Hoosein [Ḥusayn] I thought it my duty to visit them; with this auspicious determination I proceeded thither, when the rebel above named [Ibráhím Za'farání]* declared that if I came with troops he would not permit my entrance; and I ascertained that he had also prepared the means of opposition. To withdraw in this position of affairs from my publickly announced purpose was a difficult step; & should the report of it spread abroad, it might, God forbid, affect the

* In the dispatch, his name is spelt Ibrahim Zaffranee.

whole order of government, the rejection, too, of the petitions of loyal & suffering subjects, who are the most sacred charge of the deity to us, is contrary to all the rules & requirements of justice; I therefore, determined to proceed, under the Imperial shadow, and the aid of the Almighty to the punishment of the rebels, as a warning example to his equals; & if, as I hear, he is prepared for resistance he shall submit to my entrance by force. There are many subjects of Iran in the town alluded to; let there hereafter be no claims, on the part of that high power, in behalf of these persons; let them come out with their children, families and property . . . in fact they must not be in that town in the hour of hostility, as this is quite inconsistent with the state of the town & place. You must therefore in compliance with your duty in such cases, without delay, inform, all those whom it may concern, of these facts; for which friendly aid this letter is written and despatched; and, please God you will doubtless thus act on the receipt thereof, & without delay favour me with a reply to the same.'[2]

However, no warning was given to the Persians to quit Karbilá as Farrant's report makes clear: 'The Mollahs also excited the religious feelings of the peoples, making them believe it was a common cause, a religious war, a Persian seyd who was present, stated to me that many of the Persians fought or gave assistance, that he amongst many did not leave the town, thinking it would not be taken, and rumours were spread that the Shah was sending a large force to their assistance, he also stated that those Persians who were unfitted or refused to bear arms were obliged to give money . . . likewise they considered themselves safe, as their Consul did not come to order them away.'

Instead, Farrant reports: 'The Persian Consul in reply to the Pacha begged him to postpone his intended attack, that if the town was taken by assault many innocent people (Persian subjects) would suffer, who at present were unable to come away . . . that if he would delay his expedition for four or six months to give the Persians time to arrange their affairs, he would proceed to Kerbella, and bring the Persians away, and arrange everything for him.

'Three days before receiving the Pacha's letter, the Consul asserts he wrote privately to the Chief Priest Hajee Seid Kausem saying "we hear the Pacha will move on Kerbella, and if he is determined, he will certainly come, he is not an Ali Pacha—tell the Persians they had better come out—" After the receipt of the Pacha's official letter he again wrote to the Chief Priest [Siyyid Káẓim] of the Pacha's fixed determination, and requested him to tell all the Persians to quit the town—This letter he sent by a confidential person, but it appears it never reached, as the Chief Priest declares he never wrote to him, although he requested him to come to Kerbella—'

Farrant goes on to say: 'The Pacha would not listen to the propositions of the Consul—H.R.H. The Zel-i Sultan (son of the late Shah of Persia, a refugee) accompanied by Hajee Seid Kausem Chief Priest, Seid Wahab Governor* of Kerbella, Seid Hossainee and Seid Nasseroola [Siyyid Naṣru'lláh], influential people of Kerbella, came to the Pacha's camp at Mossaib and remained four days—The Pacha told them he did not wish to injure the people, that Kerbella was in rebellion and belonged to the Sultan . . .' However, he was willing to make concessions, should the people of Karbilá submit to his rule and let soldiers be stationed in their city.

Farrant further relates: 'The Pacha told His R.H. the Zel i Sultan and Chief Priest before leaving his camp to warn all Persians to separate themselves from the Geramees (and gave the Prince a paper to that effect) that if they could not leave the town, they should retire altogether to one

* The nominal Governor. He was either willingly or by force of circumstances allied to the rebels.

quarter of it, or else with their families and property seek protection in the Courts of the tombs of Hoossein and Abbas, for he was determined to proceed to extremities if the Kerbellai's refused to submit to his orders . . .'

Farrant reports a second excursion by Ḥájí Siyyid Káẓim and 'Alí-Sháh, the Ẓillu's-Sulṭán, on behalf of the people of Karbilá, this time to the camp of Sa'du'lláh Páshá, the Colonel commissioned by Najíb Páshá to invest the city. 'About the 1st January [1843],' writes Farrant, 'the Persian Consul accompanied by Seid Ibrahim Kasveenee* arrived at Najib Pacha's camp at Mossaib from Bagdad—The army had now been eleven days before Kerbella and much fighting had taken place, and many on both sides had been killed.' The talks which Mullá 'Abdu'l-'Azíz (Persian Consul) and Siyyid Ibráhím had with Najíb Páshá bore no result, and as Farrant reports: 'The Consul and Chief Priest returned to Bagdad, they had been four or five days in the Pacha's camp—The Chief Priest in Kerbella Hajee Seid Kausem it is said (he told me also the same thing) wrote to the Persian Consul and Seid Ibrahim Kasveenee begging the former to come on to Kerbella, that "his presence was necessary, it was the hour of danger"—This letter was received by them after they had quitted the Pacha's camp about two hours. Rumours in the town were very prevalent, that the Shah of Persia was sending an army of twenty thousand men to their assistance, which gave great confidence to the Persians inside—Persians have informed me that they heard these reports and many believed them, also they have most positively assured me that their Consul never wrote or communicated with them, and on learning, that he had returned to Bagdad, did not consider there was any danger. The Consul asserts he wrote to the Chief Priest Hajee Seid Kausem, which the latter most positively denies . . .

* Siyyid Ibráhím-i-Qazvíní, the adversary of Siyyid Káẓim, who had left Karbilá altogether during this turbulent period.

'... The walls were daily crowded,' Farrant writes, 'by the inhabitants who vented the grossest abuse on the Sultan, and cursed the soldiers and their religion. The chief people in Kerbella did all in their power to excite the religious feelings of the Sheeahs against the Soonies, the Priests also were most active, I have been told, and as they could not fight, repaired any damages the walls might receive. They prayed also in the Mosques encouraging and exciting the people by telling them it was a religious war.'

And then came the final assault. Farrant reports: 'Before daylight on the 13 January the storming party moved from Camp accompanied by the main body which halted at the battery, a soldier advanced and clambered up the breach, observing that the guards had left their posts, and the few who remained were asleep at the bottom of the wall round a fire—he returned to the Seraskier and reported what he had seen—

'The storming party was then ordered to move forward ...'

There was panic and slaughter. Farrant states that the sanctuary of the tomb of 'Abbás was violated, but Sa'du'lláh Pá<u>sh</u>á personally intervened to prevent the desecration of the Shrine of Imám Ḥusayn. The boastful leaders fled the city and as Farrant puts it: 'The principal cause of the late affair at Kerbella may be ascribed to the chiefs of that place who supported the Geramees in opposition to the Government, and in the time of danger withdrew from the contest and left the innocent and helpless to the fury of the soldiers.' 'Many flung themselves over the walls and were dashed to pieces,' Farrant reports, 'whilst others sought shelter in the houses of H.R.H. The Zil i Sultan and Hajee Seid Kausem [Siyyid Káẓim] Chief Priest, the latter shewed me a court in his house where 66 persons of all ages and sexes were suffocated, or crushed to death flying from the fury of the soldiers ...'

Farrant further reports: 'No Prince of the Royal blood nor any Persian of rank were [sic] killed, the sufferers were all of the poorer classes, small shopkeepers and labourers, also a few learned men—The wife of Prince Holakoo Meerza [Hulákú Mírzá] was severely wounded by a soldier (she is closely connected with the Shah of Persia being a daughter of the late Hoossein Ali Meerza Prince Governor of Fars) . . . The Secretary of Seid Ibrahim Kasveenee Chief Priest; Seid Mahomed Ali Moosvee [Siyyid Muḥammad-'Alíy-i-Músaví] was seized by the soldiers and forced to carry outside the walls some plunder for them, he stated who he was, but it was of no avail, on arriving outside the gate, they cut off his head and took it to the cashier of the Seraskier Pacha for a reward—he was a young man much respected . . . The house of Alee Werdee Khan ['Alí-Virdí Khán] (an uncle of the present Shah) was also entered by the soldiers, this house was defended by the Arabs. The Khan jumped into a well to save his life, one of his servants went and informed the Seraskier who immediately sent some men to his relief—The Khan was taken to the Seraskier nearly dead with cold, who sent him into the haram [Shrine] of Hoossein for safety—Why the Khan did not leave the town before the siege is a mystery, it is said that he was very active in advising the Persians to remain in the town—'

The exaggerated reports from Mullá 'Abdu'l-'Azíz, the Persian Agent in Baghdád, had served to heighten the crisis. He had apparently been slack in the exercise of his duties and when the siege was over, alarmed by the magnitude of the disaster, he endeavoured to make a quick getaway from Baghdád. Although the following report which he made to the Prime Minister of Írán, Ḥájí Mírzá Áqásí, is unreliable and highly-coloured, it is of sufficient interest to reproduce.

'In short,' he wrote, 'there is no one left in Kerbelah, and of those who are alive, they are either wounded, naked or destitute of property. According to what is described, about

5,000 persons were killed in the shrine of Abbass,* and property pillaged is beyond estimate—no one has anything left. Whatever the people of Persia possessed was brought to this place; afterwards it will become known, what quantity of Persian property was there . . . Whatever Ali Nakee Meerza [‘Alí-Naqí Mírzá] and Imam Verdee Meerza [Imám-Virdí Mírzá] (sons of Fatteh Ali Shah [Fatḥ-‘Alí Sh͟áh]) possessed was plundered even to the stripping naked their wives . . . The wives of the people who were not killed were made captives . . . Moollah Ali a person belonging to Ali Pasha, who is at present in the service of Mahomed Nejeeb Pasha, interceded for the women—Sadoollah Pasha (Colonel) replied, that "the troops being without women, they must remain some nights with them, after which we will dismiss them" . . .

'Besides what I have related, the two shrines were converted into barracks, and all the troops which are in Kerbelah have been quartered in the two shrines with their horses and cattle—They have tied their cattle in the apartments of the shrine and the college, and the troops have made their own quarters in the corridor and private apartments, and twice a day their drums and band play within the shrine—On whatever persons they wish to inflict punishment, it is done within the shrine of Imam Hoossein . . . The remainder of the Sheeahs, who are in Nejeff, Hillah, Kazimeyn and Bagdad are dispirited to such a degree, that they have not the courage to weep at this calamity—

'All those who were in the private apartments of Hajee Syed Kazim (Chief Priest) and in the house of Ali Shah (Zil.e.Sultan) remained in safety—at the most about 200 persons were killed in the outer apartments of Hajee Syed Kazim . . .

'From the commencement to the close of the siege occupied 24 days—and from the day that the Pasha informed me,

* ‘Abbás was a brother of Imám Ḥusayn.

he would send troops against Kerbelah until they arrived there occupied 15 days, and notwithstanding my wishes that he would delay, until the people of Persia should quit Kerbelah, he neither gave any delay nor opportunity for their doing so . . .

'On account of these circumstances, the stay of your devoted servant in Bagdad is needless—As yet I have received no money from Kermanshah, if you were graciously pleased to grant it, and wrote to the Shoojah ood. dowleh [Shujá'u'd-Dawlih], to send some money speedily to me your devoted servant, to pay some of my debts,* it is possible that I might be able to bring the Zil.i.Sultan† along with me.'[3]

'The latest accounts from Kerbella,' wrote Lt.-Col. Farrant at the end of his long report on the siege, 'state the town to be perfectly quiet and its population daily increasing.'

* Mullá 'Abdu'l-'Azíz dared not go to Karbilá because he feared his creditors. Siyyid Káẓim had urged him to visit the holy city.

† Ẓillu's-Sulṭán was not in a distressed condition, and his presence in Írán was not welcomed.

APPENDIX 2

THE MARTYRDOM OF THE BÁB

The martyrdom of the Báb was reported by Lt.-Col. Sheil to Lord Palmerston, the British Foreign Secretary, on July 22nd 1850:

'The founder of this sect has been executed at Tabreez—He was killed by a volley of musketry, and his death was on the point of giving his religion a lustre which would have largely increased its proselytes. When the smoke and dust cleared away after the volley, Bâb was not to be seen, and the populace proclaimed that he had ascended to the skies—The balls had broken the ropes by which he was bound, but he was dragged from the recess where after some search, he was discovered, and shot.

'His death according to the belief of his disciples will make no difference, as Bâb must always exist.'[1]

At the time of the martyrdom of the Báb, R. W. Stevens, the British Consul, was absent from Tabríz, and his brother, George, was left in charge of the Consulate. The latter had failed to report the event to Sheil. On July 24th, R. W. Stevens, back at his post, rectified that omission and added that the body of the Báb and His disciple had been 'thrown into the Town ditch where they were devoured by dogs.'[2] Sheil wrote to Palmerston, on August 15th, that 'Although the advice and opinions of foreign agents are generally unpalatable to the Persian Minister, I nevertheless think it my duty to bring under his observation any flagrant abuse or outrage that reaches my knowledge. I persuade myself that on such occasions notwithstanding the absence of acknowledgement on the part of the Ameer-i-Nizam [Mírzá Taqí Khán, the Grand Vizier], he may perhaps privately take steps for applying a remedy.' He went on to say that the Consul at Tabríz had reported that the body of the Báb, 'by order of the Ameer-i-Nizam's brother, was thrown into the ditch of the town to be devoured by dogs, which actually happened.'[3] He enclosed the copy of the letter he had written to the Grand Vizier on this subject. This is what he wrote to Mírzá Taqí Khán:

'Your Excellency is aware of the warm interest taken by the British Government in all that concerns the honor, respectability and credit of this Government, and it is on this account I make you acquainted with a recent occurrence in Tabreez which perhaps has not been brought to Your Excellency's knowledge—The execution of the Pretender Bab in that city was accompanied by a circumstance which if published in the Gazettes of Europe would throw the utmost discredit on the Persian Ministers. After that person was put to death, his body by orders of the Vezeer.i.Nizam was thrown into the ditch of the town to be devoured by dogs, which actually happened—This act resembles the deeds of bye gone ages, and could not I believe now occur in any country between China and England—Feeling satisfied that it did not receive Your Excellency's sanction, and knowing what sentiments it would excite in Europe, I have thought it proper to write this friendly communication, not to let you remain in ignorance of the occurrence.'[4]

Palmerston wrote back on October 8th: '. . . Her Majesty's Government approve of your having called the attention of the Ameer-i-Nizam . . . to the manner in which the corpse of the Pretender Bâb was treated after his execution at Tabreez.'[5]

APPENDIX 3

PRELUDE TO THE EPISODE OF NAYRÍZ

On February 12th 1850, Lt.-Col. Sheil, back at his post in Ṭihrán after a long leave of absence, reported to Lord Palmerston:

'. . . a serious outbreak lately took place at Yezd, which however the Governor of that city with the assistance of the priesthood succeeded in quelling—

'The exciters of the insurrection were the partizans of the new Sect called Babee, who assembled in such numbers as to force the Governor to take refuge in the citadel, to which they laid siege—The Moollas conscious that the progress of Babeeism is the decay of their own supremacy determined to rescue the Governor, and summoning the populace in the name of religion to attack this new Sect of infidels, the Babees were overthrown and forced to take flight to the adjoining province of Kerman . . .

'The tenets of this new religion seem to be spreading in Persia—Bab the founder, a native of Sheeraz, who has assumed this fictitious name, is imprisoned in Azerbijan, but in every large town he has disciples, who with the fanaticism or fortitude so often seen among the adherents of new doctrines, are ready to meet death . . . Bab declares himself to be Imam Mehdee, the last Imam, who disappeared from human sight but is to reappear on earth—His decrees supersede the Koran among his disciples, who not only revere him as the head of their faith, but also obey him as the temporal Sovereign of the world, to whom all other monarchs must submit—Besides this inconvenient doctrine, they have adopted other tenets pernicious to society . . .

'Conversion by the sword is not yet avowed, argument and inspiration from heaven being the present means of instilling or attaining faith in the Mission of Bab—If left to their own merits the not novel doctrines of this Preacher will doubtless sink into insignificancy, it is persecution only which can save them from neglect and contempt, and unluckily the proselytes are all of the Mahommedan faith, which is inflexible in the punishment of a relapsed Mussulman—Thus both the temporal and religious authorities have an interest in the extermination of this Sect.

'It is conjectured that in Teheran this religion has acquired votaries in every class, not even excluding the artillery and regular Infantry—Their numbers in this city, it is supposed, may amount to about two thousand.'[1]*

The incident at Yazd, which the British Minister was reporting to the Foreign Secretary, concerned the activities of a man named Muḥammad-'Abdu'lláh, who professed belief in the new Revelation. Vaḥíd was in Yazd at the time, fearlessly proclaiming the advent of the Qá'im. Navváb-i-Raḍaví, an influential man of the city, who hated Vaḥíd as much as Sa'ídu'l-'Ulamá had hated Quddús,† was plotting to destroy him. Despite Vaḥíd's injunction, Muḥammad-'Abdu'lláh went ahead with his own schemes which resulted in clashes with the civil authority, and his own death. Vaḥíd was forced to leave Yazd in the dead of night, on foot. His house in Yazd was pillaged, and his servant Ḥasan was seized and put to death. While horsemen sent by his adversaries were searching for him, he hid in the mountains; and by mountain tracks made his way to Bavánát in the province of Fárs. There were many in that area who gave him whole-hearted support, among them the renowned Ḥájí Siyyid Ismá'íl, the Shaykhu'l-Islám of Bavánát. Then by way of Fasá he approached the city of Nayríz.

* Part of this passage is also quoted on p. 178.

† See p. 176.

APPENDIX 4

THE SEVEN MARTYRS OF ṬIHRÁN

In the course of 1849, Prince Dolgorukov, the Russian Minister in Ṭihrán, had protested to the Persian Government that while going into the presence of the Sháh he had been forced to witness the dragging away of the writhing corpses of eight criminals, executed in front of the Sháh. Dolgorukov considered it an affront to him, the envoy of the Tsar, to be presented with such a spectacle. Sheil had backed Dolgorukov's protest.[1] Palmerston had, in turn, approved Sheil's action. On February 12th 1850, Prince Dolgorukov sent this report to Count Nesselrode in St. Petersburg:

'Minds are in an extraordinarily excited state due to the execution which has just taken place in the great square of Tihran. I have already once expressed my opinion that the method by which last year the troops of the Shah under the command of Prince Mahdi Quli Mirza exterminated the Babis will not lessen their fanaticism.

'From that time on the Government has learned that Tihran is full of these dangerous sectaries who do not recognize civil statutes and preach the partitioning of the property of those who do not join their doctrine. Becoming fearful for the social peace, the ministers of Persia decided to arrest some of these sectaries and, according to the common version, having received during the interrogation their confession of their faith, executed them. These persons, numbering seven, and arrested at random, since the Babis are counted already by thousands within the very capital, would by no means deny their faith and met death with an exultation which could only be explained as fanaticism brought to its extreme limit. The Assistant Minister of Foreign Affairs, Mirza Muhammad Ali, on the contrary affirms that those people have confessed nothing and that their silence was interpreted as a sufficient proof of their guilt.

'One can only regret the blindness of the Shah's authorities who imagine that such measures could extinguish religious fanaticism, as well as the injustice which guides their actions when examples of cruelty, with which they are trying to frighten the people, are committed without distinction against the first passer-by who falls into their hands . . .'[2]

Ten days later (February 22nd 1850), Sheil wrote to Palmerston that apparently the advice tendered by Her Majesty's Government that criminals should not be executed in the presence of the Sovereign had had some effect, because a few days before, seven Bábís, accused of conspiring to assassinate the Grand Vizier, had been put to death in public with no untoward incident. Sheil asserted that this fact proved the feasibility of public executions. Mírzá Taqí Khán had earlier stated that with executions in public there was the risk of a malefactor being snatched and spirited away. Sheil felt, however, that on this occasion there was sympathy for the executed, because the story of a conspiracy to murder the Grand Vizier was not generally believed. He further observed that the Bábís had been offered their lives, were they to recant, and they had firmly refused to do so. His own comment to the Grand Vizier had been that executing the Bábís was the surest way of propagating their doctrines.[3]

Lord Palmerston in answer to Sheil stated that Her Majesty's Government was pleased to learn that Náṣiri'd-Dín Sháh had agreed with the advice not to have executions carried out in his presence, but added, 'the punishment of men for religious belief, besides being unjust and cruel, is also an erroneous practice, and tends to encourage and propagate the belief which it is intended to suppress.'[4]

APPENDIX 5

THE EPISODE OF ZANJÁN

The episode of Zanján covered the period from May to December 1850, and much engaged the attention of the British and Russian envoys. On May 25th Sheil reported to Palmerston: 'At Zenjan . . . an attempt at insurrection was made by the Sect of the Babees whose leader is the chief priest of the town—Five hours after the receipt of this intelligence a Battalion of Infantry 400 horse and three guns marched towards Zenjan—This is an instance unexampled in Persia of military celerity, which perhaps would not be surpassed in many countries of Europe.'[1] A month later, Sheil reported: 'The insurrection at Zenjan has not yet been quelled. The Bâbees of that city continue to defend themselves with the zeal of proselytes and the contempt of life inculcated by their faith . . .'[2]

Prince Dolgorukov, the Russian Minister, commented on July 31st: 'The Government has exhausted all possible means to compel the Babis to submit voluntarily. Muhammad Ali who heads the two or three hundred of these fanatics in Zanjan, has fortified himself in one of the quarters of the said town and terrifies the inhabitants. The Amir was finally forced to take energetic measures, and the former beglerbegi of Tabriz, Muhammad Khan, has just been sent against them with an army of 2000 men and four cannons.'[3] Dolgorukov had grossly underestimated the number of the Bábís. (See pp. 185–6.)

Sheil wrote on August 22nd: 'The Bâbees of Zenjan still continue to maintain that nearly defenceless city against the

Shah's troops.'[4] On September 5th he reported: '. . . these fanatics are reduced to a few hundred fighting men, they continue to maintain a hopeless contest with undaunted resolution, refusing submission on any terms . . .'[5]

Dolgorukov reported on September 14th: 'The Babis, who are engaged there in a life and death struggle against the troops of the Shah, are still resisting the attacks of Muhammad Khan, and one can only wonder at the fierceness with which they meet the danger of their situation. Their leader Mulla Muhammad Ali, has appealed to the Turkish Minister, Sami Effendi, and also to Colonel Sheil for their mediation. However, my English colleague is of the opinion that it would be very difficult to force the Persian Government to consent to foreign intervention in favor of the above mentioned sectaries.'[6] On October 6th, the Russian Minister was in a petulant mood: 'I think it would have been better if they [the Persian Government] had given more serious attention to the affairs of Zanjan. The Babis have been fighting against 6000 of the Shah's best troops for almost five months now, and Muhammad Khan, who is already master of three quarters of the city, cannot take the quarter which they have fortified themselves and are defending . . . with a heroism and a fury worthy of a better application.'[7] In his dispatch of November 9th, Dolgorukov wrote: 'New military units have just been dispatched against the Babis of Zanjan. This time the Governor of that city, a brother of the Shah's mother, Amir Aslan Khan, is accused of provoking the resistance, which the Babis offer the Shah's army, by his incautious behavior.'[8] And, at last, on December 26th Dolgorukov could report: 'The Zanjan disturbances have ended. After a siege which lasted for almost six months the Shah's troops have destroyed the center of the rebellion. The Babis who defended themselves to the last, and whose numbers were finally reduced to twenty men, who sought refuge in a cellar, were torn to pieces. In addition to monetary expenditures, this struggle has cost Persia 1500 in killed and disabled.'[9]

Meanwhile Sheil had been reporting on September 25th: 'The disciples of Bâb have barricaded a portion of that town, from which they cannot be expelled without a greater loss of life than the assailants seem willing to encounter.'[10] And he wrote on October 25th: 'Contrary to all rational expectation the small portion of Zenjan occupied by the Bâbees continues to set at defiance the efforts of the Shah's troops to expel that sect from the City.' In the same dispatch he stated that 'General Sir Henry Bethune who visited the scene of operations, expressed a conviction that three hours with ordinary troops would finish the affair . . .'[11] Bethune was the man who had helped Muḥammad Sháh to his throne. Sheil seems to have become wearied of reporting on Zanján, for on November 23rd he wrote: 'I continue unable to make any variation in my reports relative to Zenjan—The same feeble ineffectual attempts at assault, the same repulses still mark the progress of the siege.' Then he made the extraordinary assertion that it had been affirmed that the defenders of Zanján were not Bábís at all, that they had been heard to 'proclaim from the walls in hearing of the troops, the creed that "there is no God but God, and Mahomed is his prophet."' Those men were fighting, it was said, because of the enormities perpetrated by the troops. Even more extraordinary is this fantastic and incredibly false statement in that same dispatch of November 23rd: 'Moolla Mahomed Ali, their chief, has the reputation of having proclaimed himself to be the true Bâb, and his predecessor to have been an impostor.'[12] On December 16th Sheil wrote to Palmerston: 'Her Majesty's Consul at Tabreez having informed me that great atrocities are committed at Zenjan by the soldiery particularly by their shocking treatment of such women as have been captured, I brought the circumstances to the knowledge of the Persian Minister—

The Ameer-i.Nizam thanked me for the information, and said he would take immediate steps for preventing such barbarous proceedings, which are entirely opposed to his sentiments and feelings—' '. . . the mode in which my communication was received by the Ameer. i. Nizam shows an improvement in his tone, and in the temper with which he listens to suggestions of the above nature.'[13]

On December 24th, Sheil reported to Palmerston: 'This protracted siege, if siege it can be called, is inexplicable—An English gentleman who lately passed through Zenjan informed me a few days ago that the portion of the town occupied by the Bâbees is confined to three or four houses, and that their numbers are utterly insignificant—They have adopted a mode of defence which seems to exceed the military skill of the Persian commanders—The entire of the space included within these houses is mined or excavated and connected by passages. Here the Bâbees live in safety from the shot and shells of the assailants, who evidently have no predilection for underground warfare.'[14]

Lord Palmerston on February 11th 1851 wrote to Sheil that '. . . Her Majesty's Government approve of your having called the attention of the Ameer-i-Nizam . . . to the acts of violence committed by the Persian Troops against Zenjan.'[15]

And finally, here is the last report of Sheil on the episode of Zanján. It is dated January 6th 1851. 'I have the honor to report to Your Lordship that Zenjan has been at length captured—Moolla Mahomed Ali, the leader of the insurgents, had received a wound in the arm, which terminated in his death—His followers dismayed by the loss of their chief, yielded to an assault which their relaxation in the energy of their defence encouraged the commander of the Shah's troops to make—This success was followed by a great atrocity—The pusillanimity of the troops, which the events of this siege had rendered so notorious, was equalled by their ferocity—All the captives were bayonetted by the soldiers in cold blood, to avenge . . . the slaughter of their comrades—Religious hatred may have conspired with the feelings excited by a blood feud, which among the tribes are very strong, to cause this ruthless act—Four hundred persons are said to have perished in this way, among whom it is believed were some women and children—Of the fact itself there can be no doubt, as it is admitted by the Government in its notification of the reduction of the city, though it may be presumed that in the number there is exaggeration.'[16]

APPENDIX 6

LORD PALMERSTON'S ENQUIRY

Lord Palmerston wrote to Sheil on May 2nd 1850:

'I have to instruct you to furnish me with a more detailed account than that contained in your despatch No. 20, of the 12th of February, of the difference between the tenets of the new sect of Bab, and those of the established religion of Persia.'[1]

Sheil answered Lord Palmerston on June 21st:

'In conformity with Your Lordship's instructions I have the honor to enclose an account of the new Sect of Bab—The statement contained in the enclosure numbered No. 1 is taken from an account given to me by a disciple of Bab, and which I have no doubt is correct. The other is extracted from a letter from a chief Priest in Yezd, and cannot be trusted—

'This is the simplest of religions. Its tenets are summed up in materialism, communism, and the absolute indifference of good and evil, and of all human actions.'[2]

Unfortunately both accounts sent to Palmerston are highly inaccurate. Moreover, Sheil's own comments indicate that he himself did not have an open mind. Plainly the account given to him, as he had stated, 'by a disciple of Bab', was not a verbatim rendering into English, but a reconstruction with interpolations, as witnessed by these two sentences: 'They believe in Mahomed as a Prophet and in the divine origin of the Koran: but Bâb contends that until this moment only the apparent meaning of the Koran was understood and that he has come to explain the real secret and divine essence of God's word. But it will be seen in a subsequent part of this account that the words *Prophet* and *Divine origin* have no signification.' Further evidence is provided by Sheil's rough notes with marginal additions[3] from which the account by a Bábí is drawn.

What disciple of the Báb would say: 'The intercourse of the sexes is very nearly promiscuous—There is no form of marriage; a man and woman live together as long as they please and no longer, and if another man desires to have possession of that woman, it rests with her, not with the man who has been her husband, if he can be so termed:—A man may have wives without limit; a woman has a similar licence.' This Bábí, unless his account was garnished, was either a nihilist of sorts, or totally ignorant of what the teaching of the Báb was.

Equally extraordinary, confused and contrary to the Writings of the Báb in the Persian and Arabic *Bayán* are the following lines in that account by a Bábí: 'There is no hell or heaven, therefore there is no hereafter—annihilation is man's doom in fact—he with every living and vegetable thing, in short everything whatever, will be absorbed in the Divinity—Everything is God, and therefore *absorbed*, which is the phrase of the Soofees, who consider every thing is a reflection of God—Hell is suffered and heaven is enjoyed in this world; but there is no such thing as crime, nor of course virtue, only as they concern the relations of man and man in this world. A man's will is his Law in all things . . .

'The most absolute materialism seems to form the essence of their belief—God is one—Every individual substance and particle, living or not, is God, and the whole is God—and every individual thing, always was, always is, and always will be.'[4]

The account by the Chief Priest of Yazd, which was a vitriolic attack on the Báb and Vaḥíd, and which Sheil had ruled out in his letter to the Foreign Secretary as 'cannot be trusted', was not dissimilar, in some respects, to the account by 'a disciple of Bab'.

These extracts make it clear how misinformed was Lord Palmerston, the British Foreign Secretary, by the reports of his representative in Ṭihrán.

APPENDIX 7

MYTH-MAKING

The volume of writing in the West about the Bábí and Bahá'í Faiths is not insignificant. There are copious scholarly works on the subject in Russian, French and English. We have the works of Alexander Toumansky, Baron Rosen, Mírzá Kazem-Beg, Count Gobineau, A.-L.-M. Nicolas, and Edward Granville Browne. We also have attacks and refutations, but these latter categories belong to more recent years, when the Bahá'í Faith has been making considerable headway in the Western world.

There is another genre of writing which merits attention, if only for a negative reason. These writings do not enlighten; they create myths. Generally speaking, remarks by travellers and casual visitors to Írán fall within this category, but are by no means confined to such writers.

A sizable book could be compiled of the remarks and observations which are myth-making. Here we must be content with only a few extracts. Some of these solemn pronunciations are highly amusing, as with the following which is taken from a book by Arthur Arnold:*

'The measure of injustice and oppression which these courts of the Koran inflict upon the Christians may seem mild, in comparison with the treatment by which they suppress nonconformity within the pale of their own community. We have seen an example in the sentence of "a hundred sticks", which the incautious expression of

* 1833–1902, a radical politician and writer. M.P. for Salford and editor of *Echo*.

liberal views brought upon the friend of the Zil-i-Sultan [Ẓillu's-Sulṭán],* who added to free speech the wickedness of wearing trousers of European cut. There is, however, in Ispahan a surviving heresy, the most notable in Persia, which, when proved against a man, is almost a death warrant.†

'Early in the present century, a boy was born at Shiraz, the son of a grocer, whose name has not been preserved. Arrived at manhood, this grocer's son expounded his idea of a religion even more indulgent than that of Mahommed. He is known by the name of Bāb (the gate), and his followers are called Bābis. In 1850, Bāb had established some reputation as a prophet, and was surrounded by followers as ready to shed their blood in his defence as any who formed the body-guard of Mahommed in those early days at Medina, when he had gained no fame in battle, and had not conceived the plan of the Koran. Bāb was attacked as an enemy of God and man, and at last taken prisoner by the Persian Government, and sentenced to death. He was to be shot. Tied to a stake in Tabriz, he confronted the firing party and awaited death. The report of the muskets was heard, and Bāb felt himself wounded, but at liberty. He was not seriously hurt, and the bullets had cut the cord which bound him. Clouds of smoke hung about the spot where he stood, and probably he felt a gleam of hope that he might escape when he rushed from the stake into a neighbouring guardhouse. He had a great reputation, and very little was necessary to make soldiers and people believe that his life had been spared by a genuine miracle. Half the population of Persia would perhaps have become Bābis, had that guardhouse contained

* Prince Sulṭán Mas'úd Mírzá, the eldest son of Náṣiri'd-Dín Sháh, Governor-General of Iṣfahán and the adjoining provinces.

† At the time of Arnold's visit, Mírzá Asadu'lláh Khán, a Bahá'í, was the Vizier of Iṣfahán.

the entrance to a safe hiding place. But there was nothing of the sort. The poor wretch was only a man, and the soldiers saw he had no supernatural powers whatever. He was dragged again to the firing place and killed. But dissent is not to be suppressed by punishment, and of course Bābism did not die with him. Two years afterwards, when the present Shah was enjoying his favourite sport, and was somewhat in advance of his followers, three men rushed upon his Majesty and wounded him in an attempted assassination. The life of Nazr-ed-deen [Náṣiri'd-Dín] Shah, Kajar, was saved by his own quickness and by the arrival of his followers, who made prisoners of the assassins. They declared themselves Bābis, and gloried in their attempt to avenge the death of their leader and to propagate their doctrines by the murder of the Shah. The baffled criminals were put to death with the cruelty which the offences of this sect always meet with. Lighted candles were inserted in slits cut in their living bodies, and, after lingering long in agony, their tortured frames were hewn in pieces with hatchets.

'In most countries, the theory of punishment is, that the State, on behalf of the community, must take vengeance upon the offender. But in Persia it is otherwise. There, in accordance with the teaching of the Koran, the theory and basis of punishment is, that the relations of the victim must take revenge upon the actual or would-be murderers. In conformity with this idea, the Shah's chamberlain executed on his Majesty's behalf, and with his own hand, one of the conspirators. Yet the Bābis remain the terror and trouble of the Government of Ispahan, where the sect is reputed to number more followers than anywhere else in Persia. But many of them have, in the present day, transferred their allegiance from Bāb to Behar, a man who was lately, and may be at present, imprisoned at Acca, in Arabia, by the Turkish Government. Behar represents himself as God the Father in human form, and declares that Bāb occupies the same position, in regard to himself, that John the Baptist held to Jesus Christ. We were assured that there were respectable families in Ispahan who worship this imprisoned fanatic, who endanger their property and their lives by a secret devotion, which, if known, would bring them to destitution, and probably to a cruel death.'[1]

Our second extract is from a much weightier book written by an American diplomat, Mr. S. G. W. Benjamin, the first United States Minister accredited to Írán:*

'But the most remarkable sect now in Persia is probably that of the Bâbees, or followers of the Bâb. Their importance is not so much due to their numbers or political influence, as to the fact that the sect is of recent origin, full of proselyting zeal, and gaining converts every day in all parts of Persia, and latterly also in Turkey. The Bâbees present one of the most important religious phenomena of the age. It must be admitted, however, that they very strongly resemble in their communistic views the doctrines enounced [sic] by the famous Mazdâk [Mazdak], who was executed by Chosroes I after bringing the empire to the verge of destruction by the spread of his anarchical tenets.

'In 1810 was born Seyed Alee Mohammed, at Shirâz . . . Like all the founders of oriental religions, he began his career with a period of seclusion and meditation. He accepted Mahomet and Alee in the creed which he considered himself predestined to proclaim; but he added to this the declaration that their spirits had in turn entered into his own soul, and that he was therefore a great prophet,—the Bâb, who was to bring their gospel to a legitimate conclusion. It

* 'In the winter of 1882–1883 the author was appointed by President Arthur to the Legation in Persia, just created by Act of Congress. In 1885, with the accession of the Democratic party to power, he returned to private life, in accordance with the practice of the diplomatic service of the United States.'[2]

became his mission, therefore, to announce that all things were divine, and that he, the Bâb, was the incarnate presentment of the universal life. To this doctrine was added a socialism which formulated the equality of all, sweeping away social classes and distinctions, and ordaining a community of property, and also, at first, of wives. The new doctrines took hold of the heart of the masses; men and women of all ranks hastened to proclaim their yearning for something that promised to better their condition, by embracing the wild teachings of the Bâb . . . the Government could not long remain blind to the possible results if the movement were allowed to spread unchecked. Therefore, after several serious tumults, the Bâb was seized and executed at Tabreez. This only served to add fuel to the fire. A fierce persecution broke forth; but the Bâbees were not willing to submit tamely to suppression . . . The Bâbees are now obliged to practise their faith in secret, all of those in Persia being outwardly of the Sheäh sect. But their activity does not cease, and their numbers are increasing rapidly. The sect has also extended to Turkey. The leader of the Turkish branch resides at Constantinople.

'In Persia the title of the present head of the sect is Sob-e-Azêl [Ṣubḥ-i-Azal]. As his belief in the Bâb is a secret, his name is not mentioned in this connection . . . Just now there seems to be unusual activity among the Bâbees, emissaries or missionaries are secretly pervading the country, not only seeking to make proselytes but also presenting modifications in belief. The community in wives is no longer a practised tenet of the Bâb sect, while it is proclaimed with increasing emphasis that the Bâb is none other than God himself made manifest in the flesh.'[3]

The next extract is by another diplomat, General Sir Thomas Edward Gordon, who had once been the Military Attaché and Oriental Secretary of Queen Victoria's Legation in Ṭihrán, and wrote his book after a second visit to Írán:

'The Babi sect of Mohammedans, regarded as seceders from Islam, but who assert their claim to be only the advocates for Mohammedan Church reform, are at last better understood and more leniently treated—certainly at Tehran. They have long been persecuted and punished in the cruellest fashion, even to torture and death, under the belief that they were a dangerous body which aimed at the subversion of the State as well as the Church. But better counsels now prevail, to show that the time has come to cease from persecuting these sectarians, who, at all events in the present day, show no hostility to the Government; and the Government has probably discovered the truth of the Babi saying, that one martyr makes many proselytes . . .

'An acknowledged authority on the Bab, the founder of this creed, has written that he "directed the thoughts and hopes of his disciples to this world, not to an unseen world." From this it was inferred he did not believe in a future state, nor in anything beyond this life. Of course, among the followers of a new faith, liberal and broad in its views, continued fresh developments of belief must be expected; and with reference to the idea that the Babis think not of a hereafter, I was told that they believe in the reincarnation of the soul, the good after death returning to life and happiness, the bad to unhappiness. A Babi, in speaking of individual pre-existence, said to me, "You believe in a future state; why, then, should you not believe in a pre-existent state? Eternity is without beginning and without end." This idea of re-incarnation, generally affecting all Babis, is, of course, an extension of the original belief regarding the re-incarnation of the Bab, and the eighteen disciple-prophets who compose the sacred college of the sect . . .

'The Babi reform manifests an important advance upon

all previous modern Oriental systems in its treatment of woman. Polygamy and concubinage are forbidden, the use of the veil is discouraged, and the equality of the sexes is so thoroughly recognised that one, at least, of the nineteen sovereign prophets must always be a female. This is a return to the position of woman in early Persia, of which Malcolm speaks when he says that Quintus Curtius told of Alexander not seating himself in the presence of Sisygambis till told to do so by that matron, because it was not the custom in Persia for sons to sit in presence of their mother.'[4]

It must be said that Sir Thomas Gordon's long account of the Bábís (from which only a few passages are taken) is good in many respects; nevertheless, it perpetuates myths.

Finally, here are two extracts from a book* so highly rated that, when it was published in 1915, it was put on the 'Secret List' of the British Foreign Office, and kept there for more than a decade:

'A religious heresy which was destined to produce serious political consequences in Persia made its appearance during the later years of Muhammad Shāh: this was Bābism, the creed of the Bābis or followers of the Bāb. The founder was Saiyid 'Ali Muhammad, the son of a grocer of Shīrāz, who, being sent as a youth to represent his father at Būshehr, soon left that place on pilgrimage to Makkah and afterwards sat as a student at the feet of Hāji Saiyid Kāzim, the

* Lorimer, *Gazetteer of the Persian Gulf.* Gordon Lorimer was one of the ablest members of the Indian Political Department, and held various posts in the area of the Persian Gulf. In 1904, he was commissioned by the Government of India to prepare the Gazetteer. At the end of 1913, Lorimer replaced Sir Percy Z. Cox as Consul-General in Búshihr and Political Resident in the Persian Gulf. In February a mishap with a revolver caused his untimely death. The present writer well remembers the event. The Gazetteer was made ready for publication by Capt. R. L. Birdwood.

greatest Mujtahid of the day at Karbala. On the death of his teacher he returned to Būshehr, where he proclaimed himself a prophet, the 23rd May 1844 being accounted the date of his manifestation in that character.

'"He now assumed the title of the *Bāb*, or gate, through whom knowledge of the Twelfth Imam Mahdi could alone be attained. His pretensions undoubtedly became more extravagant as time proceeded, and he successfully announced himself as the Mahdi, as a re-incarnation of the prophet, and as a Revelation or Incarnation of God himself."* The Bābi faith was ecclesiastically proscribed throughout Persia; and massacres of its adherents, with counter-assassinations of leading persecutors, became the order of the day.'

'The new Bābi religion in Persia, of which the institution may be dated from 1844, the year in which Mīrza 'Ali Muhammad, commonly known as the Bāb, declared his mission, does not appear to have obtained as yet much hold on the coast of the Persian Gulf, notwithstanding that the Bāb visited Būshehr at an early stage in his public career. It was reported that at Būshehr there were in 1905 only about 50 Bābis, chiefly employed in the Customs Department or in the Artillery; a very few others were found at the ports of Bandar 'Abbas and Lingeh, and possibly at Shehr-i-Vīrān in the Līrāvi district; but at Baghdād, which was the headquarters of the Bābi religion from 1853 to 1864, it did not appear that there are any. It is probable, however, that Bābis are to be found in places where their existence has not been ascertained.'[5]

* Curzon, *Persia and the Persian Question*, Vol. I, p. 497.

BIBLIOGRAPHY

'Abdu'l-Bahá. *Memorials of the Faithful*. Translated from the original Persian text and annotated by Marzieh Gail. Wilmette, Illinois: Bahá'í Publishing Trust, 1971.

Arberry, Arthur J. *The Koran Interpreted*. Vol. One, Suras I–XX; Vol. Two, Suras XXI–CXIV. London: George Allen & Unwin Ltd., 1955; 2nd imp. 1963.

Arnold, Arthur. *Through Persia by Caravan*. Vol. II. London: Tinsley Brothers, 1877.

Bahá'í World, The. An International Record. Vol. VIII, 1938–1940. Wilmette, Illinois: Bahá'í Publishing Committee, 1942.

Bahá'u'lláh. *Gleanings from the Writings of Bahá'u'lláh*. Trans. by Shoghi Effendi. Wilmette, Illinois: Bahá'í Publishing Trust, 1935; rev. ed. 1952; repr. 1969. London: Bahá'í Publishing Trust, 1949.

—— *The Kitáb-i-Íqán. The Book of Certitude*. Trans. by Shoghi Effendi. Wilmette, Illinois: Bahá'í Publishing Trust, 1931; 2nd ed. 1950; 3rd repr. 1960. London: Bahá'í Publishing Trust, 2nd ed. 1961.

Balyuzi, H. M. *'Abdu'l-Bahá*. The Centre of the Covenant of Bahá'u'lláh. London: George Ronald, 1971; 2nd repr. 1972 (Oxford).

—— *Bahá'u'lláh*, a brief life, followed by an essay entitled The Word Made Flesh. London: George Ronald, 1963; 4th repr. 1973 (Oxford).

—— *Edward Granville Browne and the Bahá'í Faith*. London: George Ronald, 1970.

BENJAMIN, S. G. W. *Persia and the Persians*. London: John Murray, 1887.

BROWNE, E. G. *A Literary History of Persia*. In four volumes. Vol. IV: *Persian Literature in Modern Times*. Cambridge University Press, 1924.

—— (ed.) *Materials for the Study of the Bábí Religion*. Cambridge University Press, 1918; repr. 1961.

—— (ed.) *The Táríkh-i-Jadíd or New History of Mírzá 'Alí Muḥammad the Báb*, by Mírzá Ḥuseyn of Hamadán, trans. from the Persian, with an Introduction, Illustrations, and Appendices. Cambridge University Press, 1893.

—— (ed.) *A Traveller's Narrative written to illustrate the Episode of the Báb*. Edited in the original Persian, and translated into English, with an Introduction and Explanatory Notes. Vol. I, Persian Text. Vol. II, English Translation and Notes. Cambridge University Press, 1891.

—— *A Year Amongst the Persians*: Impressions as to the Life, Character and Thought of the People of Persia, received during twelve months' residence in that country in the years 1887–8. London: A. & C. Black, 1893. 2nd ed. Cambridge University Press, 1926. 3rd ed. London: A. & C. Black, 1959.

CHEYNE, T. K. *The Reconciliation of Races and Religions*. London: Adam & Charles Black, 1914.

CURZON, G. N. *Persia and the Persian Question*. In two volumes. London: Longmans, Green and Co., 1892. Frank Cass & Co. Ltd., 1966.

FLANDIN, EUGÈNE-NAPOLÉON and COSTE, PASCAL. *Voyage en Perse* pendant les années 1840 et 1841. Paris, 1851.

GOBINEAU, M. LE COMTE DE. *Les Religions et les Philosophies dans l'Asie Centrale*. Paris, 1865 and 1866.

GORDON, SIR THOMAS EDWARD. *Persia Revisited (1895)*. London: Edward Arnold, 1896.

KAZEMZADEH, FIRUZ. *Russia and Britain in Persia, 1864–1914*. New Haven and London: Yale University Press, 1968.

KELLY, J. B. *Britain and the Persian Gulf.* 1795–1880. Oxford: The Clarendon Press, 1968.

LAYARD, SIR HENRY. *Early Adventures in Persia, Susiana, and Babylonia.* In two volumes. London: John Murray, 1887.

LORIMER, J. G. *Gazetteer of the Persian Gulf, 'Oman, and Central Arabia.* In two volumes. Calcutta, 1915 and 1908. Repr. Farnborough, Hants. and Shannon, Ireland: Gregg International Publishers Ltd and Irish University Press, 1970.

NABÍL-I-A'ẒAM (Muḥammad-i-Zarandí). *The Dawn-Breakers.* Nabíl's Narrative of the Early Days of the Bahá'í Revelation. Wilmette, Illinois: Bahá'í Publishing Trust, 1932; Repr. 1953. London: Bahá'í Publishing Trust, 1953.

NICOLAS, A.-L.-M. *Seyyèd Ali Mohammed dit le Bâb.* Paris: Dujarric & Cie., 1905.

SALE, GEORGE (ed.) *The Korân.* Trans. into English from the Original Arabic, with Explanatory Notes. London: Frederick Warne and Co. Ltd., 1927.

SHEIL, LADY MARY LEONORA. *Glimpses of Life and Manners in Persia.* London: John Murray, 1856.

SHOGHI EFFENDI. *God Passes By.* Wilmette, Illinois: Bahá'í Publishing Trust, 1944; 5th repr. 1965.

—— *The World Order of Bahá'u'lláh.* Wilmette, Illinois: Bahá'í Publishing Trust, 1938; rev. 1955; 2nd imp. 1965.

SOHRÁB, AḤMAD. *Risáliy-i-Tis'a-'Ashariyyih.* Nineteen Discourses on the Báb and His two heralds: Shaykh Aḥmad-i-Aḥsá'í and Siyyid Káẓim-i-Rashtí. Cairo, 1919.

The reader is also referred to bibliographies contained in the following works (listed above):

Balyuzi, *Edward Granville Browne and the Bahá'í Faith*, pp. 123–5.

Browne, *Materials for the Study of the Bábí Religion*, Sec. III, pp. 175–243.

Browne (ed.), *A Traveller's Narrative*, Vol. II, Note A, pp. 173–211.

Nabíl-i-A'ẓam, *The Dawn-Breakers*, pp. 491–3 (Brit.), pp. 669–71 (U.S.).

NOTES

Full details of authors and titles are given in the bibliography. Page numbers are given for the American and British editions of Nabíl-i-A'ẓam, *The Dawn-Breakers*. All Foreign Office documents (reference F.O.) are held by the Public Record Office, London. They are Crown copyright and appear verbatim by kind permission of the Controller of Her Majesty's Stationery Office.

Prologue I and II

1. See Sohráb, *Risáliy-i-Tis'a-'Ashariyyih*, p. 13, for an account of Shaykh Aḥmad's discourses. (This source is discussed in Balyuzi, *'Abdu'l-Bahá*, p. 417.)

2. *ibid.*, p. 14.

3. See note 1 above, pp. 19–20.

4. F.O. 248/108 of May 15th 1843, enclosed in letter of May 20th 1843 to Sheil.

5. *The Dawn-Breakers*, p. 33 (Brit.), p. 45 (U.S.).

6. Sheil served as the British Minister in Ṭihrán from August 1842 to February 1853, except for a period of leave from October 1847 to November 1849, when Col. Farrant deputised for him. Sheil was knighted in 1855.

7. F.O. 248/113.

8. The other pretenders were Ḥusayn-'Alí Mírzá, the Farmán-Farmá, Governor-General of Fárs, and Ḥasan-'Alí Mírzá, the Shujá'u's-Salṭanih, Governor General of Kirmán, both sons of Fatḥ-'Alí Sháh. Three of the sons of the Farmán-Farmá managed to take themselves to London.

9. Sir Henry Layard (1817–1894) was the discoverer of the ancient city of Nineveh. He was elected to the British parliament as a Liberal, and served a term as the Under-Secretary of State for Foreign Affairs. In 1877 he was appointed Ambassador in Constantinople. His account is taken from *Early Adventures in Persia, Susiana, and Babylonia*, Vol. I, pp. 257–61.

10. The Ambassador recalled was Sir John MacNeill and the quarrel between Írán and Britain was over the city of Hirát. This beautiful city had always been considered an integral part of the province of Khurásán, but since the assassination of Nádir Sháh, the Afshár king, in 1747, Hirát had passed into possession of Afghán rulers. Muḥammad Sháh was intent on regaining Ḥirát, but Anglo-Russian rivalry and the British fear of Russian designs on India, hitherto almost non-existent, had become dominant factors in the international scene, bound to shadow the destiny of Írán; the British believed that the acquisition of Hirát by the Persians would, in the main, benefit Russia. They took counter-measures in the Persian Gulf and occupied the island of Khárg, close to Búshihr.

11. F.O. 60/95 of February 14th 1843.

12. *ibid.*

Chapter 1: All Hail Shíráz

Opening quotation: Gertrude Lowthian Bell (1868–1926), *Poems from the Divan of Hafiz*, Wm. Heinemann Ltd., London, 1897, No. xxx.

1. Browne, *A Year Amongst the Persians*, (1926 ed.), p. 284.

2. Curzon, *Persia and the Persian Question*, Vol. I, p. 497, n. 2.

3. Browne (ed.), *A Traveller's Narrative*, Vol. II, p. 309.

4. Since they originated from the small town of Baraghán, they were known as Baraghání.

5. Qurratu'l-'Ayn's words are quoted in *The Dawn-Breakers*, p. 56 (Brit.), pp. 81–2 (U.S.); and in verse form in *A Persian Anthology*, trans. by E. G. Browne, ed. by E. Denison Ross, Methuen & Co., London, 1927, p. 72.

Chapter 2: He Whom They Sought

Opening quotation: T. K. Cheyne, *The Reconciliation of Races and Religions*, p. 74.

1. Mír Muḥammad-Riḍá's father was named Mír Naṣru'lláh, his grandfather Mír Fatḥu'lláh, and his great-grandfather Mír Ibráhím.

2. For details of this unedifying transaction, see Kazemzadeh, *Russia and Britain in Persia, 1864–1914*, ch. 4. The contract was signed on March 8th 1890.

3. Translated by H. M. Balyuzi.

4. Shaykh Muḥammad was known as Shaykh 'Ábid, and also as

Shaykhuná and Shaykh-i-Anám. That his real name was Muḥammad is attested by this verse in the Arabic *Bayán*, one of the last works of the Báb: 'Say O Muḥammad, My teacher, do not beat me ere my years have gone beyond five.'

His school was in the quarter called Bázár-i-Murgh (Poultry Market), housed in a mosque-like structure which went by the name of Qahviy-i-Awlíyá'. It was close to the house of Ḥájí Mírzá Siyyid 'Alí, the uncle-guardian of the Báb. In its courtyard were a number of graves: three were particularly revered as those of saintly personages, one of whom was called Awlíyá'—though no one really knew whose were the graves.

It is known that Shaykh 'Ábid wrote a monograph on the childhood of the Báb, but the manuscript has always been in the possession of people not well-disposed to the Faith of the Báb and Bahá'u'lláh, and they have persistently refused to give it up or to divulge its contents. Shaykh 'Ábid was also destined in later years to accept the Faith proclaimed by his former Pupil.

5. Account taken from Mírzá Abu'l Faḍl's unpublished writings.

6. Nicolas, *Seyyèd Ali Mohammed Dit le Báb*, pp. 189–90.

7. Written in several volumes during the reign of Náṣiri'd-Dín Sháh by Lisánu'l-Mulk of Káshán, whose soubriquet was Sipihr.

8. *The Dawn-Breakers*, pp. 20–2 (Brit.), pp. 25–9 (U.S.).

9. *ibid.*, pp. 22–3 (Brit.), p. 30 (U.S.).

10. Ḥájí Mírzá 'Alí's father was named Mírzá 'Ábid.

11. By Dhikr, he means Himself. Repeatedly in the *Qayyúmu'l-Asmá'*, the Báb refers to Himself as Dhikr, and was known to His followers as Dhikru'lláh-al-A'ẓam (Mention of God, the Most Great), or Dhikru'lláh-al-Akbar (Mention of God, the Greatest), and sometimes as Ḥaḍrat-i-Dhikr. 'Ḥaḍrat' prefixed to the name of a Manifestation of God has been translated as 'His Holiness'. But this English rendering is totally inadequate, for 'Ḥaḍrat' has no English equivalent when placed prior to the name of a Manifestation of God. It conveys also the sense of His Honour, His Eminence, His Excellency, and the like.

12. From the *Qayyúmu'l-Asmá'*, translated by H. M. Balyuzi.

Chapter 3: Ṭihrán

Opening quotations: Bahá'u'lláh, (1) *Gleanings*, LVI (2) *Kitáb-i-Íqán*, p. 161 (Brit.), p. 252 (U.S.).

1. *The Dawn-Breakers*, p. 58 (Brit.), pp. 86–7 (U.S.).
2. *ibid.*, p. 66 (Brit.), p. 96 (U.S.).
3. Two works of the Báb are entitled *Bayán* (Utterance): the larger one is in Persian, and the other which is much shorter is in Arabic.
4. *The Dawn-Breakers*, p. 69 (Brit.), p. 99 (U.S.).
5. *ibid.*, p. 70 (Brit.), pp. 100–1 (U.S.).
6. *ibid.*, pp. 71–4 (Brit.), pp. 104–8 (U.S.).
7. See Foreword, paragraph 4.
8. Shoghi Effendi, *God Passes By*, p. 9.

Chapter 4: The First Martyr

Opening quotation: T. S. Eliot, 'Choruses from *The Rock*', I. 'The Eagle soars in the summit of Heaven'. *Collected Poems 1909–1962*, Faber & Faber Ltd., London, 1963.

1. London 1856, p. 177.
2. *The Dawn-Breakers*, pp. 61–2 (Brit.), pp. 90–1 (U.S.).
3. Throughout his life Áqá Muḥammad-Muṣṭafá served the Faith which he had embraced, with zeal and distinction. He spent many years in Beirut where he attended to the needs and requirements of pilgrims. His son, Áqá Ḥusayn Iqbál, did the same in subsequent years, with great devotion. Another son, Dr. Zia Bagdadi (Dr. Ḍíyá Baghdádí) resided in the United States, where his services were inestimable.
4. 'There gathered Shaykh Najaf, the son of Shaykh Ja'far, and Shaykh Músá from Najaf; Siyyid Ibráhím al-Qazvíní from Karbilá; Shaykh Muḥammad-Ḥasan Yásín and Shaykh Ḥasan Asadu'lláh from Káẓimíyyah; Siyyid Muḥammad al-Álúsí and Siyyid 'Alí, the Naqíb-al-Ashráf, and Muḥammad-Amín al-Wá'iz and Shaykh Muḥammad-Sa'íd, the Sháfi'í Muftí from Baghdád. There were others also besides these.' (Áqá Muḥammad-Muṣṭafáy-i-Baghdádí.)
5. Translated by H. M. Balyuzi. Áqá Muḥammad-Muṣṭafáy-i-Baghdádí's autobiography is no more than 24 pages long. It is the second of two booklets printed together in Cairo. There is no publication date.
6. Major-General Sir Henry Rawlinson (1810–95) was one of the outstanding European figures in the nineteenth century. It was he who transcribed the cuneiform inscriptions on the rocks of Bísitún in Western Írán, which record the achievements of the great Darius. He discovered the key to decipher them.

Like Sir John Malcolm, he entered the service of the East India Company at the age of seventeen. Six years later, he went with two other British officers to train the Persian army, but after two years he was dismissed because Muḥammad Sháh had begun to quarrel with the British. Next he served in Qandahár. By his own wish he was transferred to 'Iráq, because he wanted to be close to Western Írán and continue his research. He also continued the unfinished work of Layard at Nineveh. The British Museum has a wealth of archaeological finds donated by him. From 1859–60, he briefly occupied the post of British Minister in Ṭihrán. Then to the end of his life he served on the India Council in London and devoted his time to writing and to scientific pursuits. From 1870–84, the Trustees of the British Museum issued four volumes of cuneiform inscriptions under his close supervision.

7. F.O. 248/114 of January 8th 1845, enclosed in Rawlinson's letter to Sheil of January 16th 1845.

8. *ibid.*

9. *ibid.*

10. F.O. 248/114 of January 16th 1845.

11. F.O. 248/114 (undated). Translation by Rawlinson, enclosed in his letter to Sheil of January 16th 1845.

12. F.O. 195/237 of April 15th 1845.

13. F.O. 195/237 of April 30th 1845.

14. F.O. 195/237 of February 18th 1845.

15. F.O. 248/114 of February 28th 1845.

Chapter 5: Pilgrimage to Mecca

Opening quotation: translation by H. M. Balyuzi.

1. His son, Ḥájí Shaykh Yaḥyá, succeeded him as Imám-Jum'ih, and lived till 1919 to an advanced age. He extended his protection to the Bahá'ís on every possible occasion.

2. Ḥájí Mírzá Ḥabíbu'lláh's narrative.

3. *The Dawn-Breakers*, p. 91 (Brit.), p. 131 (U.S.).

4. *ibid.*, pp. 90–1 (Brit.), p. 130 (U.S.).

5. *ibid.*, p. 92 (Brit.), pp. 132–3 (U.S.).

6. *ibid.*, pp. 93–5 (Brit.), pp. 134–6 (U.S.).

7. *ibid.*, pp. 96–7 (Brit.), pp. 138–40 (U.S.).

8. *ibid.*, p. 97 (Brit.), p. 140 (U.S.).

CHAPTER 6: FORCES OF OPPOSITION ARRAYED

Opening quotation: Isabella in *Measure for Measure*, Act II, sc. ii.

1. Published by Leavitt, Trow & Co., New York & Philadelphia.

2. *The Dawn-Breakers*, p. 99 (Brit.), p. 142 (U.S.).

3. *ibid.*, pp. 100–1 (Brit.), p. 144 (U.S.).

4. Cited Kelly, *Britain and the Persian Gulf*, p. 310.

5. Eugène-Napoléon Flandin (1809–76) was an archaeologist and painter of note. He and Coste, an architect, were members of the suite of M. de Sercey, Louis-Philippe's envoy to the Court of Muḥammad-Sẖáh. They stayed in Írán, after the envoy's departure, to draw her ancient monuments. The result of their labours, *Voyage en Perse*, was published in 1851 by the French Government.

6. *Early Adventures in Persia*, Vol. I, pp. 326–8.

7. Father of Mírzá Ḥusayn Kẖán, the Musẖíru'd-Dawlih and Sipahsálár, who was the Persian ambassador in Constantinople in 1863, at the time of Bahá'u'lláh's exile to Adrianople. Mírzá Ḥusayn Kẖán later rose to be the Ṣadr-i-Aʿẓam (Grand Vizier).

8. Ḥájí Mírzá ʿAlí-Akbar, the Qavámu'l-Mulk, was a younger son of Ḥájí Ibráhím Kẖán, the Grand Vizier who concluded a treaty with Sir John Malcolm, and later fell into disgrace and was barbarously put to death by Fatḥ-ʿAlí Sẖáh. Most of his family perished with him. However, the young Mírzá ʿAlí-Akbar survived to be restored to favour in later years and given the title of Qavámu'l-Mulk. He and his descendants, over several generations, greatly influenced the destinies of the inhabitants of Fárs.

9. Sartíp was a high rank in those days both in the civil and the military establishment; today it means brigadier. The Farmán (Firman) was to be read in the Masjid-i-Naw. Quarters of a city either belonged to the Niʿmatí-Kẖánih or the Haydarí-Kẖánih.

10. F.O. 248/113 of August 7th 1844, enclosed in a letter of August 14th 1844, from Hennell to Sheil.

11. F.O. 248/113 of November 24th 1844, enclosed in Hennell's letter to Sheil of December 11th 1844.

12. F.O. 248/113 of December 24th 1844, enclosed in Hennell's letter to Sheil of January 4th 1845.

13. *The Dawn-Breakers*, p. 104 (Brit.), pp. 148–9 (U.S.).

Chapter 7: Belief and Denial

Opening quotation: *An Essay on Man*, Epistle II.

1. *The Dawn-Breakers*, p. 105 (Brit.), pp. 149–50 (U.S.).
2. Arberry (ed.), *The Koran Interpreted.*
3. See Foreword, paragraph 4.
4. Arberry (ed.), *The Koran Interpreted.* Verse numbers for the first extract are 49–50, although Arberry gives 50–1.
5. *The Dawn-Breakers*, pp. 105–6 (Brit.), p. 150 (U.S.).
6. Arberry (ed.), *The Koran Interpreted.*
7. *The Dawn-Breakers*, pp. 125–6 (Brit.), pp. 174–6 (U.S.).
8. *ibid.*, p. 126 (Brit.), p. 176 (U.S.).
9. *ibid.*, pp. 126–7 (Brit.), p. 176 (U.S.).
10. *ibid.*, p. 127 (Brit.), p. 177 (U.S.).
11. Browne (ed.), *A Traveller's Narrative*, Vol. II, p. 8.
12. Masjid-i-Vakíl: built by Karím Khán-i-Vakíl, the founder of the Zand dynasty.
13. *The Dawn-Breakers*, pp. 107–9 (Brit.), pp. 153–4 (U.S.).
14. Browne (ed.), *A Traveller's Narrative*, Vol. II, p. 7.
15. 'Andalíb (Nightingale) was the soubriquet of Mírzá 'Alí-Ashraf of Láhíján in the Caspian province of Gílán. 'Andalíb was a poet of superb accomplishment and an eloquent teacher. He met Edward Granville Browne in Yazd in the year 1888. A very long letter exists, in his handwriting, addressed to Edward Browne, in which he cites proofs from the Bible, in support of the Bahá'í Faith, and encourages Browne to visit Bahá'u'lláh in 'Akká. It is not known whether a copy of the letter ever reached Browne.
16. Nicolas, *Seyyèd Ali Mohammed dit le Bâb*, p. 233.
17. Browne (ed.), *A Traveller's Narrative*, Vol. II, pp. 9–10.
18. *The Dawn-Breakers*, pp. 128–9 (Brit.), p. 179 (U.S.).
19. See footnote ch. 4, p. 62.
20. Browne (ed.), *A Traveller's Narrative*, Vol. II, p. 11.

Chapter 8: The City of 'Abbás the Great

Opening quotation: *The Contention of Ajax and Ulysses*, 1659.

1. It has been stated by one writer that Áqá Muḥammad-Ḥusayn-i-Ardistání was also with the Báb on this journey.
2. Layard, *Early Adventures in Persia*, Vol. I, pp. 311–12.
3. Arberry (ed.), *The Koran Interpreted.*
4. *The Dawn-Breakers*, p. 145 (Brit.), p. 202 (U.S.).

5. *ibid.*, p. 146 (Brit.), p. 204 (U.S.).
6. *ibid.*, p. 148 (Brit.), pp. 205–7 (U.S.).
7. Ṣadru'd-Dín Muḥammad of Shíráz, who died in the year A.H. 1050 (A.D. 1640–1) is generally known as Mullá Ṣadrá. Shaykh Aḥmad-i-Aḥsá'í wrote commentaries on two of his works: *Ḥikmatu'l-'Arshiyyah* (Divine Philosophy) and *Mashá'ir* (Faculties).
8. *The Dawn-Breakers*, p. 150 (Brit.), p. 209 (U.S.).
9. *ibid.*, pp. 150–1 (Brit.), pp. 209–11 (U.S.).
10. Browne (ed.), *A Traveller's Narrative*, Vol. II, p. 13.
11. Nicolas, *Seyyèd Ali Mohammed Dit le Bâb*, p. 242, n. 192.
12. *The Dawn-Breakers*, pp. 152–3 (Brit.), p. 213 (U.S.).
13. 'Abdu'l-Bahá states in *A Traveller's Narrative*, Vol. II, p. 13, that the Báb's sojourn in the private residence of Manúchihr Khán lasted four months.

Chapter 9: The Antichrist of the Bábí Revelation

Opening quotation: Act II, sc. ii.
1. See Shoghi Effendi, *God Passes By*, p. 164.
2. In the early days of Islám, these people were ranked with those groups of zealots who had earned the generic term of Ghulát (Extremists, or 'those who exaggerate'). They identified 'Alí, the first Imám, with the Godhead. 'Abdu'lláh Ibn-Sabá, a Jewish convert to Islám who originated this doctrine, was put to death by 'Alí himself. ''Alí is not God but is not separate from Him either' is the statement attributed to them today.
3. *The Dawn-Breakers*, p. 156 (Brit.), p. 217 (U.S.).
4. *ibid.*, p. 161 (Brit.), pp. 224–5 (U.S.).
5. The account of this journey is given in *The Dawn-Breakers*, pp. 156–62 (Brit.), pp. 217–27 (U.S.).
6. Browne (ed.), *A Traveller's Narrative*, Vol. II, p. 14.
7. *The Dawn-Breakers*, pp. 162–3 (Brit.), pp. 228–9 (U.S.).
8. Browne (ed.), *A Traveller's Narrative*, Vol. II, pp. 14–15.
9. *ibid.*, pp. 15–16.
10. *The Dawn-Breakers*, p. 163 (Brit.), pp. 230–1 (U.S.).

Chapter 10: Where the Aras Flows

Opening quotation: translation by H. M. Balyuzi.
1. *The Dawn-Breakers*, pp. 165–6 (Brit.), p. 235 (U.S.).
2. *ibid.*, p. 166 (Brit.), p. 236 (U.S.).

3. *ibid.*
4. Browne (ed.), *The Táríkh-i-Jadíd*, pp. 220–1.
5. *The Dawn-Breakers*, p. 167 (Brit.), p. 238 (U.S.).
6. Browne (ed.), *A Traveller's Narrative*, Vol. II, p. 16.
7. *The Dawn-Breakers*, pp. 173–4 (Brit.), p. 247 (U.S.).
8. *ibid.*, p. 174 (Brit.), pp. 247–8 (U.S.).
9. Dossier No. 177, Ṭihrán, 1848, pp. 49–50 and p. 360. See Appendix 5, n. 2.
10. See Foreword, paragraph 4.
11. Browne (ed.), *A Traveller's Narrative*, Vol. II, p. 16.
12. *The Dawn-Breakers*, p. 175 (Brit.), p. 249 (U.S.).

Chapter 11: The Grievous Mountain

Opening quotation: *In Memoriam A.H.H.* (Prologue, v. 5.)
1. *The Dawn-Breakers*, p. 219 (Brit.), p. 303 (U.S.).
2. After the martyrdom of the Báb, a number of His followers turned to Dayyán for guidance. They were known as 'Dayyáníyyih'. Most of them lived in the provinces of Ádharbáyján and Gílán. It has been thought that Dayyán claimed to be 'He Whom God shall make manifest', but Bahá'u'lláh refuted this in his *Kitáb-i-Badí'*. When Dayyán came into the presence of Bahá'u'lláh in 'Iráq, He fully recognized His station.
3. *The Dawn-Breakers*, p. 220 (Brit.), p. 304 (U.S.).
4. *ibid.*, pp. 21–2 (Brit.), p. 305 (U.S.).
5. See ch. 2, n. 7.
6. Browne (ed.), *A Traveller's Narrative*, Vol. II, pp. 278–89. The questions and replies are extracted from this much longer report of the trial.
7. *The Dawn-Breakers*, pp. 230–1 (Brit.), pp. 316–19 (U.S.). The quotations are taken from these pages; one reply of the Báb is paraphrased.
8. Browne, *Materials for the Study of the Bábí Religion*, pp. 260–2.
9. *The Dawn-Breakers*, p. 234 (Brit.), p. 323 (U.S.).
10. Ḥájí Qásí's end was sad. Some seventeen years later, in spite of assurances given to him, he was strangled on the platform of Persepolis, and his corpse was left dangling there, by the orders of an uncle of Náṣiri'd-Dín Sháh, Ḥájí Sulṭán Murád Mírzá, the Ḥisámu's-Salṭanih, who was on his way to take up the reins of governorship in Shíráz.

Chapter 12: That Midsummer Noon

Opening quotation: 'The Báb' in *The Bahá'í World*, Vol. VIII, p. 945. Beatrice Irwin (1877–1956) was a British Bahá'í of Irish descent, who lived a good part of her life in the United States, but travelled both in her work and as a Bahá'í teacher to many parts of the world. Educated at Cheltenham College and Oxford, she was a pioneer in the field of lighting engineering, and also devoted much of her life to advancing the cause of world peace. Her writings include *The Gates of Light*, *The New Science of Colour*, and *Heralds of Peace*.

1. In later years he became known as Mírzá 'Alíy-i-Sayyaḥ (Traveller), married a daughter of Shaykh Ḥasan-i-Zunúzí and made his home in Karbilá. He was one of the four Bahá'ís sent with Ṣubḥ-i-Azal to Cyprus, by the Ottoman Government. He died there on August 4th 1871.
2. See Foreword, paragraph 4.
3. *The Dawn-Breakers*, p. 314 (Brit.), pp. 430–1 (U.S.). Account of Siyyid Ḥusayn-i-Yazdí (or 'Azíz).
4. *ibid.*, pp. 370–1 (Brit.), p. 505 (U.S.).
5. *ibid.*, p. 371 (Brit.), p. 506 (U.S.).
6. *ibid.*, p. 372 (Brit.), p. 507 (U.S.).
7. *ibid.*, pp. 223–4 (Brit.), pp. 307–8 (U.S.).
8. Cited Shoghi Effendi, *The World Order of Bahá'u'lláh*, p. 101.
9. *The Dawn-Breakers*, p. 373 (Brit.), p. 508 (U.S.), and Sohráb, *Risáliy-i-Tis'a-'Ashariyyih*, p. 74.
10. *The Dawn-Breakers*, p. 374 (Brit.), pp. 509–10 (U.S.).
11. *ibid.*, p. 375 (Brit.), p. 512 (U.S.).
12. *ibid.*, p. 376 (Brit.), p. 514 (U.S.).
13. *ibid.*, p. 378 (Brit.), pp. 518–19 (U.S.).

Chapter 13: The Dawn-Breakers

Opening quotation: *Díván-i-Miṣbáḥ*. 'Azízu'lláh Miṣbáḥ (1876–1945), poet, educationalist, master of *belles-lettres*, was an eminent Bahá'í of Írán. A book of his prose: *Munshi'át-i-Miṣbáḥ*, reprinted many times, became a textbook, for use in schools.

1. Shaykh Muḥammad Shibl and his son, Áqá Muḥammad-Muṣṭafá (then about ten years old); Shaykh Sulṭán-i-Karbilá'í; Siyyid Aḥmad-i-Yazdí, the father of Siyyid Ḥusayn (the amanuensis of the Báb); Shaykh Ṣaliḥ-i-Karímí and Mullá Ibráhím-i-Maḥallátí were of that number.

2. Browne (ed.), *A Traveller's Narrative*, Vol. II, xliii.

3. He was variously named as Mullá 'Abdu'lláh, Mírzá Ṣáliḥ, and Mírzá Ṭáhir, the Baker.

4. 'Abdu'l-Bahá, *Memorials of the Faithful*, p. 201.

5. *The Dawn-Breakers*, pp. 215–16 (Brit.), p. 299 (U.S.).

6. *ibid.*, p. 253 (Brit.), p. 351 (U.S.).

7. Nicolas, *Seyyèd Ali Mohammed dit le Bâb*, p. 296.

8. *The Dawn-Breakers*, p. 240 (Brit.), p. 332 (U.S.).

9. F.O. 60/144.

10. Bahá'u'lláh, *Kitáb-i-Íqán*, p. 142 (Brit.), p. 223 (U.S.).

11. Cited *The Dawn-Breakers*, p. 284n. (Brit.), p. 395n. (U.S.). Also in another translation in 'Abdu'l-Bahá's *Memorials of the Faithful*, p. 7.

12. They were al-Ḥáj Muḥammad al-Karradí and Sa'íd al-Jabbáwí. Ḥájí Muḥammad was nearly eighty years old. In his younger days, he had led a hundred men in the war between the Ottomans and Ibráhím Páshá, son of the celebrated Muḥammad-'Alí Páshá of Egypt.

13. *The Dawn-Breakers*, p. 298 (Brit.), p. 411 (U.S.).

14. In 1970, the present writer received, through the good offices of his cousin, Abu'l-Qásim Afnán, the photostatically-produced copy of a manuscript describing this episode in Bábí history. It is in the handwriting of Áqá Muḥammad-Báqir-i-Ṭihrání, a merchant, whose brother, Mushiru't-Tujjár, was one of the 'Five Martyrs' of Sárí. (These five were murdered in the early years of the Constitutional Movement in Persia: see Balyuzi, *Edward Granville Browne and the Bahá'í Faith.*) Áqá Muḥammad-Báqir states, in a short introduction, that he visited Bárfurúsh sometime in the year 1319 A.H. (April 20th 1901–April 9th 1902), where he chanced upon a manuscript of the history of the Bábís at Shaykh Ṭabarsí, written by one of them, which he copied for himself and the benefit of others. He does not mention the name of the owner of the original. This history begins with an account of the author joining Mullá Ḥusayn; by this he can be identified, although he nowhere names himself. There is no doubt that he was Mírzá Luṭf-'Alí or Luṭf-'Alí Mírzá of Shíráz, a descendant of the Afshárid monarchs of the 18th century A.D. He was one of the few survivors of Shaykh Ṭabarsí, who managed to escape in the company of Mullá Ṣádiq-i-Muqaddas-i-Khurásání, but in the holocaust of August 1852 (see Balyuzi, *Bahá'u'lláh*, p. 18) he died a martyr's death.

On receiving and examining this chronicle, the present writer recalled that E. G. Browne mentions, in his *Materials for the Study of the Bábí Religion*, a manuscript history of the episode of Shaykh Ṭabarsí by Luṭf-'Alí Mírzá, sent to him by Mírzá Muṣṭafá, the Azalí scribe. As this manuscript is now in Cambridge University Library, a photostatic reproduction was obtained by the kindness of the Librarian. According to the scribe (whose real name was Ismá'íl-i-Ṣabbágh-i-Sidihí), the manuscript which he copied for Prof. Browne was faulty, but he could find no other for comparison.

Luṭf-'Alí Mírzá's chronicle ends abruptly, and Áqá Muḥammad-Báqir, the copyist, incorrectly concludes that the author must have died of starvation, since the last lines of his chronicle describe the state of famine caused by the siege.

The present writer is currently engaged in collating the two manuscripts.

15. *The Dawn-Breakers*, p. 285 (Brit.), p. 396 (U.S.).

16. F.O. 60/150, See Appendix 3.

17. Mullá Báqir, the imám of the Chinár-Súkhtih quarter; Mírzá Ḥusayn-i-Qutb, the Kad Khudá (Headman) of the Bázár quarter; and Ḥájí Muḥammad-Taqí, a prominent and wealthy merchant, who later earned the surname of Ayyúb (Job) from Bahá'u'lláh, because of his intense sufferings, his patience in tribulation and his steadfastness—these were among the notables who went out to the village of Runíz in the district of Fasá to meet Vaḥíd.

18. *The Dawn-Breakers*, pp. 353–4 (Brit.), pp. 479–80 (U.S.).

19. They were commanded by Mihr-'Alí Khán-i-Núrí, the Shujá'u'l-Mulk, and Muṣṭafá-Qulí Khán-i-Qaráguzlú, the I'timadu's-Salṭanih.

20. *The Dawn-Breakers*, pp. 361–2 (Brit.), pp. 488–9 (U.S.).

21. Shoghi Effendi, *God Passes By*, p. 47.

22. Browne (ed.), *The Táríkh-i-Jadíd*, p. 255.

23. *ibid.*, p. 253.

24. Browne, *A Year Amongst the Persians*, p. 81. (1926 ed.).

25. F. O. 60/153. K. W. Abbott's dispatch of August 30th 1850, enclosed with Sheil's report of September 5th 1850 to Palmerston.

26. F. O. 248/142 of December 9th 1850, R. W. Stevens, Consul at Tabríz to Sheil.

27. *The Dawn-Breakers*, p. 419 (Brit.), p. 572 (U.S.).

28. F.O. 60/158 of January 6th 1851.

Epilogue

1. Shoghi Effendi, *God Passes By*, pp. 273–4.

Appendix 1: The Siege of Karbilá

1. F.O. 248/108, of May 15th 1843, enclosed in Farrant's letter to Sheil of May 20th 1843. All quotations unidentified by a number in this Appendix are taken from this document.
2. F.O. 248/108, of November 18th 1842, enclosed in Farrant's letter to Sheil of May 2nd 1843.
3. F.O. 60/95 (undated), enclosed in Sheil's letter to Aberdeen of February 4th 1843.

Appendix 2: The Martyrdom of the Báb

1. F.O. 60/152.
2. F.O. 248/142, of July 24th 1850.
3. F. O. 60/153
4. F.O. 60/153, of August 3rd 1850, translated by Taylour Thomson.
5. F.O. 248/140.

Appendix 3: Prelude to the Episode of Nayríz

1. F.O. 60/150, of February 12th 1850.

Appendix 4: The Seven Martyrs of Ṭihrán

1. F.O. 60/145, of July 27th 1849.
2. Dossier No. 133, Ṭihrán, 1850; pp. 100–5. Translation by Dr. Firuz Kazemzadeh in 'Excerpts from Dispatches Written During 1848–1852' by Prince Dolgorukov, Russian Minister to Persia; quoted by kind permission of *World Order*, A Bahá'í Magazine, Vol. I, No. 1, 1966. The dispatches were published as an appendix to M. S. Ivanov's book, *The Babi Uprisings in Iran.*
3. F.O. 60/150. See Appendix 3.
4. F.O. 248/140, of May 2nd 1850.

Appendix 5: The Episode of Zanján

1. F.O. 60/151, of May 25th 1850.
2. F.O. 60/152, of June 25th 1850.
3. Dossier No. 133, Ṭihrán, 1850; pp. 470–1. See Appendix 4, note 2, for details.
4. F.O. 60/153.
5. *ibid.*
6. Dossier No. 134, Ṭihrán, 1850; p. 562. See Appendix 4, note 2, for details.
7. Dossier No. 133, Ṭihrán, 1850; p. 582. *op. cit.*
8. Dossier No. 134, Ṭihrán, 1850; p. 99. *op. cit.*
9. Dossier No. 134, Ṭihrán, 1851; p. 156. *op. cit.*
10. F.O. 60/153.
11. *ibid.*
12. F.O. 60/154.
13. *ibid.*, of December 16th 1850.
14. *ibid.*, of December 24th 1850.
15. F.O. 248/143.
16. F.O. 60/158.

Appendix 6: Lord Palmerston's Enquiry

1. F.O. 248/140.
2. F.O. 60/152.
3. F.O. 248/141.
4. F.O. 60/152, enclosed with Sheil's letter to Palmerston.

Appendix 7: Myth-Making

1. Arnold, *Through Persia by Caravan*, Vol. II, pp. 32–5.
2. Benjamin, *Persia and the Persians*, Preface.
3. *ibid.*, pp. 353–5.
4. Gordon, *Persia Revisited*, pp. 81–91.
5. Lorimer, *Gazetteer of the Persian Gulf*, Vol. I, part 2, pp. 1966–7 and 2384.

INDEX

'Abá, 5, 138
Abbas ('Abbás), brother of Imám Ḥusayn, 193, 197, 198, 200
'Abbás the Great, Sháh, 106, 107
'Abbás, Shaykh, of 'Iráq, 60
'Abbás Effendi, *see* 'Abdu'l-Bahá
'Abbás Mírzá, Prince (the Náyibu's-Salṭanih), 8, 9, 10, 149
'Abbás Mírzá Mulk-Ára (the Náyibu's-Salṭanih), 135, 139
'Abbás-Qulí Khán-i-Láríjání, 172, 174
'Abbásábád, 139
'Abdu'l-'Alíy-i-Hirátí, Mullá, 102
'Abdu'l-'Azíz, Mullá, 64, 197, 199, 201
'Abdu'l-Bahá ('Abbás Effendi), 5, 32, 93, 95, 96, 99, 105, 114, 118, 128, 132, 139, 149, 167, 168, 175, 191, 192
'Abdu'l-Báqí, Siyyid, 118
'Abdu'l-Hádí, of 'Iráq, 60
'Abdu'l-Ḥamíd Khán-i-Dárúghih, 97, 104, 105
'Abdu'l-Karím, Mírzá, of Shíráz, 103
'Abdu'l-Karím-i-Qazvíní, Mullá (Mírzá Aḥmad-i-Kátib), 92, 102, 104, 115, 120, 151, 152
'Abdu'l-Vahháb, Ḥájí Mírzá, 27
'Abdu'lláh, Mírzá, of Shíráz, 170
'Abdu'lláh Ibn-Sabá, 236
'Abdu'lláh Khán-i-Turkaman, 174
'Abdu'lláh-i-Bihbihání, Áqá, 164
Aberdeen, the Earl of, xi, 12, 63, 68
'Ábid, Mírzá (grandfather of the Báb's wife), 231
'Ábid, Shaykh, 34, 35, 36, 230, 231
Abraham, 31, 70, 184
Abú-Háshim, Shaykh, 69, 70, 78, 99
Abú-Lahab, 86
Abú-Ṭálib (uncle of the Prophet Muḥammad), 86
Abú-Ṭalib, Mullá, 78
Abú-Turáb, Shaykh (Imám-Jum'ih, of Shíráz), 69, 89, 94, 95, 99, 103
Abu'l-Faḍl-i-Gulpáygání, Mírzá, 32, 39, 125, 231
Abu'l-Ḥasan, Ḥájí, 69, 70, 71, 103
Abu'l-Ḥasan Khán, Mírzá (the 2nd Mushíru'l-Mulk), 98
Abu'l-Qásim, Ḥájí Mírzá (brother-in-law of the Báb), 46, 106, 107
Abu'l-Qásim, Mírzá (Qá'im-Maqám-i-Faráhání), *see* Qá'im-Maqám
Abu'l-Qásim-i-Labbáf, Mashhadí, 103
Adhán, 78, 128
Ádharbáyján, 79, 124, 125, 131, 132, 136, 137, 140, 143, 149, 152, 170, 204, 237
Ádí Guzal, Mullá (Mírzá 'Alíy-i-Sayyáḥ), 149, 238
'Ádil Sháh, *see* 'Alí-Sháh
Adrianople, 128, 189, 234
Afghán, 230
Afnán, 46
Afshár, Afshárid (kings), 103, 161, 230, 239
Aga Khan I (Ḥaṣan-'Alí Khán), 122
Ahl-i-Ḥaqq, 118
Aḥmad (son of the Báb), 46, 47
Aḥmad, Ḥájí, of Mílán, 160
Aḥmad, Mírzá (Imám-Jum'ih, of Tabríz), 140
Aḥmad, Siyyid Mír (brother of 8th Imám), 103
Aḥmad-i-Aḥsá'í, Shaykh (founder of Shaykhí sect): early years, 1; pilgrimage and death, 2; teaching, 19, 162, 166, 229, 236
Aḥmad-i-Azghandí, Mírzá, 56
Aḥmad-i-Ibdál-i-Marághi'í, Mullá (Letter of the Living), 26, 131

Aḥmad-i-Kátib, Mírzá, *see* 'Abdu'l-Karím-i-Qazvíní, Mullá
Aḥmad-i-Mu'allim, Mullá, 56
Aḥsá, 1
Ájúdán-Báshí, *see* Ḥusayn Khán
Akhbárí, 62, 101
Akhund, Ḥájí, 189, 190
'Akká, 128, 145, 166, 191, 192, 219, 235
'Aláu'd-Dawlih, 145
Aleppo, 68
Alexander, 223
Alexander I, Tsar, 8
'Alí ('Alí ibn Abí Ṭalib, the first Imám), 18, 95, 194, 200, 236
'Alí, Ḥájí Mírzá (father of the Báb's wife), 46
'Alí, Ḥájí Mírzá Siyyid (uncle of the Báb), 33, 105, 150, 183–4, 231
'Alí, Ḥájí Mullá, 25
'Alí an-Naqí, Imám, 41
'Alí Bishr, Siyyid, 60, 162, 163
'Alí Khán (warden of Máh-Kú), 122, 128, 129, 131, 135
Ali Pasha, 200
'Alí Qabl-i-Muḥammad (the Báb), 78
'Alí-Akbar, Mírzá, of Shíráz, 103
'Alí-Akbar Big, 125
'Alí-Akbar-i-Ardistání, Mullá, 78
'Alí-Akbar-i-Shahmírzádí, Ḥájí Mullá (Ḥájí Ákhund), 189, 190
'Alí-Aṣghar, Mírzá (Shaykhu'l-Islám, of Tabríz), 140, 145
'Alí-Aṣghar Khán, of Nayríz, 179
'Alí-Ashraf, Mírzá, *see* 'Andalíb
'Alí-'Askar, Ḥájí, 128
'Alí-Mardán Khán, fort of, 185
'Alí-Naqí, Mírzá, 200
'Alí-Sháh (the Ẓillu's-Sulṭán), 5, 10, 12, 196–8, 200, 201, 218
'Alí Virdí Khán, 199
'Alíy-i-Basṭámí, Mullá (Letter of the Living), 27, 28, 37–8, ch. 4, 162, 166, 232
'Alíy-i-Rází, Mullá, *see* Khudá-Bakhsh-i-Qúchání, Mullá
'Alíy-i-Sayyáḥ, Mírzá, *see* Ádí Guzal, Mullá
'Alíy-i-Tafrishí, Ḥájí Mírzá Siyyid (the Majdu'l-Ashráf), 190
'Alíy-i-Zunúzí, Siyyid, 153
Alíyu'lláhís, 118, 164
Alláh-u-Akbar, pass of, 16; invocation, 128
Alláh-Yár, Ḥájí, 159
Alláh-Yár Khán (Áṣafu'd-Dawlih), 9
Alváṭ (pl. of Lúṭí), 83
America, American, 1, 77, 145, 220
Amínu's-Sulṭán, 145
Amír Niẓám, *see* Taqí Khán, Mírzá
Amír-i-Díván, *see* Nabí Khán-i-Qazvíní, Mírzá
Amír-i-Kabír, *see* Taqí Khán, Mírzá
Ámul, 172, 174
'Andalíb (Mírzá 'Alí-Ashraf of Láhíján, poet), 96, 235
Antichrist, of the Bábí Revelation, 117, 140; *see also* Áqásí, Ḥájí Mírzá
Applications, science of, 141
Áqá Ján Khán-i-Khamsih, 158
Áqá Muḥammad Khán, 7
Áqá-Bálá Big (the Naqqásh-Báshí), 138
Áqáy-i-Kalím, *see* Músá, Mírzá
Áqásí, Ḥájí Mírzá (Grand Vizier), 11–12, 13, 93, 111–12, 114, 117, 119, 121–3, 128, 131, 132, 136, 137, 139–40, 147, 148, 199
Arab, Arabic, 108, 136, 141, 165, 176
Arabia, 219
Aras (Araxes, river), 9, 124
Arberry, Prof. A. J., 3
Archives, *see* International Archives
Ardistán, 114
Armenians, 147, 158
Armenian Socialist Soviet Republic, 117
Arnold, Arthur, 217, 218
Arthur, President, of the U.S.A., 220
Asadu'lláh, Ḥájí, 167
Asadu'lláh Khán-i-Vazír, Mírzá, 218
Asadu'lláh, Mírzá, of Khuy, *see* Dayyán
Asadu'lláh, Shaykh, of Shíráz, 99
Asadu'lláh-i-Iṣfahání, Mírzá, 191
Asadu'lláh-i-Qumí, Siyyid, 139
Asadu'lláh-i-Rashtí, Ḥájí Siyyid, 50, 112, 113
Aṣlán Khán, 84
'Aṭṭár, gate, 118
Azalí scribe, 240
'Aẓím, *see* Shaykh 'Alí, Mullá, of Khurásán

Báb, The (Siyyid 'Alí-Muḥammad): meeting with Mullá Ḥusayn and declaration, 17–22; arrival of Quddús, 23–4; accepts Qurratu'l-'Ayn, 24–6; His disciples, 24, 26–7; sends Mullá 'Alí to 'Iráq, 28; addresses Letters of Living, 28–31; family, youth, education, 32–7; merchant in Bus͟hihr, 37, 39–41; journey to holy cities and meeting with Siyyid Káẓim, 41–6; marriage and son, 46–7; sends Mullá Ḥusayn to Bahá'u'lláh, 48–50, 52–7; letter to wife, 57; pilgrimage to Mecca, 57, 69–71; declaration in Mecca, 71; challenge to Muḥít, 72–4; Tablet to S͟haríf of Mecca, 74–5; returns to Írán, 77; advance contacts with S͟hiráz, 77–8; arrest at Dálakí, 84, 105; returns to S͟hiráz, 85, 88–9; birth of Bábí community, 89–90, 103; Vaḥíd accepts, 90–4; at Vakíl mosque, 94–8; Ḥujjat accepts, 100–1; leaves S͟hiráz, 104–6; resides at Iṣfahán, 109–16; S͟háh calls to Ṭihrán, 116, 118; stops at Kás͟hán, 118–19, Qumrúd, 119, Kulayn, 119–21; receives communication from Bahá'u'lláh, 120; meeting with S͟háh prevented, 121–3; consigned to Máh-Kú, 122, 124, 128; arrives Mílán, 126–7; stays at Tabríz, 127–8; events at Máh-Kú, 128–33; removal to C͟hihríq, 131–2, 134–7; summoned to Tabríz, 137; stops in Urúmíyyih, 138; His portrait, 138–9; examination at Tabríz, 140–5; bastinadoed, 145–7; returned to C͟hihríq, 147–8; followers visit, 148–50; receives news of persecutions, 150–1; sends Writings, etc., to Bahá'u'lláh, 151–2; composes Arabic *Bayán*, 152; martyrdom, 152–9, 202; remains rescued, concealed, 159–60, 189–91; final mission to Mullá Ḥusayn, 171; anticipates 'Seven Martyrs', 185; His Shrine, 191–2; inaccurate reports of life, teachings, 203, 204–5, 214–16, appendix 7; claim and station, 18–19, 71, 141–2, 143–4, 167, 189; Writings, 20, 39, 73, 91–2, 110, 132, 136, 141, 147, 163, *see* index for *Bayán*, *Qayyúmu'l-Asmá'*
Bábís, 26–7, 89–90, 134–6, 145, 146, 159, 164–7, 169–78, 180–7 *passim*, 204–12 *passim*, 215, 219–24, 239
Bábí Faith, 224
Bábíyyat (Gatehood), 96
Bábíyyih, 56, 173
Bábul, *see* Bárfurús͟h
Bábu'l-Báb, *see* Ḥusayn-i-Bus͟hrú'í, Mullá
Badas͟ht, conference of, 167–71
Bagdadi, Dr. Zia (Bag͟hdádí, Ḍíyá), 232
Bag͟hdád, 41, 59, 60–1, 63, 64, 66, 67, 68, 131, 135, 162, 163, 164, 176, 191, 193, 197, 199–201, 224, 232
Bág͟h-i-S͟háh, gate, 109
Bág͟h-i-Tak͟ht, palace, 104
Bahá, 152; *see also* Bahá'u'lláh
Bahá'í, Bahá'ís, 138, 145, 182, 192, 218, 233, 238
Bahá'í Faith, 235
Bahá'u'lláh (Mírzá Ḥusayn 'Alí): receives communication from Báb, 55, 152; sends message to Báb, 120; rescues Ṭáhirih, 167; arranges Badas͟ht conference, 167–8; attacked at Níyálá, 170–1; goes to Núr, 171; visits S͟hayk͟h Ṭabarsí, 173; attempts to join defenders, 174; protects remains of Báb, 189–91; chooses site for Shrine of Báb, 191–2; quotations from, 48, 174–5; mentioned, 9, 27, 56, 78, 109, 120, 125, 128, 135, 138, 145, 154, 165, 183, 188, 235, 237, 240; *see also* 'He Whom God shall manifest'
Baḥrayn, 1
Baḥru'l-'Ulúm, 36
Bak͟htíyárí, 108, 109
Bandar-'Abbás, 224
Banú-Ṣak͟hr, 1
Báqir-Ábád, mosque, 78
Báqir, Mírzá, of Tabríz, 155
Báqir, Mullá, imám, 240
Báqir-i-Tabrízí, Mullá (Letter of the Living), 27, 151, 168, 174
Baqíyatu'lláh (Remnant of God), 78, 155

Baraghán, 230
Bárfurúsh (Bábul), 23, 172, 173, 176, 184, 239
Bashír an-Najafí, Shaykh, 60
Başrah, 104
Bavánát, 205
Bayán: Arabic, 152, 215, 231, 232; Persian, 50, 71, 132, 154, 215, 232
Bázár-i-Murgh, 231
Bázár quarter, of Nayríz, 182
Beirut, 166, 191
Bell, Gertrude Lowthian, 230
Benjamin, S. G. W., 220
Bethune, Sir Henry Lindesay, 10, 211
Bible, 147, 235; New Testament quoted, 127, 155, 156, 158–9
Birdwood, Capt. R. L., 223
Bísitún, 232
Black Standard, 171, 172, 176
Bombay, 37, 57
Bonaparte (Napoleon I), 7, 8
Bonnière, M. de, 115
Boré, M., 79, 80
British Museum, 233
Britain, British, 1, 8–10, 12, 58, 61, 63, 77, 79, 109, 186, 193, 194, 202, 203, 205, 209, 216, 223, 230, 233; *see also* England
Browne, Edward Granville, 16, 141, 146, 152, 166, 186, 217, 235, 239, 240
Burgess, Mr., 80
Burújird, 93
Búshihr (Bushire), 2, 15, 16, 37, 39–41, 57, 71, 75, 77, 78, 79, 81, 83, 84, 87, 104, 105, 107, 223, 224, 230
Bushrúyih, 4
Buzurg, Ḥájí Mírzá, 96
Buzurg-i-Núrí, Mírzá (Mírzá 'Abbás, father of Bahá'u'lláh), 54
Byron, Lord, 117

Cain (by Byron), 117
Campbell, Sir John, 10
Canning, Sir Stratford (first Viscount Stratford de Redcliffe), 6, 61, 63, 66, 67, 193
Carmel, Mount, 191, 192
Caspian Sea, 3, 9
Caucasus, 9, 117
Chahár-Lang, 108
Chashmih-'Alí (tribe), 190
Cheltenham College, 238
Cheyne, T. K., 32, 168, 230
Chihríq, 132, 134–7, 147–50, 153, 159, 167, 183, 185
China, 203
Chinár Súkhtih (quarter of Nayríz), 178, 182
Cholera, 104, 105
Chosroes I, 220
Christ, *see* Jesus
Christian, 147, 217
Communism (-istic), 214, 220
Congress, Act of (U.S.A.), 220
Constantinople (Istanbul), 5, 63, 66, 67, 79, 163, 193, 221, 234
Cormick, Dr., 145
Cox, Sir Percy Z., 223
Cyprus, 238

Dalá'il-i-Sab'ih (The Seven Proofs), 132
Dálakí, 84, 105
Damascus, 68, 182, 191
Dáráb, 90, 101, 178
Darius, 232
David, 127
Dawn-Breakers (followers of the Báb), 90, 161, 188
Dayyán (Asadu'lláh, Mírzá, of Khuy), 136, 237
Dayyáníyyih, 237
Declaration, of the Báb (anniversary), 20, 150
'Deliverer of the Latter Days', 3
Democratic Party (U.S.A.), 220
Dhikr (the Báb, also Dhikru'lláh-al-A'ẓam, Dhikru'lláh-al-Akbar, Ḥaḍrat-i-Dhikr), 46, 132, 231
Dhi'l-Ḥijjah, month of, 70, 71
Dispensation of Bahá'u'lláh, The, 167
Díván-Khánih (the Court), 81
Divine origin, Divinity, 215
Dolgorukov, Prince Dimitri Ivanovich, 131, 206, 209, 210, 241

East India Company, 233
Ecbatana, *see* Ḥamadán
Echo (English publication), 217
Eclectic Magazine of Foreign Literature, Science and Art, 77
Eliot, T. S., 58

England, English, 80, 145, 203, 210, 214, 217; *see also* Britain
Erivan, *see* Íraván
Esther, 165
Ethiopian servant, of the Báb, 17, 49, 57, 71, 84
Euphrates, 108, 182, 193
Europe, European, 146, 209, 217

Fará'id (by Mírzá Abu'l-Faḍl), 39
Farmán-Farmá, *see* Firaydún Mírzá and Ḥusayn-'Alí Mírzá
Farrant, Lt.-Col. T., 5, 135, 173, 193, 195–9, 201, 229
Farrásh (farrásh-báshí, lictor), 145, 146, 156, 157
Fárs, 49, 109, 169, 178, 199, 205, 234
Farsakh (farsang), 114
Fasá, 104, 205, 240
Fatḥ-'Alí Sháh, 7, 8, 9, 138, 200, 229, 234
Fatḥu'lláh, Mír (great-grandfather of the Báb), 230
Fáṭimih (daughter of the Prophet Muḥammad), 47, 74
Fáṭimih-Bagum (mother of the Báb), 33, 103
Faylí (a clan), 82
Finkenstein, treaty of, 8
Firaydún Mírzá (the Farmán-Farmá), 80, 81
Firman (royal edict), 81, 234
Fírúz Mírzá, Prince (the Nuṣratu'd-Dawlih), 180
Fírúzábád, 82
'Five Martyrs', of Sárí, 239
Flandin, M., 80, 234
Foreign Ministers, British, *see* Aberdeen, Palmerston
France, French, 1, 7, 8, 79, 80, 194, 217, 234
Futúḥ-ar-Rasúl (boat), 69

Galata, 79
Gandum-Pák-Kun, *see* Ja'far, Mullá
Gardanne, General, 7, 8
Gazetteer of the Persian Gulf, 223
George III, 8
Georgian, 108
'Geramees', 6, 196, 198
Ghulát, 236
Gílán, 237
Gobineau, Count, 217
Golgotha, 127
Gordon, Sir Thomas Edward, 221, 223
'Great Sophy', 107
Greeks, 124
Guardian of the Bahá'í Faith, *see* Shoghi Effendi
Gulistán, treaty of, 8
Gulpáygán, 4
Gurgín Khán, 116, 117

Ḥabíbu'lláh (the Prophet Muḥammad), 46
Ḥabíbu'lláh Khán-i-Afghán, 174
Ḥabíbu'lláh-i-Afnán, Ḥájí Mírzá, 32, 34, 35, 39, 41, 45, 71, 96, 98
Hádí, Mírzá, 167
Hádíy-i-Nahrí, Mírzá, 51, 102
Hádíy-i-Qazvíní, Mírzá (Letter of the Living), 27
Ḥaḍrat, 231
Ḥáfiẓ, 15, 16, 35, 69, 124
Hagar, 184
Haifa, 191
Ḥajar al-Aswad (The Black Stone), 72
Ḥájí (the Báb), 87
Ḥájí-Bábáy-i-Afshár, Mírz (Ḥáájí Bábá, Mírzá), 9
Ḥajj, 70, 71
Ḥajj-i-Akbar, 70
Ḥakím, Dr. Lutfu'lláh, 165
Ḥakím Masíḥ, 165
Hamadán, 12, 102, 164, 165
Ḥamzih Mírzá (the Ḥishmatu'd-Dawlih), 152, 153, 170, 171, 172
Ḥanafí, 13
Ḥanbalí, 13
Hand of the Cause, 139, 189
Ḥaram, *see* Masjid
Ḥasan, servant of Vaḥíd, 205
Ḥasan, Ḥájí Mírzá Siyyid (brother-in-law of the Báb), 46
Ḥasan, Siyyid, 124, 128, 129, 146, 156
Ḥasan al-'Askarí, Imám, 41, 119, 142
Ḥasan Ja'far, Siyyid, 60
Ḥasan-'Alí, Ḥájí Mírzá (uncle of the Báb), 33
Ḥasan-'Alí Khán (Aga Khan I), 122
Ḥasan-'Alí Mírzá (the Shujá'u's-Salṭanih), 229

Ḥasan-i-Bajistání, Mullá (Letter of the Living), 27
Ḥasan-i-Núrí, Mírzá, 112
Ḥasan-i-Vazír, Mírzá, 190
Ḥasan-i-Zunúzí, Shaykh, 103, 104, 115, 120, 129, 132, 137, 143, 153
Háshim, Háshimite, 44, 59, 74, 86
Ḥaydarí (Ḥaydarí-Khánih), 82, 234
'He (Him) Whom God shall make manifest' (Man-Yuẓhiruhu'lláh), 154, 191, 237; *see also* Bahá'u'lláh
Hebrew, 136
Hennell, Captain (later Colonel) Samuel, 79, 81, 83, 104, 109
Ḥijáz, 49
Ḥikmatu'l-'Arshíyyah, 113, 236
Ḥillah, 200
Hirát, 230
Ḥishmat, poet, 103
Hizárih, tribe, 102
Holy Land, 139, 191
Ḥujjat (Ḥujjat-i-Zanjání, Ḥujjatu'l-Islám), 100, 125, 147, 185–7, 209–12
Hulákú Mírzá, Prince, 199
Ḥurúf-i-Ḥayy (Letters of the Living), 24; *see also* Letters of the Living
Ḥusayn, Imám, 1, 6, 32, 41, 43, 111, 182, 193, 194, 197–200
Ḥusayn, Siyyid, of Nayríz, 182
Ḥusayn Khán (Ájúdán-Báshí, Niẓamu'd-Dawlih, Ṣaḥib-Ikhtíyár), 68, 79, 83, 85, 88, 89, 90, 92, 93, 97, 98, 104, 105, 123
Ḥusayn Khán, Mírzá (the Mushíru'd-Dawlih), 234
Ḥusayn Khán, Siyyid (Syed Hussein Khan), 81
Ḥusayn-'Alí, Mírzá, *see* Bahá'u'lláh
Ḥusayn-'Alí Mírzá (Hoosein Ali Meerza, the Farmán-Farmá), 199, 229
Ḥusayn-'Alíy-i-Iṣfahání, 191
Ḥusayn-i-'Arab, Shaykh (the Náẓimu'sh-Sharí'ih, Ẓálim), 78, 89, 97, 98, 99
Ḥusayn-i-Bushrú'í, Mullá (Bábu'l-Báb): mission from Siyyid Káẓim, 4, 7, 13, 15, 16; meeting with Báb and His declaration, 17–22; encounters Quddús, 23–4; Letter of the Living, 26; mission to Bahá'u'lláh, ch. 3; returns to Shíráz, 102; visits Máh-Kú, 131; description of, 166; Báb sends to rescue Quddús, 171–3; besieged at Shaykh Ṭabarsí, 173–4; death and Bahá'u'lláh's tribute, 174–5; mentioned, 149, 150, 168, 170, 239
Ḥusayn-i-Hamadání, Mírzá, 126
Ḥusayn-i-Mutavallí, Mírzá, of Qum, 135, 174
Ḥusayn-i-Qutb, Mullá, of Nayríz, 240
Ḥusayn-i-Turshízí, Siyyid, 184
Ḥusayn-i-Yazdí, Siyyid (also Kátib, 'Azíz; Letter of the Living), 27, 115, 118, 124, 129, 132, 146, 156
Ḥusayní, Siyyid (Seid Hossainee), 196

Ibn-i-Sa'd, 153
Ibn-i-Zíyád, 153
Ibráhím, Mír (great-great-grandfather of the Báb), 230
Ibráhím, Siyyid, of Nayríz, 182
Ibráhím Khán, Ḥájí (the I'timádu'd-Dawlih), 8, 234
Ibráhím Páshá, 239
Ibráhím-i-Khalíl, Siyyid, 138
Ibráhím-i-Maḥallátí, Shaykh, 165, 166
Ibráhím-i-Qazvíní, Siyyid, 6, 59, 197, 199
'Íd-al-Aḍḥá ('Íd-i-Qurbán), 70
Iḥrám, 71
Ijtihád, 13
Ílbagí, 84
Ílkhání, 82, 84
Ilyáhú, Mullá, 165
Imám(s), 11, 13, 41, 62, 65, 95, 98, 119, 121, 132, 142, 160, 194, 200, 236; *see also* Ḥusayn, Riḍá, Imáms
Imámate, 65
Imám-Jum'ih: of Iṣfahán, 109–13 *passim*; of Kirmán, 33; of Shíráz, 233, *see* Abú-Turáb, Shaykh; of Tabríz, 140
Imám Mehdi (Mihdí), 67; *see also* Mihdí
Imám-Virdí Mírzá, 200
Imám-Zádih Ḥasan, shrine of, 189
Imám-Zádih Ma'ṣum, shrine of, 189
Imám-Zádih Zayd, shrine of, 191

'Imárat-i-Khurshíd, 116
India, 27, 37, 137, 223, 230
International Archives, of the Bahá'í Faith, 132, 139, 166, 190
Iqbál, Áqá Ḥusayn, 232
Írán, 3, 113, 161, 166, 194, 199, 201, 204, 206, 209, 217–21, 223, 224, 230, 233, 238
'Iráq, 1, 4, 27, 28, 37, 41, 45, 58, 60, 135, 147, 163, 165, 166, 176, 237
Íraván (Erivan), 117, 128
Irish, 238
Irwin, Beatrice, 148, 238
Iṣfahán (Ispahan), 49, 50, 105, 106–11, 114–17 *passim*, 169, 191, 218–20 *passim*
Ishmael (Ismá'íl), 184
Ishráqí School (Platonism), 112
Iskandar, Mullá, 100, 101, 125
Iskí-Shahr, 135
Islám, Islamic, 13, 78, 88, 93, 99, 111, 167, 180, 181, 182, 185, 236
Ismá'íl, Ḥájí Siyyid (Shaykhu'l-Islám of Bavánát), 205
Ismá'íl, Mírzá (Mámaqání), 143
Ismá'íl, Siyyid, 151
Ismá'íl-i-Qumí, Ḥájí Mullá, 184
Ismá'il-i-Sabbagh-i-Sidihí (Muṣṭafá, Mírzá), 240
Ismu'lláhu'l-Aṣdaq, *see* Ṣádiq-i-Muqaddas, Mullá
Istanbul, *see* Constantinople
Ithná-'Asharís (Twelvers), 119

Jabal-i-Básiṭ (Máh-Kú), 134
Jabal-i-Shadíd (Chihríq), 134
al-Jabbáwí, Sa'íd, 239
Jacob, 19
Jaddih, *see* Jiddah
Ja'far, Mullá (Gandum-Pák-Kun, the 'Sifter of Wheat'), 51
Ja'far-i-Kashfí, Siyyid, 70, 90, 94
Jalíl-i-Urúmí, Mullá (Letter of the Living), 27
Jamádíu'l-Úlá, month of, 150
Jamál-i-Burújirdí, Áqá, 145, 189, 190
Jání, Ḥájí Mírzá, 40, 52, 118, 126, 174
Javád, Ḥájí Siyyid (Imám-Jum'ih of Kirmán), 33
Javád, Mullá (cousin of Ṭáhirih), 25
Javád-i-Baraghání, Mullá, 102
Javád-i-Karbilá'í, Ḥájí Siyyid, 35–40 *passim*, 46, 90
Javánshír, 'Abbás-Qulí Khán-i-, 139
Jerusalem, 3, 127, 128, 158
Jesuit, 79
Jesus, 31, 35, 127, 128, 155, 156, 158, 159, 220
Jewish, 31, 165
Jiddah (Jaddih), 57, 69, 75
John, the Baptist, 220
Jones, Sir Harford, 8
Joseph, Súrih of, *see* *Qayyúmu'l-Asmá'*
Julfa, 79

Ka'bih (Ka'bah), 69, 71
Kalántar, Maḥmúd Khán-i-, 171
Kangávar, 102
Karbilá, 1–7 *passim*, 12, 15, 23, 25, 26, 36, 37, 41, 42, 51, 58–65 *passim*, 73, 74, 102, 150, 162, 171, 224, 238; siege of, 193–201; tragedy of (martyrdom of Imám Ḥusayn), 153, 182
Karím Khán, Zand ruler, 161
Karkúk, 68
al-Karrádí, al-Ḥáj Muḥammad, 239
Káshán, 49, 52, 118
Kashfí, *see* Ja'far-i-, Siyyid
Kátib, *see* Ḥusayn-i-Yazdí, Siyyid
Kawthar, Súrih of, the Báb's commentary on, 91–2, 141, 163
Káẓim Big, Mírzá (Kazem-Beg), 142
Káẓim-i-Rashtí, Siyyid: joins Shaykh Aḥmad and succeeds him, 2, 3; role in siege of Karbilá, and death, 4–7; anticipates Promised One, 15, 18, 19, 23, 134; Qurratu'l-'Ayn contacts, 25–6; mentioned, 13, 36, 50, 59, 140, 162, 166, 184, 201, 223–4
Káẓim-i-Zanjání, Siyyid, 104, 106, 109, 185
Káẓimayn (Káẓimíyyah), 41, 58, 60, 131, 162, 200
Khadíjih-Bagum (wife of the Báb), 46, 103, 142
Khájih, fort of, 179, 181
Khárg (Karrack), 79, 109, 230
Khudá-Bakhsh-i-Qúchání, Mullá ('Alíy-i-Rází, Mullá, Letter of the Living), 27

Khurásán, 4, 49, 56, 122, 167, 170, 171, 176, 230
Khusraw-i-Qádí-Kalá'í, 172, 173
Khuṭbiy-i-Qahríyyih (Sermon of Wrath), 147
Khuy, 136
Kinár-Gird, 119
Kirand, 164, 169
Kirmán, 33, 169, 204
Kirmánsháh, 2, 102, 164, 169, 191, 201
Kitáb-i-Íqán (The Book of Certitude), 48, 87, 174
Koran, *see* Qur'án
Kúfih, 16, 50, 60
Kulayn, 119, 120, 121
al-Kulayní, Muḥammad ibn Ya'qúb, 119
Kunár-Takhtih, 105
Kurds, Kurdish, 11, 128, 135

Labaree, Rev. Benjamin, 145
Lálizár, Mullá, 165
Lawḥ-i- Ḥurúfát (Tablet of the Letters), 136
Layard, Sir Henry, 11, 79, 108, 109, 230, 233
Letters of the Living (Ḥurúf-i-Ḥayy): meaning, 24; list of names, 26–7; *also* 51, 89, 104, 131, 150, 151, 168, 174, 177
Lingeh (Lingih), 224
Líráví, district, 224
Literary Gazette, The, 76, 77
London, 68, 79
Lord of Hosts, 191; of the Age, or Religion, *see* Ṣáḥibu'z-Zamán
Lorimer, Gordon, 223
Louis-Philippe, French king, 80, 234
Lucifer, 117
Luke, St., 155, 156, 158, 159
Luristán, 93, 108
Luṭf-'Alí, Mírzá (chamberlain), 93
Luṭf-'Alí Khán, Zand ruler, 7
Luṭf-'Alí Mírzá, 103, 239, 240
Lúṭí, 82

Macneill, Sir John, 230
Madákhil (perquisites), 161
Madrisih (school), of Páminár, 53; of Mírzá Ṣálih, 52
Máh-Kú (Mákú), 121, 122, 124, 128–35 *passim*, 139, 163
Maḥmúd, Ḥájí Mullá (the Niẓámu'l-'Ulamá), 140–44 *passim*
Maḥmúd, Mírzá (uncle of the Báb's father), 33
Maḥmúd, Mullá, of 'Iráq, 60
Maḥmúd al-Álúsí (Muftí of Baghdád), 162
Maḥmúd-i-Khu'í, Mullá (Letter of the Living), 27
Mahomet, *see* Muḥammad
'Mahometan schism', 76
Makkah, *see* Mecca
Malcolm, Sir John, 8, 223, 233, 234
Malik Qásim Mírzá, 138
Málikí, 13
Man-Yuẓhiruhu'lláh, *see* 'He Whom God shall manifest'
Manifestations of God, 150
Manúchihr Khán (the Mu'tamidu'd-Dawlih), 50, 108–17 *passim*
Marághih, 79, 149
Marḍíyyih (sister of Ṭáhirih), 26
Mark, St., 127, 128
Mashá'ir (by Mullá Ṣadrá), 236
Mashhad (Meshed), 2, 56, 85, 119, 171
Mashíyyatu'lláh (martyr), 27
Masjid: al-Aqṣá, 3; al-Ḥarám, 3; i-Ílkhání, 18; i-Jum'ih (of Nayríz), 179, 182; i-Máshá'u'lláh, 190; i-Naw, 234; i-Vakíl (of Shíráz), 94, 96, 99
Mas'úd Mírzá, Prince Sulṭán (Ẓillu's-Sulṭán), 10, 218
Ma'ṣúmih (sister of Imám Riḍá), 52
Materialism, 214
Maydán, 114
Maymand, 83
Mazdak, 220
Mázindarán, 27, 131, 149, 150, 171, 174, 184
Mecca, 2, 21, 69, 70, 71, 72, 74, 77, 89, 134, 223
Medina, 2, 21, 73, 74, 75, 89, 218
Memorials of the Faithful, 128, 168, 175
Menchikov, Prince, 9
Messenger of God (Rasúlu'lláh), *see* Muḥammad (The Prophet)

Mihdí (Mahdí), 3, 61, 67, 96, 142, 171, 204, 224
Mihdí (Bábí of 'Iráq), 60
Mihdí, Mírzá (Ṣábir, the poet), 103
Mihdí Khán, Ḥájí Mírzá, 159, 160
Mihdíy-i-Khu'í, Mullá, 120
Mihdíy-i-Kujúrí, Ḥájí Shaykh, 78, 99
Mihdí-Qulí Mírzá, Prince, 172, 175, 176, 206
Mihr-'Alí Khán-i-Núrí (the Shuja'u'l-Mulk), 240
Mílán, 126, 127
Mír-Ghaḍab (executioner), 76
Mi'ráj, 3
Mírkhund (Mírkhwand), 141
Mírzá Áqá Khán-i-Núrí, 152
Mírzá-Áqá, Áqá (nephew of wife of the Báb), 32
Mírzá-Áqáy-i-Rikáb-Sáz, 103
Mírzáy-i-Shírází, *see* Muḥammad-Ḥasan, Ḥájí Mírzá
Miṣbáh, 'Azízu'lláh, 161, 238
Mohammedans, *see* Muslims
Mordecai, 165
Morier, James, 9
Moses, 31
Mosul, 61
Mubárak, *see* Ethiopian servant
Muḥammad, the Prophet, 3, 44–8 *passim*, 86, 95, 98, 111, 167, 171, 177, 181, 182, 211, 214, 218, 220
Muḥammad, Ḥájí Áqá, 145
Muḥammad, Ḥájí Mírzá Siyyid (uncle of the Báb), 33, 40, 107
Muḥammad, Mullá (husband of Ṭáhirih), 25
Muḥammad, Shaykh, *see* Shaykh 'Ábid
Muḥammad, Siyyid, of Shíráz, 36
Muḥammad, Siyyid (Sulṭánu'l-'Ulamá), *see* Imám-Jum'ih, of Iṣfahán
Muḥammad-'Abdu'lláh, 205
Muhammad Ali, Mirza (Persian minister), 207
Muḥammad-'Alí, Ḥájí Mírzá (cousin of the Báb), 87
Muḥammad-'Alí, Mírzá (1st Mushíru'l-Mulk), 98
Muḥammad-'Alí, Mírzá (secretary of Ḥájí Qavám), 82
Muḥammad-'Alí, Mullá, of Zanján, *see* Ḥujjat
Muḥammad-'Alíy-i-Bárfurúshí, Ḥájí Mullá, *see* Quddús
Muḥammad-'Alíy-i-Ḥamzih, Ḥájí, 176
Muḥammad-'Alíy-i-Maḥallátí, Mullá, 78, 99
Muḥammad-'Alí Mírzá (Rukni'd-Dawlih), 2
Muḥammad-'Alíy-i-Músáví, Siyyid, 199
Muḥammad-'Alíy-i-Nahrí, Mírzá, 51, 102
Muḥammad-'Alí Páshá, 239
Muḥammad-'Alíy-i-Qazvíní, Mírzá (Letter of the Living), 26, 168
Muḥammad-'Alíy-i-Zunúzí, Mírzá, 153–8
Muḥammad Áqá Yávar, 164
Muḥammad-Báqir, Mírzá (Letter of the Living), 26
Muḥammad-Báqir Khán (the Biglar-bagí), 69
Muḥammad-Báqir-i-Qá'iní, Mírzá, 56, 173, 175
Muḥammad-Báqir-i-Rashtí, Ḥájí Siyyid, 4, 13, 50, 162
Muḥammad-Báqir-i-Ṭihrání, Áqá, 239, 240
Muḥammad Big-i-Chápárchí, 118, 120, 121, 124–6
Muḥammad-Bisáṭ, Ḥájí, 103
Muḥammad-i-Furúghí, Mullá Mírzá, 56
Muḥammad-Ḥasan, Ḥájí Mírzá (Mírzáy-i-Shírází), 33
Muḥammad ibn-i Ḥasan al-'Askarí, *see* Twelfth Imám
Muḥammad-Ḥasan-i-Bushrú'í, Mírzá (Letter of the Living), 26
Muḥammad-Ḥasan Khán (the Sálár), 122
Muḥammad-Ḥasan-i-Najafí, Shaykh, 59
Muḥammad-Ḥusayn, Mírzá (father of the Báb's mother), 33
Muḥammad-Ḥusayn-i-Ardistání, Áqá, 235
Muḥammad-Ḥusayn-i-Kirmání, Mírzá, *see* Muḥít-i-Kirmání
Muḥammad-Ḥusayn-i-Marághi'í, Áqá, 184, 185

Muḥammad-Ibráhím-i-Ismáʻíl Bag,
Áqá, 34, 35
Muḥammad-Ibráhím-i-Kalbásí, Ḥájí,
50
Muḥammad-Ismáʻíl-i-Gulpáygání,
Ḥájí, 3
Muḥammad-Jaʻfar, Siyyid, 60, 163
Muḥammad-Jaʻfar-i-Ábádíʼí, Ḥájí,
112, 113
Muḥammad-Karím, Áqá, of S̲h̲íráz,
103
Muḥammad-Karím-i-ʻAṭṭár, 191
Muḥammad-Karím K̲h̲án-i-Kirmání,
Ḥájí Mírzá, 52, 102, 134
Muḥammad-Káẓim K̲h̲án (farrás̲h-
bás̲h̲í), 145
Muḥammad K̲h̲án (former Biglar-
bagí of Tabríz), 209, 210
Muḥammad-i-K̲h̲urásání, Ḥájí Mírzá,
53
Muḥammad-i-Mámaqání, Mullá, 140,
143, 144, 155, 156
Muḥammad-Mihdí, Áqá, 111
Muḥammad-Mihdíy-i-Kindí, Mullá,
120
Muḥammad Muʻallim-i-Núrí, Mullá,
53
Muḥammad-Muṣṭafáy-i-Bag̲h̲dádí,
Áqá, 60, 162, 166, 232
Muḥammad-Qulí K̲h̲án-i-Ílbagí, 81,
84
Muḥammad Rawḍih-K̲h̲án-i-Yazdí,
Mírzá (Letter of the Living),
27
Muḥammad-Riḍá, Siyyid (or Mír,
father of the Báb), 32, 33, 142,
230
Muḥammad-Ṣádiq-i-Muʻallim, Ḥájí
Mírzá, 96, 98
Muḥammad-Ṣáliḥ, Áqá, 23
Muḥammad S̲h̲áh, 10, 12, 80, 81, 83,
90, 93, 99, 100, 102, 109, 112, 113,
115, 117, 121, 122–3 (letter to the
Báb), 135, 137, 139, 147, 148, 149,
165, 170, 175, 178, 185, 211, 221,
230, 233
Muḥammad S̲h̲ibl, S̲h̲ayk̲h̲, 60, 162,
166
Muḥammad-Taqí, Ḥájí Mullá (uncle
of Ṭáhirih), 25, 166
Muḥammad at-Taqí, Imám, 41
Muḥammad-Taqí, Mírzá, of Sárí, 171

Muḥammad-Taqí, S̲h̲ayk̲h̲ (Máma-
qání), 143
Muḥammad-Taqíy-i-Ayyúb, Ḥájí,
240
Muḥammad-Taqíy-i-Hirátí, Mullá,
110
Muḥammad-Taqíy-i-Juvayní, Mírzá,
173
Muḥammad-Taqí K̲h̲án (Bak̲h̲tíyárí
chief), 108
Muḥammad-Taqí K̲h̲án (Lisánuʼl-
Mulk-i-Sipihr), 141, 231
Muḥammad-Taqíy-i-Kirmání, Ḥájí,
184
Muḥammad-Taqíy-i-Mílání, Ḥájí,
128
Muḥammad-i-Zarandí, Mullá (Nabíl-
i-Aʻẓam), 40, 93, 94, 100, 114, 119,
122, 132
Muḥarram, month of, 32, 71
Muḥibb-ʻAlí K̲h̲án, 66
Muḥít-i-Kirmání, Mírzá (Muḥam-
mad-Ḥusayn, Mírzá), 72, 73, 74
Muḥsin al-Káẓimí, Siyyid, 60
Muʻínuʼs-Salṭanih, Ḥájí, 41
Mujtahid, 1, 50, 60, 67, 224
Mulk, Súrih of, 20
Mulk-Árá, see ʻAbbás Mírzá
Muqaddas, see Ṣádiq-i-Muqaddas-i-
K̲h̲urásání, Mullá
Murád Mírzá, Ḥájí Sulṭán (Ḥisámuʼs-
Salṭanih), 237
Múrc̲h̲ih-K̲h̲ár, 115
Muríd (disciple), 112
Murs̲h̲id (guide), 40, 112
Murtaḍáy-i-Zanjání, Siyyid, 184, 185
Murtiḍáy-i-Anṣárí, S̲h̲ayk̲h̲, 162
Murtiḍá-Qulíy-i-Marandí, Mullá
(ʻAlamuʼl-Hudá), 140, 155
Músá, Mírzá (Áqáy-i-Kalím, brother
of Baháʼuʼlláh), 55
Músá al-Káẓim, Imám, 41
Musayyib, 4, 196, 197
Mus̲h̲íruʼl-Mulk, 98
Mus̲h̲íruʼt-Tujjár, 239
Muslim (Musulman), 98, 108, 146,
147, 178, 205, 222
Muṣṭafá, Mírzá (Ismáʻíl-i-Sabbág̲h̲-i-
Sidihí), 240
Muṣṭafá-Qulí K̲h̲án-i-Qarág̲h̲uzlú
(Iʻtimaduʼs-Salṭanih), 240
Muʻtamid, see Manúc̲h̲ihr K̲h̲án

Nabí Khán-i-Qazvíní, Mírzá (Amír-i-Díván), 81, 82
Nabíl-i-A'ẓam, *see* Muḥammad-i-Zarandí, Mullá
Nádir Sháh, 161, 230
Najaf, 1, 41, 45, 49, 59, 60, 64, 65, 193, 200
Najaf-'Alí, Áqá, 145
Najíb Páshá, 4, 5, 12, 60, 63, 64, 66, 163, 194, 196, 197, 200
Narjis (mother of 12th Imám), 142
Násikhu't-Tavárikh, 40, 141, 142
Náṣirí regiment, 158
Náṣiri'd-Dín Sháh, 9, 33, 135, 140, 141, 145, 148, 152, 207, 218, 219, 237
Naṣru'lláh, Mír (grandfather of the Báb), 230
Naṣru'lláh, Siyyid, 196
Navváb-i-Raḍaví, 205
Naw-Rúz, 118, 119, 131, 132, 192
Nawrúz-'Alí, 163
Náyibu's-Salṭanih, *see* 'Abbás Mírzá, Prince, and 'Abbás Mírzá Mulk-Ára
Nayríz, 178–82, 186, 204–5
Náẓimu'sh-Sharí'ih, *see* Ḥusayn-i-'Arab, Shaykh
Nesselrode, Count, 131, 206
New Day, Dispensation, 20, 90, 162, 172
Nicolas, A.-L.-M., 39, 99, 104, 115, 152, 172, 217
Ni'matí-Khánih, 81, 234
Ni'matu'lláhí dervish, 184
Nimrod, 31
Nineveh, 229, 233
Niṣf-i-Jahán, 108; *see also* Iṣfahán
Níyálá, 170–2 *passim*
Níyáz-i-Baghdádí, Ḥájí, 74
Niẓámu'd-Dawlih, *see* Ḥusayn Khán
Niẓámu'l-'Ulamá, *see* Maḥmúd, Ḥájí Mullá
Nubuvvat-i-Kháṣṣih, 111
Nuqṭiy-i-Bayán, 137; -i-Úlá, 48 (The Báb)
Núr, 53, 171
Nuṣayrí, 118

Ottoman, 12, 59, 63, 238, 239
Outray, M., 80
Oxford, 238

Palm Sunday, 127
Palmerston, Viscount, xi, 12, 79, 173, 178, 180, 202, 204, 206, 207, 209, 211, 212, 214, 216
Páminár (Páy-i-Minár), 53
Paris, 79, 80
Peel, Sir Robert, xi
Persepolis, 237
Persia, *see* Írán
Persian(s), 136, 140, 146, 147, 163, 165, 176, 194–7, 199, 206, 210–12, 218, 230, 234
Persian Gulf, 109, 223, 230
Platonism, 113
Polygamy, 223
Pope, Alexander, 85
Portuguese, 107
Presbyterian Mission, American, 145
Primal Point (The Báb), 189

Qahru'lláh (a dervish), 137
Qahviy-i-Awlíyá', 39, 231
Qá'im, 3, 18, 33, 48, 50, 51, 70, 71 (Báb's declaration in Mecca), 74, 87, 96, 98, 111, 134, 143, 144, 145, 156, 167, 170, 178, 185, 186, 205
Qá'im-Maqám (Abu'l-Qásim, Mírzá), 8–9, 10, 148
Qájár, 7, 108, 113, 219
Qandahár, 233
Qashqá'í, tribe, 81, 82, 84
Qásim, Siyyid, of Rasht, 3
Qavámu'l-Mulk, Ḥájí, 81, 82, 84, 234
Qayyúmu'l-Asmá' (Commentary on Súrih of Joseph), 19, 20, 21, 46, 47, 58, 99, 101, 141, 211
Qazvín, 108, 124, 125, 131, 164–7
Qiṣaṣu'l-'Ulamá (Chronicles of the Divines), 141, 142
Qubád Khán, 82
Quddús (Muḥammad-'Alíy-i-Bárfurúshí, Ḥájí Mullá), Letter of the Living: recognises the Báb, 23–4, 26, 33; accompanies Him to Mecca, 48–9, 71, 74; is separated from Him, 77, 78, 149, 150; at Badasht, 167–70; arrest, 171; at Shaykh Ṭabarsí, 173, 175, 177; martyrdom, 150, 176, 205
Quintus Curtius, 223
Qum, 49, 51, 119, 135, 151, 174
Qumrúd, 119

Qur'án (Koran), 13, 28, 29, 30, 61, 62, 64, 65, 74, 75, 87, 88, 90, 91, 101, 110, 141, 144, 172, 175, 181, 186, 204, 214, 217, 218, 219
Quraysh, 86
Qurbán-'Alí, Mírzá, 184
Qurratu'l-'Ayn (the Báb), 47
Qurratu'l-'Ayn, *see* Ṭáhirih

Rabí'u'l-Avval, month of, 116
Raḥím, Mírzá, of Shíráz, 103
Ra'ísu'l-'Ulamá, of Hamadán, 165
Ramaḍán, month of, 57, 191
Rangoon, 192
Raqshá' ('She-Serpent'), 109
Rashíd Khán-i-Sartíp, 81
Rasht, Rashtí, 3, 162
Rawḍatu'ṣ-Ṣafá, Supplement to, 141, 142
Rawlinson, Sir Henry, 61–7, 232
'Remnant of God', *see* Baqíyatu'lláh
Resurrection, Day of, 98, 150
Riḍá, Imám, 52, 56, 85, 103, 119
Riḍá, Mírzá (British Agent), 81, 82, 83
Riḍá Khán-i-Turkamán, 173
Riḍáy-i-Qásí, Ḥájí, 147, 237
Riḍá-Qulí Khán-i-Afshár, 134
Riḍá-Qulí Khán-i-Hidáyat, 141
Riḍá'íyyih, 135; *see* Urúmíyyih
Risáliy-i-Fiqhíyyih, 39
Risáliy-i-Tis'a-'Ashariyyih (Nineteen Discourses), 229, 238
Rodwell, J. M., 88
Rosen, Baron, 217
Ruknábád (fountain overlooking Shíráz), 15
Rukni'd-Dawlih (Muḥammad-'Alí Mírzá), 2
Runíz (Fárs), 240
Russell, Lord John, xi
Russia, Russian, 7–10, 124, 131, 132, 159, 206, 209, 210, 217, 230
Rustam-'Alí, *see* Zaynab

Ṣábir, *see* Mihdí, Mírzá
Sabzih-Maydán, of Bárfurúsh, 176; of Ṭihrán, 183
Sa'dí, 16
Ṣádiq, Mullá (a pretender), 132
Ṣádiq-i-Muqaddas-i-Khurásání, Mullá, 51, 78, 165, 239
Ṣadrá, Mullá, 113, 236
Ṣadr-i-A'ẓam, *see* Ḥusayn Khán
Sa'du'lláh Páshá, Sar'askar, 4, 5, 197–200
Ṣafar, month of, 77
Ṣafavid, 107, 108, 161, 162
Safíhu'l-'Ulamá, *see* Muḥammad-Mihdí, Áqá
Ṣáḥib-Ikhtíyár, *see* Ḥusayn Khán
Ṣáḥibu'z-Zamán (Lord of the Age, or Religion), 13, 15, 18, 24, 50, 96, 142
Ṣaḥífiy-i-Baynu'l-Ḥaramayn (Epistle between the Two Shrines), 73
Ṣaḥnih, 164
Sa'íd-i-Hindí, Shaykh (Letter of the Living), 27, 137
Sa'ídu'l-'Ulamá, of Bárfurúsh, 172, 174, 176
St. Petersburg (Leningrad), 9
Sale, George, 168
Salford, 217
Ṣáliḥ, Ḥájí Mullá, 25
Ṣáliḥ, Mírzá, 239
Ṣáliḥ-al-Karímí, Shaykh, 60, 165, 166
Saljúqs (Seljucids), 107
Sám Khán, 157
Sámarrá, 41, 142
Sami Effendi (Turkish minister), 210
Sar-Chishmih, 189
Saráy-i-Amír (a caravanserai), 36
Sárí, 171
Sartíp, 134, 234
'Seal of the Prophets' (Muḥammad), 95
Sercey, M. de, 234
'Seven Goats', *see* 'Seven Martyrs'
'Seven Martyrs of Ṭihrán', 182–5, 206–8
Sha'bán, month of, 75, 151
Sháfi'í, 13
Shaftí, 162
Sháh 'Abdu'l-'Aẓím, 140, 190
Sháh Chirágh (a shrine), 103
Sháh Muḥammad-i-Manshádí, Ḥájí (Amínu'l-Bayán), 190, 191
Shahr (Shehr)-i-Vírán, 224
Shakespeare, 76, 107
Sharíf (Sherif), of Mecca, 21, 74, 75
Shavvál, month of, 194

Shaykh 'Alí, Mullá, of Khurásán ('Aẓím), 57, 103, 137, 151
Shaykh-'Alí Mírzá, 103
Shaykh-i-Anám, *see* 'Ábid, Shaykh; 231
Shaykhí, 1, 5, 38, 42, 53, 59, 62, 72, 74, 140
Shaykhu'l-Islám, of Tabríz, 140
Shaykhuná, *see* 'Ábid, Shaykh; 231
Sheil, Lady, 58
Sheil, Lt.-Col. (later Sir Justin), 63, 64, 81, 135, 177, 180, 186, 187, 202–15 *passim*, 229
Sherley brothers, 107
Shí'ah, 1, 12, 13, 33, 50, 59, 62–8 *passim*, 162, 163, 198, 200, 221
Shikastih Nasta'líq (a script), 54
Shíráz, Shírází, 2, 16–18 *passim*, 22, 23, 32–40 *passim*, 45, 46, 48–52 *passim*, 56, 57, 61, 62, 67–9 *passim*, 76–88 *passim*, 90, 94, 99–107 *passim*, 143, 147, 150, 166, 169, 170, 179, 182, 204, 220, 223, 237, 239
Shirley, James, 106
Shish-Parí, Siyyid-i-, 95
Shíshván, 138
Shoghi Effendi (Guardian of the Bahá'í Faith), 139, 167, 183, 189, 192
Shujá'u'd-Dawlih, 201
Shukru'lláh Khán-i-Núrí, 69
Ṣiddíqih (the Truthful), 163; *see also* Ṭáhirih
Sipihr, *see* Muḥammad-Taqí Khán
Sisygambis, 223
Síyáh-Dahán, 124
Siyyid, 17, 23, 51, 70, 72, 99, 121, 136, 140, 146, 147
Siyyid 'Alí, 171; *see also* Ḥusayn-i-Bushrú'í, Mullá
Siyyidu'sh-Shuhadá, *see* Ḥusayn, Imám
Stevens, R. W., 202
Ṣubḥ-i-Azal, *see* Yaḥyá, Mírzá
Sublime Porte, 61, 63, 66, 163
Ṣúfí, 215
Sulaymán Khán, of Tabríz, 149, 159, 160, 189
Sulaymán Khán-i-Afshár, Ḥájí, 125, 134
Sulṭán al-Karbilá'í, Shaykh, 60, 166
Sulṭánu'l-'Ulamá, *see* Imám-Jum'ih, of Iṣfahán
Sunní, 12, 13, 63, 64, 65, 68, 163, 198
Surra-man-Ra'a, *see* Sámarrá
Súrih (Súrah), 19; *see also* (Súrihs of) Joseph, Kawthar, V'al-'Aṣr, 'al-Wáqi'ah
Syria, Syrians, 8, 193
Syriac, 136

Ṭabarsí, Shaykh, 29, 51, 135, 150, 165, 171–7, 180, 185, 186, 239
Ṭabas, 57
Tabríz, 10, 124, 126–8, 138, 140, 145, 152, 154, 157–9, 167, 169, 202, 203, 209, 211, 218, 221
Ṭahá, Siyyid, 163
Ṭáhir, Mírzá (the Baker), 239
Ṭáhir, Mullá, 166
Ṭáhirih (Qurratu'l-'Ayn, Letter of the Living), 24–7, 58, 124, 162–71, 176, 230
Talbot, Major Gerald F., 33
Taqí Khán, Mírzá (Amír Niẓám, Amír-i-Kabír), 146, 148, 152, 184, 185, 203, 207, 209, 212
Táríkh-i-Jadíd (New History of the Báb), 78, 126
Tennyson, Alfred, Lord, 134
Ṭihrán, 26, 36, ch. 3, 63, 66, 69, 81, 90, 102, 104, 113, 115, 119–25 *passim*, 131, 140, 145, 147, 149, 152, 166, 167, 177, 178, 183, 185, 189, 205, 222, 233
Tilsit, 8
Times, The (London), 77
Titow, M. de, 63
Tobacco Régie, 33
Toumansky, Alexander, 217
Traditions, of Islám, 13, 90, 98, 141
Traveller's Narrative, A, 105, 114, 118, 120, 121, 141, 152
Tsar, of Russia, 8, 10, 206
Túpchí (gunner), 81
Turkumancháy, treaty of, 9
Turkey, Turkish, 63, 104, 124, 132, 136, 210, 219–21 *passim*; *see also* Ottoman
Twelfth Imám, 65, 119

Umm-Salamih, *see* Ṭáhirih
United States, 220, 238

Urúmíyyih (Riḍá'íyyih), 131–5 *passim*, 138, 145, 169
Uṣúl-i(al)-Káfí, 119
Uṣúlís, 62, 64

Vaḥíd (Siyyid Yaḥyáy-i-Dárábí), 70, 90–4, 99, 101, 103, 178–82, 205, 215, 240
Vakíl, mosque of (Shíráz), 94, 96, 99, 103
V'al-'Aṣr, Súrih of, Commentary on, 110, 141
Valí-'Ahd (Crown Prince), 144; *see also* Náṣiri'd-Dín Sháh
Varqá (martyr-poet), 138
Varqá, Valíyu'lláh, 139
Vazír Niẓám (Mírzá Ḥasan Khán), 152, 153, 203
Vicegerent of God, 21
Victoria, Queen, 221

Wahab, Siyyid (Seid Wahab), 196
'al-Wáqi'ah, Súrih of (The Event), 168
Wellesley, Marquis of, 8
World Order of Bahá'u'lláh, The, 167

Yaḥyá, Ḥájí Shaykh (Imám-Jum'ih, of Shíráz), 233
Yaḥyá, Mírzá (Ṣubḥ-i-Azal), 174, 238
Yaḥyá Khán (warden of Chihríq), 135
Yaḥyá Khán, of Tabríz, 149
Yaḥyáy-i-Dárábí, Siyyid, *see* Vaḥíd
Yazd, 4, 102, 116, 178, 184, 205, 214, 215
Yazíd, 182
Yúnis Khán-i-Afrúkhtih, Dr., 190
Yúsuf, Mírzá (the Mustawfíu'l-Mamálik), 139
Yúsuf-i-Ardibílí, Mullá (Letter of the Living), 27
Yúsuf, Súrih of, see *Qayyúmu'l-Asmá'*

Za'faráni, Ibráhím, 194
Ẓálim, *see* Ḥusayn-i-'Arab, Shaykh
Zand, 7, 161
Zanján, 100, 101, 125, 131, 134, 178, 185–8, 209–13
Zarrín-Táj, *see* Ṭáhirih
Zaynab (Rustam-'Alí), 186
Zayni'd-Dín, Shaykh, 1
Zaynu'l-'Ábidín, Áqá Mírzá (cousin of the Báb's father), 32
Zaynu'l-'Ábidín Khán, 178–80
Ẓillu's-Sulṭán, *see* 'Alí-Sháh and Mas'úd Mírzá, Prince Sulṭán

The writer is very grateful to Farhang Afnan for his valuable help in compiling the index.